Why readers love *Mine* ...

'A beautifully written and tightly plotted novel with themes of love, family, redemption, grief, and mental health. One of my books of the year, without a doubt'

'I loved Clare Empson's debut *Him*, but *Mine* is even more exquisitely glorious. Best book I've read this year, a must read!'

'What a book – a heartbreaking account of what it means to be loved. *Mine* is a masterclass in story telling by an extremely talented writer'

'A clever, confident, intelligent and engaging joy of a book'

'A beautifully written heart-rending story exploring the after-shocks of adoption. *Mine* packs a punch with such an unnerving twist'

'All the grip of a thriller with the emotional impact of a love story. Highly recommended!'

'This is a book of love stories in all their different guises . . . the love we feel for our children; romantic love; platonic love; and the love of a child for his parents'

Clare Empson is a journalist with a background in national newspapers. Since the publication of her debut novel, *Him*, Clare is a full time author and freelances for a wide variety of publications including the *Daily Telegraph*, the *Guardian* and the *Daily Mail*. Clare lives in Wiltshire with her husband and three children.

Also by Clare Empson

Him

MINE

Clare Empson

ORION

An Orion paperback

First published in Great Britain in 2019
by Orion Fiction,
This paperback edition published in 2020
by Orion Fiction,
an imprint of The Orion Publishing Group Ltd.,
Carmelite House, 50 Victoria Embankment
London EC4Y 0DZ

An Hachette UK Company

1 3 5 7 9 10 8 6 4 2

A CIP catalogue record for this book
is available from the British Library.

ISBN (Paperback) 978 1 4091 7776 0

Typeset by Deltatype Ltd, Birkenhead, Merseyside

Printed in Great Britain by Clays Ltd, Elcograf S.p.A.

www.orionbooks.co.uk

To Cindy and John, with love

Adoption can damage a child's sense of identity. It brings with it a rash of existential questions that remain un-answered. Who am I? Why am I here? Why did my mother give me away?

Who Am I? The Adoptee's Hidden Trauma by Joel Harris

Now

Luke

London, 2000

The woman standing in front of me, shy, hesitant, an exact mirror to my own awkwardness, is so unexpectedly beautiful that for a moment I have no words.

'Hello, Alice,' I manage to say.

'Luke.'

She speaks my name as if she is trying out a new language. I reach out my hand, but Alice ignores it and pulls me into a quick, fierce embrace instead. We sit opposite each other at a table laid up with knives and forks, glasses, a pitcher of water.

'Water?' I offer, and when I pick up the jug, I see my hands are shaking.

'Wine,' Alice says, and this first smile, revealing teeth whiter than my own and grooves around her eyes that hint at her real age, lodges itself somewhere near my heart.

With the wine ordered and menus on the way there is nothing to do but look at each other. Alice sent recent photographs of herself along with her introductory letter, so her beauty should not have come as such a shock, not like this. But she is clearly struggling with my appearance too.

'You look so like your father, I'm completely ... stunned.'

'Richard Fields? He's my girlfriend's favourite artist. We just couldn't believe it.'

There is something in Alice's face here, a lightning flash of pain or sorrow, but she steels herself to carry on.

'What made you decide to find me?'

I turn over different beginnings in my mind. The years on the rugby pitches looking at the touchline and wondering if my real mother was one of the women gathered there: the blonde in the fur coat, the lady with the ponytail. And later, the years spent locked in my bedroom, curled up in fury after another row with my parents, consoling myself with the thought that at least my actual mother, the person I truly belonged to, was someone different. And then once I'd met Hannah, the endless questioning. 'Don't you want to meet her?' 'Don't you want to know what she's like?'

It's true that my girlfriend's persistent fascination with my real parentage was a driving force behind this sudden reunion. But the real reason – my tiny brown-eyed, long-lashed boy – lies draped in his mother's arms several miles away.

'I think it was the day Samuel was born.'

'That would do it,' Alice says.

I watch her swallowing back tears, but I feel no guilt. She had a baby and gave him away. I'm a father myself now and I will never understand it.

'How old is he?'

'Three months.'

Alice places a hand against her heart as if she's compressing a wound.

'Oh,' she says, though the 'oh' is really a gasp of pain. 'I think this is going to be even harder than I thought.'

We look at each other, this woman and I, both wanting to run but trapped by the glass and cutlery-lined beechwood table between us, by the polite convention of going through with our hastily arranged (leisurely repented?) lunch.

'It's all right,' Alice says with a brief, businesslike smile, as though she's shrugging herself into the position of adult, of parent. 'If we take it slowly, we'll be fine. Let's start with the easy stuff. Tell me about your girlfriend.'

I met Hannah at the opening of a mutual friend, Ben, who has had the balls to dedicate his life to painting, subsisting on government handouts, sleeping on sofas and working right through the night to produce edgy, instantly recognisable portraits that have been compared, strangely enough, to Richard Fields. Hannah was filing a piece about him for her paper and I watched her walking around the gallery with her notepad, pausing in front of each painting before she scribbled down her thoughts. I wondered what she was writing. Who she was. Whether she was single. I liked the way her curly dark hair fell across her face, obscuring her eyes. She pushed it back, tucked a thick strand behind her ear, but moments later it broke free again.

When she started talking to Ben, dressed in an unfamiliar suit with his dirty white trainers, I decided to head over and say hello. A moment's awkwardness while I waited for Ben to finish speaking.

'There's never been any question in my mind that I'd do anything but paint. It might have been nice to earn lots of money doing something else, but that wasn't an option. I'd never let anything get in the way of my painting.'

He looked up and saw me.

'God. Don't just stand there listening to me being a dick.'

Our friendship goes back to prep school; two misfits in a blur of dull entitlement.

'This is Hannah,' he said. 'She works for *The Times*. She does have a proper job.'

'What about you?' Hannah asked me. 'Artist or proper job?'

'Oh, I prefer to feed off other people's talent.'

'Luke's an A&R man,' Ben said, with the note of pride that is always there when he tells people about my job. 'He was running his own record label at twenty-five.'

'Now you've made *me* sound like a dick,' I said, and Hannah laughed.

Ben's parents came over then and we were swept up in a plan to go out for dinner.

'There's a lovely little Italian around the corner, we've booked a couple of tables,' Ben's father said, and Ben hissed, low-voiced, 'Don't worry, they're paying.'

I liked Ben's parents, they were good, kind people who invited me on holiday to France with them every year, but without saying anything Hannah and I dropped back, slowing our pace until soon we lost sight of Ben's entourage altogether.

'We're right next to Chinatown,' Hannah said, and I didn't hesitate. Within minutes we were sitting opposite each other in a booth in one of my favourite restaurants.

I liked her impeccable rolling of pancakes: two slivers of spring onion laid head to toe alongside a neat stripe of hoisin sauce, modest slices of duck that she took time to select, no fat, no skin. While we ate, she told me about growing up in north Cornwall in a house by the sea.

'Our house is on the path to the beach. When the tide's coming in you can be swimming in the sea in three minutes flat. We used to time it. I was surfing by the age of eight. And when I was older I spent every summer working as a lifeguard.'

She told me about warm nights spent on the beach, sleeping out in the open, first with her parents, then with friends. They'd gather mussels and cook them over a campfire, drinking hot chocolate from a thermos.

'On Midsummer's Eve the whole village goes down to the beach and builds a big bonfire. People bring food and tell stories and everyone is there, young and old. I miss it sometimes. When I'm late for work and shoving my way onto the Tube without bothering to apologise, I wonder what the hell has happened to me.'

She laughed as she said this, but all I could think was: you're perfect. That's what's happened to you. I've always been greedy for information about other people's families, but I'd never felt like this, as if not just my mind but my whole body was attuned to every word she spoke.

'You're very good at not talking about yourself,' Hannah said. 'You ask a lot of questions.'

'That's because I've nothing to tell. I had a nice, safe, comfortable childhood in Yorkshire with parents who were quite a bit older. I'm an only child. They adopted me when I was just a few weeks old.'

'You're adopted?' Hannah said, now vehemently interested, a reaction I find peculiarly female. Men basically don't give a shit how you came into the world. 'I love a mystery,' she said.

And that was the first time she asked me about my birth mother.

'So this is Hannah?'

Alice has laid out the photographs I brought with me like a hand of solitaire and she examines them one by one. She's looking at my favourite photo of Hannah. In it, she's behind the wheel of a tiny little phut-phut boat we hired on a whim one afternoon in Falmouth. It had a top speed of about ten miles an hour, this boat, and Hannah, who has a powerboat licence, who surfs and sails and could probably skipper a hundred-foot yacht if you asked her to, found it hilarious. She's laughing so hard in this picture you can see both rows of teeth, her eyes are scrunched and her head is tipped right back. It makes my heart ache a little just to look at her and to remember that most perfect afternoon. Just this – I would be lost without her.

'She looks like a good person to have on your side.'

Alice's astuteness is a chest thump to the heart. As though this woman, this stranger, who once carried me in her womb, is still so connected to me she can read my innermost thoughts.

'That's me on my seventh birthday,' I say, pointing to an image of me and three other friends holding sausages on sticks ready to cook on the barbecue. My birthday falls in May and I can still remember the scorch from that day. We had home-made lemonade that was too bitter for my friends and a cake in the shape of the Tardis.

'And here I am at school playing rugby.' I point to the adjacent photo.

'You went to boarding school? How old?'

'Eight.'

'That's far too young,' Alice says, before softening it, 'in my opinion.'

I wonder if I should tell her about the tearful departures, the utter desolation of the Sunday-night drive back to school. The first time my parents dropped me off I was too shocked and excited to cry much. The second time I knew what was coming and I clung to the car door handle and ran halfway down the drive with them before my father accelerated away.

I'd hesitated before including the photograph of Christmas lunch, me aged twelve, sitting at the table with my parents and grandparents. My father is standing up to carve the turkey, my mother is handing me a plate crammed with meat and vegetables. We are all wearing paper crowns and there is cracker debris scattered across the table. When I look at this photo, I think: quiet, lonely, bored. To me it is glaringly obvious that I didn't fit in. But Alice sees something different. She sees the way my mother is smiling at me as she hands me my plate. She sees tenderness. Familiarity. Ownership.

'So that's her,' she says, without looking up.

And now I understand. My adoptive father means nothing to Alice. It's all about the woman who replaced her.

'How does she feel about you seeing me? Your ... mother?'

I hear how the word hurts her.

'She doesn't know. I haven't told her. I probably could, but ...'

How to explain my mother's froideur around the circumstances of my birth. She told me I was adopted when I was eight, just before I went away to school.

'Why did she give me away?' I asked.

It is, after all, the only question.

'She was a young girl who got pregnant by mistake and she needed to get on with the rest of her life.'

'Do you think she ever wonders about me?'

'She doesn't need to wonder about you. She knows you are happy, that you have a wonderful life, one she could never have given you. She knows you are lucky.'

Lucky, so lucky, the mantra of my childhood.

I cannot bring myself to share this detail with Alice, who seems nothing like the casual, carefree girl my mother described as she sits all broken-looking, surrounded by my childhood photographs.

'Luke?' she says, and it still sounds as if she's testing out my name, as if she expects me to be called something else. Charlie. The name she gave me.

'I won't ever try to be a mother to you. That would be foolish.

7

Shall we settle for friends?'

She picks up her wine glass and waits for me to do the same. We clink glasses, this beautiful forty-seven-year old woman and I, two strangers in a restaurant, connected by a past I have yet to understand.

Then

Alice

London, 1972

The hard slap of a magazine dropped from above makes me look up.

'*This* is what sex looks like.'

The voice, strangely gravelled for a non-smoking nineteen-year-old, belongs to Rick. The face and torso now displayed beside my pseudo-Cubist still life is Jacob Earl, the dark-eyed, high-cheekboned singer of Disciples. He's on the front page of *Sounds* magazine, black shirt unbuttoned, chest gleaming, objectified just like a Page Three girl.

'Gig at the Marquee tonight. We're going,' Rick says, glaring down at my canvas. 'Think the apple might work better in blue?'

He says it lightly, to be helpful, but with each new and perfect intuition I feel the familiar drifting to self-doubt. Am I as good as everyone else? Do I truly deserve my place here, one of only twelve students accepted on the fine arts degree at the Slade, renowned as the best art school in the country?

Rick is the kind of artist (slash sculptor, ceramicist, embroiderer; he can excel in any medium) who doesn't really need to be here. He's already *it*, the tutors' darling, the art school's mascot, the collector's early hunch. Last week he sold a self-portrait

9

– his whole face rendered in vertical stripes of green – to a man who turned out to be the owner of San Lorenzo. I can imagine Mick and Bianca eating their gazpacho while Rick gazes down at them with his sharp blue eyes.

This afternoon's session, printmaking with Gordon King, is the one I dread the most. A former pop artist (he distanced himself from the movement some years ago and now speaks about it only with distaste), his work sells for thousands of pounds and hangs in the permanent collection of the Whitechapel Art Gallery. He swept into the Slade four years ago and turned its printmaking department on its head. It is said that he can make or break a career, and three of his protégés now sell on Cork Street.

Rick is his favourite; he can stand beside him eulogising his colour choices for a full five minutes.

'Gather round, people. See these pinks and greens and browns. See how the cherry blossom gorgeousness is offset by sludgy olive and shit brown? This is colour calibration at its best.'

Today I am working on a lithograph of a favourite tree and I am hopeful that all the nights I've spent frying my brain reading about tonality and chromaticism might finally pay off. Once I've drawn the outline of my tree (a mesmerising, strangely humanised oak) onto a block of limestone, I'm going to wash over it in a restricted palette of yellow, red, black and white. I've been practising for this moment all week, mixing up little tubes of paint in my student bedroom until I came up with three perfect shades of skin. Soon the tree's branches will become flesh-coloured limbs, the thick round trunk a torso, its ribs defined by hand. I'm going to call it *Metamorphosis 1*, a pleasingly Kafkaesque title and the first in a series of tree people.

But Gordon doesn't wait to see this transformation.

'Surely not another tree?' he says, arms folded, mouth tight, hovering beside me. 'What is it with you and trees?'

And something crumples inside me. Instead of standing up to him, as I do every day in my mind, I say, 'I don't know. I just like them.'

'Well, I like ice cream, but I don't paint it every bloody day. Move on now. We need to see some development. This is sub-A-level standard.'

In the pub, Rick feeds me gin and tonic and holds my hand while I cry.

'I shouldn't be on this course, I'm going to drop out.'

We have the same conversation every week, always after Gordon King's class.

'What is it with you and trees?'

Rick can mimic Gordon perfectly, his soft Anglicised Scottish voice at odds with his bitter personality.

'The man's a bully. And you're his victim. We have to find a way of changing that.'

He glances at my half-full tumbler of gin.

'Drink up, tree girl. We have a gig to get to.'

There's time for another drink before the show starts, but the bar is packed full, three hundred drinkers crammed into a tiny space, most of them smoking, the air a greenish grey. Rick holds my hand and hauls me through the crowd.

"Scuse us. Sorry,' he says as we tread on feet and squeeze in between couples. And then, five feet from the bar, he stops dead and I smack into him.

'What?' I ask, but Rick doesn't answer.

Perhaps it's his pheromones, some kind of chemical energy anyway, that makes me look where Rick is looking. Jacob Earl is standing at the bar, two elbows leant on it, a pound note held in one hand. He's ordering drinks and there seems to be an invisible force field around him, a whole room full of people who can look but not touch.

He has his back to me, but even that is intriguing, the way his dark, almost black hair curls over the collar of his shirt, the skinniness of his hips in their tight black jeans, his snakeskin boots.

'Wait till he turns round,' Rick says, and at that moment, Jacob does.

The face is astonishing, it's true, a perfect blend of male and female, though not in the Bowie way, for he is even prettier, with his curly hair and big brown eyes, his full lips. Around his neck he wears a flowered choker and several gold chains. His shirt, like in the photo, is open almost to his waist. It's impossible not to stare.

'Oi, Jacob!' Rick calls out unexpectedly, and the singer turns around. 'Get us a couple of ales while you're there, would you?'

He does this, Rick, asks for the impossible with an optimistic grin, and people often fall for it.

'All right,' Jacob says, and he begins to smile slowly in return. 'Pints or halves?'

'Pints. Please.' Rick passes over a pound note.

'For your girlfriend too?'

'She's not my girlfriend,' Rick says, too fast, and Jacob laughs. 'You sure about that?'

'Positive. This is Alice. I'm Rick. We're at art school together.'

'Art school? Whereabouts?'

'The Slade.'

'Hey, Eddie. EDDIE.'

Another man in head-to-toe black turns around from the bar and looks at us without interest.

'These guys are art students,' Jacob says. 'They're at the Slade.

You know the Slade, right? The best art school in the country. Remember what we were talking about earlier?'

'Oh yeah.'

Whatever it was, Eddie clearly couldn't give a toss.

'So maybe we should talk to them? About our idea?'

Eddie shrugs. He looks at his watch.

'There's no time. We're on in ten.'

Jacob nods, reluctantly it seems to me.

'You're right, we should go.'

He looks at me with a final heart-shattering smile and I return his gaze, heat flooding to my cheeks.

'Well, enjoy the show,' he says. 'See you for a drink afterwards?'

Waiting for the band to come on, the small, dark room now crammed with bodies and pulsing with the collective energy that accompanies anticipation, I am preoccupied with the beautiful singer. I am physically affected by those brief seconds of interaction, stomach tense, heart banging in my chest, whole body framed in some kind of expectation.

I assume I'm going to like the band, everyone else seems to, but when they finally come out onto the stage, all of them in black, the density of their opening chord – simultaneous drums, guitar and a long-drawn-out vocal – leaves room for nothing else. I am immersed in the music in a way I never have been; my eyes scan each musician – the drummer, the bass guitarist, the backing singers, two girls, one guy – before returning each time, as if magnetically pulled, to Jacob. Never have I seen someone so effortlessly at ease with himself. Singing so close to the mic that his lips almost touch it. Dancing across the stage between vocals, though dancing is not the right word for this strange, hip-swinging side-shuffle. It might look odd on anyone else, but not him, with his pretty-boy thinness and his cool, jerky moves.

But it is the words he sings that tip me head-first over an invisible line to a place where I can no longer remember a time when Jacob wasn't the headline in my thoughts.

The first song, 'Sarah', about breaking up with a girl, is the embodiment of sadness. I want to be Sarah, I want to immerse myself in Sarah's sorrow.

'Does he write his own songs?' I ask Rick without taking my eyes off the stage.

Rick laughs, also without shifting his attention.

'Of course. He's a god.'

What to say about the next hour, the two of us rapt in sound and visuals and private fantasy? As a whole – an all-male three-piece consisting of singer/guitarist, bass player and drummer, plus for tonight the trio of backing singers – the band seems to exist in permanent frenzy, explosive riffs, each one longer than the last, extended drum solos that are exhausting in their demand for focus. But it's the quieter moments I like best, the slow, somnambulant drift into ballad, lyrics that pierce the heart with their compelling sadness. For the final, tortured love song, Jacob sits on the edge of the stage, singing into the microphone with his bluesy Americanised voice – honey flecked with gravel.

He walks from the stage first, one hand raised in salute, guitar slung around his neck – even his casualness is arresting – and then, in turn, the bassist and drummer both take a final solo before following him.

No encore, just the explosive sound of audience rapture.

'Christ, they're bloody amazing.'

'His voice,' Rick says. 'David Bowie, but better.'

'His face. Mick Jagger, but cuter.'

Rick raises his brows and tilts his head to examine me.

'And finally,' he says, 'the girl made of ice begins to thaw.'

Now

Luke

We live in a four-bedroomed Victorian terrace in Clapham, bought with a legacy from my father. None of our friends live in a house like this, but then our friends still have both parents intact; my father died from spleen cancer two years ago, a hard, horrible ending that left my mother and me alone. Ours has always been the tricky relationship, and now we no longer have my father's childish jokes and penchant for expensive wine to take the edge off. When my mother discovered Hannah was pregnant after only three months of our being together, she begged us not to 'make this mistake'.

'Don't put so much pressure on your relationship when you hardly know each other. I'll pay for you to go to a private clinic; it's all so easy these days.'

Recommending abortion to an adopted person – well, the irony is writ pretty large. Don't make the same mistake your mother made. There's that. And then the rather devastating underpinning: kill this embryo, scrape away this nucleus, before it has a chance to wreck your life. Don't get me wrong, choosing to have a child with Hannah was no mercy mission, a debt repaid for the life I was given (I was born in 1973; abortion was front-street and fully available by then). Simply that the prospect of beginning a life with this cloudy-haired girl, with her pink Cornish cheeks and the optimism that precedes her into every room, was an adrenaline shot to the heart. And I wanted a child, this child, in a way I'd never wanted anything before.

This afternoon, arriving home after my momentous lunch, the front door is wrenched open even before I have my key in the lock, as if my girlfriend has simply been waiting the other side of it.

'Oh my God,' she says, grabbing my hand and pulling me into the house. 'How. Are. You?'

The way Hannah cares about me, her concern, her interest, sometimes I feel I can never get enough of it. I try to be nonchalant, never to show how much I crave the full beam of her attention. But inside I'm just like a child. Look at me, Hannah. Look at me.

'I'm good, I think,' I say, kissing her. 'Where's the baby?'

'He's asleep. Come on, he won't wake for a while and I want to hear *everything*.'

Sitting across the table from Hannah, holding hands, I feel the first small rush of elation. I've found my real mother. I like her. I like having her in my life.

'Start at the beginning. What does she look like?'

How to describe another beautiful woman to your girlfriend? With honesty, I decide.

'She's tall and dark and sort of amazing-looking. People were staring at her. It was like having lunch with Helena Christensen. And before you ask, no, I do not fancy my own mother.'

Instantly, Hannah is laughing.

'I'm not surprised she's beautiful,' she says, getting up from her side of the table and walking round to mine. She presses her lips to my mouth; a quick pinch to my inner thigh and my groin fires in response.

'Shouldn't we be making the most of him being asleep?'

I slide both hands inside her T-shirt, inch by inch moving up her belly towards her breasts.

'Oh God,' she says.

What I love about Hannah is that our passion is equally matched. One expert touch and she'll drop everything, the burn between us mutual and instantaneous. Harder with a baby, of course, especially when that baby sleeps sandwiched between you at night.

She pushes my hands away.

'Later,' she says. 'I need to hear about Alice.'

I tell her the few details my birth mother shared about her life. She lives in Chiswick, she's single with no other children, she's an artist. She paints portraits of pets for rich old ladies.

'What about Richard?'

Hannah is a diehard Fields fan. We have a print of one of his most famous paintings – *The Exhibitionist* – on the wall opposite. It's a portrait of a show-off dancing for her enraptured parents. She's overweight and dressed in a sequinned purple leotard and top hat; you can tell she isn't very good by the gawkish positioning of her limbs.

'She and Richard are still best friends. They talk every day, see each other most weeks. She didn't tell me much about them being together; I got the impression it was just a fling. He's gay, after all.'

'Do you think he might be up for an interview?' Hannah has the grace to laugh as she says it.

At the *Sunday Times* Culture section where Hannah works, there is an unwritten hit list of ultimate but almost impossible-to-get interviewees. Richard Fields is at the top of that list and Hannah has been trying to get a profile piece with him for years.

'You're a hard and ruthless woman. Doesn't my twenty-seven-year heartache mean anything to you?'

'Your heartache is the perfect in. Surely he wants to meet his son? You've a lot of catching-up to do.'

'I get the feeling it's just me and Alice for now. She didn't mention Rick much. That's what she calls him, not Richard.'

'Can I meet her?' Hannah grabs hold of my hands. She kisses one, then the other. Her excitement is so different to mine: pure, uncomplicated. She sees Alice as the plot twist in my story, the beginnings of a mystery solved. 'We could ask her for lunch. She can meet Samuel. Her grandson.'

'It might be too soon for her,' I say, thinking it's definitely too soon for me.

'Did she tell you what happened? Why she couldn't keep you?'

'Not really. I got the feeling it was too painful for her to talk about. I guess he – Richard – didn't want to go through with it. They weren't in love or anything.'

Hannah smiles and reaches for my hand. The parallels in our stories – albeit twenty-seven years apart – are uncannily similar. Except that we chose to have the baby, to keep the baby, to treasure the baby. I'm sad suddenly for Alice and for myself, for the life we were never allowed to have.

I remember so well the day Hannah turned up on my doorstep, red-faced from crying. Instantly, I feared the worst. Here it comes, the ending I project over and over. Rejection that burrs in my veins no matter how hard I try to ignore it.

But it was the exact opposite of what I thought.

'I'm pregnant,' she said, and it was all I could do not to laugh, for those seemed like perfect, shimmering words to me. I wondered why she was crying.

'Is that so bad?' I asked her, and she stared at me, confused, for just one moment before her face slid into a grin that cracked my heart in two and we springboarded into a future neither of us had anticipated.

Then

Alice

I love the life drawing class, it's the highlight of my week. I love Josef, the Spanish model, who sits huddled in his blue dressing gown, waiting for the lecture to finish and the drawing to begin. I love Rita Miller, the life tutor, who speaks so passionately at the beginning of each class and always fills me with renewed confidence for my time here. Gordon King takes me down, Rita Miller builds me back up, week after week. And I also love the fact that within thirty seconds of seeing Josef stark naked, I am able to scrutinise and measure his genitals as if sketching an arrangement of fruit.

Every week Rita tries to teach us about observation.

'Beginners think freedom is the greatest thing,' she says. 'But most beginners don't have any freedom because they are in bondage to their limitations. Before you can be spontaneous, first you must learn to see and have a command of the language that enables you to express what you are seeing.'

She flicks her hand towards the small platform at the front of the class.

'Josef, I think we're ready for you.'

The life model removes his dressing gown and folds it carefully on the chair before ascending the platform. He drapes himself over a green hessian screen, notes of a crucified Jesus there, a posture that has clearly been pre-designed by Rita. Head turned to the side and tilted down, each arm stretched out, wrists limp, hands dangling. He is rather Jesus-like, with his sculptured face, and his thin, impeccably defined body. Flat stomach, those strong, muscular thighs, hands with long fingers, curved now into the position of claws.

'Think about what you see,' Rita says. 'Think. Not gawp. I'm not talking about folds of skin or the underlay of bones.' She points to Josef with a flourish and he gazes back dispassionately. 'What we're looking for are those links and underlying patterns, those insights and sensitivities that at first seem hidden. Without observation you have no content.'

When I look at Josef, I imagine his backstory. A young man who was tempted away from a traditional life in provincial Spain by the wild hedonism of seventies London, a place where sex shops and pornography cinemas and strip shows and prostitutes line the grimy, litter-strewn streets and marijuana is smoked like cigarettes (right now there will be four or five students on the roof of the Slade sharing a joint). Perhaps he is gay. Or he's ardently heterosexual, here for his promised sexual revolution, in a city where women – drunk, stoned women – dance topless at parties and engage in acts of defiant promiscuity. Perhaps, though, he is neither of these things. Perhaps I just have sex on the brain.

True to say I went to bed and woke up thinking about Jacob, the beautiful singer with his pencil-thin cheekbones, and the poetry of his songs. Never before has music affected me in this way. Yes, I collect the albums of the day – T. Rex, The Doors, The Rolling Stones (*Sticky Fingers*, released last year, played so often the grooves of the record have stretched and turned a whitish-grey). But something happened to me as I stood in that densely packed, smoke-saturated room watching Jacob sing

of endings and premature goodbyes. I think it's that I com-
prehended – physically, rather than intellectually – the unity
of sound and voice, the notes of each instrument, as though
my entire physiology was absorbing it. And still it was more
than that. The words Jacob had written, the words he sang, he
believed in them, he knew them to be good. Self-assurance was
the drug that drew me to him.

Now when I gaze at Josef I want to import these new sensa-
tions from last night, a feeling of longing, lust, envy, admiration.
While I draw Josef's eyes – haunting and mesmeric they seem to
me now – I hear Jacob singing his lament to a girl named Sarah.

The sketch turns out to be the best thing I've ever done.
This time when the students are told to gather round, it is my
drawing they come to see.

'Observation is fed by the imagination,' Rita says. 'What
Alice has done wonderfully here is capture a sense of character
that she can only have imagined. See the look of sadness in
Josef's eyes? A sort of yearning, wouldn't you say?'

After class there seems to be some kind of commotion on the
ground floor. The high-pitched voice of Muriel Ashcroft, the
Slade's receptionist, shrieks up towards us as Rick and I walk
down the spiral staircase.

'I'm sorry, but if you don't have an appointment then I really
must ask you to leave.'

'But I'm here to talk to two of your students about a potential
commission.'

'Which students?'

'A girl and a guy; the girl was called Alice.'

'But which Alice? We have two.'

'Oh well, this Alice is very – how shall I put it? She's a girl
that stands out.'

Rick and I arrive on the ground floor and Jacob Earl is standing there, his whole face breaking into a smile as soon as he sees me. There is no time to prepare, and this first sighting causes another chemical reaction: bones, cells, blood, heart clamouring and craving beneath my skin. And I find that I'm grinning back at him, stupidly I should imagine. If I could freeze one moment in my life, perhaps it would be this.

'There you are. This is my Alice,' Jacob says to Muriel, who is looking really quite flustered in the presence of this beautiful man. Perhaps she's human after all.

And how that 'my' sounds on his lips …

'Very well,' Muriel says. 'Perhaps you'd like to take your "business meeting" outside?'

Jacob is taller than I'd realised and dressed again in black, a shirt with flowing sleeves, a long scarf patterned with brown and cream feathers, flared black jeans and the snakeskin boots of last night.

The three of us walk out of the front door, down the steps and into the courtyard.

'Thought you guys were going to stick around for a drink?' Jacob says.

'The bar was packed,' Rick replies. 'The bell for last orders had rung, we wouldn't have got served. Not much point sticking around when you can't get a drink.' He laughs, and Jacob does too.

'So. I wanted to talk to you about a potential project. A drawing project.' He nods at our sketchbooks. 'I'm guessing you're pretty good at drawing?'

'Alice is the star,' Rick says. 'You should see what she's just drawn in class. What's the project?'

'Potentially our next album cover. Eddie and I had this idea of having a sketch of the band on stage, but very posed, a bit like a still life.'

24

'Rick is who you need,' I say, hoping Jacob doesn't notice the tremor in my voice. 'He's the most talented artist we've got. He's already selling his work.'

'Sweet, you two. Like a couple of newly-weds. Buy you a coffee and we can talk about it?'

In the flesh, in the mid-afternoon light, Jacob looks older than he did on stage, around thirty, I'd say. But still hauntingly beautiful. Eyes, cheekbones, mouth. Slim neck, pronounced collarbones, the dip between them around the size of my thumb.

'You go, Alice,' Rick says, unexpectedly. 'You're the best at drawing and it'd be good for you.'

'Wait. No. Hang on.' I try to stop him, but Rick just smiles and walks away.

'I'm meeting someone,' he throws back over his shoulder, which is obviously a lie.

'Don't worry, Alice,' Jacob says. 'Strictly business.'

Though the way he says it, with eyes that are serious, a twisted mouth that isn't, makes me wish it wasn't just business.

'Do you like coffee?'

'Yes, sure, coffee, tea, Coke, anything.'

Jacob leans in, his face now only inches from mine.

'I meant real coffee. Italian coffee. Coffee that's more of a religious experience. Coffee to blow the mind.'

'I'm not sure I've ever had one like that.'

'Then we're going to Bar Italia.' He nods at the sketchbook under my arm. 'Bring your etchings.'

Now

Luke

The psychological wound of an adoptee is internalised at the very beginning of life. There's a prevailing sense of 'there must be something wrong with me, I am a disappointment, I am not worth keeping'. Over time, these hidden insecurities can develop into something potent and perilous.

Who Am I? The Adoptee's Hidden Trauma by Joel Harris

Hannah has a new title for me.

'The man with two mothers,' she said last night in the darkness, stretching out across the baby to place her hand on my thigh.

Today, with the arrival of my mother Christina for the weekend, it feels particularly apt.

I return home from work and see her navy-blue Golf parked up outside the house with a complicated cocktail of feelings. There is, I always feel, an undertow of resentment on both sides: mine in having to feel gratitude for my rescue, hers for me not being the child she actually wanted. Her own flesh-and-blood baby was stillborn in her last month of pregnancy and I don't think she will ever get over it.

I find her pacing around the kitchen in tight little circles with Samuel draped across one shoulder. She is winding him maternity-nurse style, or so I imagine, having never actually come across one of these mythical creatures (I picture someone large and humourless in a starched white cap).

'Hello, darling,' she says and we attempt an air kiss with the baby lodged between us.

Hannah is sitting at the kitchen table with about one quarter of her normal presence. This is the thing I notice first when the two women in my life get together, how my mother saps my girlfriend's energy until she becomes almost someone I can't recognise. She says hi, limply, and immediately I know something is up.

'When did you arrive?' I ask Christina, trying to piece together potential disaster.

'Oh, just after lunch. I found Hannah asleep in that chair with Samuel virtually sliding off her lap. So I persuaded her to go to bed while I looked after the baby.'

There's a small silence, which my mother breaks with, 'I cannot believe it was Samuel's first time in his cot. You two are hilarious. He screamed the house down.'

I don't look at Hannah; I know her tragic eyes will break my heart. One of the many things we are united on is our attitude to parenting. This baby – our son, no one else's – will never be allowed to cry, not if we can help it. He will be cocooned in safety, a nest of reassurance, powered by our heartbeats. No need for psychoanalysis – I was wrenched from my natural mother's arms and deposited in an alien environment, where, as Christina loves to recount with a seeming lack of perception, 'you cried and cried and cried for the first few weeks'. Let's just say I am physiologically programmed to detest the sound of a baby crying.

'Mum, I've told you that Samuel doesn't sleep in his cot.'

I fight the instinct to grab my son back and go instead to the fridge, where I take out a bottle of beer.

'Drinks,' I say. 'What would you like, Mum? I think we've still got gin from last time you were here.'

My mother is here for forty-eight hours and already I am struggling to think of things to say to her. The conversation never flows the way it does when Hannah's parents come up from Cornwall – those lovely, semi-drunken, laughter-filled nights when everyone talks at once. When I first met her family, I was stunned by what I initially saw as a lack of respect. Don't they ever listen to each other? I thought, as the sisters interrupted and vaulted from one topic to the next, no sentence finished, gravity, whenever possible – even the saddest of tales – traded for their easy laughter. And the touching – my God. I'd never seen anything like it. Knee-sitting and hair-stroking and hand-holding; these people were so goddamn tactile, and not just with each other, but with me too. Maggie, Hannah's mother, hugged me the first time I was introduced, a sluice gate, it seemed, for cheek-pinching and hair-ruffling and the regular chest punches from Peter, her father, the slightly alarming knee-sitting from her younger sister Eliza. If you wanted the North and South Pole of families, then mine and Hannah's could step up as the perfect candidates.

I realise as I mix a gin and tonic and begin chucking ingredients from the fridge onto the kitchen table that I have slipped into my default position of high alert, a state I assumed throughout my childhood. Keep busy to stay out of trouble was the maxim I lived by. The trouble, I think, was simply my mother's notice and the likelihood of being forced into worthy pursuits I couldn't bear. 'Why don't you cycle over to Andrew's and see if he'll go blackberry-picking with you? We could make a pie later.' (I was around fourteen at this time.) 'Let's ring up the girls from the Grange and invite them over for a game of cards.' (A pair of sisters so beautiful and cool I'd rather have cut off my own testicles than make that phone call.)

She is a good woman, my mother, and I do love her, albeit a textbook kind of love that is layered with guilt, gratitude and frustration. Complex, like I said.

There are more shocks over supper when it transpires that she has rung up a nanny agency on our behalf and invited two prospective au pairs for interview tomorrow. Interfering doesn't quite cover it.

'Don't be cross with me,' she says, correctly interpreting our shocked silence. 'Hannah, it's really not that long before you go back to work and it can take time to find the right person. I thought it might help if I was here for a second opinion.'

'Oh Christina,' Hannah says, instant tears in her lovely eyes. 'I can't bear to think about leaving Samuel, not yet.'

My mother reaches out to pat her hand.

'If you change your mind about going back to work, I'll make sure you don't suffer financially.'

For the best possible reasons, Christina thinks Hannah should be a stay-at-home mum. She doesn't perceive the raging torment, the utter wrench, that is the choice for Hannah between leaving our beautiful boy and returning to a job she loves.

And so next morning to the prospective au pairs, the first one arriving at 10.15. My mother has spent the morning cleaning, and the house looks as if it belongs to someone else. She has found a home for every piece of clutter – a new cupboard for nappies, trainers rehoused in neat rows beneath the stairs – and she has even been out to buy flowers (lilies, which Hannah dislikes on account of their overpowering smell).

The way Hannah and I take against Nicole, the first

interviewee, before she's even taken her coat off, is pretty comical. It's as if she marks a cross in every box on the way down.

First thing she does is marvel at Samuel sleeping on his sheepskin rug in the middle of the floor. She looks at her watch.

'This is his mid-morning nap, isn't it? Do you think he might sleep longer in his cot?'

'They don't allow the little thing to sleep in his cot,' says my mother, laughing. 'They cart him around everywhere they go and then wonder why they're all exhausted!'

There follows a terse little discussion about Gina Ford, whose childcare manifesto was published last year. First present my mother gave us was *The Contented Little Baby Book*, an advocate of early starts, rigid routines and controlled crying, that last the most heinous in our minds. Nicole swears by Gina Ford, so there's little point her even sitting down.

My mother asks the questions, the au pair provides the correct answers – certified first-aider, recent, impeccable references, experience with newborns – while Hannah and I commune with our eyes. And I realise, looking at my girlfriend slouched in her chair, punishing Nicole with her feigned indifference, that none of this really matters. Hannah, me and Samuel, our tribe of three versus the rest of the world.

We actually like the next au pair, Carla, who grew up in Buenos Aires looking after her six siblings while her parents went to work. She falls upon Samuel, now awake and tentatively smiling, and asks if she can hold him.

It's me and Hannah asking the questions this time – equally coded – and Carla aces every one.

'Do you think it's good to let a baby cry sometimes?'

'My babies hardly ever cry. I wrap them up in a papoose and keep them close to me. They are happy.'

She laughs a lot, which reminds me of Hannah, and she

kisses Samuel's cheek without asking us if it's all right (it is).

But even so, after Carla has left, my mother says, 'I could tell you liked her,' and Hannah shakes her head.

'Yes. But not enough. I can't imagine leaving Samuel with her. I can't imagine leaving Samuel full stop.'

And seeing Hannah's closed-up face, my mother has the good sense to leave it there.

'You'll find someone when you're ready,' she says. 'And if you want me to help out to begin with, you only have to say.'

An afternoon at the park, a garlicky roast chicken for supper, an intense evening watching our latest LoveFilm offering, *American Beauty*, with its opening masturbatory shower scene at which none of us laugh.

Towards the end of the film, my phone pings with an arriving text and I pick it up, idle, scarcely even curious until I see who it is from. ALICE. Name in lights, in red, inferno-esque flames. My heart on the floor. My mother oblivious. My adoptive mother. My real mother, despite the confusing terminology. Guilt I am used to, but this is something else. I feel like a cheat.

Luke, the message reads, *shall we have lunch again? It would be so lovely to see you!*

Back in our bedroom, I show the message to Hannah and she says, instantaneous reaction, 'Fantastic, let's invite her over!' and then claps her hand over her mouth. Christina, the mother who has brought me up for the past twenty-seven years, lies just feet away in the bedroom next door.

When I was young, the facts of my birth and adoption were rarely mentioned. But I do remember hearing my mother telling one of her friends, 'Oh, Luke has absolutely no interest in finding his birth mother. He isn't curious about her at all.'

My story was mapped out for me, carefully drawn and plotted like an Ordnance Survey map. Here you are, Luke, the blueprint for your life, no need to deviate. Questions? Why on earth would you have any of those? On my first day at prep school, my mother said, all nonchalant and casual, 'By the way, I wouldn't mention that you're adopted. People tend to make such a big deal out of it.'

I could read between the lines. Keep your adoption secret, she was saying, and mostly I did. I was biddable back then, and desperate to fit in.

'Oh God,' Hannah says, 'this is so complicated.' I feel the flat of her hand resting on my thigh. 'You know you're going to have to tell her, don't you?'

What, tell my mother about my mother? Impossible to even consider it.

Christina, I fear, would be totally displaced by the presence of Alice in my life. For within her is the same instinct that festers in me, the same unanswered question. Is the genetic flesh-and-blood connection different? Is it better, deeper, more natural? Deep down, we both suspect that it is.

Hannah's title has never felt more appropriate. The man with two mothers, that's me.

Then

Alice

Walking through Soho with Jacob, mind like a snowstorm. I'm relieved he doesn't try to make conversation as we pick our way through the litter of Berwick Street, polystyrene cartons spilling out the remnants of lunch – flaccid baked potato skins, bits of burger – stallholders calling out to one another as they pack away their crates of apples and oranges and pears. Jacob walks fast, fractionally ahead of me, with his feathered scarf flapping behind him, and I spot the stares as we cross Brewer Street and turn into Wardour. Is it his beauty that makes people look twice, or do they recognise him, this boy, this man I barely know?

He points out Bar Italia. There are tables outside crowded with men wearing suits and drinking coffee from little white cups; all around us the undulating, fast-paced rhythm of Italian.

'I know this place,' I say as we walk into the café with its terracotta floor and the vast chrome coffee machine behind the bar. At one end of the long, thin room there is a television, a crowd of customers sitting on stools in front of it, shouting. 'They come to watch the football.'

'For the football, the coffee, the chat. It's a kind of religion.'

At the counter, a man wearing a waiter's white shirt and bow tie greets Jacob.

'Hey, Luigi. This is Alice.'

Luigi extends a hand over the top of the counter.

'Two espressos?'

'Alice would like a cappuccino,' Jacob says, and Luigi rolls his eyes.

'Cappuccino is for breakfast. Espresso now.'

'She's never had one. She has to try it.'

'OK, Alice. But is not good for your digestive system.' He waggles his finger like a schoolteacher. 'Milk in the afternoon will make you sick.'

Sitting beside Jacob at the little red and white Formica table, I fight through a wave of self-consciousness. When he looks at me with a small smile, I wonder if he can read my mind.

'Come on, then. Show us your etchings.'

I open up the sketchbook halfway through. I won't bore him with the early staged tableaux: the solitary pear on a carefully pleated tablecloth, the vase of flowers, the basket of apples. As it happens, the page I show him is a portrait of Rick, drawn in the first week at college. He is sitting at his desk, chin propped in his hand, staring straight at me; it makes me smile just to see him.

'Your friend is right. You're very good. It's exactly like him.'

'It's the first time I drew him and still the one I love best.'

'Really not your boyfriend?'

'No. Everyone thinks we're together, but we're not. Sometimes I wonder if Rick might be gay.'

It comes out before I can stop myself.

'I shouldn't have said that.'

'Why? I don't care.'

'I might be wrong. I probably am.'

He smiles and says, 'Alice, I believe you,' and I feel foolish for protesting so much. But I am as confused as everyone else that nothing has developed between Rick and me. He's indisputably handsome, he is the funniest, kindest person I have ever met and since day one we have been inseparable. We are as close as any lovers but, so far anyway, without even the tiniest spark of chemistry.

Jacob flips a few more pages and then he comes to my oak tree.

'A tree that's actually a man. Or a man that becomes a tree?'

And suddenly I'm telling him about my fascination for all trees, but particularly oaks. When I was a child, growing up in Essex, I spent every spare hour in the fields behind the house. And the trees, especially in the dusk light, seemed to take on their own characters. I don't feel stupid telling him that they were like my friends. Or that even as I've grown older, the character of a tree – the oaks in Battersea Park, the cherries and limes lining the streets of Notting Hill – has remained visible to me, as if I perceive trees in a way that no one else does.

Luigi arrives with our coffees.

'Cappuccino for the young lady. Espresso for you.'

I've had proper coffee before. My parents were devotees of Rombouts; they treated themselves to one of the little plastic filter cups every Sunday after lunch, although I wasn't always offered one – it depended on my father's mood. This is something different.

Jacob watches me while I take my first sip.

'God. It's delicious.'

Another sip.

'It's like – well, I've never had nectar, so …' What would be the most accurate description of this creamy, mouth-exploding taste? 'Hot ice cream.'

Jacob laughs.

'That's exactly what it's like.'

I tell him about the Rombouts coffee. My father deciding whether or not I'd earned the right to one depending on my behaviour that week. Homework done the day it was set. Dressing properly for church. Being on time. A whole mental checklist for him to riffle through each week.

'He sounds like a bit of a jerk.'

'He's a canon at our local church.'

'There you go.'

'I don't like him very much. He's not nice to my mother. He preaches about human kindness in church and then treats her like she's a slave. He has a vicious temper and you never know when he's going to lose it.'

'Sounds like it was time to get away.'

'I'd like never to go back.'

'Well you don't have to. You're a free woman now. How old are you?'

'Almost nineteen,' I say, and Jacob laughs. I've let myself down with the 'almost'.

'How old are *you*?'

'How old do you think I am?'

I am confident enough now to look at him properly, examining his features as an artist might. The grooves around his eyes are quite deep, especially when he smiles. His front teeth are a little bit crooked and slightly yellowed from nicotine. Not that any of this detracts from his beauty; more I am measuring his flaws as an indicator of age. Like looking into a horse's mouth. Or counting the rings of an oak.

'I think you're thirty.'

'Cheeky. Twenty-six.'

Seven years older, I find myself thinking. Is that an acceptable gap? And perhaps he is having the same thought, because he says, 'Quite a lot older than you.'

'That doesn't matter,' I say, and he smiles.

'It doesn't, does it?'

He looks at his watch. It's ten minutes to seven.

'If we walk slowly, the French House will be open by the time we get there. Are you up for it?'

More than I have been up for anything, ever. I wish I could communicate with Rick telepathically. If I could, I'd tell him that right now, right in this moment, I have never felt happier.

Now
Luke

Reunions between an adopted child and his birth parent are often characterised by an intense honeymoon period which can feel a bit like a love affair. The bonding process that normally takes place in the first six years of a child's life remains dormant and is reawakened when they meet as adults.

Who Am I? The Adoptee's Hidden Trauma by Joel Harris

Samuel lies on his little sheepskin rug in the corner of the kitchen. Hannah arranges and rearranges the flowers she bought from the florist earlier; I am stirring apple sauce, checking the slow-roasting pork, salting the potatoes, and all with an undertow of frenetic excitement. Alice is coming for lunch.

Earlier today I got out the paint pot we keep under the stairs and painted over every single fingermark and smudge of dirt I could find. Hannah polished the dark brown furniture my mother gave us, clunky mahogany antiques that feel too old-fashioned for our home. A few minutes ago she lit a Diptyque candle she'd been given for her birthday and now the kitchen smells deliciously of roasting meat mixed with fig and fern. The table is laid with linen napkins bought earlier from the gift shop. I have even polished the wine glasses. Ridiculous levels of over-preparation, but it's the only way either of us can keep calm.

When there's a knock at the door – one o'clock, she's exactly on time – my stomach swoops and I am momentarily paralysed by a desire to run. Not towards the front door but away from it.

'It will be fine,' Hannah says, and she takes hold of my hand and pulls me out into the corridor, a gentle shove in my back until I am leading the way.

I open the door and find Alice standing there, and there's a rush of chemicals, no other way to describe it, coursing through my veins, a surge of intensity that is like nothing so much as the feeling of being in love.

She stands on our doorstep dressed in a blue denim shirt and white jeans, a paper wrap of sweet peas held against her chest.

'These are for you.' She thrusts them at Hannah as she walks through the door and Hannah presses them to her face and inhales.

'My absolute favourites. Oh Alice,' she says, looking up at my birth mother. 'You look exactly like Luke. And Samuel looks just like you too.'

Her voice wavers dangerously and Alice reaches forward to pull her into a brief, spontaneous hug.

'Believe me,' Alice says, 'I've done nothing but cry for the past few days.'

She releases Hannah and looks at me – a fractional pause; you'd need to be deeply attuned to notice it – and then we embrace too. How can I explain what it's like, this shyness, this shall-we, shan't-we first-date-ness between mother and son? It's easier for Hannah and Alice, that's all.

In the sharp bright light of our kitchen, Alice spots Samuel on his rug and gives a little cry of anguish that seems familiar to me, perhaps from a lifetime ago, perhaps recorded somewhere in my cellular memory, who knows?

'Just look at your little boy,' she says. 'He's you exactly, isn't he? Those eyes, my God.'

But then she moves away to look out at our little garden with its tiny bed in full bloom: irises, freesias, delphiniums (my other mother's handiwork; she's a fanatical gardener).

'What a place you have here,' she says, and does Hannah notice the way Alice's voice shakes, her fight for composure? Her examination of the garden, I understand, is simply a decoy while she gets herself back together.

And yet with the presence of Hannah and Samuel, the relaxed setting of our own home, this lunch is the antithesis of our first one.

The food is perfect. Roasts are my speciality and I've really put my back into this one. The pork is scented with fennel seeds and cloves, the potatoes are hot, exploding little mouthfuls of crunchy sweetness.

And within minutes it seems Alice and Hannah are like old friends. They have art in common and a shared passion for Rodin. Alice tells us she still goes to the V&A at least once a month to sketch a Rodin nude.

They talk of the Young British Artists, Hirst, Emin, the Chapman brothers, and Charles Saatchi's *Sensation* show a few years back, which Hannah loved and Alice hated.

'I can't stand this trend for fleeting, button-pushing art. The portrait of Myra Hindley was shocking. And? What are you left with? So Marc Quinn filled a head with blood. Cheap, disposable emotion, nothing particularly thought-provoking or enduring, to my mind.'

When Alice tells us about her and Richard's time at the Slade, I find myself mesmerised.

'There was a restaurant everyone went to at the time – everyone famous, that is, not poor students like us. San Lorenzo, you might have heard of it? Well, they bought one of Rick's self-portraits and hung it in the restaurant, and after that, collectors and galleries were sniffing around him, even in our first year. That doesn't happen very often. Rick was the real deal right from day one.'

Hannah says, 'We literally couldn't believe it when we found out he was Luke's father. He's a god as far as I'm concerned.'

'You must meet him. He's keen to get to know Luke, but we thought it was a good idea for us to meet first.'

'What happened with you and Rick? Do you mind me asking?' Hannah says.

'You probably know he's gay?'

'So how …?'

'It was much harder to be gay back then. There was a lot of homophobia around. And Rick was always hoping he'd become straight, that was the goal.'

She breaks off to sigh.

'Poor Rick. You can't change who you are. The thing you need to know is that both of us wanted to keep you, and we tried so hard to make it happen. But my father was very insistent on your being adopted.'

'If you and Rick wanted to keep me, surely it was none of his business?'

'You'd have to meet my father to understand, and that's never going to happen. I haven't seen him since you were born.'

'How awful,' Hannah says.

'My father went behind my back to bring in the adoption agency. I'll never forgive him for that. He refused to give me any financial support and the only way for us to survive was for Rick to drop out of college and get a job. And in the end

I couldn't let him make that sacrifice. He had to finish at the Slade. He needed to become Richard Fields. And we'd have been so poor, you and I, living in council housing and relying on social security handouts. I didn't want that for you, Luke. I'm sorry.'

Alice seems exhausted after this admission, exhausted and a little broken. Hannah, who has been feeding Samuel on her lap, instinctively hands him to her. I see Alice's reluctance as the baby is settled in her lap; fractional, just the slightest hesitation, but I catch it. And I also register the seconds of pain that flash through her eyes.

'Goodness,' she says. 'The weight of him. The feel of him.' She sniffs his head. 'That wonderful baby smell. What is it, milk, soap? There's a sweetness, isn't there? I'd quite forgotten.'

She is wearing a long necklace of black beads, and Samuel, nestled against her chest, grabs hold of it in his fist and pulls.

'Oh you cheeky thing,' Alice says, pulling a puppet show of facial expressions, eyes wide, mouth in a round, exaggerated 'O'. And Samuel laughs, for the first time in his life, a deep-bellied chuckle that neither of us has ever heard before.

'Oh Alice,' Hannah cries, 'you made him laugh.'

And Alice does it again, no trace of self-consciousness as she performs for our son, eyes open, eyes shut; a simplistic version of peekaboo that triggers another outburst of giggles.

'You are such a sweet boy.' She presses her lips against Samuel's scalp.

There is this great big dent in my heart, no other way to say it. Once upon a time, Alice would have pulled faces for me too.

Perhaps in the silence that follows we are all thinking the same thing.

Hannah leans forward and says, voice low, 'Oh Alice. Poor you.'

Alice closes her eyes for a second; she nods.

'I tried, Luke, I really did. But in the end I couldn't keep you. And after you'd gone, well, to say that I regretted it ...'

Hannah says, 'I'm sorry,' and I know from the break in her voice that she is fighting tears. I hear the words she leaves unsaid. Sorry for asking about it. Sorry for what happened, for losing your son.

'You did the right thing for me,' I say, even though I believe the opposite is true. Take a child from its natural mother? How could that possibly be the right thing? But instinctively I understand that this woman, this real live mother of mine, cannot cope with the truth. 'It was brave of you. You gave me a life with the security of two parents, even though it was the last thing you wanted.'

Alice reaches out to cover my hand with her own, and it's the first relaxed physical contact between us.

'Luke,' she says. 'You have grown into the nicest human being.'

Then

Alice

Here at the French House (actual name the York Minster, though no one calls it that), Jacob is famous. Everyone knows him: young, old, the red-faced, bad-tempered barman, who redeems himself when he shouts, 'What's your girl drinking, Jake? Gin or beer?'

It's halves of beer and pressing ourselves into a tightly packed corner, no tables or chairs or anywhere even to put down my sketchbook. I keep it wedged beneath one arm until Jacob notices, takes it from me and stashes it behind the bar.

The white noise of a hundred or so people talking and laughing, the air putrid with smoke and spilt alcohol, our bodies unnervingly close. We try to talk a few times but it's like puppet theatre. I'm mouthing words, like I'm underwater; he's shaking his head.

'Nope,' he shouts. 'Still can't get it.'

And then he looks at me in a way that makes me aware of my heart thudding, pulsing, and my breath, which I let go in one long rush. He doesn't drop his eyes and I don't drop mine and the look, the half-smile, lets me know that he feels as I do. There is a conclusion to this, an obvious one, and I understand it here in this densely packed bar where the noise is like a cocoon, just me and Jacob at its very centre, no room for anyone else.

I've made a decision and the decision is this. If there's a

chance to sleep with Jacob tonight, I'm taking it. The desire to touch him, with my hands, my mouth, to press my cheek against his, it's exactly the same pull I felt when I watched him on stage at the Marquee.

'What are you thinking about, Alice?' he shouts. He pulls his face into a comical frown.

I'm thinking that I would really, really like to kiss him, though I can't say that.

'Shall we find somewhere quieter after this?' I shout back, and he smiles again.

'Come on.' He takes hold of my hand, and just that first contact is an electrical charge that judders through my bones.

Outside, it's a crowded Friday night in Soho. There are people everywhere, the streets now vivid with neon signs for strip joints and peep shows and girlie bars. When I first arrived in London, a few weeks ago, I was shocked by the blatant, frenzied sexualness of Soho. Not like my father, who decries it as a snake pit of immorality (he's always been unoriginal in thought); more the fact that these bodily desires I'd always considered secret, and possibly shaming, were to be honoured and celebrated instead. I took the trouble to lose my virginity in my last year at school; nothing special, a few pleasant-enough skirmishes with a boy from school I liked but didn't love. One thing I knew was that I wasn't going to arrive in London with the tag of virginity tied around my neck.

Drinkers pool on the pavement outside every pub we pass, and quite often we walk in the middle of the street just to get around them, still hand in hand, Jacob now with the sketchbook beneath his arm.

'Are you hungry?' he asks, and I tell him yes, wanting to stretch the evening out for as long as I can.

'Chinatown then.'

*

Our 'business deal', such as it is, is struck in a red and gold restaurant over bowls of chicken in black bean sauce and egg-fried rice.

'What we have in mind is a charcoal drawing of the three of us on stage, something very posed and stylised, almost like a classical painting, but it's a sketch.'

He flips through the final pages of my sketchbook and comes to the last drawing of Josef.

'This is incredible, Alice. You have so much talent.'

I can't hide the glow of pleasure at his words.

'There are some classic poses that life models always adopt. Maybe we could incorporate some of those?'

'Are you suggesting we do this in the buff?'

I start to laugh, but it dies halfway through because now all I can see is him naked.

'We'll get you some money from the record label, of course. How much do you want? Fifty pounds? A hundred? Let's call it a hundred.'

'A hundred pounds is far too much.'

'Most people would actually be quite pleased. Most people would ask for more. Stick it in the bank or something, you might need it someday.'

In my head I'm storing up these extraordinary moments to recount to Rick, but they are coming at me too fast. Me earning a hundred pounds in the course of one brief conversation? Rick sold his painting to San Lorenzo for thirty, and at the time that seemed unthinkable to us.

'What shall we do now? We could go to a club, but there's nothing open for an hour or so. But maybe you want to go home?'

'I don't want to go home.'

'So …' A slight hesitation. 'I live in Soho. You could come to my flat for a bit, if you wanted? But is that what you want?'

I nod, because it's impossible to speak.

The way we grin at each other then, a mutual smile that tips into almost-laughter, is an agreement signed.

In darkness now, we pass doorways with red lights above them, others where girls stand outside, bare legs with fur coats, the standard uniform. Sometimes Jacob says hello.

'Hi, darling,' he calls, and the girls always know his name.

'Hi, Jake.'

'Should I call you Jake?' I ask, and he laughs.

'I should think so. My grandparents were the only people who called me Jacob, and you wouldn't want me to associate you with them.'

His flat is at the far end of Dean Street, three floors up, he tells me, though the moment he has opened up the front door of the thin, tall house and pulled me inside, he kisses me, both hands clasping my face, the sketchbook thudding to the floor.

'Next time,' he says, stooping to pick it up, 'let's leave the etchings behind.'

The front door of his flat opens into a large sitting room, painted wine red with purple and gold strips of fabric hanging from the ceiling like rows of hammocks. There are candles everywhere, dark red ones, stuffed into empty wine bottles with swollen bases. Beneath the window there's a low-slung sofa made of brown corduroy, almost hidden beneath a covering of cushions, twenty or thirty of them, in orange, red and purple, each one embroidered in gold and glinting with tiny mirrors.

Jake picks up a box of matches and begins to light the candles.

There are records everywhere – in boxes on the floor, in piles stacked up against the wall – and I watch him flipping through the first pile, taking his time to select one. *Exile on Main St.*

I've played it so often on the turntable in my teenage bedroom, the soundtrack will always be imbued with memories of home.

'They wrote this album in the south of France. And we're going to do the same thing in Italy. We've rented a house in Fiesole, just outside Florence, for the summer.'

Jake lights the last candle and comes to sit next to me on the sofa.

'There's a lot of pressure with this second album,' he says. 'The first one made it to number six; they're expecting the next one to be even bigger. And it's complicated because – well, you saw the show – our music is very varied, not one thing to define us, and that can be hard to sell.'

He leans forward to kiss me.

'Shall we have some wine? There's a bottle in the fridge.'

'Wine would be good,' I say, feeling that I need it. I'm not much of a drinker – Rick can testify to my weak head – but it's hard to ignore the undercut of nerves, my whole body clenched with … desire? Fear at what comes next?

Jake returns with an opened bottle of Frascati and two glasses, which he places on a wooden coffee table covered in music magazines, including *Sounds*, with its arresting picture of him. This, more than anything, underlines the surreality of the situation. I'm about to sleep with a rock star; there on the table is the evidence.

He sits next to me and kisses me again, more insistently this time, and I close my eyes, expecting more, but he draws away.

'I think we both want the same thing. But any time you want to stop you just have to say. OK? I'm a lot older than you and you don't have to do anything you don't want to do.'

'I want to do everything,' I say, and Jake laughs.

'Oh me too. All of it. Shall I tell you what I thought when I saw you at the Marquee for the first time? I thought you were the most beautiful girl I'd ever seen and that whatever happened that night I must make sure I talked to you. And then you disappeared. Not to say that the album cover project is a ruse, but I had to find you.'

He sketches an outline of my features with his finger, stroking my eyelids, nose, mouth, chin.

'You're so lovely,' he says, manoeuvring himself so that somehow we are both lying down on the sofa, Jake on top of me, his hips pressing against mine, bony and a little painful. But his touch is so light, hardly there, as he strokes a pathway from my neck to my chest, veering outwards, exactly, expertly sliding back and forth across my T-shirted breasts, as though he is touching my nipples. The T-shirt needs to go, that's all. I sit up and begin to peel it off, but he stops me, taking hold of my hand.

'Let's take it slowly.'

He presses his mouth lightly on top of my breasts, first one, then the other, then moves his hand inside my T-shirt, seeking each nipple in turn.

'I'm not sure I want to take it slowly,' I say, and though his face is buried against my chest, I know he is smiling.

'You will want to, Alice Garland.'

I love the way he says my name, all the time, almost every sentence. On his lips it seems to transcend into something else, something poetic, majestic. He lifts his head again and stays there, not touching, not kissing, but the way he looks at me, the gravity of his dark-eyed stare, is more intensely sexual than anything that has come before.

'The waiting is the thing. The wanting is the thing. You'll see.'

Now

Luke

Adoptive parents often feel as if there's a chapter missing from the instruction manual. They can't understand the child's anxiety and feelings of shame, don't recognise the pervasive layer that runs right through them, the sense that 'I am flawed'.

Who Am I? The Adoptee's Hidden Trauma by Joel Harris

We are on our way to have lunch with my father. My real, actual father, who just happens to be the renowned artist Richard Fields. Fields the artist is public property. His paintings sell for millions and hang in the world's most famous galleries – MOMA in New York, the Tate Modern, the Pompidou. We had to wait weeks to get tickets for last year's exhibition at the National Portrait Gallery. And yet little is known about the man himself, which is why Hannah is hoping to get an interview with him. He's gay, apparently, though never seen out with a lover. Alice says he is married to his art. And to her, of course, a couple throughout all these years it would seem, just without the sex. Or the baby.

In the missing years – twenty-seven of them – I have always been focused on my longing to know more about the woman who carried me in her womb and who must, I figured, have felt some connection to unborn me. Now I am about to come face to face with my biological father, and I'm not sure how I feel about it. Do I want a relationship with him, this man who supposedly nurtured me through the first weeks of life? If you'd asked me this before I knew my father was Richard Fields, I suspect I wouldn't have cared too much either way. Now it's impossible to get beyond the fact that my flesh-and-blood father has two whole pages dedicated to him in *Who's Who*.

Richard lives in a converted warehouse on the edge of Smithfield Market, its walls painted blue-black like the old factory buildings in downtown New York. I press the bell. While we wait for him to answer, Hannah says, 'I'm nervous,' and I nod my agreement.

But it's Alice who opens the door, in a white shirt and dark jeans, her feet bare, toenails painted a surprising cobalt blue. Again, that strange, tilting feeling just to see her.

'Hello, little family,' she says, instantly putting us at ease.

We follow her along a dark corridor, navy walls hung with Richard's distinctive portraits. If I were to describe them, I'd say they combined the wide-eyed psychological intensity of Lucian Freud with the angularity of Francis Bacon, the crudeness of Beryl Cook.

The corridor leads into an open-plan space painted entirely white – walls, floor, ceiling – and here at the other end of the room is Richard, coming towards us gripping a bottle of champagne by its neck. He is taller than I thought and almost boyish-looking with his blonde hair and tanned, handsome face. I feel suddenly, excruciatingly shy and I force myself to meet his gaze while my stomach lurches with unease. But Richard puts down the bottle and opens his arms wide.

'Surely this is one of those moments when we have to hug?'

he says, and his smile is so warm and friendly I feel myself beginning to relax.

'My goodness,' he says once he has released me. 'Let me look at you. Do you know, I'm embarrassed to tell you this, but I once tried to draw you as an adult, or rather how I imagined you would look as an adult. A bit like a police photofit. It was terrible and I see now that I got it completely wrong. You're far more handsome. You look … well, you look just like … your mother.'

For him, like me, it's clearly a difficult word.

'Wait till Samuel wakes up,' Alice says. 'He's exactly like Luke, you will be amazed.'

Samuel is in his papoose, face buried in Hannah's chest, only his fine covering of dark hair visible.

'Let's get stuck into this champagne,' Rick says, leading the way to a pair of sofas at the far end of the room.

I notice a tremor in his hands as he eases the cork from the bottle, and I am glad. I think perhaps he feels the same as me. It is entirely overwhelming meeting him, on two counts. First, most incontrovertibly, for the fact that he is my real, actual father. But also his fame. I've never met anyone as well known as Richard Fields; it's a shock just to see him up close.

A word about the apartment, quite the coolest, most lavish space I have ever been in – what you'd expect from a famous artist, only more so. The walls are hung with paintings – not just the portraits he is known for, but abstract landscapes too, with his well-documented fetishising of colour: hills in burnt orange, trees that are neither purple nor silver but somewhere between the two. Above our heads is a chandelier, a waterfall of glass baubles suspended from thin wires. Even the sofas, low, leather and segmented to make up two corners, feel like they belong in a design museum.

Rick walks over to the record player and puts on *Blood on the Tracks*, my favourite Bob Dylan album if I had to choose. We talk about music and they marvel at the fact that we like all the same bands.

For the first ten minutes or so I'm happy to sit back and watch. Hannah is used to talking to artists, and the three of them run through a précis of the biggest names, some of whom – Freud and Hockney – Richard actually knows. They are engrossed in their world and it is the perfect foil for my observation. Surreptitiously, I'm looking at Richard whenever I can. I'm noticing his physique, slim and fine-boned like mine, though he is a good few inches shorter than I am. His blonde-ness, his fair skin, his blue eyes are all his own; there's no doubt that I take after Alice. Personality-wise, he's funny, warm and absurdly talented. I'd be happy to inherit any of that.

Samuel wakes up crying. It always astonishes me, the nought-to-sixty journey from comatose to full-blown rage, the few emotions he can express so stark and extreme.

'I'll warm up his milk,' Hannah says, passing him to me and following Rick out into the kitchen. It's impossible to talk or even think as Samuel arches his back and screams into my ear. I'm trying to console him, standing up, walking around, jiggling, shushing, but his rage, his hunger, clamour against my brain.

There is something in his cry that taps into a primal instinct in me, each wail provoking a wash of instant coldness. When we brought him home from the hospital the first day, he woke in the middle of the night raging with hunger. And while we, brand-new parents, switched on lights and found breastfeeding pillows and handed this tiny, red-faced, screaming package from one to the other like an unexploded bomb, there was an unstoppable flow of tears running down my face.

We got Hannah propped up against her pillows and the baby latched on and the lights switched off, and she reached out and took my hand in the darkness.

'I had a feeling this was going to be difficult for you,' she said, with the piercing insight that defines her.

Now, as Samuel gears up for full-force rage, Alice is across the room in seconds. 'Shall I take him for you? I remember how distressing it is when your baby cries. The pitch of the cry is designed to provoke you. Biological programming or something like that. I used to hate it.'

She takes Samuel and sits down with him in her lap, and though he still continues to cry, Alice is right. From a distance, the sound is more tolerable.

He twists his head from side to side, opens his mouth and closes it again.

'It's coming, little bird,' Alice says, and when Hannah re-appears with a bottle, she offers to feed him.

'You can drink your champagne and look at Rick's paintings. I'm sure you never get a break.'

It's such a touching gesture this, and also seeing Alice sitting there with our baby on her lap – my mother, in fact, with her grandson – fills me with unexpected joy.

Rick's homosexuality is more apparent here in his private collection. Many of the paintings are of young men, one a reclining nude on a sofa draped in velvet that makes me think of Manet, an inverted Olympia perhaps, but Hannah says, 'A tribute to Modigliani,' and she would know. We are engrossed in the art, the privilege of being allowed to see the paintings Rick has kept for himself. It amuses me to watch Hannah and see the look of intensity in her eyes. I understand that in her head she is constructing a profile piece on Richard Fields, storing up one detail after another, the artist as you've never seen him before.

So it's a shock when Rick comes out of the kitchen, cries, 'Oh Alice!' and drops a basket of bread all over the floor. 'He's identical,' he says, his voice devastated.

'I know. But, Rick, isn't it wonderful?'

Approaching the sofa, stooping to collect the scattered bread, I feel as if Hannah and I are intruding on a private, interior conversation. When Rick turns to us, he has tears in his eyes and he uses his index fingers to prevent them from spilling out onto his cheeks.

'Sorry to be emotional. You couldn't possibly understand. But for me, it's like déjà vu. It's you, Luke. He is exactly the same as you. It's like being taken back in time to see our baby again.'

'Our baby'; the casualness with which he claims me as their own. I'm not sure whether to feel elated or destroyed.

'I felt that too,' Alice says. 'It is a shock, the first time.'

Rick seems speechless for a good minute or two; he stares at Samuel, shaking his head. And it is left to Alice to expertly defuse the moment.

'Look at that.' She waves the empty bottle at us. 'He's such a good baby. Aren't you, little bird, a very good baby? Is lunch ready? Need a hand?'

Lunch is a work of art in itself; how many dishes on the table? Six or seven at least. Salad studded with pomegranate and feta, bulgur wheat flecked with parsley and tomato, an earthenware pot of chicken tagine, little dishes of hummus and baba ganoush, strips of flatbread, a plate of caramelised squash. It is almost too beautiful to eat.

We sit opposite each other – Hannah and I on one side, Rick and Alice on the other – and from this vantage point I see how they are really the same as any couple. They pass each other dishes without asking for them and discuss the flavours – 'More cumin this time?' 'I like it better with the feta, don't you?'

Rick even calls her 'my love'. 'More champagne, my love?' he says.

And soon, with Hannah's talent for unobtrusive but expert questioning, they are talking about when they first met at the Slade.

'There were only twelve students,' Alice says. 'And they were all brilliant, although Rick, of course, was the best by miles. It was absolutely terrifying. On our first day, Gordon King came into the studio with lots of balls of string and said, "Use the string, however you want," and so we strung it up in a sort of complicated cat's cradle right across the room. And the next day, it was a different tutor called Mick Moon, and he told us to dance in between the string and so we had to come up with a performance piece. It was excruciating.'

'Alice, remember Josef, the life model?'

'How can I forget? He was beautiful,' Alice says. 'I think we were both a bit in love with him.'

'Alice was so talented. The star of our year.'

'You were the one selling paintings to famous restaurants.'

'And you were working on an album cover. We were all jealous of that.'

'Really?' I ask. 'Which band?'

And Alice says, 'No one you'd have heard of. They broke up after that album, career over.'

'Enough about us,' Rick says. 'I want to hear about your childhood. I can't tell you how often I thought of you and wondered how the adoption was working out. Hoped it was, prayed it was, but we had nothing to go on. You can't imagine what that silence feels like. You make the decision to give up your child for adoption – and then you never hear anything about them again.'

'There's not much to tell. My parents were quite a bit older than me and my dad died a couple of years ago. I grew up in Yorkshire, in a village near Harrogate, and went to boarding school in Suffolk. My mother' – always a word to snag upon – 'is very different to me. She's wonderfully kind and generous and she loves me a lot, but the truth is …' I take a swig of champagne, Dutch courage for this surprising burst of honesty, 'we are not interested in the same things. I've never felt she understood me and I don't say that to complain. I think I've been a mystery to her and that makes me feel guilty. I was perfectly happy throughout my childhood, but I never felt like I fitted in. I was all wrong at school. I didn't care about rugby or cricket or being in the school play or any of that stuff. And it was the same at home. It's not that it didn't work; just, I think, that we all wanted it to work better than it did.'

I catch Hannah's eye and she reaches out to squeeze my arm. She understands how I'm feeling, relieved to admit the truth, guilty at what feels like a betrayal of my mother.

Rick says, 'That makes sense to me. Can you take a child from one environment and expect them to fit perfectly into another, alien one? One they are not genetically programmed for?'

His comprehension is hard to bear. He understands it now. Why, why did neither of them understand it then? Alice talks with derision of the life she and I might have had, living in a council flat, surviving on benefits. But what I see, crave, long for, is the true connection between mother and son that has always been denied me.

Rick says, 'The only thing Alice and I wanted to know was whether we had made the right decision for you.'

They are both looking at me now, intense dual stares that verge on pleading. I tell them what they need to hear.

'It was a good childhood. I wanted for nothing.'

*

There's orange polenta cake with crème fraiche for pudding and Persian coffee in tiny coloured cups – royal blue, dark pink, jade and lavender – painted gold on the inside. Everything Richard Fields owns a statement of immaculate taste.

Rick says, 'Before you leave, I have something to show you,' and I catch Alice's tiny, barely perceptible nod, the silent communication between these ex-lovers who have spent a lifetime as best friends.

He goes over to a Chinese cabinet, another jaw-dropping possession, black lacquer covered with tiny birds in gilded cages, and comes back with a piece of paper in one hand and a pen in the other.

He places the paper down on the table in front of us.

It's a pencil sketch of Samuel, or at least that's what you would think; a close-up of him sleeping: long lashes, fine dark hair, the pronounced bow of his lips captured to perfection, his head resting on a small clenched fist. But at the top of the drawing, the year of my birth, 1973, and a name. Charlie.

'It's you,' Hannah whispers, and I'm glad she has spoken because I'm not capable of it. I don't look at Alice, I don't look at anyone.

Rick uncaps his pen and signs the bottom of the drawing with a flourish. *Richard Fields*, the same curlicue signature, instantly recognisable to me from the print we have at home. He slides it towards me.

'It's for you, Luke,' and my heart turns itself inside out.

I pick up the drawing – this tiny time bomb from my past – and clasp it against my chest. I shake my head, too blown apart to speak. But Rick understands, I can see that. He reaches out and squeezes my shoulder quickly.

'It's absolutely miraculous to have you back in our lives,' he says.

Then

Alice

Sex with Jacob turns out to be a lesson in longing. And waiting. He wasn't joking about that. The teasing, the painfully slow removal of each garment, the stroking of one part of my body, his touch so devastatingly effective that I no longer care about the noise I am making, and then, just when I think this is it, he begins all over again somewhere else. I didn't know that the feeling of his lips pressed against the arch of my foot could trigger a short, sharp pathway of desperation that leads straight to my groin. Or that talking, non-stop in Jacob's case, could drive me to the edge of insanity. He tells me what he's going to do, he tells me what he likes.

'I think this might be my favourite part,' he says, before pressing his mouth very exactly beneath my hipbone, a light line of kisses from one side to the other.

I sit up and try to kiss him too.

But he pushes me down again, gently.

'I'd like to do things to you as well.'

'And you will. I'm looking forward to that.'

Always in his voice I hear the smile.

He turns me over and I wait, unseeing, for the feel of his lips, always longer than I want to wait, never where I expect them to be. He smoothes his palm over the curve of my bottom, follows it with the light flicker of his tongue.

'This I like very much,' he says.

He slides his fingers inside me, first one, then another, moving them backwards and forwards until I think I have reached the point of no return. My mind is empty, my body moves to its own rhythm, thrusting, pulling, wanting more. Yet just as I am about to tip over into orgasm, he stills his fingers and begins kissing my neck instead. And this goes on for more than an hour.

When we finally make love, I'm so riven by need I grip his shoulders tightly with my fingers and he laughs and says, 'Ow, that hurts.'

And then neither of us is laughing; there's just the feeling of him being inside me at last and the euphoria of being able to finally give in. Afterwards, we lie in stillness, hearts racing, and then Jake lifts his head from my chest and says, 'Some business meeting,' and my laughter verges on hysteria. Everything with him is magnified and I can't quite work out why. There's my inexperience, but I don't think it's that. I think Jake, somehow, is just more; he exists in high relief.

We sit up, both naked on his corduroy sofa, but after his leisurely exploration of my body, I feel no self-consciousness, none at all. Jake passes me a glass of wine and I take two big gulps, one after the other; I need the alcohol to calm me down.

He says, 'I feel completely wired. What have you done to me, Alice? There's no way I can go to sleep. Shall we smoke something?'

For the record, I'm the world's worst pot smoker, though I try to persevere. I watch him crossing the room again, and this time he comes back with a sweet tin, the kind my father keeps in the glove compartment of the car, and a blue striped blanket, which he hands to me.

I wrap the blanket around myself and watch him work, opening up his tin to reveal Rizla papers, a lighter and a foil packet that contains grass. I've seen joints being built numerous times, but something about his skinny-fingered expertise connects with my brain and my heart and my groin. Already, only minutes later, I long to be in bed with him again.

He lights the joint, an elongated, tightly packed three-skin, inhales deeply and passes it to me.

'This is probably the moment to warn you that I'm a lightweight.'

'It's very mild, you'll be fine.'

I take several long, deep tokes, hearing the little seeds of grass crackle and pop, the tip of the joint burning vivid orange with flecks of yellow. I hold the smoke down in my lungs for a few seconds and exhale in a pleasing, dragon-like plume. I've kept going with the smoking thing because everyone does it and I want to fit in. I want my university years here in London to be the thing I dreamed of in my teenage bedroom, this vibrant, free-spirited, technicolour world where everything is possible.

'What are you thinking about?'

'How much I want to be in bed with you,' I say, surprising myself, though Jacob smiles.

'So now you can read my mind?'

He stubs out the joint in the ashtray, stands up and leans down to scoop me up into his arms, carrying me across his sitting room like a threshold bride.

Now

Luke

If Hannah and I were ever to get married, Ben would be my best man. I've told him this countless times and he finds it hilarious that I am forecasting a wedding in which my girlfriend apparently has no interest.

'Don't be such a groomzilla,' he said last time I raised it. 'You don't need a church service and a piece of paper. You and Hannah are the real thing.'

Tonight we're meeting Ben and his girlfriend Elizabeth at Kensington Place. Favourite restaurant and favourite people. I could not be looking forward to it more.

Hannah is wearing a black dress from pre-pregnancy days, with tiny straps and multicoloured zigzags across the front. Her wild hair is pulled back in a velvet scrunchy and twisted up into a knot; she is wearing gold hoop earrings and dark lipstick. She is so beautiful, it seems to me she could trigger a cardiac arrest. I tell her this as we pass through the restaurant's revolving doors, and she laughs.

'I can't decide whether you're good for my ego or appalling. I might become horribly conceited if you carry on like this.'

Ben and Elizabeth are sitting at the back of the restaurant, side by side on a red leather banquette. He half rises when he sees us and raises his fist in a comrade salute, an old prep-school joke we haven't managed to shake.

Ben, like Hannah, comes from tactile parentage, and he grasps us into a three-way hug that goes on for too long. He enjoys my discomfort; it makes him laugh to see me squirm.

It's six weeks since we've seen each other, and there are vital topics to discuss. Most pressingly, what's it like having found my real parents?

'I can't believe you haven't met them yet,' I say casually, shrugging on this suit of normalcy to see if it will fit. Me, son of Richard Fields and Alice Garland. He's my dad, didn't you know?

But I will never fool Ben.

'And how many times have *you* seen them exactly? Twice?'

'Alice three times, Rick once.'

'I can't get my head round it,' Elizabeth says. 'I have two prints of his in my sitting room at home. It's like finding out you're related to Van Gogh.'

We all laugh at this, and when the waiter comes over with menus, Ben orders a bottle of champagne.

'You've found your real parents. This is big. This is huge. We should be celebrating.'

Ben knows better than anyone how much I've fantasised about this reunion over the years. He was the only one at school who knew I was adopted – I followed my mother's advice and kept the facts of my birth tightly wrapped in secrecy. There was one year when we shared a room, and after lights-out the conversation invariably went the same way. In darkness I could run with the fantasy. Was she a musician or an actress, this beautiful, loving girl who had fought hard to keep me? Did she live in London or Paris or Rome? Did she think of me every day as I thought of her? Turns out I wasn't so far from the truth.

When the waiter comes back, we order without looking at the menu. Chicken and goat's cheese mousse to start for all four of us, followed by scallops for the girls, calves' liver for me and Ben. When you've found your favourite restaurant serving your favourite food, why would you bother to change?

Ben wants to know every detail we can remember from the lunch with Rick. At art school, he was dubbed 'the new Richard Fields' on account of his gritty, overexaggerated portraiture. To say that Rick is his hero is missing the point. In his head, Ben *is* Richard Fields.

'Everything he owns is wildly beautiful,' Hannah says. 'Even the sofas are a work of art. And he's an incredible cook.'

Elizabeth says, 'And can you see them as a couple? Back in the day?'

'They still are in a way, aren't they?' Hannah looks at me. 'It was like we were a couple and they were a couple. If you didn't know, you wouldn't be able to tell the difference.'

'So why did they break up?'

Elizabeth is a child psychologist, and gentle persistence is her defining trait. The number of times she has pushed me through a conversation I haven't wanted to have.

'Pretty obvious, isn't it? He's gay. I imagine it just took him a while to come out.'

'But they could have kept you, couldn't they? Couldn't Richard, Rick, have supported Alice? Couldn't he have left art school and gone out on his own? He had the talent.'

Ben intervenes as I knew he would. He picks up the bottle of champagne and pours the rest of it into our glasses, painstakingly divided so we all end up with the same amount.

'Elizabeth,' he says. 'My love, my darling. You are trampling on our friend's feelings with six-inch platform boots. He needs time to get used to it. Don't grill him.'

'Sorry, Luke,' Elizabeth says, blowing me a kiss. 'You can always tell me to shut up, you know that.'

Over dinner, Ben tells us about his latest portrait: a forty-something hedge fund manager, commissioned by his wife.

'The really gratifying thing is that they collect art. Weird, outré stuff they buy from graduate shows. And they've encouraged me to go to town on his absurdities. He has what I would call ...' Ben breaks off to laugh, 'an excessively strong nose. And I've exaggerated it to become the focal point. And he loves fishing, so we've got him in his waders with a Picassoesque trout in the background.'

'This is what I miss,' Hannah says. 'I'm dreading leaving Samuel, but I cannot wait to start writing again, interviewing artists, going to shows.'

'Have you found an au pair yet?' Elizabeth asks.

'Not yet. The ones we like are always too expensive.'

The reality, the one we try to avoid, is that we can't really afford for Hannah to go back to work. She's going down to three days a week, which means her salary is virtually halved, and every childcare option we've looked at, including a nursery where the babies slept lined up in cots like a Romanian orphanage (Hannah cried when we left), would eat up all her income. We discuss the should-she-shouldn't-she quandary endlessly. And we have decided that she should go back to this job she loves, arts correspondent on a national newspaper at only twenty-seven. If she doesn't return, someone else will be parked up at her desk in a nanosecond. And although she tears herself apart each night, talking, thinking, fretting about leaving Samuel, we tell ourselves she has at least to try it. But she'll effectively be working for free, just a hundred pounds or so left over at the end of each month.

'If only my mum lived closer,' Hannah says. 'Or yours.'

There is a weighted silence while the unmentioned mother – *the other mother* – hovers in the air between us.

'We don't really know Alice yet,' I say, 'and also, she works. She's an artist too.'

'Not a bad idea, though,' Hannah says, kissing my cheek. 'We've got three mothers between us; maybe they could job-share.'

We are paying the bill and ordering cabs to take us home when my phone pings with an arriving text. Alice.

'There you go,' I say, flashing the phone at my friends, pleased, as if I needed to prove her existence. 'She wants us to meet up with her and Rick on Sunday,' I tell Hannah.

'Great, invite them for lunch. It's our turn.'

And then, catching the look of wistfulness on Ben's face, she says, 'Why don't you both come too? You're Luke's best friend, it's time they met you.'

Then

Alice

I slide into class ten minutes late, wearing the jeans of yesterday with a blue striped shirt Jake has lent me, which Rick notices immediately. He makes his eyes enormous and hisses, 'Alice Garland, have you been collecting scalps?'

We are in Gordon King's class, which is unfortunate because my mind is fried, my face raw from this morning's intense kissing, my groin aching, not unpleasantly, from a full night of lovemaking.

I fetch the lithograph of the oak I made in the last session and begin to mix paint, four specific colours: titanium white, yellow ochre, cadmium red and ivory black. This restricted palette, made famous by the Swedish painter Gustav Zorn, gives me all the scope I need for the microscopic metamorphosis from bark to flesh, or rather, a hue that can be perceived as both. There is an art to getting the right shades to effect the transformation, almost a kind of wizardry. I know exactly what is needed and begin with the gradual reduction of black and yellow ochre; I will use the resulting greens and browns for the first wash of colour.

Just looking at these tones of bark can transport me back to the old oak tree in the field behind my house, with a hollow big enough for me to hide in. I might make a version with the hollow painted on afterwards, symbolic of the emptiness inside my tree. Not much of a leap to remember the first time I hid within the oak, aged twelve, the day my first full report arrived home from boarding school. A rash of B minuses and the occasional C (plus D for needlework, which I claimed privately as a triumph).

My father called me into his study.

'Well, hello, Miss Average,' he said as I walked through the door.

The words held an edge of jokiness that didn't meet his tone. I realised in the next fifteen minutes as he railed against weakness and mediocrity that trying to please him would never be enough. I was a different girl when I left his study, with the whole of the long, lonely summer holiday ahead. I knew my father didn't love me, couldn't love me, wouldn't love me, and from that moment on, my childhood became simply something to get through.

I am absorbed in my preparation, and Gordon's voice, his presence right in front of me, comes as a shock.

'What is this, Alice?'

His voice is quiet, and I know, from a whole childhood of experience, that a quiet, measured voice can be the most vicious.

'It's a tree,' I say; not to be facetious, more as a preparation for what comes next, for the groundswell of indignation that will accompany my defence.

I am a woman who paints trees, humanised ones. I am being paid a hundred pounds to capture the likenesses of a band who are being talked about as the new Rolling Stones.

'If you'd been on time, you would have heard what I said at the beginning of class. If your idea isn't working, then start again with a fresh approach. Don't waste your time and mine with repetition of a weak concept.'

'Gordon, if you would hear me out, I'd like to explain why I'm painting trees and what it is I'm trying to convey.'

He nods his assent, his sharp-featured face tensed into acute irritation.

I tell him about the series of people trees, caught at the exact moment of metamorphosis. I talk about why I've chosen the Zorn palette, to find not just skin tone but the exact shade for bark, lichen and moss. I tell him that when I look at certain trees, I can see character and emotion, traits and flaws displayed in the gnarl and twist of the branches; I see gender, history, triumph and disappointment.

'Very well, Alice. Since you're so passionate about it, carry on.'

His voice is neutral, unexpressive, hard to read. But I am instantly buoyed by his change of heart, the first time he has ever listened to me.

I am immersed in my work and the next hour and a half flashes past, no thought for anything except the personality of my tree. Strong, bold, confident. The way I am feeling today, as if I am wearing Jake's self-assurance along with his shirt.

At the end of class, Gordon leans against the edge of his desk and waits for us to listen.

'In art, intellect is everything. Passion is everything. Curiosity is everything. If you have an intrigue, the essence of something you can dig and scrape away at until it becomes an actual concept, then pursue it. That curiosity and passion is the whole reason you are here.'

Across the other side of the room, Rick catches my eye and winks. Victory to you, tree girl, the wink says.

Our second 'business meeting' takes place in the Coach and Horses, a chance to get to know the band, Jake says, and so I bring Rick along for moral support.

The pub is crowded, but they're easy to spot, gathered in a corner, their own little pocket of black. Jake has his back to me, so it's Eddie who sees us first.

'The art students are here,' he says.

Jake whirls around, pint sloshing over his hand, laughing as he pulls me into his arms. He kisses me on the mouth, briefly, though just the lightest touch of his lips is a pathway of electrons leading straight to my groin.

'Come and meet the boys,' he says, introducing us to Eddie first, a James Taylor lookalike with the same strong brows and dark, shoulder-length hair; then Tom, the drummer, who jumps up and shakes both our hands.

'Jake's been telling us all about you. A pair of geniuses according to him.'

'He's exaggerating. Wildly.'

'Speak for yourself,' Rick says.

Jake has swooped upon a table littered with empty fag packets and scrunched-up bags of crisps, which he sweeps to one side. Tom brings over a tray of drinks, including a couple of pints for me and Rick. Jake, I notice, has switched to whisky, which he drinks neat without ice.

He says, 'As you know, Alice is going to be working on our artwork for the album cover. We should probably tell her a bit about the record.'

'It's a rock album,' Eddie says. 'But with more ballads than the last one. So we need the artwork to reflect that.'

'And the love songs are sorrowful and melancholic,' Tom says. 'That's the mood we want to convey.'

'Can we see the drawing you did the other day? The expression on that guy's face is exactly what we're talking about. She's unfazed by nudity, by the way. We could all take our kit off and

Alice would be there with her pencil measuring the distance between our eyes.'

Everyone laughs, including me, I feel myself beginning to relax. I'm not at all self-conscious flipping the pages of my sketchbook, until we come to the latest drawing of Josef.

'Wow, he's beautiful,' Tom says, and there's a wistfulness in his voice. 'What a face.'

'Jake is right. This is incredible work,' Eddie says, and his approval, coming after a coolness I do not understand, gives me a little rush of satisfaction.

'Are you sure you want a charcoal sketch? You don't want to try oils?'

'Definitely black and white and sort of sketchy,' Jake says. 'I liked your idea of us posing as if we were the life models.'

'We could try out very classical poses so you look like statues but you're on a stage and you have your instruments around you. Almost as if you've been turned to stone.'

'See? I told you she was good. Robin is going to love this artwork.'

'Who's Robin? Your manager?' Rick asks.

'He's an art dealer, kind of our patron really. He spends a lot of time with musicians and actors and writers. He has a whole scene going on.'

'Please don't tell me you're talking about Robin Armstrong?'

'Yeah, that's him. He likes to support new talent. He did a lot for the Stones at the beginning.'

Rick clutches a hand to his chest, miming cardiac arrest.

'The man is a god. And here you are just casually dropping his name into the conversation.'

Jake says, 'You can meet him if you want. We'll introduce you.'

And I know Rick feels exactly as I do, that this chance meeting with Jacob Earl, lead singer of Disciples, is causing ripples and repercussions in our lives, his and mine, that seem miraculous.

I marvel at Jake's confidence when he kiboshes a suggestion for the five of us to go out for a curry.

'Alice and I might make other plans,' he says, standing up from the table and holding out a hand to me. And though Rick whistles and Eddie rolls his eyes and Tom laughs, no one seems to care.

The moment the door to his flat closes behind us, things turn frantic. Grabbing each other, kissing, wrenching off clothes. I am torn between the urgent desire to feel Jake on top of me, our skin melding together, his ribs pressing painfully into mine, and wanting to slow down, like he did, wanting to make him wait. He puts his arms around my waist as if to carry me to bed, and I say, 'Hold on, not yet.' I begin to kiss a pathway down his chest and hear his sharp intake of breath as I fall to my knees and move closer and closer to his groin.

And so it will be a game of control between us, I realise, as I reach his erection, harder and fuller than I could ever have imagined, and take him tentatively in my mouth.

Jake says, 'Oh God,' and the tortured tone of his voice is a shot of aphrodisiac. After a few seconds I return to the slow exploration of his body, first my lips, then my tongue, and this time he gives a long, low moan and grips hold of my head with his hands, his fingers laced into my hair.

'Fucking hell, Alice,' is what he says.

Afterwards, we lie on his sofa, wrapped up together, the room lit only by the lamps outside. Soho is in full night-time swing, the rattle of cabs in the street below, the drunken laughter of strangers.

Inside, though, we are silent, as if it is impossible to put into words what is happening between us.

Jake smoothes his palm along the side of my body, rhythmically, as if he's stroking a cat. It feels comforting to be touched like this, it stirs something inside me, something that goes way back.

'I like the way you touch me,' I tell him, and he smiles.

'Same.'

I reach for his hand, holding it in my own, rubbing circles in his palm with my thumb. Instinctively, I press my thumb up and down, right in the centre.

'That feels good. Reflexology?'

'I don't even know what that is.'

I carry on with my thumb-pressing, working my way slowly up to the base of his hand and then his wrist. My thumb hits a thick ridge of scar tissue, confusing at first. I stop pressing and start stroking, learning its shape. Jake just watches me.

'What's this?'

He takes his other hand from where it rests on my thigh and brings both wrists together.

'Two of them, actually. A matching pair. Stupid mistake when I was sixteen.'

I'm so shocked I can't find any words. Instead, I kiss each of his wrists in turn.

'But why?' I say finally, and Jake shrugs.

'I think the correct term is a cry for help.'

'I hate that you were once so sad,' I say, and my throat feels tight with unshed tears.

'Seems to me you didn't like childhood much either. Lots of people don't. It really doesn't matter.'

He moves even closer so that he can kiss me, eyes first, nose, then mouth.

'Don't look like that, Alice. The past is over. You and me, here, in the now. That's all there is.'

Now

Luke

Reunions between adopted children and their natural parents can feel deceptively celebratory at first. There's relief on both sides, a passionate desire for it to work. But fast-tracking these fragile new bonds can end in disaster if both parties are not careful.

Who Am I? The Adoptee's Hidden Trauma by Joel Harris

I'm always in charge of the food when people come over, and today I've decided to keep it simple. It would be foolish to try and compete with Rick's cooking, so I've made a casserole instead. Shin of beef from Moen's, the butcher, simmered for three hours in a lethal combination of sherry and red wine, fresh thyme to lift it into something sublime. I'll serve it with mashed potatoes, the cardiac variety, whipped with butter and cream until they are as soft and melting as a mousse. We have beautiful cheeses and plenty of red wine – a classic Chianti I've fallen in love with; the table is laid with our favourite plates, flowers and six bright orange candles that Hannah picked up in the Design Museum. It's beginning to feel like a party.

'This is exactly the celebration we should be having,' Hannah says, because she can always read my mind. 'Having Ben and

Elizabeth here makes it special. We are introducing your best friends to your parents.'

There is nothing to do but laugh at the absurdity of this statement, and for a moment hilarity overtakes us.

'Christ,' I say, remembering seconds before they turn to mush, 'I need to turn the potatoes off.'

Alice arrives first. The moment she sees Samuel, she swoops him up from his little rug, lifts his T-shirt and blows raspberries against his stomach. We do this too, but Samuel always laughs hardest with Alice. And it's an addictive sound, these deep-bellied chuckles of his. Even when she has stopped, he sits on her lap, smiling at her, waiting patiently for the next trick, and she obliges, playing peekaboo behind the flat of her hand.

Today she has brought a toy with her, an octopus with different sounds hidden within each of his legs – a bell, a rattle, the crunch of crackly paper. It's a slightly ugly thing, this octopus, bright blue with black and white stripes and sinister eyes, but Samuel loves it. He grips one of the legs in his small fist and doesn't let go.

Rick arrives in a cab twenty minutes later. He hands over a bottle of champagne and says, 'I was going to drive, but I changed my mind at the last minute in case we want to get pissed.'

'Rude not to when we have all this,' I say, gesturing to six bottles of Chianti lined up on the worktop.

Alice says, 'Oh Rick, look, Chianti Classico. The labels are still the same.'

'We used to drink this in Italy,' Rick says. 'Alice was there for a whole summer and I went out to visit. A long time ago now.'

I catch something here, an edge of melancholia between the two of them. But there is no time to examine it, because Ben and Elizabeth arrive, the way they always do, in a maelstrom of noise and excitement. Ben is dressed in his yellow and black Rupert the Bear suit, bought in a charity shop ten years ago and worn relentlessly ever since, Elizabeth is holding an enormous bouquet of flowers and a chocolate cake she made herself.

Ben and Rick begin talking instantly, and while I race around the room filling wine glasses and checking the casserole and mashing the potatoes, I try to listen in.

Rick says, 'I checked out your website this morning. I really like what you're doing. Are you with a gallery?'

I'm quietly proud when Ben tells him that he has already had two solo shows in London and one in New York.

'Sit down anywhere,' I say, carrying the casserole over to the table, and it turns out that Ben and Rick are opposite each other at one end while Alice, Hannah and Elizabeth sit at the other. I perch in the middle, perfectly poised for both conversations.

The casserole and the wine are good and the noise level ramps up the way it does when your oldest friends come around. Already there's a strange familiarity about Rick and Alice, almost as if we have known them for years.

And Hannah clearly feels the same, for I overhear her saying to Alice, 'Funny how quickly you've fitted into our family. Like we've known you for ever.'

A confusing stab of anguish at this, my girlfriend's faint disloyalty to my adoptive mother. Hannah and her family, wild, Cornish free spirits that they are, have tried and failed to connect with Christina.

When Hannah first got pregnant and we decided to keep the baby, they invited my mother and me to Cornwall. I'd been there once before, a golden weekend where I learned to surf and Hannah's mother, Maggie, took us on a walk over the cliffs and taught me the names of the wild flowers that grew there. We'd built a fire on the beach and drunk hot cider from a flask, and when the tide came in, Peter, her father, took us cave-wading, a dangerous torchlit pursuit that left us up to our necks in freezing water. On the train journey back to London I felt strangely bereft, pining for a county and a family never known before.

When my mother came to stay, she drove the eight hours from Yorkshire and arrived in her navy-blue Golf with her Jack Russell on the passenger seat beside her. Seeing my mother arriving or leaving anywhere solo swamps me in sadness, I can't help it. And as she entered Hannah's brilliantly ramshackle house, stepping over surfboards and wetsuits slung down in the hallway, the family's effervescence seemed to leak away. They'd been waiting with a home-made carrot cake and the teapot on standby, excited about the impending meeting, the projection of our shared future, the conversations we would have about the baby. But, instead, my mother's formality (a mask for shyness, I've always thought) set them all on edge and suddenly no one was acting like themselves. Peter, one of the best conversationalists I know, seemed capable only of asking about the journey; Maggie, too, tested out topics – gardening, Tony Blair, the failing NHS – and dropped them one by one, until we were left with virtual silence. I was completely torn. Wanting so much to belong to this family but feeling physically divided, as if by an estuary: me and my mother on one side, the pink-skinned, curly-haired Robinsons on the other. I don't want to be on my mother's island, but I don't want to leave her there either. Complicated being me.

Throughout this lunch, which becomes louder and more amusing with each new bottle of wine, I am happy to sit back and listen. I want to absorb the sensation of my old-new parents conversing with my best friend. Rick and Ben are talking about portraiture and what it is that makes a painting endure.

Rick says, 'I always think good art reveals itself slowly over time. That's what collectors want. They want a work that shows you a little bit more of the process each time you look at it. For every hour of making, I try to spend another one looking. The critical thing is what you observe when you go back to your work.'

Hannah says, 'Rick, this is exactly why you should give interviews sometimes. People love to hear about the process.'

'I hate the press. I have no need of them, my work sells. Why should I tell people about my private life?'

'Because you are public property in a way. People are fascinated with you, your art, your influences and inspirations. Isn't it a bit hard-hearted not to share those details?'

'I do share them. There's always a press release that goes out with each show.'

'Oh come on. Richard Fields, the persona behind the portraits. No one knows that. There's virtually nothing true or honest written about you; it's all conjecture.'

Alice says, 'Maybe Hannah could interview you? You could trust her not to write something you didn't like.'

'Oh Rick, would you? I've so wanted to ask you but haven't quite dared. I'd give you full copy approval. And anything else you wanted.'

Hannah's lovely face is aglow with possibility; how could he resist? We are all watching Rick as he considers it, his reluctance is clear. Finally he smiles.

'Hannah, of course. For you I'll make an exception. It might even be fun. When would you like to do it?'

'I'm back at work in two weeks and it would be amazing to have something lined up. My editor won't believe it.'

'Have you found an au pair yet?' Elizabeth asks.

'Not one we like and can afford. I'm getting panicky about it. Although Luke's mother,' Hannah stumbles infinitesimally on the word but carries on, 'will step in if we're stuck.'

Samuel is sitting on Alice's lap, one hand clasped around her long jet necklace, his head nestled against her chest. I am sure we are all thinking the same thing, but it's Elizabeth who hints at it.

'Look how comfortable he is with you, Alice. Shame you can't look after him.'

There's a flash of intensity around the table; Hannah and I are unable to look at each other.

But Alice says, 'Oh my goodness, wouldn't that be great? He's such a gorgeous baby. I wonder if there's a way to make it work.'

Hannah says, 'Could you, Alice? Even in the short term? I'd feel so happy leaving him with you.'

'I'd love to help.'

'We'd pay you, of course.'

'What about your work, Alice?' Rick says.

'Huh. Painting pooches for rich old ladies? I can do it in my sleep. You know I can.'

'I'm not sure it's such a great idea. You did say you wanted to take things slowly.'

Elizabeth says, 'But isn't there something so lovely about the idea of Alice looking after her son's son. Sort of full circle.'

A silence falls on the table again. Alice presses her lips against Samuel's scalp, lightly, once.

'It must have been so hard on you having to give Luke up,' Elizabeth says, and I glance at Alice quickly. I recognise the fight for composure. It's a battle I'm going through myself.

'You have no idea.'

The pain in her face is almost shocking to see. I love Elizabeth, but for someone with a career dependent on her people skills, she can be immensely tactless.

Alice has made a hammock of her arms; Samuel is lying

across them, feet and head balanced on her elbows. When she strokes his cheek, he smiles at her, full beam, irresistible.

'It's tempting, little bird, isn't it?' she says, and Hannah leaps up from the table.

'Luke, wouldn't that be the perfect solution? Let's have tea and some of Elizabeth's delicious cake,' she says, just stopping herself, it seems to me, from adding 'to celebrate'.

Then

Alice

Jake is cooking for Tom, Eddie, Rick and me, and he has thrown himself into it with his usual vigour and intensity. Not for him the standard student fare of spaghetti Bolognese or macaroni cheese. We are having bouillabaisse, made from fish bought at Billingsgate Market this morning (he left the flat at six to get there before it closed), and tomatoes cooked in his oven for hours until they collapsed into a sweet, garlicky mess.

He has made a rouille to go with it, and a green salad dressed with olive oil bought from the chemist, with day-old panini donated by Luigi, grilled and rubbed with cut cloves of garlic.

'Where did you learn to cook like this?' I ask him as I lay the table with additional knives and forks bought hastily from a junk shop near college.

'Books,' he says. 'I found an old Elizabeth David cookbook and I used to read it at night when I couldn't sleep. I've been collecting second-hand recipe books ever since.'

I want to ask him why he couldn't sleep, but we are so brand new, he and I, and his face closes up whenever he talks about his childhood, so I allow the moment to slide.

Rick arrives first, a relief for me, with a bottle of wine wrapped in a twist of white tissue paper on which he has drawn felt-tipped stars and crescent moons interspersed with smiley faces. He is wearing purple corduroy bell-bottoms and a white peasant top, bought, he told me, in a boutique in Neal Street selling exclusively female fashion.

'Let me tell you,' he said, 'I was not the only male browsing the rails. And they were not shopping for their girlfriends.'

'Wow,' he says now, looking around Jake's burgundy, orange and purple sitting room. 'This place is cool. The vibe of a strip joint, if you know what I mean.'

Eddie and Tom arrive and we all squash around the tiny kitchen table with our tumblers of Mateus Rosé. Jake and I have been together for almost three weeks, and I know he is holding this dinner so I can get to know the band.

'We're family to each other,' he told me. 'Especially me and Eddie. The two of us grew up in the same town. There's nothing we don't know about each other.'

I forced myself to ask Jake about Eddie then.

'Why is he so distant with me? It's as if he doesn't like me.'

'How could anyone not like you?' Jake said. 'It's just that he's protective of me. He knew my family – especially my wicked grandfather …' he laughed as he said this, but I caught the sudden darkness in his eyes, a film of gloom, 'and he's been looking out for me ever since.'

I can tell Jake has relayed some of this conversation to Eddie, because there's a noticeable difference in the way he treats me tonight, asking me questions about college and home.

'Alice's father is a prize jerk by all accounts,' Jake says.

'Oh yeah, the wannabe vicar. Isn't he a churchwarden or something, Alice?' Rick asks.

'A canon. He gets to dole out communion on Sundays. He loves that. And sometimes he gives the sermon – and if he doesn't, he gives it to my mother and me at the lunch table. He did a whole sermon about Soho that he called Soho-dom and Gomorrah.'

Everyone laughs at that.

Eddie says, 'Have you heard about this gay and lesbian march that's happening? Your father will be apoplectic when he finds out. Apparently everyone is going to walk to Hyde Park, kissing and holding hands in the street. I think it's brilliant. We should all go along and show our support.'

Am I the only one who sees how still Rick becomes when he hears this? I've suspected he is gay all along, but he keeps his sexual identity resolutely hidden, even from me, his best friend.

'Are you gay, Rick?' Jake says, casually, almost in passing, and for a moment the air around me freezes. I force myself to meet Rick's gaze and I see the shock that comes into his face. Shock, confusion, then something else. All of a sudden he's laughing.

'Oh my God! Fuck! Yes, I am gay.' He says it slowly, like an announcement. 'I just haven't admitted it to anyone before.'

He's looking at me and I'm looking at him; it's often this way with us. As if there is no one else in the room. I reach out across the table to grab his hand.

'Alice,' he says.

'I'm so proud of you,' I tell him.

And then we are all laughing and Eddie thumps Rick on the shoulder and says, 'Well done, mate. Who the fuck cares? Gay, straight, bisexual, whatever.'

Rick shakes his head.

'That was so much easier than I thought.'

'When did you find out you were gay? Or did you always know?' Tom asks.

'At school, when I was maybe sixteen or seventeen. Up until then I was putting up posters of Brigitte Bardot and hoping I might feel something. I've spent years hiding who I am, pinning my hopes on marriage and kids and the whole heterosexual dream. Like that was ever going to happen.'

The night turns into a celebration. More bottles of wine are opened and the bouillabaisse is, hands down, the most delicious thing I have ever eaten. None of us manages to do much more than groan as we dip our toasted Italian bread into the tomatoey, fishy sauce. Even the salad, with its sharp garlicky dressing, is an explosion of flavours in the mouth.

After dinner, Eddie rolls a joint, which he lights and passes to me. 'Ladies first,' he says with a formal mock bow, and I take a couple of tiny tokes before I move it on.

We listen to the new album from Stone the Crows, a blues act whose star is in ascension. They were playing exactly the same size venues as Disciples – the Rainbow Room, the Marquee – but overnight their popularity has soared. Tom, Eddie and Jake unpick the music, what they like, what they don't, and throughout the entire record Rick sits in silence with a half-smile that never leaves his face. I glance at him whenever I can. No one else realises it, but tonight is monumental, the landmark moment when he catapults from one way of life to another, no turning back.

After everyone has left, Jake and I lie together on the sofa and I tell him, 'You are a miracle worker, did you know that? Did you see how happy Rick was? He left this place looking like he was going to conquer the world.'

'Next mission, Tom,' Jake says. 'But I think we've got a long way to go with that one.'

'You think he's …?'

'I'm sure he is. But Tom doesn't. Not yet.'

'It must be so hard having to keep it all inside, and feeling so ashamed when there's no reason to. But unless you tell people, they can't help.'

'And that, Alice Garland,' Jake leans over to kiss my forehead, my nose, finally my mouth, 'is the crux of everything. You can't conquer your demons if you don't bring them out into the open.'

I'm surprised by his lack of self-perception, this man who keeps his sadness trapped inside him. Later, in the darkness, my fingers reach for his hands, brushing lightly over his ragged, bumpy wrists, and I vow to myself that one day, someday soon, I will wrestle Jake's demons from him and banish them for good.

Now

Luke

Adoptees may try to integrate their birth parent into their lives too quickly. They are anxious to traverse the missing years as quickly as possible and forge a strong mother/child bond. Inevitably this may backfire.

Who Am I? The Adoptee's Hidden Trauma by Joel Harris

Alice is to become our nanny. However many times I say that to myself, I still can't quite take it in. In other words, Alice, my actual mother, whom I have known less than two months, will be here week after week ensconced in our family lives. As reunions go, you'd have to say this one has been pretty phenomenal.

We struck the deal, Alice, Hannah and I – and Samuel, of course, cocooned on his grandmother's lap – over tea and eclairs in the French Café. Alice will arrive at 9.30 a.m. and leave at 6 p.m., Tuesday to Thursday, though she has offered to work extra days whenever Hannah needs it. She won't accept any more than a hundred pounds a week, which is considerably less than any of the au pairs we saw. We tried to insist on paying more, but she wouldn't hear of it.

'Look at him,' she said, stroking the back of Samuel's neck

with her index finger. 'He's so adorable, frankly I should be paying you.'

'You're just saying that to make us feel better,' I said, and Alice laughed.

'Luke, it works for all of us. You need someone you can trust and I'm ready for a change in my life. It's perfect.'

On our last night before Hannah returns to work, I cook fillet steak and open a bottle of our favourite Rioja. Candles burning on the table, Samuel wide awake and passed across the table from one to the other as we take turns to eat.

'I'm going to miss him.'

'Of course you are, but it's only for three days. And once you're in the office, working on a piece, you'll forget about him.'

'I will not,' Hannah says, a little fierily. 'But at least I won't have to worry about him. We couldn't find a safer pair of hands if we tried.'

'Are we asking too much of Alice?'

'No, I think she genuinely wants to do it. She's so close to Samuel already. It's almost uncanny.'

'I hope it brings Alice and me closer too.'

'Alice has bonded so quickly with Samuel *because* he reminds her of you.'

'Far easier to deal with a baby than the weird, fucked-up grown-up version.'

Hannah laughs. 'Exactly.'

We're making tea and getting ready to go up to bed when the phone rings. It's 9.30, which means it's my mother, also making her last-minute preparations for bed, including her nightly phone call.

'Hello, darling, just ringing to wish Hannah good luck tomorrow.'

'Hi, Mum. Would you like to speak to her?'

'No, no, I'm sure she's busy getting ready. Send her my love. So the new au pair is starting in the morning? What's her name?'

Duplicity is hard. It steals the words from your tongue, the breath from your lungs.

'Alice.'

'Alice?' my mother says, and I wonder in my coldly alert, paranoid state if her mind is whirring with all the Alices she has known. Alice, Alice, now where have I heard that name before? 'Alice who?'

'Oh, er, God, I can't remember her surname.'

'Darling, you are hopeless.' My mother is laughing. 'How old is she?'

'Um, fortyish, I think.'

'Oh, quite old then. What's her situation?'

If only I'd insisted on passing the phone to Hannah; she would have dealt with this inquisition so much better than me. She is sitting on the bench, Samuel asleep in her arms, watching me intently.

'How do you mean, Mum? She's a part-time painter. Looking to supplement her income, I guess.'

'But what's her experience with babies? She is a proper au pair, isn't she?'

'Of course she is. Mum, let's talk tomorrow. Hannah is keen to get an early night.'

I hang up and join Hannah on the bench, bent double with the drama of it all.

'Oh babe,' she says, 'this is so complicated, isn't it? But the moment your mum knows about Alice, it's going to feel easier.'

'I can't tell her.'

'Not yet. But soon. Things will become much simpler once Christina knows who Alice really is.'

Such prescient words. If only I'd listened. If only I had told my mother the truth.

Then

Alice

Jake shows me a different way to live. He cares about nothing and wants to try everything; to say that he has opened my eyes sexually in the space of a few short days is a dramatic under-statement. But it's more than that. His whole life is dedicated to small acts of pleasure, from the ritualistic Italian cappuccino to a night spent watching shooting stars in Hyde Park (we broke in by climbing over the locked gates, and spent hours on a bench wrapped up in blankets, and I think it might be the most romantic thing I will ever do).

It's his idea to spend a whole weekend in bed, forty-eight hours of decadent living during which we get dressed only once, to visit the little shop across the road for provisions.

Amir, the owner, laughs when he sees what we have lined up on the counter.

A bottle of cava, another of white wine, milk, a jar of Nescafé's Blend 37, a loaf of Mother's Pride, a packet of ginger nuts.

'All the essentials, yeah?' he says.

'Think we've got it covered,' Jake says, wrapping an arm around my shoulders.

In the kitchen, we unpack the shopping together like any married couple: milk in the fridge, tea and biscuits in the cup-board, champagne into the fridge. I am boiling the kettle for

91

tea, my back turned to Jake, when he surprises me with his hands inside my shirt, the sharp cold of two ice cubes against my nipples.

I cry out, but then I feel the warmth of his mouth against my neck and it turns into a gasp of pleasure instead.

I try to turn around to kiss him, but he whispers, 'No,' and I am used to this game of taking turns. I love it. I live for it.

'We're going to need a lot of time, a lot of weekends,' he says afterwards, as we lie on the brown sofa, and our future of committed eroticism stretches out in front of us, a whole infinity of lovemaking.

Jake carries the television into his bedroom and we watch one show after another: *Doctor Who*, *The Goodies*, *Parkinson*. There's an *Omnibus* on Andy Warhol, and the two of us watch entranced. Like everyone else, we're fascinated with Warhol. So much has been written about him, but it's rare to see him on TV, the man famed for his fiercely guarded privacy.

'Rick is going to be as big as Warhol, if not bigger,' I tell Jake. 'I overheard Gordon saying so the other day.'

Jake picks up my hand and kisses it without taking his eyes away from the screen.

'I live in hope that one day, Alice Garland, you might actually believe in yourself. You're just as talented as him.'

We drink the champagne at two o'clock in the morning out of cheap tumblers bought with Green Shield stamps; I recognise them because we have the same ones at home. My father often makes my mother a gin and tonic in one of these glasses, his own evening whisky in fine crystal inherited from his parents; small, everyday acts of pettiness intended to grind her down.

'Why do you put up with him?'

'Because we're frightened of him. His temper. The rages that can blow up from nowhere. He's tolerable most of the time, but when he drinks, it's a nightmare.'

'Alcoholic?'

'I don't really know. It doesn't seem to take much to make him turn. Three glasses of wine and he'll fly off the handle. It's like he's just waiting for me or my mother to say the wrong thing so he can start yelling at us. You get inured to it after a while. My mother just drifts off into her dreamworld and I suppose I closed down a bit more each time. I felt like I was marking out the time until I could leave.'

'Poor baby,' Jake says, kissing me. 'I hope he never hurt you. Physically, I mean.'

'No. Thank God. Sometimes I thought he might. But he always pulled himself back at the last minute.'

Jake is quiet for a moment.

'My grandfather was violent. All the time. But I never let him break me.'

'You really hate him, don't you?'

He shrugs. 'He's dead, so … I guess I just need to let it all go.'

Instinctively, I want to reach for his poor scarred wrists, but I hold myself back and try to believe in this cloak of imperturbability he shrugs on whenever I question him, as if the past cannot touch him. I think his wrists are proof of exactly the opposite: the past did break him.

In the morning, we are in the bathroom together, Jake shaving in front of the mirror, me about to have a shower, when I open up the cabinet to look for soap. And there inside are two boxes of medication I am instantly drawn to. I take them out and look at their names. Phenelzine and Largactil. They look nothing like the antibiotics I was prescribed throughout most of my childhood for recurring tonsillitis.

'Phen-el-zine.' I sound out the word like a child learning the alphabet. 'These look heavy-duty. What are they?'

Jake puts down his razor and turns to me, his half-shaved chin segmented by white foam.

'Antidepressants and antipsychotics. I've been on them for years. Ever since I was sixteen.'

'Psychotics?'

'That doesn't make me a psycho, if that's what you're thinking. Just a depressive. But not any more. I stopped taking them a while ago. I hate the way they fur up my brain. I can't write properly when my mind is all blurry, it slows me down.'

He takes the first packet of pills from me and starts popping them out, one by one, into the lavatory.

'What are you doing?'

'Moving on. Like I should have done a long time ago.'

This is all happening too fast. I want to stop him, to snatch the pills out of his hands and put them back in the cupboard. Just in case. I am just getting used to the information that Jake has spent the past ten years on heavy medication, and now, in a heartbeat, he is throwing it away. What if his symptoms come back? I feel in this moment completely out of my depth.

'Jake! Stop. Shouldn't you talk to the doctor first?'

'Do I seem depressed to you? Or euphorically happy?'

'Well, happy right now, but …'

I watch, helplessly, as he picks up the next packet and empties out the contents.

'Come here,' he says.

He closes the loo seat and sits down, pulling me onto his lap.

'I promise there's nothing to worry about.'

'What's it like?'

'Depression?'

I nod, too full of the moment for words, too fearful of what I'm about to find out.

'It's like being underwater while the rest of the world rushes by. You'd like to come up for air, only you have no energy, none at all; you might as well be paralysed. So instead you exist in a curled-up ball of bleakness.'

I press my cheek against his, eyes squeezed shut. My tears are a weakness when he's been through so much.

'Alice, look at me.'

I open my eyes, and he kisses me.

'There's no need to be sad. You have to believe me when I tell you that it's over. I've felt good for a long time, even before the cataclysmic, life-changing arrival of you. Do you believe me?'

'Yes.'

'Good. In that case, only two rules for the rest of the weekend,' he says. 'No clothes to be worn at any time. And no more questions.'

I was in love, you see. And I wanted more than anything to believe him.

Now

Luke

When Alice arrives each morning, Samuel and I are waiting for her. She always knocks, never uses her key, and I throw open the door with a flourish; it's part of our stand-up routine. Alice pulls one of her funny faces, mouth and eyes remoulded into a surprised 'O', and is rewarded with an instant chuckle. Samuel stretches out his arms and leans his whole torso towards her. This day after day after day.

'Traitor,' I say, handing him over with a goodbye kiss, and Alice says what she always says: 'Don't worry about us, we'll be fine.'

It's hard to know how we managed without her. As well as looking after Samuel all day, she washes and irons his clothes, cleans the house and cooks for us. Hannah and I come back to these beautifully prepared dishes – shepherd's pie, tagine, lasagne – classic fare but always with an undercut of sharpness, chilli or ginger or preserved lemon. I find myself looking forward to her food from mid-afternoon onwards.

She buys us things too, even though we ask her not to: fresh flowers every week, clothes and toys for Samuel, little gifts of chocolate from the delicatessen.

Today Hannah is interviewing Rick, a lead feature for the *Sunday Times* Culture section. Returning to work with a

Richard Fields profile in the bag, she jumped straight to the top of the class. Her editor said, 'Thank God you're back, we've really missed you,' and she came home that first day jubilant.

I'm back just a few minutes after six, the official end to Alice's day. In the kitchen, I find her stirring a chicken casserole at the hob, Samuel bathed and dressed in a clean sleepsuit, flopped up against a beanbag.

There is something consoling about the care she takes in creating beautiful food for me, her son, reunited after twenty-seven years apart. I like to think that Alice – who I find more reserved and conversationally restrained than I expected – pours her love into cooking for us instead.

We'd like to see more of her at the end of the day, but she always rushes off, refusing our offer of a glass of wine.

'You need your time with Samuel,' she says.

I did persuade her to have a drink with us once, and I came to regret it. She sat at the table with her glass of wine and told us about the things she had done with Samuel – a visit to the library to look at picture books, a walk around the park – and it felt, this drink I had forced upon her, exactly like the sum of its parts. Two parents catching up with their nanny. Nothing more. Nothing less. I've decided that our relationship, Alice's and mine, needs to be conducted outside the restraints of the parent–nanny dynamic.

When Hannah arrives home, moments later, she is euphoric from a whole day spent in Rick's studio.

'Oh Alice,' she says, slinging her bag down on the floor and holding out her hands for Samuel, 'he was so generous. We talked for hours and hours. About everything. His time at the Slade. His relationships with significant others, or rather the lack of them. He says there's only ever really been you.'

'Did he talk about the early days with Luke? When it was just the three of us?' Alice asks.

'Not really.'

Hannah shoots a look over at me. She knows how I long to find out about the first weeks of my life.

'It's hard for both of us to go back to those days. Such painful memories.'

'I understand,' I say, although I don't really.

I think these parents of mine have a duty to share everything they can remember about newborn me. Missing me. The me I can never access. It's not that I want them to feel pain, far from it; more that this surging quest for identity runs right through me. Sometimes I feel it's all there is.

'How was your day?' Hannah asks, so I tell her about Reborn, the new band I'm obsessing over.

'I went to meet them at lunchtime, H, and they are even better than I thought. They're so political, like The Clash re-invented for the noughties, but with a disco edge. I feel like I've been looking for them my whole life.'

Hannah leans forward to kiss me and deposits Samuel in my arms.

'You say that every time.'

Alice says, 'The casserole is on low, ready to eat whenever you want it.'

'Sit down for five minutes before you go?' Hannah asks as she does every night.

'I can't, I'm afraid, I have to be somewhere. I'm already late.'

Alice is off, coat on, striped canvas bag over her arm, and I watch her leave the kitchen with a strange mixture of gratitude and regret. Wanting something, but not quite knowing what.

Then

Alice

This, exactly this, is what I spent my teenage years dreaming of, holed up in my bedroom, surrounded by sketchpads and pencils, as if I could somehow draw myself away from my father's scorn into a world of decadence and liberation.

From my first incendiary meeting with Jake a few weeks ago, I have morphed into the band's 'artist in residence', a title he jokingly bestowed upon me when I sketched them picnicking in St James's Park.

The idea has grown from me creating an image for the album cover to documenting the fledgling stages of a band already being talked about as the new Rolling Stones. I've drawn them on stage, drinking halves of beer in the French House, playing football in the park. My favourite is one of Jake dressed in a black polo neck and his flared black jeans, cross-legged on the floor, a mug of coffee beside him. I like the everydayness of it, the reminder that I see him in a way no else does; he is mine, that's what I think when I look at this drawing.

Sometimes, especially when he's stoned, Jake talks about the times we're living in, this age of reinvention and aspiration, where anything might happen and you can be whoever you want.

'We're young at exactly the right time, when people are

prepared to take a chance on us. When we can make our own success.'

The first time he said this, I thought: it's all right for you, you're already halfway there, the front cover of *Sounds* magazine, two Top 20 singles under your belt. Me? I'm a nobody. Just an undergraduate art student racked with ambition and the need to impress her father. But his self-belief is infectious, and with the band's flattering and constant acclaim, I'm beginning to hope that perhaps I might be halfway there too.

And then the most extraordinary thing happens. A casual Tuesday at the Slade, no classes, and I'm in the studio working on a painting of the boys, Eddie, Jake and Tom all in black, lounging on a violet sofa, that wonderful juxtaposition of masculine and feminine. I'm interested in the pale purple slashes of this fabric, the mottling of silver grey where the material has rubbed, and I'm trying out a tight stippling technique to achieve it. Next to me, Rick has almost finished a portrait of David Bowie, borrowed from a Sunday supplement photograph but colour-washed in red. The effect is like a red-based sepia; it looks amazing.

Neither of us has spoken for hours, there have been no tea breaks; our absorption is absolute.

When Lawrence Croft, the principal, walks through the door, without warning or ceremony, accompanied by Robin Armstrong, the famous gallery owner and patron of Disciples, it takes us a few seconds to register their presence.

'Hard at work, I see,' Lawrence says. 'These two always are. I don't think workaholic is too strong a word.'

'Mind if I take a look?' Robin asks, and inwardly we both recoil – I know this without looking – but Rick says, 'Of course,' and stands up to allow him a clearer view.

'I always see Bowie in red too,' Robin says, after a good

minute or two of looking. 'It must be the Ziggy Stardust light-ning flash. I liked your self-portrait in San Lorenzo, by the way. I've been keeping an eye on you.'

It's hard to keep a straight face, knowing how this remark will have Rick doing inner cartwheels of joy, but we both remain nonchalant, casual.

'Do you plan on staying with portraiture? Unfashionable right now, of course.'

'I don't really care about that,' Rick says. 'I'm interested in people. I want to catch that moment of honesty when you get a glimpse of who they really are. I'm quite ruthless. If there's no chemistry between me and the sitter, I'll just abandon it halfway through.'

Robin nods at this, and a glance passes between him and Lawrence before he turns to examine my painting.

'I've come to know these boys rather well and your likenesses are exceptional. Jake tells me you're documenting this phase of their career with informal sketches?'

'To begin with I was working on artwork for the new album. But the project has sort of grown.'

'I think there might be something more interesting to be done with this, given that Disciples have a record to promote, one I'm keen to support however I can. Why don't you and Jake pop into the gallery tomorrow evening? Bring any finished sketches with you and we'll have a proper chat.'

The Robin Armstrong Gallery is in Duke Street, next door to the Bernard Jacobson Gallery, which has a Lucian Freud char-coal in the window, a nude woman with unevenly sized breasts and cartoonish kohl-rimmed eyes. Freud gave a lecture in our first term, one hundred per cent attendance from students and tutors and a relatively forgettable seminar about colour. The thing I remember most clearly is the coffee afterwards, where he was to be seen locked in earnest conversation with a gaggle of pretty female students.

To see Freud displayed in the next-door window, to know that I am about to have an informal chat with one of the most revered gallerists in London, is to tremor with nerves. But I have Jake by my side, the top half of his body almost hidden behind my one finished canvas, the boys picnicking in Hyde Park. He pauses just before we reach the door.

'Alice,' he says, lowering the canvas so that I can look into his eyes. 'There is absolutely nothing to worry about.'

The gallery is closed, but an assistant unlocks the door for us and shows us into Robin's office, bypassing walls hung with his most famous clients: Gillian Ayres, Peter Sedgley. In contrast to the sparse white-walled gallery, the office has the feel of an old gentleman's club, or at least how I'd imagine one: deep-red and chocolate-brown colours, a magnificent leather-topped desk where Robin is sitting, an ancient-looking chesterfield sofa for his visitors. The room is crammed with artefacts: carved ebony heads, an exquisite marble nude, a framed series of painted gradient circles, each one more intensely coloured and mesmerising than the last; you realise on entering that here is a man who has dedicated his life to beauty. He is dressed in a navy velvet suit with a pale yellow silk shirt, and he stands up as we walk in, arms around Jake in an enveloping hug, for me a European kiss on both cheeks.

He gestures to the sofa, and the three of us sit like podded peas, me in the middle, flipping through my sketchbooks.

At first Robin says nothing, and I fill the silence with background noise about each sketch. It's easier when I'm talking about Jake, my specialist subject; I'm able to tell him why I think something works and what I was trying to achieve.

Together we examine a drawing of Jake sitting up in bed bare-chested, notepad balanced on his knees. He is songwriting and completely absorbed, one of the best times to draw him. I've caught the abstraction in the way he concentrates, an almost dreamlike quality, yet his focus is so absolute it's as if he is surrounded by an impenetrable wall.

'For me this works because Jake is unguarded, lost in thought. It's obvious to the viewer that he's thinking about a song, and I think it shows the effort and intensity that goes into the creation of the music.'

'Do you know, Alice, I rather think you're on to something.'

Robin stands up and walks back to his desk.

'You'll be with the band in Italy, I assume?'

Jake says, 'We haven't got around to that, but of course you should come. If you'd like to.' He looks at me quickly and squeezes my leg.

'It's an important stage in the band's career,' Robin says. 'I'll cover all your expenses, no need to worry about that.'

'I've longed to go to Florence,' I say, and he smiles for the first time.

'Every art student should spend time in Florence, in my opinion; it really ought to be a prerequisite for a fine arts degree.'

He leans forward on his desk.

'Your style is still developing, I can see. But what I like is the way you capture the casual immediacy of a snap. And I wonder if this should be your definition, those off-camera moments, a behind-the-scenes glimpse into the life of an up-and-coming band. All the normal stuff – cooking, washing, eating – alongside the making of music.'

'That's sort of what I'm trying to do already, but I also want the paintings, in particular, to be stylised and instantly recognisable rather than an almost photographic likeness.'

'Yes, I'd agree with that. Shall we have a glass of champagne? I've had rather a good idea.'

While Robin is out of the room fetching the champagne, I ask Jake, 'What do you think he means?'

He shrugs. 'I don't know. But I can tell he likes you. He's rarely so complimentary, trust me. If he thinks something is shit, our songs included, then he says so.'

Robin opens the bottle expertly, a gentle sliding out of the cork, no pop, no fizz, and pours it into three pale turquoise glasses, so thin and fragile I am almost afraid to touch them.

'Venetian,' he says, when I ask. 'Eighteenth century.'

He raises his glass and the three of us clink.

'You know, it seems to me that the two of you are having a moment. Your careers are heading in the same direction and at exactly the same time. You're connected not just as lovers but as artists, and I think we should capitalise on that.'

He pauses, but his eyes never leave my face.

'Alice, how would you like to have your own show here at the gallery? Focusing on your drawings and paintings of the band, documenting six months in the life of Disciples. We could tie the show and the album launch together – maybe do both here at the gallery next year. What do you think?'

I put my glass down on the table with precision, even though my hands are beginning to shake and my heart is racing.

'What do I think?' I say, trying to sound considered and sensible, though it's hard with this gigantic grin that is spreading across my face. 'I think that sounds incredible!'

'Excellent,' Robin says, and he raises his glass again. 'A toast, then. To Jacob Earl and Alice Garland, whose moment has well and truly arrived.'

Now
Luke

Opposite-sex reunions may become fraught. Quite often the birth parent will still be young and attractive and the child may mistake its craving for connection as a kind of infatuation.

Who Am I? The Adoptee's Hidden Trauma by Joel Harris

I'm on a date with my mother, or at least that's how it feels when I arrive home and find Alice applying lipstick in front of the mirror. She's coming to the Reborn gig with me, a pressurising prospect to be sure.

I'm in a state of high anxiety; my default setting, Hannah would say. Partly I'm nervous about all the other A&R sharks circling around Reborn, because I want to sign them so intensely, so savagely, it's beginning to hurt. I haven't signed a successful act yet and I am desperate to prove myself.

And then there's the fact of hanging out with my birth mother, whom I scarcely know despite her almost constant presence in our lives. I've been craving time alone with her, but now that it is here, I feel almost afraid.

As usual, Alice puts me at ease.

'Luke, don't worry about me tonight. I know you'll have lots of people you need to talk to, and I'm good at blending into the background. You won't even know I'm there.'

This I doubt very much. Alice is the kind of woman people look at wherever she goes; she stands out, I think that's it. She looks pretty incredible for her age, tall and slim, her shoulder-length dark hair without one strand of grey. She dresses well, too, tonight in dark jeans and a checked blue and white shirt, a pair of navy Converse on her feet. She won't look out of place at the gig – not that at forty-seven there's any reason why she should. Meeting Alice has recalibrated my views. I used to think late forties seemed far off and incalculable; now it feels scarcely any different to my own age.

A moment of awkwardness when Hannah arrives home from work to babysit and Samuel refuses to go into her arms. He clings to Alice and starts to cry, and Hannah's face – embarrassed, devastated – destroys me.

'Don't be so silly.' Alice uncurls his hands from around her neck and passes him over, walking quickly from the room. But the moment sears, it really does.

'Just 'cos he's tired,' I say, kissing Hannah goodbye, then a quick kiss to my baby's head. 'You've got him all to yourself now.'

But I see the slight shame in her downcast smile, that her baby, whom she carried on her hip for the first six months of his life, should prefer anyone other than her.

On the tube to Camden, Alice and I discuss Samuel's minor betrayal, a meaningless moment of tiredness that will have preyed on Hannah's insecurities, I know.

Alice says, 'It's only because he's teething and I've been carrying him around all day. But still. I know exactly how Hannah feels.'

'She's struggling so much with the whole working-mother

thing anyway. Loving her job but feeling she's missing out on him. She was in tears about it the other night. She feels like she's letting him down.'

'There's never an ideal solution, it's always some kind of sacrifice.'

Walking along Camden High Street, minutes away from the gig, I broach the subject of how Alice and I should refer to each other. I can't ask her to lie about our relationship. But full disclosure will trigger unbearable interest, which neither of us wants.

'So, I was thinking of introducing you tonight as a friend, if that's OK?'

'Friends is what we are, Luke,' Alice says, smiling at me.

I feel the release in my body, a slight loosening of my limbs, and it's only then that I realise how much tension I have been carrying. It's not a straightforward thing, the introduction of my secret birth mother to a gathering of colleagues I see day in, day out.

The pub is packed and already I spy a hefty sprinkling of A&R men, circling around the bar. On the surface, back-slapping and man-hugging and exchanging news, but beneath that, each man is clenched with the desire to win. There's so much pressure in A&R. Sign an act that goes stratospheric and you secure the entire record company's future; that's everyone from the packers in the warehouse to the designers in the art department. Everyone treats you like a god. Waste money on a flop and you've the prowess of a donkey.

It's a relief to catch sight of Ben at the bar.

'Thank fuck,' I say. 'I wasn't sure you'd come.'

'Problems?'

'Just my own weirdness.'

With me and Ben there's never any need to explain. We

take three beers over to the corner, where Alice, I see to my horror, is talking to Gareth the accountant. Gareth is in his fifties and he has an unchanging gig uniform: plain round-neck white T-shirt, jeans that are not definitely made of denim and may well be elasticated. Not that it matters. The problem with Gareth is twofold: he's intensely boring – a job prerequisite, you might say – and woefully lecherous. And Alice is clearly in his sights. Christ, this I really didn't need tonight.

'Hello, Luke,' says Gareth, though he doesn't take his eyes off Alice. 'Just been chatting to your lovely friend.'

Alice hugs Ben and asks after Elizabeth.

'Working late, catching up on her notes. She wanted to come but she's snowed under.'

'There'll be plenty more times, I'm sure. Luke says the band are amazing.'

When Alice's phone rings moments later, I can tell from her tone of intimacy that the caller is Rick.

'That's a shame,' she says to me. 'I was hoping Rick would come, but he's in the middle of something, working late.'

As she goes to put her phone away, it slips out of her hand and lands face down on the floor.

'Oh shit,' she says, as I crouch down to pick it up. 'Is it cracked?'

I turn the phone over in my hand and examine it, and I feel the cold creep of dismay. For her screen saver is a picture of Samuel I've never seen before. Why is there a picture of my baby on her phone? And if she's going down that route, shouldn't it actually be one of me? For a moment I'm too shocked to speak and I don't even know why.

'Isn't that your baby, Luke?' Gareth asks, and Alice and I speak at the same moment.

'Yes, I look after him while Luke and Hannah are at work.'

'Alice is my birth mother.' The surprising admission slips out. 'She's Samuel's grandmother.'

There's a tense little moment of silence while Alice and I stare at each other, heat rising in her cheeks.

'Uh-oh, cat's out of the bag,' Ben says.

'It is rather,' Alice says, but she's smiling. 'We're still getting used to it. And actually, Gareth' – he looks thrilled that she's remembered his name – 'it's meant to be a secret. Luke's mother doesn't know yet. So we're keeping it quiet.'

'My lips are sealed,' Gareth says. 'And let me tell you, you look nothing like a grandmother.'

It's the moment of levity we need.

'I'll catch you all a bit later on,' Alice says, grabbing the opportunity to move away. 'I'm not good in crowds. I'll probably stand at the back.'

Reborn aren't due on for another ten minutes, but it's already impossible to get anywhere near the stage. *Time Out* ran a feature last Friday; I guess that's how the punters have got hold of it. I think, momentarily, about the band in the dressing room. Wonder if they're nervous or revelling in their moment in the sun. While I wait, I exchange nods with the other A&R men, all of whom I know. There's an unspoken code at a gig like this, one where we are all fierce competitors – every label wants to sign Reborn, though only three or four of us have the money – and it's nonchalance. If conversations must be had – and we're all keen to avoid them – the subject matter is kept light and brief. I spy Joel Richardson, boss of Universal, in a corner, flanked by two of his A&R guys, Matt and Tommy, both friends of mine, if that's what you'd call our nights out on the lash. Pre-Hannah days, Friday nights that might start at a gig and move to a club, then someone's flat to see in the dawn. Too much booze, too many drugs, hangovers that destabilised me even then. Good times that felt in retrospect like anything but.

Ben and I are standing in the middle of the crowd, jostled and jarred from every side, toes stepped on, elbows in backs, the slosh of spilt beer as it lands like raindrops on my jeans. I'm happy here, a few rows back from the mosh pit but up close enough to see, feel, immerse myself in the act. No place for a chat, but I find myself shouting above the noise anyway.

'Did you think it was weird that Alice had that picture of Samuel on her phone?'

'Weird how? She's looking after him all day. Of course she's going to take pictures.'

'You're right. I'm the weirdo. I forgot.'

Ben laughs. 'Alice is in for a shock when she finds out what you're really like.'

The band are about to come on; there's a surge, a momentum, both the pushing as the crowd tries to pull closer and the palpable energy of expectation. How many people in this tiny room? A hundred and fifty at most. Yet as the band walk out – Daniel, the lead singer, first, then Arlo the drummer, Ingrid the guitarist and finally Bex on bass – it's the cheer of a stadium. Straight into their first song, 'Special', a punky electro number that is a guaranteed hit, I'd say.

The first three songs are classic Reborn, emotional turbulence and political rant hidden in a skilful wrap of classic songwriting. Then they surprise the crowd with new material – a song I've never heard before and one that has veered into unapologetic disco – and an extraordinary thing happens. Halfway through, I realise the audience is dancing. A&R men don't dance. A bit of gentle nodding at most, foot-tapping if you must. So this feels kind of momentous. I glance across at Universal, still clustered together, a trio of men, and see that even Joel Richardson is

swinging his hips and padding the air with his palms, an enthu-
siastic post-rave gesture that is almost endearing.

The band leave the stage after exactly thirty minutes to overwhelming rapture. It's no longer a question of whether they
will be huge, or even when; their fame is here, their moment
has come.

The bar is rammed, of course, and it takes Ben and me a good
ten minutes to get served, all the time looking around for Alice.
How can someone as conspicuous as her – tall, head-turningly
good-looking – have evaporated like this? I wonder if she aban-
doned the gig halfway through.

'How can Alice have just disappeared?' I say more than once.
'Do you think she bailed?'

'Mate,' Ben says, 'you're alarming me. Just relax about Alice,
OK? She's a grown-up. She does her own thing. And she probably doesn't get off on pints of beer being chucked all over her.'

Alice appears from nowhere just as we've got our drinks, and
Ben passes her his beer.

'Have this,' he says. 'I'll go and get another one.'

'Oh, no need. I'm off now. Just wanted to say goodbye. And,
Luke, the band are fantastic. You're really on to something. I
can see why you're excited about them.'

'Won't you stay for a quick drink? I've hardly seen you.
Where were you standing?'

Ben is staring at me intently, probably trying to communicate
the integral message of 'be cool', as he has so many times before.

'At the back. I get panicky if I can't find my way out.'

'Well at least let me walk out with you to say goodbye.'

'Don't worry about that. You'll want to talk to the band,
won't you? Don't miss your chance. We'll catch up when I
come next week.'

'Do we need to have words?' Ben says when Alice has gone,

our catch-all phrase for when one or other of us (usually me) is losing our shit.

'I can't help being a bit needy. I'm an adoptee.'

'With two brand-new flesh-and-blood parents and one extremely loving adoptive mother. Don't make this harder than it needs to be.'

'You're right,' I say. 'I know you're right.'

'You know what Elizabeth would say right now? Boundaries, my friend. Alice has them, but you don't. We all need boundaries.'

Then

Alice

We glide down the King's Road in Robin's open-top car, a shining cream and silver work of art that draws cheers and yells of appreciation from pedestrians and hoots from other drivers.

'E-type Jag,' Jake says, incredulous that I don't know. 'The most beautiful car ever made.'

We have borrowed Robin's car so that we can drive to Essex to have lunch with my parents, more of an order than an invitation. When I rang home to ask if they'd post my passport, my father said, 'If you're planning on going to Italy with some youth we have never met, think again. You can come and get it yourself.'

My mother wrote to me the same day and I spied her round, girlish handwriting with the same pit of gloom that accompanied most of my childhood. Her missives, dictated by my father, have been chequering my life since I started at boarding school.

We thought you might have the decency to introduce your new boyfriend to your family. We haven't heard from you all term. Come for lunch on Sunday.

Driving out of London along the Bayswater Road, lined with its cheerful display of bad art, clunky nudes and one-dimensional still lifes proudly tacked to the railings, T. Rex turned up to distortion volume on the car stereo, I feel I've never been happier.

But the moment we turn off the A12 and begin the approach to my village, past the house where I took Scottish dancing lessons as a child and the courts where I learned to play tennis, past Huskard's, the grim-looking old people's home with its barred top windows, I become twelve again. Frightened of my father, ashamed of my mother, her weakness, her cowardice, her lack of self-respect. I suppose I love her in some far-off way, but she never once stood up for me; she watched my father berate me for kicks and allowed her silence to be his accomplice.

'You're quiet,' Jake says, reaching out to take my hand. 'How bad can it be?' but I can't find any words to answer him.

'Christ, you didn't tell me you lived in a mansion,' he exclaims as we turn into our drive.

'We only own part of it,' I am still too choked for proper conversation.

It is a vast and beautiful house, mostly red brick, with black and white gables and three tiers of long, thin windows running across its facade. It was bought as a whole by my grandparents in the fifties and then carved up, so that we only live in the middle section, a large-roomed, high-ceilinged flat overlooking the rose gardens below. A retired schoolmaster lives in the top flat, originally the servants' quarter, and a couple of bad-tempered Scottish pensioners inhabit the ground floor, and this, growing up, was my day-in, day-out demographic.

I hesitate at the side door, the entrance to our flat, and consider ringing the bell. But the door is open and I remind myself that I am not a visitor, that this is my home.

'Hello?' I call, and my voice sounds thin and false even to myself.

In these last moments, I'm uttering a silent plea. Please can it not go too badly. Please can my father be all right.

The stairs lead to a landing where I would expect my parents to be waiting, but it's empty.

'They must be in the kitchen,' I say, and we follow the smell of roasting chicken down the dark corridor.

'Smells delicious,' Jake says, still believing this is a normal family gathering. 'I'm starving.'

In the kitchen, black and white tiled floor of my youth, both parents are at the Aga with their backs to us.

'We're here,' I say, and my mother turns immediately, a wooden spoon held aloft. I see that she is wearing make-up, lipstick, blusher and eyeshadow, an unusual event in her world. She's dressed up too, in a bright blue trouser suit, the jacket zipped and belted, an orange silk collar peeking out of the top.

'Hello,' she says, holding out her hand.

'Hi, Dad,' I say, but my father doesn't answer; he continues to stir a pan as if he hasn't heard us.

I see Jake dart his eyes at me and then my mother, trying to gauge the situation. Are we being ignored?

'Hello, Dad,' I say, louder this time, and I watch my mother slide her eyes away from me; she's not going to help. She doesn't offer Jacob a drink – always my father's domain; if he doesn't give her a glass of wine then she goes without. She stands with her gaze averted, as though she's fascinated by the rose bushes below.

Eventually, perhaps only a couple of minutes later, though it feels longer, my father turns around. He is smiling, if you can call it that, and I see that while he has been making the gravy, he has drunk two thirds of a bottle of red wine.

'Hello, daughter,' he says, a name he never calls me. 'Or perhaps you have absconded from that role? Perhaps you are now emancipated from your parents?'

'Of course not. Dad, this is Jacob.'

The best recourse when my father is in this mood is to try and move things on, although with four glasses of wine inside him, I'm not optimistic.

'Good to meet you, Mr Garland.' Jake extends his hand, which my father ignores. Instead he allows his eyes to travel over Jake in expressionless assessment. I feel him registering the shoulder-length hair, the flowered choker at Jake's neck, the long bead necklaces I considered asking him not to wear.

'Well, lunch is ready, come and sit down.'

We are eating in the kitchen, the table already laid with knives, forks and four glasses, although my father doesn't pour me any wine. He refills his own, and then pours a couple of inches for Jake and my mother. Our boundaries are set; lunch is to be an endurance test.

You throw a new lover into a situation of extreme awkwardness and you see a different side to them. I would never have expected Jake to try so hard with my mother, asking her about the roses in the garden below.

'I think they are classic tea roses, and perhaps the purple ones—'

My father cuts across her.

'It's not our garden.'

'But you have a garden here? There's so much space.'

'Yes. An acre, the other side of the house.'

'We grow vegetables,' I say, surprising myself and perhaps my parents with the pronoun. 'Courgettes and beans, potatoes and carrots, all the usual. We have fruit cages too, with redcurrants, blackcurrants and raspberries in the summer.'

'My grandparents lived on a farm; I spent a lot of my childhood there. My grandmother grew every vegetable you could think of. They were almost self-sufficient.'

'Sounds idyllic,' my mother says, and I feel hot with shame. Jake's childhood was the exact opposite of idyllic.

'This trip to Italy.' My father has no interest in small talk. 'Who pays for it?'

'Well, the record label is paying all our recording costs, and we have a sponsor who has rented the house for the summer.'

'And why does Alice need to be there?'

'She's making a series of drawings of the band. Didn't she tell you? She's going to have an exhibition at the Robin Armstrong Gallery.'

'Alice doesn't communicate with her parents any more,' my father says, refilling his glass.

I could protest but what would be the point? When I started at art school, I told myself I would ring home once a week. Then once a fortnight, before it slipped to every month. What happened, I think, is that with the space and distance to review my teenage years of repression and isolation, my parents morphed into grotesque caricatures: the tormenting bully, the muted wife. For the first time in my life I was away from them, I could be whoever I wanted to be, and the freedom was addictive. I didn't want to be reminded of my home life, which became in my head a swirling underworld of doom; it suited me to live as if my parents didn't exist.

'Student life is pretty hectic,' Jake says. 'It doesn't leave much time for anything else.'

'Art school? Swanning around drawing some pretty nude model, you mean? I hardly think so. We wanted Alice to go to Oxford, but she didn't have the brains.'

There's a tense little moment of silence. It's not so much what my father says but the scorn in his voice as he says it. I wonder if perhaps he has hated me all along.

'Alice has a real gift. Perhaps you don't know of Robin

Armstrong, but he's a big deal in the art world. I would have thought you'd be proud of her.'

My mother looks down at her plate of food; she's hardly touched it, and her hands are fluttering around her knife and fork as if she's forgotten how to use them. Inside me now is just one burning intention. I will never be like her.

We all watch my father draining and refilling his glass. His greed, his selfishness, his sad, old-fashioned patriarchy: it makes me feel ashamed.

'I'm sure Jacob would like another glass of wine,' I say, and my father looks at me in disgust. But he picks up the bottle and empties the rest of it into Jake's glass.

'I'm not sure we approve of Alice spending her summer in Italy. She should live here and get a job like everyone else.'

'I don't think you understand,' Jake says. 'Alice is being commissioned to do a show, and for that she needs to be in Italy, working on her drawings of the band.'

'A vanity project, that's all this is. I don't want Alice hanging around some band with a dubious lifestyle. Don't think I don't know what you lot get up to. She's far too young.'

I would speak, but the threat of tears keeps me quiet, and I will not cry in front of my father. My mother and I are frustrating victims; we don't react. What happens is that my father's scornful put-downs escalate; he needles away at us, childlike in his quest for victory.

'I think you might be surprised by how hard-working we are.' Jake's voice is soft, polite, but I know without looking at him that inside he is clenched with anger.

'Hah!' My father takes a sip of his wine. Jake, I notice, hasn't touched his. I understand the rebellion.

'What is it, if you don't mind me asking, that you object to? Alice is being paid for her work. This commission will earn her far more money than a summer job washing dishes or whatever else you had in mind.'

'I object,' the word imbued with hostility, viciousness, the way only my father can, 'to all of it. Our daughter is nineteen. We don't want her spending a summer with your lot, picking up all your habits. Drugs, free love, whatever else it is you're into.'

'It's not up to you,' I say, pushing my plate away and standing up.

'I think you'll find it is for as long as this is your home.'

The moment erupts.

'I don't want it,' I say. 'I don't want this home.'

'If I were you, daughter of mine, I would take that back right now.'

We stare at each other, my father and I, with our matching masks of rage. Why, on the one day when it mattered to me, could he not have behaved? Hate does not have enough bite for how he makes me feel.

'No. I won't take it back. Because I meant it.'

'Then get out. Go on, get out right now.'

My father's face, always flushed, has turned an alarming shade. Purple madder would be the closest; I used it in Gordon King's class last week.

'Fine,' I say, and now Jake is standing up too. 'I just need my passport.'

I've already spied it on the dresser. I'm wondering if I should make a dash for it, just in case. But my father saves me the trouble. He shoves back his chair, a screech of metal across parquet, picks up the passport and hurls it at my face. The corner catches me just beneath my eye, and the shock of it, more than the pain, and the absolute humiliation, makes me cry, an unguarded, instantaneous reaction.

'For God's sake.' Jake stoops to pick up the passport, then wraps his arm around my shoulders. 'Let's just go.'

My father says, 'You're going to have to choose between your family and this inappropriate love affair of yours, which, mark my words, you will come to regret.'

I look right into his eyes while the anger coruscates inside me like fuel. I know the answer, of course I do, but I'll make him wait for it. Ten, nine, eight, seven, six … Mentally I'm counting down until I say the words that will make my family life implode.

'In that case, I choose Jacob.'

Now

Luke

The absence of a biological mother and father feels as intense as death to the adopted child. He is submerged in unexplained loss. And unless the facts of his birth are discussed openly, untold grief will be at the root of his character.

Who Am I? The Adoptee's Hidden Trauma by Joel Harris

I wouldn't admit this to anyone, but I feel a little bit pissed off when Hannah goes off for her second tête-à-tête with Rick. Like she's getting to know him and I am not.

The *Sunday Times* is running her interview as the Culture section lead and flagging it on the front page of the newspaper. In conference, the editor described it as 'the scoop of the year'.

Rick has been customarily indiscreet, spilling confidences about Grace Jones, Mick Jagger and Lucian Freud, nothing off the record.

'It's all true,' he told her. 'So write what you like.'

For a man who hates intrusion, he has been extraordinarily generous.

I am immensely proud of Hannah and slightly put out. And my jealousy – there, I admit it – is compounded by the easy, relaxed way Alice and Hannah communicate at night. Alice loves to hear Hannah's stories about the other journalists she works with, the shows she is reviewing, the artists she has met. When Hannah gets back from work, Alice will often stay for a cup of tea, while with me she invariably rushes off. She doesn't seem to care that I am working my arse off trying to sign Reborn; since they are a band she has seen and liked, I would have thought she might be more interested.

I have no right to feel like this, I know that. This week, when Hannah has had to work extra days to finish her Richard Fields profile, Alice stepped in to cover without any complaint and refused to take any more money for it.

'I love looking after Samuel,' she said. 'You never need to feel bad about asking me.'

She is lovely, always, but slightly withdrawn.

'You can't bridge a gap of twenty-seven years overnight,' Hannah said yesterday when I tried to tell her how I was feeling. 'I know it's hard, but you have to give it time.'

Today, however, there's no time for reflection. Industry gossip tells me that Universal have made a colossal offer for Reborn; figures are not known, but it's expected to be a million. There's no way my label, Spirit, can match it, but I do have a brilliant idea up my sleeve and the trump card of allowing the band creative control when it comes to mixing their album. With Universal, they might as well be signed to Simon Cowell and have done with it. Cash-rich and the say-so of a monkey. That's no choice at all.

As if there could be any doubt, my boss, Michael, calls me into his office at four o'clock when the rest of the company have decamped to the pub for the traditional Friday piss-up. He offers me a drink from the fridge behind his desk – neat rows of Red Stripe, Chablis and Bollinger lined up – which I refuse. I try to stay sober around Michael.

'I took a risk on you, Luke, didn't I? Giving you your own label to run when you weren't yet twenty-six?'

'You did. And I appreciate it.'

'I'll cut to the chase, shall I? We had a directors' meeting. The accountants were in, and two of the directors – I won't name names – were in favour of closing Spirit down. Cutting our losses, as it were.'

'Michael ...' I try to speak but the words won't come out.

I have dreaded, projected, catastrophised about this possibility endlessly. Take Spirit away from me – my own label, the thing I care most about in the world (aside from Hannah and Samuel) – and I hate to think what I would do. Spirit is my sanity, my security; it gives me a blueprint of how to be.

'Don't look at me like that, Luke. You have my support one hundred per cent. All I'm saying is you need to close the deal with Reborn. You've got them on the hook and the whole of the industry wants to sign them. Be the one who does.'

'What if I can't?'

'We'll cross that bridge when we get to it. We need a little triumph here.'

It's after five when I call Steve Harris, the band's manager, a miserable, diminutive Scot whom nobody likes.

'Luke! How're you doing?'

He is uncharacteristically warm and I realise within a few seconds that, like everyone else, Reborn have been whiling away their Friday afternoon in the pub.

No is not an option when Steve says 'Come and join us?' even though I'm due home at six for Alice (Hannah is working late again). I tell myself I'll only stay for one, and if I get a cab, I'll still make it back in time.

But I hadn't factored in the drunkenness of the band, who are in an optimum state for me to make my pitch. Steve stands up and embraces me and the rest of them follow suit, hugs all round.

'Shall I get us a bottle of champagne?' I say.

Drinks are always on the record company, and with a fledgling band, champagne never fails to impress.

The lead singer, Daniel, follows me up to the bar.

'It's good you came,' he says, while I put in my order for not one, but two bottles of champagne. 'Thing is, we all really like you, but we've had a pretty incredible offer.'

'I heard. But I have an idea that could really transform this next album into something pretty epic.'

With the champagne poured, matching ice buckets to emphasise the flashiness, I outline my plan.

'Your songs already have an edge of disco,' I say. 'I think we should amp it up, a full-blown disco record but reworked for the twenty-first century. Your lyrics, your political message, only come through on second or third hearing. It's subliminal, and that way we reach the masses, the people who don't think they care and then find out that they do.'

'I like it,' says Daniel. 'I like it a lot.'

'Like it?' shouts Bex, the bassist, slamming down her glass so that champagne slops out onto the table. 'It's genius!'

I refill everyone's glass and bask a little in the acclaim. I feel almost light-headed from the spectre of success. No one is saying it, but I can feel how close I am to clinching this deal.

It's only when I'm on my way home in the back of a cab that I register the travesty of my lateness. It's already past seven o'clock. Hannah will be furious; she reminds me on an almost daily basis that we must never take advantage of Alice.

I'm just about to walk through our gate when the sight of a

navy-blue Golf parked up outside the house stops me dead. My mother's car. I stand there staring at it, frozen in the horror of the moment, champagne fizzing in my veins. How can I have allowed this to happen? I remember now that my mother is on her way back from a painting trip and said she might spend the night. And I, stupid moron that I am, have forgotten. My heart bangs against my ribs as I slot my key into the lock and push open the front door with no idea what I'm walking into.

My two mothers are sitting together at the kitchen table.

'There you are, darling,' says Christina. 'We were starting to get worried. Has something happened at work?'

'Hi, Mum,' I say, my voice fading on the word. 'Alice, I am so sorry. I tried to call but my phone was flat. I had a last-minute meeting with Reborn. It feels like they're going to sign to us and it was impossible to get away without seeming rude. I can't tell you how sorry I am.'

'It's fine, Luke. I understand. Samuel is asleep in his cot. Your mother' – she says the word evenly, but to me it is laced with pain – 'put him down ten minutes ago. I was just about to leave.'

'It's been so lovely to meet your au pair,' says my mother, and instantly the term seems insulting, belittling. 'I do think you were sensible finding someone a bit older. You don't mind me saying that, Alice, do you?' Christina laughs but Alice doesn't.

'That's fine.'

'You're so wonderful with the baby. He clearly adores you. Do you have your own children?'

Inside I'm howling like a wounded dog. No. Please, no. I try to meet Alice's eyes; the sorrow I am expecting to find there will be my punishment. But Alice doesn't look at me.

'Sorry to rush, Christina,' she says, ignoring the question. 'But I must get going. I have to go and see someone and I'm already late. Have a nice evening, I'll see myself out.'

My mother crosses the room for one of her air kisses – 'Darling, hello' – and I hear the click of the front door with a plunge of sadness.

'Do you know, I had the strangest feeling that I'd met Alice before. Of course, that's impossible, isn't it? She's nothing like I expected. How did you did find her? Was it through the agency?'

Communication is impossible, throttled as I am by panic, by guilt, a tide of self-loathing that rises from my chest to my neck to my brain.

'Mum, I'm just going to check on Samuel. You know we don't put him in his cot.'

'All right, darling.' My mother laughs. 'Though he's absolutely fine. The painting trip was lovely, thanks for asking.'

We painted Samuel's bedroom one weekend shortly before he was born, back in the days when Alice was no more than a figment of my imagination. We chose a vivid lemon yellow – neither of us favours those generic saccharine pastels meant for babies – with lime green for the woodwork and a little second-hand chest of drawers that we painted orange. We bought an armchair and a reading lamp for Hannah, who planned to catch up on novels while the baby slept – a concept that now seems hilariously naïve. In the first weeks after Samuel was born, she barely had time to brush her hair, let alone cross Tolstoy off her list.

I peer over the cot at my beautiful sleeping boy, who has one arm flung out, the other curved around a soft toy I don't recognise. I don't know what makes me look twice at this teddy, an old-fashioned one with sewn-on glass eyes, the kind Hannah has forbidden as a potential hazard. I retrieve it carefully from Samuel's grasp and sit down in the chair, bear balanced on my knee. Its fur feels rough and matted beneath my fingers. On an impulse, I press it to my face and inhale. The mustiness of age, and behind it something faint, but it's there, a sharp, citrusy smell I recognise. Alice's perfume. It must have belonged to her.

And then, slowly, devastatingly, the truth of this bear's origin smacks me between the eyes.

Then

Alice

Emancipation from my parents is at once exhilarating and terrifying. I have stood up to my father for the first time in my life, and although I cry throughout most of the journey home, Jake driving with one hand on the steering wheel, the other clamped around my own, beneath the tears is the fierce thrust of pride. I am not like my mother and I never will be.

'Actually this is all very hip,' Jake says, emphasising the word, because he always knows how to make me laugh. 'We are living through the decade of liberation, and you, Alice Garland, are at the coalface.'

I move my belongings – two paltry black bin liners of clothes and books and about a hundred sketchpads – out of my student lodgings into Jake's flat. My bottles of shampoo and conditioner line his bath, my clothes in two drawers he has cleared out for me.

'Let's buy you things to make this place feel more like yours,' he says on the first night, as we lie naked and entwined on his brown corduroy sofa, surrounded by candlelight.

'Everything I need is right here,' I say, smoothing my hand across the S of his body, his thigh curving into his hip, the dip of flesh beneath his ribcage.

But Jake shakes his head.

'I'm serious. I want this flat to feel as much yours as mine.'

He takes me to Nice Irma's Floating Carpet to stock up on wine-coloured beanbags, joss sticks, a rug of swirling brown and orange, a wall hanging of a bejewelled Shiva.

He loves to surprise me with gifts, small things to begin with: an orange jug he has filled with sunflowers, a pair of striped woolly socks he bought at the market because my feet are always so cold, second-hand copies of *A Room with a View* and *The Leopard* in preparation for our trip to Italy.

Then one afternoon I come back to a little wooden desk in the corner of the sitting room, the kind we used to have at school, with a lid and a hole for the inkwell. Jake has filled it with my sketchpads and watercolours, my pencils in a holder made from a baked beans can rewrapped in bright blue paper. It's so touching, this gesture, that unexpectedly I find myself crying, and he pulls me into his arms, his face anxious.

'It's meant to make you happy.'

'I am happy,' I say, crying even more, though I'm laughing too.

'I'm your family now. And you are mine. We don't need anyone else.'

Now our evenings are spent working, me drawing at the little desk, Jake on the sofa or the floor, picking out chords on his guitar, writing lyrics in his notebook. If he's songwriting we work in silence, the focus of one motivating the other so that often it will be one or two in the morning before we stop.

We'll go to bed exhausted and fall asleep straight away, but then I'll wake again a few hours later and realise I'm alone. I'll stumble through to the sitting room and Jake is always there, surrounded by candlelight, hunched over his guitar. Once I stood in the doorway watching, and the expression on his face shocked me; I knew I was witnessing something private, something he always tries to hide. I crept away and went back to bed, but it was impossible to forget the pain I'd seen, pain and something even more menacing. To me, standing there, it looked like hatred or despair. I lay awake, waiting for him to join me, promising myself that somehow I would find a way to make him tell me about his past. Together we would eradicate those memories, we would make him strong.

With his music, at least, Jake's self-belief is unfaltering. He never has any doubt about whether he has what it takes to succeed.

When Robin offered me a show at his gallery, I had second thoughts immediately afterwards.

'I'm not ready for this,' I told Jake again and again, until he finally became impatient.

'How can you expect people to believe in you if you don't believe in yourself? Robin hasn't offered you a show as a favour to me. He's a businessman; he thinks your work will sell. He knows it will.'

Jake tells me – and I know he is right – that a childhood lived in the shadow of a volatile and vengeful father has corrupted my self-confidence. But slowly I am learning.

Robin Armstrong, more than any other dealer and gallerist in London, has the power to accelerate an artist's career; it's hard not to feel like an imposter when it's me, not Rick or any of the other star students from the years above, who is getting this break.

As soon as Lawrence Croft hears of my impending show, he calls a meeting with Gordon and Rita.

'I can safely say we've never had this happen to a first-year student before. Congratulations, Alice,' Lawrence says. 'What an opportunity. We must think how we can best support you.'

'You deserve this,' Rita says. 'The work you've been doing in class recently is outstanding. You've really put the hours in.'

That, at least, is true. These past two weeks, Jake and I have barely slept, working through the nights. And how I have loved it, the silent consensus that the two of us are wholly committed to our art. It is Jake who has made me feel like an artist and not a fraud.

Gordon says, 'It seems to me that next term Alice should be allowed to focus solely on her work for the show, and this can count towards her degree. Rita and I can oversee her progress with one-to-one tutorials. It's true that you have great skill, Alice, and you deserve to succeed. But the thing that really distinguishes you from your associates is your grit.'

Later Jake takes me to Kettner's, our customary haunt for celebrations big and small. We order four seasons pizza and drink house white from a small carafe.

'The thing about you, Alice Garland,' he says in a mock-Scottish accent, 'is that you're full of grit.'

Later, though, in the darkness, curled around each other in bed, he reaches for my hand.

'He's right, you know,' he says. 'You do have grit. And it's your childhood that's done it, weathering the years with your pig of a father. Standing up to him like you did the other day. I'm proud of you.'

I cannot see his face clearly, but I know that he is watching me, doing that thing where he hopes to transfer all his thoughts to me without words.

'You're a survivor, Alice,' he says just before we both fall asleep.

A throwaway line that would turn out to be more prescient than I could ever have imagined.

Now

Luke

The trickier reunion to navigate is often that of the adopted child and his birth father. With a male child in particular there may be a feverish desire to attach coupled with an instinct to emulate his absentee role model. Jung aptly described this obsession as 'father hunger'.

Who Am I? The Adoptee's Hidden Trauma by Joel Harris

Lunch with Rick at Nobu, summoned by text earlier today after the travesty of the colliding mothers. You don't say no to lunch with this famous artist, who by some bizarre quirk turns out to be my father, or to one at Nobu, which is still one of the toughest places to get a table, unless you happen to be him. I arrive at Park Lane clenched with a toxic permeation of dread and anxiety, even though he assured me in his text that there was nothing to worry about.

Bottom line, I screwed up massively, which are my first words when I'm shown to his table, black-clad waiters tearing up and down with their enormous trays of sushi.

'Rick, I'm sorry. I completely messed up last night.'

'Complicated situation. Not entirely your fault. Don't beat yourself up about it.'

He stands up and we hug a little awkwardly.

Rick is wearing a pink and orange checked shirt, electric, loud, look-at-me colours in a known celebrity hangout, and here I was thinking he was a recluse. A waiter comes over with a Sapporo beer for me, which I didn't see being ordered, and starts talking to Rick about his work.

'Last year's show at the National Portrait Gallery was incredible. Would I be able to get your autograph before you go?'

'Sure.'

'I thought you didn't like being recognised?' I say once the waiter has gone. 'That's what Alice says.'

'Some days I do quite like it. Some days I need it.'

He passes me the menu.

'Have whatever you like. I come here a lot, I know this menu inside out.'

It's a masterclass just watching him talk the waiter through our choices – a tuna sashimi salad and rock shrimp tempura with ponzu sauce first, then blackened cod and grilled beef teriyaki, followed by a selection of sashimi and sushi.

'We'll have a carafe of sake served cold, please.'

The hallmarks of a great lunch are here and I should be relaxed, but instead I'm counting down to the serious conversation I know is coming. And sure enough, the moment the first cup of sake is poured, Rick says, 'Right, Luke, I'm just going to come straight out with it. I don't think Alice should be working as your nanny.'

'But she loves—' I say and Rick holds up a hand.

'Hear me out. I haven't said this to Alice because I know it would break her heart. As you say, she adores Samuel, she loves looking after him. But you've got this whole thing back to front. It's you and her who need to be spending time together. And her working for you puts the relationship on an awkward footing, doesn't it? Like what happened yesterday. I can't really believe either of you thought it was a good idea.'

'So you're saying we should find a new au pair? We should ask Alice to leave?'

'I felt like I should tell you my concerns. The whole thing makes me uncomfortable. You see, there's a lot about Alice you don't know. She's fragile. After she lost you, she wasn't very well. Something like yesterday, when she was having to pretend to be someone she wasn't, like you were actually ashamed of her, could push her over the edge.'

'God, the opposite is true. I'm proud of Alice. I think she's amazing. I'm so happy she's my mother.'

Here Rick smiles, a full beam of a smile; he adores her, that much is clear. If I didn't know differently, I'd think he was in love with her.

Our sashimi salad arrives – a whole mound of raw tuna slices on a bed of rocket, covered in some kind of dressing – and Rick says, 'Let's pick this up later. Nothing should spoil your tuna. Death row meal for me.'

The rock shrimp tempura, arriving next, is outrageously good: hot, crunchy mouthfuls of prawn dipped into a sauce I'd really like to eat by the spoonful. Rick constantly refills our glasses and orders more sake with the merest hand signal, one finger raised to a waiter who always happens to be looking. (This guy is so cool, my feelings towards him are growing ever more complex. Never mind that he's my father; like Ben, I might actually want to *be* him.)

Over lunch he talks about some of the commissions he is working on. A nude portrait of a pregnant film star: 'Not a fluffed-up Demi Moore,' he says. 'She's very brave and self-confident, this woman; she's allowed me to draw her slumped back in a chair, legs apart, breasts drooping. Not a flattering portrait in the traditional sense, but to me very feminine and rather wonderful. And she loves it.'

There's a member of the royal family sitting for him – he won't say who – where again he was asked to do something mould-breaking.

'People who come to me tend to know about art. They are looking for something that will interest them and they think I can deliver it,' he says, without a note of arrogance, just the self-belief that must come with years of acclaim. 'When the papers get hold of this particular painting, they will go ballistic. I can hardly wait.'

We talk about Graham Sutherland's portrait of Churchill, the one he hated.

'That was a groundbreaking portrait in many ways. Presenting such a famous man warts and all. Of course, others before him had done that – Rembrandt's commitment to naturalism was considered merciless at the time. But it was unusual for someone so famous to have a portrait without all those conciliatory nips and tucks.'

Fuelled by sake and beautiful food, our mood lightens throughout lunch.

I tell Rick about a recent meeting Hannah had with Jay Jopling, sharing the most salacious details, and he retaliates with gossip about Lucian Freud.

'He was a guest lecturer when we were at the Slade; only interested in the girls, and Alice in particular. She was – still is, I think – so extraordinarily beautiful, but she wore it carelessly. She had no idea how good-looking she was and I think that made men want her even more. It still breaks my heart what happened to her. She had everything – and then suddenly nothing.'

'I don't know anything about that time. Alice never wants to talk about it.'

'She was so talented. The only one in our year to have a show, which was unheard of for an undergrad. She would have made it as an artist, definitely.'

'But why couldn't she go back to it? After me?'

'She was traumatised. She shut down inside and it took her years to be able to function again. And she lost her character, her spark; it never came back. That must sound dramatic to you, but that's how she was. And she never talks about that time now, not even to me. Because I don't think she can say the actual words.'

I notice that Rick has tears in his eyes as he tells me this; I feel a little like crying myself.

'But that's exactly why Hannah and I wanted her looking after Samuel. Because of the way she lost me. We could tell it wrecked her life.'

'One baby can't make up for another. You know that really, don't you?'

'It's more that we wanted Alice to become part of our family. Only it's not really working. I feel childish saying this, but I'm jealous of the way Alice and Samuel have bonded. I feel a bit left out.'

'Luke, that's exactly it.'

'But I don't see how we can ask her to stop looking after him. Even if we wanted to – which we don't.'

'You're probably right. Let's try a different tack. I think you and Alice need to get to know each other better. Spend more time together. That's what's missing at the moment. You know, don't you, that you're going to have to tell your adoptive mother about Alice sooner or later.'

There is time now to examine my reasons for not being honest with my mother.

Number one, I'm an only child and my mother is a widow. I was shipped in many years ago to resolve the grief of her infertility, a wound that still fuels her sadness almost three decades later.

Secondly, my mother has made it clear – many times – that she thinks I have no interest (for which read no business) in finding my real parents.

'Controversial suggestion,' Rick says, when I tell him this, 'but how about you put yourself first for a change?'

It's a radical idea, given that I have carved a career out of pleasing other people.

'I'm not sure I could do that.'

'Why not?'

'I'm scared of rocking the boat. I've spent my whole life trying to keep it steady. My mother is prone to depression, but I've only recently understood that. As a kid, I thought her black moods, those periods when she pretty much refused to talk, were something to do with me. I thought I didn't live up to her expectations. I wasn't the child she wanted.'

'You were the only one we ever wanted.'

He says it quietly, carelessly, but his choice of word, this use of 'we', wedges itself inside my heart.

'Why didn't you keep me then?'

It is the only question, and he must have known I was going to ask it, yet I see real pain flash into Rick's face.

'It was Alice's decision and she made it for my sake, though she'd never admit it. She thought I would jeopardise my career by not going back to art school. We were so young and we had no money, and she didn't want you to grow up poor. She convinced herself that giving you up was the ultimate sacrifice. Trouble was, she never got over it.'

Impulsive and fuelled by sake, I just want to make amends. I want Alice and me to fast-forward through the decades of pain, hers and mine, the two of us grieving in our separate universes.

It's my suggestion to extend the day and go and find her. And Rick knows exactly where she will be.

'Weekends she's always in her studio. We won't phone her. Let's make it a surprise.'

Mentally I haven't prepared for this impromptu meeting, I realise as we stand outside the door of Alice's studio half an hour later, Rick camouflaged by an enormous bunch of sunflowers.

'Sure we shouldn't have warned her?'

'Don't worry, she'll be thrilled. You and I are her favourite people after all.'

And she does seem ecstatically happy to see Rick, who is standing a little in front of me – 'I've brought you a surprise!' – though her face falls instantly when she realises that the surprise is me.

'Luke. I can't possibly let you into my studio.'

She looks a little older in this light, without make-up, streaks of white and blue paint in her hair. But lovely, always. She's wearing a paint-spattered shirt and loose blue trousers, a pair of espadrilles on her feet.

The sake swirls through my veins, my brain, while I try to make sense of what she is saying. Her body language is chilling, arms spread out as if physically barring us from entering the studio. I've allowed the lunch with Rick to lull me into a false sense of security; Alice is clearly reeling from yesterday's cataclysmic collision.

'I'm so sorry, I know how much last night must have upset you.'

'It's fine, Luke. Really. You mustn't worry about that. The thing is – and now I'm going to completely spoil it –I'm working on a present for you and Hannah and it isn't ready to show you yet. If you come in, it will ruin it.'

I laugh, relieved. 'You had me worried there. I thought you couldn't bear to see me. With good reason; it was inexcusable to forget about my ... about Christina coming.'

'Don't be silly,' she says. 'I understand. It's awkward for all of us. I'm just a bit protective of my "art", that's all.' She makes ironic speech marks with her fingers.

'In that case,' Rick says, 'let's go to the pub. Luke and I are well on our way to getting completely smashed. May as well finish the job.'

He takes hold of Alice's arm.

'Just the three of us,' he says. 'A bit like old times.'

Then

Alice

None of us expected the unlikely alliance between Tom and Rick, a friendship that hovers on the tightrope of something more.

'Are they lovers?' Jake asks me one night when we've left them drinking alone in the pub.

'I don't think Rick has lovers as such, not in the relationship sense. None that he admits to anyway. I think he's still getting used to the fact that he can be open about being gay.'

Tonight it's the four of us for Pink Floyd's *The Dark Side of the Moon* gig at Earls Court, a show we've been talking about for weeks. There has been so much hype around this album; everyone I know has had it on their turntable for the past six months. But to see it performed live in an arena like Earls Court, with a troupe of backing singers and musicians, a backdrop of films and special effects culminating in the sound of an aeroplane crashing onto the stage during 'On the Run', well, our minds are collectively blown.

'Us and Them' is my favourite song on the album. I love its slow, soothing church-like beginning, the heartbreaking sweetness of Dave Gilmour's vocal when he sings 'we're only ordinary men'. And then the exploding crescendo of the chorus, so dramatic and powerful and shockingly loud that my chest feels tight and I realise I am close to crying.

Most of all I love to watch Jake, who stands motionless, expressionless, as if he is in a trance. I want to grab his hand and tell him, 'This is going to be you,' but he is lost to everything but the music.

It feels after the final encore – 'Eclipse', two minutes – as if we have witnessed something momentous. When the band finally leave the stage, there's a fragment of stunned silence before the screaming begins.

Afterwards, we try to find a pub that's still serving, but everywhere is shut.

'We can't just go home after that,' Jake says. 'We need to mark tonight. We need an adventure.'

'Let's go somewhere,' Tom says.

'Like a road trip?' Rick asks.

'Exactly. Where shall we go?'

'My aunt has a place in Southwold, right by the sea,' Rick says. 'She says I can use it whenever I want.'

We leave London an hour or so later in Tom's beaten-up Austin Maxi, a wreck of a thing the colour of French mustard. Tom drives, Rick navigates and Jake and I sit in the back, my head resting on his shoulder, his hand tucked between my thighs. Before we're even out of town, I've fallen asleep, and when I next wake it is as if to a dream, the car parked up beside a row of pastel-coloured beach huts – primrose yellow, mint green, sky blue – and in front of us this vast flat sea, grey with flecks of silver. The sky is beginning its transition – we couldn't have timed it better – and the four of us jump a few feet down from the car park straight onto the beach. It is perhaps the best sunrise I have ever seen, a sheet of deep purple with flashes of hot pink and orange, the slow backlighting of yellow and gold.

I think: I'll remember this when I'm old. It's one of those moments so intensely visceral it must be burnt onto my memory.

The house is one street back from the beach, a sloping two-up, two-down terraced house painted pale blue with a bright yellow front door. It is so close to the beach you can hear the waves crashing from every room in the house. Rick opens up an airing cupboard and finds clean sheets for us – Jacob and me in the room with the double bed, Tom in the single room – and Rick says, 'Oh, don't worry about me, I can sleep anywhere,' which tells us to ask no questions.

We go to bed for a few hours and the sex is prolonged and intense. When Jake is on top of me, propped up on his hands but staring down into my eyes with a look I have come to know so well, I am filled with love so fierce and strong that the words spill out.

'I love you,' I say. And then again, again. I love you. I love you. Once I start, I cannot stop. And we lie together in the bright morning sunshine, laughing and telling each other the three words that sentiment cannot cheapen.

The way I feel when I'm with him, it's as if everything is magnified, and I don't want to miss a single second of it.

'I never expected to feel this way,' I say as we drift towards sleep, and Jake reaches for my hand, holds it between both of his.

'Shit childhoods, low expectations. I think that makes it even better. Don't you?'

I don't know much about his early years, though I've tried to fill in the gaps. A father who walked out when he was three, his choice cheap, gut-rotting alcohol that killed him off, alone in a bedsit, when he was thirty-nine. A mother who resented the burden of bringing up Jake and farmed him out whenever she could, mostly to her parents, whom he will never talk about. Once, only once, when we were very drunk, he said, 'My grandfather was an appalling human being. Him being dead isn't enough.'

The look on his face as he said it – not anger, but a kind of defeat – made me understand that whatever it was this man did or said was in some way connected to the scars my fingers seek out at night in the darkness, almost instinctively. It's as if all his pain is held there in those ridges of tissue, and I want more than anything to draw it out of him and throw it away.

There is no sound from Tom's room and no sign of Rick when we wake in the early afternoon.

'Let's leave them to it,' Jake says, and we spend the rest of the day alone.

We do all the things you're meant to do in an old-fashioned seaside town. We eat fish and chips, heavily doused in salt and vinegar, on the seafront. We walk along the pier with its hall of mirrors and its bizarre penny slot machines – like Crankenstein, a behind-bars monster who cranks into life with glowing eyes and a ferocious sneer – and we sit right at the end of it, feet dangling high above the water, salt wind on our cheeks.

'I don't think I've ever felt this good in my life,' Jake says after a long moment of silence, and I understand exactly what he means. There's a euphoria between us today, partly that shared post-coital glow, but mostly, I think, the acknowledgement of love, which has propelled us into a different place.

He wraps an arm around my shoulders and pulls me close, the water beneath us, a grey, peaked mass.

'I know it's too soon to say this and you're too young, but I want us to spend our lives together. Since I've met you, I've started to want things I've never wanted before. Stability. Kids. Not now, but one day. We could buy a house together. Am I saying too much?'

'I want those things too,' I tell him, though I feel shy saying it. 'All of them.'

We walk to the harbour talking of the house we'll buy one day, a conversation had by lovers everywhere, especially when they come upon the picture-postcard perfection that is Southwold. Our favourite house is painted salmon pink and has turrets either side like a toy palace. We stand outside it fantasising about a future that would allow us to buy it.

The thing is, we need each other equally. I might be adrift without my parents, but Jake has caught hold of me and mapped out my future. And me? I'm on a mission to chase away his darkness, to replace it with warmth and light and love.

At the harbour, we find a fisherman selling crates of mussels from his boat. We pick up brown bread and butter from the high street, Muscadet from the wine merchant, who tells us it is the only thing to drink with seafood.

And perhaps the sea air is pumped full of pheromones, because when we return to the cottage, the boys are up and the charge between them is undeniable. Tom is bare-chested and barefoot, wearing only his faded jeans. It feels strangely intimate seeing his torso, with its pronounced definition that speaks of hours in the gym. Both of them are smiling, wide, ludicrously happy grins.

Rick throws an arm around Tom moments later and says, 'So. We're a thing. You probably guessed?'

We're laughing so hard, all four of us, that it's a while before Jake is able to say, 'Well, thank Christ for that. The suspense was killing us.'

There's a little portable radio in the house that Jake tunes to Radio 1, and the distinctive drumbeat and guitar line of 'All Tomorrow's Parties' kicks in, a Velvet Underground song we have listened to so often we had to replace the record. Jake turns it up to full volume while Rick uncorks the first bottle of wine, I tip the mussels into a sink of water and Tom sits down at the kitchen table to roll a joint.

We sing the chorus, shouting it, a little delirious, and when the song finishes, Jake grabs me into his arms and kisses me, and Rick and Tom do the same, which makes us laugh even more.

Once we've rinsed and de-bearded the mussels, Jake shows me how to cook them, steaming them open in a pot with wine so that the kitchen is scented with hot, sweet alcohol. He adds cream and parsley at the last minute and we eat huge bowls of them, crowding around the little red-topped Formica table, dipping quarters of buttered brown bread into the sauce.

After supper, we decide to walk down to the beach, taking a detour first to show Rick and Tom the pale pink fantasy palace that will one day be ours.

'See the matching turrets,' Jake says, impersonating an estate agent with a nasal Kenneth Williams voice. 'This is rococo architecture at its finest. I think the four of you will be very happy here,' he adds. 'There's plenty of room for all your requirements.'

Tom laughs and wraps his arm around Rick and the two of them kiss briefly on the mouth. And at exactly this moment an elderly couple pass on the street, out for a night-time walk with their low-slung dachshund.

'How disgusting,' the man says, and his voice is vicious and bitter. 'You should be ashamed of yourselves. This is a respectable town; we don't want people like you here.'

People like you. Tom and Rick spring apart, and Rick's face, crestfallen and ashamed, makes my heart ache.

'Ah, but you see, I think you're the one who is disgusting,' Jake says, voice calm but cold as metal. 'With your judgement, your belief that you have the right to insult a complete stranger.'

Down on the beach, the four of us lying on our backs staring up at the stars, the boys' good humour is restored. They are holding hands again, I'm happy to see.

Jake picks out the constellations, stargazing another of his childhood pursuits; not just the obvious ones – the Plough, Orion, the Great Bear – but poetical-sounding ones like Ursa Minor and Cassiopeia. I love this name, its romance; a good title for a song, I say. And Jake, who seems to possess a brain stuffed full of extraneous knowledge, tells us where the name came from, a Greek goddess who was extraordinarily vain.

And then he says, apropos of nothing, 'The day will come when you guys will be able to walk down the street holding hands and kissing and no one will care.'

And, as usual, his generosity of spirit, his bravery, his innate sense of right and wrong breaks me up a bit. I know why I love him, why we all do, me, Rick and Tom. He's bigger than us, bigger than everyone. He is our mentor. And without him we'd be lost.

Now
Luke

The adopted child grows up keeping his innermost feelings secret. A habit may be formed that leads to clandestine behaviour in the adult.

Who Am I? The Adoptee's Hidden Trauma by Joel Harris

Lunchtime on a regular Tuesday, me and Alice and Samuel in the park. One of the benefits of working in the music industry is that long lunches go with the territory, so there is plenty of time for me to pop back home, make myself a sandwich – smoked salmon and avocado on bread that has seen better days – and then head out to Clapham Common.

I'd expected Alice to be here with Samuel napping on his little sheepskin rug, but instead the house is empty. It's my house, so why do I creep around it like an intruder, picking up Alice's things and scrutinising them? A scarf that hangs over the banister, long, thin and made of blue silk patterned with red and cream flowers. I hold it between my fingers; the material is beautifully soft. The instinct to put it up to my face and inhale comes from somewhere deep inside me. I've registered her scent – that same sharp, citrusy smell, more aftershave than perfume – before I drop it back on the banister, riddled with self-mockery. What kind of loser am I?

In the kitchen, I see that Alice has already made something for our supper. Our orange Le Creuset dish sits above a gas ring ready for our arrival. I lift the lid and look inside – beef casserole with squishy-looking root vegetables and the delicious waft of red wine. She made us this casserole once before and it lifts me up to think of her doing it, lovingly preparing a meal for her long-lost son, one she never expected to see (though I suspect she doesn't romanticise it in quite the same way).

There are fresh flowers on the kitchen table, which means she must have been out to the high street this morning. I picture her and Samuel buying beef from the butcher, carrots from the greengrocer, irises from the florist. I lean over to inhale the subtle sweet smell of the flowers. Hannah loves irises; uncanny how Alice always picks the right flowers, the two of them so easily, so flawlessly, connected. A needlepoint of jealousy right there.

My hand hovers over Alice's sketchpad on the kitchen table; it will contain drawings of Samuel and I long to see them. Any reason why I shouldn't? I have a little argument with myself while my hand remains poised, ready to flick the cover open. Most people in their own home, knowing a sketchpad is filled with drawings of their son, would just idly take a look. Wouldn't they? And yet, somehow, I cannot shake the sense that I am snooping, that looking at Alice's sketchpad is tantamount to reading someone's private diary. I won't allow myself to stoop that low. I'm hoping Alice will soon transfer some of her affections onto me; I'd hate to let her down.

Instead, I make my sandwich, clearing up the debris – plate and knife washed, dried and returned to the cupboard, crumbs swept from the worktop – and then walk out into the early-afternoon sunshine. I look at my watch. All this and it's only 1.30; there is still time to take a quick stroll around the park before I go back to the office.

Our house is a ten-minute walk from Clapham Common, depending on which way you go. I take the shortcut through Grafton Square, a classical square with white Regency houses facing out onto a little playground, quick scout around to see if anyone is there, before coming out at the zebra crossing on the outskirts of the park. By entering the common here, you pass the hippy café, purple walls with spray-painted flowers on the outside; ramshackle furniture, vegan brownies and obligatory bare knockers (the breastfeeding kind) on the inside. There are several mothers at the picnic tables, chatting over bowls of lentil soup while their toddlers fight over the Little Tikes seesaw. That will be us soon. I love Samuel at six months so much, his perma-smile, his wild, addictive laughter, his solemn brown eyes and fat pink cheeks. I know I will mourn the passing of each stage.

At the new skate ramp there are two teenage boys – fifteen? sixteen? – passing each other like synchronistic weathermen as they execute their perfect mid-air turns. I wonder why they aren't at school, then wonder why I even care. I'm twenty-seven, not fifty. I can imagine Hannah laughing at me: 'So go report them, Grandpa.'

Just beyond the skate park is the pond, filled with fat brown ducks gliding above a sheen of emerald scum. I search its perimeter casually, looking out for a tall, dark-haired woman pushing a buggy; she's easy to spot, this most beautiful mother of mine.

And at this moment, just as I'm about to leave, Alice and Samuel come into view. They are too far away to see me, loitering under a tree on the other side of the pond. From this distance it looks like Samuel is asleep, Alice walking slowly behind him, steering the pram with one hand, taking her time. The obvious thing to do, the *only* thing to do, is go and meet them, say hello, a quick chat with Alice, a cuddle with my son if he happens to wake up.

Instead, I stand, rooted in the shadows, watching until my eyes hurt. For it's like watching a video of the missing weeks of my childhood, this unguarded view of my mother and the small child in her care. I am silent, motionless, transfixed, addicted to this fragmental scrutiny of everything I lost.

Then

Alice

The months in Italy are, without question, the happiest time of my life. Here, in a country that celebrates pleasure in all its forms, Jake is in his element. Although the band are writing and recording much of the time, we always walk to the café in the little square in Fiesole for our morning cappuccino, and at night Jake cooks pedantically Italian food – polenta, beans, pasta or risotto – and we drink Chianti that we buy from a vineyard in five-litre flagons.

This is the time when the band become my new family. Tom has always been warm and welcoming, but now I am becoming closer to Eddie too. I have understood his initial coolness towards me was fuelled by a wariness that comes from having known Jake most of his life. He knows the troubled boy who once tried to take his own life, and at times he seems to watch over him with the intentness of an overanxious parent. One morning when we are both up earlier than the others, Eddie and I go for a walk through the hills of Fiesole. At this time of day there's a coolness in the air and the surprising ripple of a wind feathering through the Italian oaks, still clinging to their greenness despite the months of sun.

Eddie finds a porcupine spike on the dusty trail we're

following and he hands it to me, ceremoniously, as if passing over a gift.

'You're good for Jake,' he says, out of nowhere. 'He's more stable than he's been.'

'He still drinks too much. That worries me.'

'We all do.'

'But with him it's different. It's like a mood comes over him.'

'He drinks to block things out. His childhood specifically.'

'What happened, Eddie? Will you tell me?'

'His father was absent and his mother didn't care much. The real calamity was that he got left with his grandparents a lot of the time and his grandfather was not a nice man. But you know that, don't you?'

'Not the details.'

'I'm sure Jake will tell you when he's ready. But there's more to it than that. Depression is part of Jake. He needs to control it but he also has to tap into it sometimes because those intense emotions feed into his songwriting. You're good for him, though. I hope you stay together,' Eddie says, and I wonder how he could even conceive of a time when we might be apart. This is no longer a love affair; it's a combining of our souls and passion. We are everything to each other now, lover, parent, mentor, muse, all of it.

There is no darkness in Jake in these weeks; instead he is inflamed by the writing and recording of new material, the dedication to music, to self-expression, that is his holy grail. If life allowed him to exist like this, in a cocoon where he is loved and nothing is expected of him, I think his despair would be lifted for ever.

He throws himself into his work, so that even when we're talking or drinking coffee or making love, his mind is only half there; less than that. He switches to autopilot, he is present in the smallest way, yet this, to me, is an inspiration. I want to live like this too, fully absorbed, selfish in my commitment to drawing, to art.

During the days, I often take the bus to Florence and immerse myself in the Renaissance. At the Uffizi, I spend whole hours looking at the flat, two-dimensional paintings of the twelfth century, amateurish alien eyes drawn into foreheads not faces, perspective that is clumsy and unsuccessful. Only once I have fully understood the failings of these paintings – still miraculous and rather beautiful on one level, not least for their immaculate preservation – do I move on to Michelangelo, Botticelli, Leonardo, Caravaggio. This intense study of the Old Masters teaches me more, far more, than my first year at the Slade.

I stare at these paintings – Botticelli's *Birth of Venus*, Caravaggio's *Medusa* – until they are imprinted behind my eyelids. I dream of them at night. I wake thinking of the vividness of Caravaggio's work, smiles that are twisted and cruel, toenails that are ragged and dirty. I am infatuated with his rendering of Italy's seventeenth-century streets: dark, dusty, full of shadowy corners. Doorways with worn-away lintels and peeling paint, rooms with bare walls and rough brick floors, the raw underbelly of Italy painted with a photographic precision. Gradually my style begins to emerge. I have listened to Robin's advice, and my sketches and paintings combine the informality of a frozen moment with the classical influence of the Renaissance masters. I paint Jake, bare-chested, in his faded, patched jeans, leaning against a womb-pink wall in the garden of our villa. He has one knee bent, foot pressed up against the wall, and he looks off canvas, his face in profile. I photographed him in the early-evening sun and I work hard to capture the theatrical interplay of light and shadow that characterises Caravaggio's work, with my futuristic beam of gold picking out the boniness of his chest.

During these months, there is one painting I am drawn to inexplicably. Every time I go to Florence I find I must revisit *The Deposition of Christ* by Stefano Pieri, which shows Mary holding up the dead body of her son. There is something about the sorrow on Mary's face and the beautiful, naturalistic slump of Jesus's body curved into her lap that I find irresistible. That concentration of emotion, a melancholia I love to immerse myself in. When I show Jake the painting, he proclaims it 'utterly depressing'.

He indulges me, though, when I want to make my own version of it. I ask Eddie to photograph me leaning against the terracotta garden wall with Jake asleep, his head in my lap. Wearing only his ripped jeans, his dark hair wilder and longer than I have ever seen it before, with a long, beaded rosary around his neck, there is something of the modern deity about him. Unlike Pieri's Jesus, his corpse a depressing greenish grey, my Jesus is suntanned and there is an almost imperceptible smile on his sleeping face, there only to those of us who know.

'Take the fucking shot, Eddie!' he shouted after half an hour of posing.

Catholicism was inflicted on Jake by his grandparents, theirs the menacing, unforgiving kind, but he is still drawn to its trappings. Rosaries, incense, crucifixes, candles. Iron grilles for confession, the gilded robes of the priest. He loves this canvas, loves the fact that he is immortalised in a 1970s rock-and-roll pietà.

He takes a photograph of the painting and mails it to Robin in London, and a few days later we receive a telegram.

Congratulations. Your album cover, I think? Call it Apparition.

The word fits the picture, I can see that, but why does it give me that familiar tug of unease, the way I once felt when my father's mood threatened to turn?

Eddie says, 'Album cover. And also album title. *Apparition*, by Disciples. It's perfect.'

The working album title has been *Cassiopeia*, named for our night of star-gazing in Southwold, and Eddie, perhaps because he wasn't there, perhaps because it was a little clichéd, didn't like it.

Jake fetches a bottle of sparkling wine and we toast the second album.

'To *Apparition*,' we say, clinking glasses, inspired, proud and wholly unaware that this spectre would soon implode our lives.

Now

Luke

The power of the internet continues to astonish me. Less than six months ago, I typed my birth mother's name into a search engine and *ping!* a match came back with an artist named Alice Garland living in Chiswick. After several days and several drafts, I sent her a letter to introduce myself and tentatively enquire about the two of us meeting. And the rest is history. Except, of course, that it isn't. For the dream I had when I wrote that letter is not reaching fruition in the way I expected. My real, natural mother might come to my house three days a week, but I know little more of her than I did when I first typed her name into Google.

Today in the office I find myself googling my birth mother again. Richard Fields and Alice Garland, I'll try that. There's a picture of the two of them – my real live parents, still hard to take in – at the opening of Rick's retrospective at the National Portrait Gallery. I stare at them, Rick in a checked three-piece suit, Alice wearing a slim-fitting black dress, her hair up and exposing her neck, which is almost unfeasibly long and swan-like. She must have been so beautiful when she was young.

I find a small article about her that I haven't seen before, in a local magazine called *Chiswick Life*. There's a picture taken in her studio, Alice wearing a paint-spattered shirt and sitting in front of a comical portrait of a pug, exaggerated squinty eyes and rolls of fat on its tiny-toy body.

A quote from her makes me laugh: 'This pug has a lion-sized character, the resilience and determination of a giant.' Inside I know she's amusing herself; outside she's pitching for more business from her clientele of pooch-obsessed old ladies.

When I type in *Alice Garland, the Slade 1973*, nothing comes up. I realise there are no press articles from that time on Google; if I wanted to find out more I would have to go somewhere like the British Library and sift through reams of microfiche. Or I could ask Hannah to look up Alice and Richard in the cuttings library at *The Times*. But what would I say? Hannah, I'm beginning to think my birth mother is not exactly who we think she is; can't put my finger on it, just a feeling I have.

Samuel is bathed and ready for bed by the time I get home, and dressed in something I don't recognise. Instead of his usual white sleepsuit, a pair of pyjamas, navy with ladybirds on them, sweet though not exactly to mine and Hannah's taste.

'You bought him some pyjamas, Alice,' I say, scooping him up from his sheepskin rug. He's sitting up now, though Alice has him propped against a beanbag just in case. 'How kind of you.'

'Oh, I made them, actually. I thought I might have forgotten how, but it came back straight away.'

'You made these? I'm so impressed.'

Alice laughs, pleased. 'Well, I'm glad you like them. I could make him other things if you wanted. Dungarees? I used to make those for you ...' Her voice fades, but I press ahead, keen to glean something from the past we briefly shared.

'You dressed me in dungarees? I'd love to see some photos. Do you have any?'

'I don't think so. I'll have a look.'

'Really? No photos from that time? How long was it we were together? A month? Six weeks?'

I hate myself for the way I press her, but she leaves me no alternative. Surely it can't go on, this reluctance of hers to discuss our past?

'That's right,' she says. 'It felt like barely any time at all.'

She gives me a sad smile and then turns away to pick up her handbag, and I curse myself for reminding her.

'The fish pie is ready to go into the oven. It will take around forty-five minutes. What time will Hannah be back?'

Hannah is working late again but she promised to be home in time for supper.

'Around eight, I think,' I say.

'Well, have a good evening and I'll see you tomorrow. Goodnight, little bird.'

She blows Samuel a kiss as she leaves the room, and I succumb to the now familiar dip of disillusionment.

The fish pie is perfectly brown by the time Hannah arrives, and I've laid the table with napkins, candles, a bottle of white wine.

'Thought we ought to celebrate your success,' I say, pouring her a glass.

Hannah serves the pie, a gorgeous yellowy mess studded with prawns and chunks of salmon. We've eaten it several times before and it's become our favourite.

'God, that's good,' she says. 'We are so lucky with Alice.'

We have a variant of this conversation most nights and I usually agree, but now I allow a little of my bleakness out.

'Lucky in one way, I guess. But in another way this whole thing is starting to do my head in. I don't feel I'm getting to know her at all.'

Hannah looks up at me in surprise, mid-mouthful, fork frozen in the air. She puts it back down untouched.

'How do you mean? I thought you liked her. I thought we felt the same.'

'Of course I like her. But I don't know her. And wasn't that the whole point? Mother and son being reunited. Spending time together. Forming some kind of bond. The only bond being formed here is between Alice and Samuel.'

I take a big drink of wine. I've said more than I meant to. But Hannah is looking at me with concern. She gets up from her side of the table and comes around to mine.

'Budge up.' She squeezes in next to me on the bench. 'Poor baby,' she says, reaching up to kiss the side of my face. 'This is harder on you than we realised, isn't it?'

I can't rely on my voice just yet, so I have another swig of wine and allow Hannah to do the talking.

'You do know, don't you, that this is ridiculous. But *completely understandable*.' Firm emphasis on the words. 'The thing is, Alice has to form a bond with Samuel just by the fact of being his carer. If she didn't, we would be bloody worried. In fact, we'd have to sack her.'

She pauses, expecting me to laugh, but I can't.

'Luke, it's going to take time for you and Alice to have the kind of relationship you want. In a way, I think there's too much hurt on both sides. Yours at the fact that she gave you up, hers at the fact that she had to and she still feels guilty about it. And when you feel guilty, you get defensive, you put up barriers. It's going to take time to break those barriers down, but that's all right. Time is something we have. You're young and so is Alice; she's not even fifty. You've got years and years to get to know each other.'

'You know me. Always wanting to rush things.'

'The thing is, you're actually quite lucky. So few people get the chance to form a relationship with their parents as an adult; they have all the baggage of childhood, all those disappointments and rows that get in the way. You and Alice have a clean slate.'

And, for the first time ever, I think: Hannah doesn't get it. The baggage is what I want. The history is what I crave. I'd like to pick up that clean slate and dash it to the ground, little fragments of black scattered across our immaculate, Alice-swept, Alice-washed oak floor.

Then

Alice

In August, the heat becomes unbearable. The little basement studio where the band are recording is anvil-hot, tolerable only in the coolness of night. Jake declares a week's holiday.

Tom and Eddie are content to lie around the pool deepening their suntans, playing cards and drinking vats of cheap red wine at night. But after just one day of this, Jake takes the bus into Florence and comes back driving a tiny lemon-yellow bubble car. All three of us, Eddie, Tom and I, gather around to watch him unfolding his long, thin body from the confines of the car; at six foot two, it's a miracle he managed to get inside it in the first place.

'We're going on a road trip,' he says. 'Just you and me.'

'In Noddy's car?'

'This magnificent machine is a Cinquecento. We couldn't possibly travel in anything else.'

Cars, cappuccinos – authenticity is Jacob's drug.

The Cinquecento has a top speed of around eighty kilometres per hour, so we decide upon a few nights in Siena, just a short drive up the road. The euphoria of those first hours, the two of us alone at last, puttering through a backdrop of Tuscan hills now burnt bronze from the weeks of scorching sun. It looks as I'd imagine Africa to look, beautiful but parched, bleached, bleak from the lack of green. Jake turns on the radio and the opening bars of 'All Along the Watchtower' start up, and he says, 'Fuck.' We listen in silence, volume right up, and afterwards he tells me about seeing Jimi play in a tiny little Soho pub called The Toucan.

'You knew he was different right away, even before the mental guitar solos. He had it like no one else, not Jagger, not Bowie, certainly not The Beatles. That was the moment I knew nothing else mattered apart from music. I came back from that gig and I began playing guitar obsessively, all the way through the night. Sleep felt like a waste of time. I wanted to be just like him. I taught myself to play bass and rhythm guitar, I felt like I needed to be able to do everything better than anyone else.'

He holds my hand and we're quiet again and I know he's thinking about Jimi, his death, a drug overdose that could have been prevented, people said, if only his girlfriend had reacted sooner. I remember her name, it's scorched into my memory: Monika Dannemann. If she had dialled 999 half an hour earlier, he would probably still be alive.

'But he might have been brain-dead,' Jake says, as if we've been having this conversation out loud instead of in our heads.

'What must it be like to be Monika?'

'Hard to see how she'll ever get over it.'

Hendrix's manager found a poem he'd written hours before his death, 'The Story of Life'. A love song, really, to Monika, which talked of love being a series of hellos and goodbyes. A beautiful poem or a suicide note? No one will ever know.

Jimi Hendrix's death affected all of us, but with Jake you can tell it's still raw. He rarely talks about his past and always tries to steer away from anything negative, but right now there's a surround of sorrow in our tiny little car. I reach out my hand, tanned brown from our summer of sun, and place it on his thigh. He picks it up with one hand and kisses it quickly before returning it to his leg. No words are ever needed.

When we see a sign for a vineyard, Jake pulls off the road. We drive at around five kilometres an hour up a bumpy track riddled with potholes, olive groves on either side, and finally, after a long and jarring five minutes, a farmhouse comes into view, standard Tuscan fare of cream stone walls and a red tiled roof. Behind it the sweep of a vineyard, acres and acres vanishing into the horizon.

An elderly woman comes out to greet us, talking in fast, lyrical Italian that neither of us understands. We stare at each other in confusion.

'*Mangiare?*' she says bringing her fingers to her mouth.

'*Si, signora, grazie,*' Jake answers with the only Italian he knows. He mimes putting a bottle to his lips, head tipped back like a drunk, and she laughs.

'*Ovviamente*! Chianti Classico.'

There could be no more perfect place for lunch than this. A little wooden table set up beneath the shade of a sprawling cypress tree. A cheerful blue gingham tablecloth, tumblers filled with red wine, a plate of home-cured salami, a basket of bread and a bowl of the fattest olives I have ever seen. We eat greedily, assuming that this is it, but we are in Italy and we should have known better. Soon we are given bowls of truffle tagliatelle, wide ribbons of pasta that gleam with oil and taste more intoxicating, more sublime than anything I have ever eaten before.

'Oh my God,' we say to each other, over and over again.

Jake, with his hamster store of extraneous knowledge, can tell me all about black truffles. The specific breed of dog used to hunt them – Lagotto, he even remembers its name – the wars that break out between locals when one stumbles across another's secret stash.

'It's a bloodthirsty business,' he says. 'People die for truffles. You can see why.'

'Sometimes I think I've fallen in love with the *Encyclopaedia Britannica*. How do you know all this stuff?'

He laughs, then takes hold of my hand.

'By the way, will you marry me? Any time you like,' he says. 'Today, next week, in five years.'

'Should I answer?' I say when I manage to speak, and now he smiles, tilting his head as he observes me.

'I'd have thought so.'

'Then yes, of course I will. Any time. Today, next week, in five years.'

Siena in August is empty of Italians; just foolish tourists like us braving the heat, spending our days cowering within the thick walls of the Duomo. Not that it's a hardship to be in this mind-bending building, more opulent, more dramatic than anywhere I have ever seen, in life or textbook. Acres of marble, columns that are striped and preposterously tall, a frescoed ceiling so gilded it is almost blinding. There is an altarpiece with four saints sculpted by a teenage Michelangelo, each one perfection, and I find it hard to take this in, that here in Siena, we casually stumble across Michelangelo.

'Can we live here one day?' I ask Jake as we brace ourselves for the burning sun of the piazza.

'Just what I was thinking,' he says.

We rent a hot little room above a bar and spend our days seeking out shady restaurants, eating long, indulgent lunches of wild boar pappardelle and a porcini risotto with pecorino cheese that amazes us. It's hard to sleep at night, so we have afternoon siestas instead, knocked out by our calorific lunches and carafes of red wine, waking thirsty and fuzzy-headed when the sky is turning dark grey. I love the evenings best of all, walking through streets so narrow we must go in single file while on either side tall coloured buildings lean towards each other like lovers. We'll stop at our favourite café in the square and drink espressos, sometimes with a balloon of grappa.

The sketches I love best come from this time, Jake freer, happier than I've ever seen him. While I'm drawing, he'll scribble lyrics in his little leather notebook or take sips from his coffee or stare up at the sky, searching for the hallmarks of his childhood, stargazing his consolation from those demons he will never share. We are so relaxed with each other in these days that I'm tempted to ask him. What happened? What is it that sometimes makes you so sad? But then I look at him, almost absurdly beautiful in his loose black shirt, hair that now reaches his shoulders, and he smiles back at me, raising his brandy in a salute, and I know that I will never do anything to recast him in gloom.

Now

Luke

To tell you the truth, I'm a little bit addicted to my amateur sleuthing. I'm good at it, that's the thing. I have Alice and Samuel's timings down to perfection; I know exactly where they will be during my lunch hour. I have a little argument with myself most mornings. Today you will not follow your mother and son, I say as I sit down at my desk. But by midday the craving is upon me. I need the fix of looking, watching, examining; I like to catch the scent of Alice in the air – lemons or cedar or fig, an indefinable yet instantly recognisable perfume that is beginning to drive me mad.

Alice, I discover, is a creature of habit. After Samuel has had his lunch at midday – relentlessly puréed slops, poor sod – she always walks up to the park or the high street, depending on whether or not she's had a chance to go shopping in the morning. Sometimes they stop off in the library. I haven't had the nerve to follow them in there. I stand outside the old sandstone building watching its passage of visitors: Clapham mummies wrestling buggies up the steps, pensioners who go to read the papers or perhaps in the hope of a random hello, a shaggy-haired tramp once, who was ejected minutes later.

It's better when, as today, they head for the shops and I can follow at a distance. I love walking behind Alice; there is much to glean from the unguarded posterior view. I see that she is happy and relaxed, occasionally I'll even hear a fragment of a song she is singing – she has a good voice, clear and strong. Mostly I observe how devoted she is to Samuel, talking to him softly if he's awake, constantly telling him about his surroundings. I can't hear exactly what she says from this distance, just a muffle of words. Sometimes she stops, sharply swivelling the buggy in front of a shop window, where she'll point out something of interest. The butcher's, with its hanging pig carcasses, feels a little indelicate after his lunch of carrot mush.

I was in danger of getting caught once, when they slammed to a halt in front of Arcadia, the gift shop. I stood exposed, terrified of Alice glancing to the left and seeing me, her son, Samuel's father, loitering with intent. A moment of reckoning, that time.

What the fuck, dude?

I tell myself that I am checking in on Alice from time to time, as any other new father would, making sure that the woman who cares for his child is doing a good job.

I've been standing at the top of Clapham Manor Street for only five minutes when Alice and Samuel walk right past me. I catch her perfume in the air, sharp, citrusy, a little floral. They might be going to Woolies; Alice goes there a lot. I've risked lurking amidst the pick 'n' mix once or twice just to see her at the back of the shop, examining cake tins and oven gloves that appear in our house later. Another little Alice gift, something useful, thoughtful, transformative – like the corkboard she tacked up to the kitchen wall.

'So we can leave each other notes,' she said. 'And I can buy stuff you need.'

Such a simple thing. So obvious, I wonder now how we lived

without it. Alice bestows these gifts upon us with such ease and grace, it's easy to accept.

I was right, they have turned into Woolworths, which is perfect. I always think it's the kind of place I might easily pop into to pick up some pens or a notepad on the pretence of having left mine at the office.

As always, Alice wheels the pram towards the back of the shop. She is looking not at kitchen equipment or stationery but the selection of toys on the left-hand side of the store. From a distance I watch her pick up a glove puppet, an orange, yellow and brown chicken made of felt. She puts her hand inside it, snaps the beak at Samuel and gives a pretty perfect rendition of a cockerel. Cock-a-doodle-doo. The whole of Woolworths must catch Samuel's hysteria, a joyful, infectious sound. I creep a little closer, addicted to the tableau between woman and child. I'm lurking three rows away, amidst a job lot of Caterpillar boots, taking a pair from its box, sliding my hand inside one and holding it out for closer examination.

The puppet routine continues. Alice has moved on to a furry alligator, emerald green with a lemon-yellow stomach and a crimson mouth. She snaps its jaw, hovering right in front of Samuel's face until she swoops down and pecks his nose. More wild laughter and Alice is laughing too. There is no end to the fun these two can have together. I'm about to leave my post when a blonde girl with a toddler walks up to them.

'Hi there,' she says. 'I've seen you at circle time in the library. How old is your baby? He's gorgeous.'

'Six months, almost seven,' Alice says. 'How about yours, he looks around a year older?'

'Yes, he's eighteen months. I'm Kirsty, by the way.'

'Lovely to meet you. I'm Alice. And this—'

'Would you like to try them on?'

The girl in front of me, green Woolies shirt of nylon, has a quizzical look on her face. Perhaps she's been watching me. Perhaps she's wondering why a young guy like myself is peeking over the shelf of boots to observe a middle-aged woman and a baby.

But my mind is heavy with new intelligence and it's an effort to speak. Alice didn't explain that Samuel wasn't her baby, a child she looks after three days a week. She acted as if he was hers.

'No, I don't, thanks.' I'm barging past the shop assistant, incapable of civility.

Outside on the pavement, I run down the street, realising after a minute or two that I am running away from the Tube, not towards it, so preoccupied am I with this latest development. Is Alice pretending Samuel is her baby? Or am I, increasingly paranoid freak that I am, jumping to conclusions? If I told Hannah, apart from thinking I was a lunatic for spying on my mother in my lunch hour – *not spying, H, checking up* – she'd tell me not to be so ridiculous. I can even hear the words she would choose.

'Alice looks far younger than she is; she probably gets mistaken for Samuel's mum the whole time. Sometimes it's too boring to explain, that's all.'

And she is probably right. But that doesn't stem the cold spread of concern I feel in my lungs, my stomach, my heart. I'm your baby, Alice. Me. Not Samuel.

I hear how that sounds. Infantile, immature, borderline psychotic. But here is the thing. I am and always will be the child that was given away. I am needy. I am fucked up. I am desperate to be noticed.

I'm brushing away tears as I walk down into Clapham Common station, as the hard, ugly truth strikes me. I am jealous of my own son.

Then

Alice

In the autumn, we are both working so hard we barely see each other. Jake is out most nights mixing the album; I might stay at college until ten or eleven, painting in a kind of fever. All those ideas and sketches from Italy now morphing into their colour-heightened reality, snapshot meets Renaissance, a style I am working and working on until I can perfect it.

If I was expecting favoured treatment at college – the girl with the make-or-break art show – the reality turns out to be different. The tutors are working me like a dog, even Rita Miller.

I now have sixteen drawings and five oils that I consider ready to show.

But Rita says, 'Good. But good is not enough. You are capable of better.'

Gordon walks around the studio considering each work in silence.

'Not there yet,' he says, although he loves the mock pietà, Jake asleep on my lap.

'This is sheer brilliance, Alice, and I'll tell you why. It's be-cause I can see the layers in this painting. There's an intensity here, and the feeling that you're almost mothering this boy in your arms. It's painted with sorrow, or at least that's how I see it. I want to feel like this about every single painting. I want to look at them, stare at them until the hidden meaning becomes apparent.'

I am learning to immerse myself in feeling before I begin to paint. Each day I take one of the drawings – today it's Jake bare-chested, in flared jeans, lying back against the lacy, absurdly feminine pillows of our Italian bed, the wrought-iron bedstead framing his face – and think about what he meant to me in that moment. The drawings took a long time, sometimes a full hour, and you can see that he has forgotten I am here; he is lost in thought. Now, with intense scrutiny, I see I have caught his unguarded melancholy, an innate sadness he tries his best to hide. And I am on a journey of imagining. With his indisputable good looks, Jake has been portrayed as a sex object in the media. I see something different. I see a man on the brink of success if only his inner torment will allow it. I worry for him. I wish that he wouldn't keep his private anguish locked away, out of reach of everyone. There's something I could help him with, I feel it, I know it. Yet every time I approach the subject, asking him about his childhood, and, once or twice, his suicide attempt, he shuts the conversation down.

'The past is over. It's just you and me now.'

All of this goes into my painting. I've captured Jacob's beauty, but also his darkness, the side of himself he refuses to show.

When Gordon King next comes into the studio, he stares at the painting in silence.

Finally he says, 'Bravo, Alice. This is what will distinguish you. Viscerality. Emotion so potent you feel you can touch it.'

The band are putting the finishing touches to their album with the producer Brian Eno. If all goes to plan, the record will be mastered next month and released in February, timed to coincide with my show.

Brian thinks there are four definite hits on the album, one a ballad called 'Cassiopeia', written after our night on the beach stargazing. It's bittersweet, a song not about our love, Jake's and mine, but about Rick and Tom, their shame at the vitriol of passers-by. Every time I hear the refrain, 'They built each other up but you tore them back down', it pierces my heart.

Our lives fall into a routine as September leans into October. We wake at eight and go for breakfast, always together, always Bar Italia. The owner, Luigi, is our friend and he brings our cappuccino and croissants without us having to ask for them. More often than not he won't let us pay.

'It's my gift,' he says, 'to the musician and artist who will soon be very rich. You can look after me when I'm old.'

I leave for the Slade half an hour later and Jake walks me partway there. We kiss goodbye on Wellington Street, sometimes for a long time, long enough to draw wolf whistles from people passing, sometimes with his tongue searching my mouth, my hands drawing his hips towards me.

'And you think I can concentrate now?' he says, every time.

Once at college, though, my focus is absolute, and I've barely looked up from my canvas, it seems, when Rick comes in at lunchtime and suggests going out for a sandwich. And it happens that on this lunchtime in early October, the leaves on the trees beginning their dramatic burn of yellow, gold and crimson, I am overcome by a sudden feeling of nausea, so that I sit down in the middle of the street, hand clamped against my sweating forehead.

'Alice?'

Rick squats down beside me.

'I'm going to be ...' The last word gets lost as I retch the watery contents of my stomach onto the pavement.

'Something you ate?' Rick says, pulling me up and skilfully sidestepping us away from the pile of puke.

'I've barely eaten in the past few days. Maybe that's the problem.'

But when we get to our favourite sandwich shop, as I hold my standard tuna and cucumber order in my hands, I find I must vomit again, lurching out onto the pavement. The moment I've been sick, I feel a little better.

'I'm not ill,' I say to Rick.

He looks at me, head on one side, taking bites out of his ham and cheese bap.

'Well you look a bit green. And, if you don't mind me saying so, like you've put on weight. You're such a skinny thing normally.'

'That's what Jake says. Says he likes his women big.'

The evidence is there, swirling all around us, but it still takes time to piece the facts together.

'I'm exhausted, that's all it is. We've both been working so hard.'

Rick looks at me again.

'What?'

'Alice, my love, do you think you might be pregnant?'

'I'm on the pill. How could I be pregnant?'

'Sweetheart, I'm a gay man. How on earth would I know? But let's go and find out.'

Rick, who has had his fair share of transitory sexual diseases, is a face around the Marie Stopes Clinic on Tottenham Court Road. The receptionist recognises him instantly. 'Oh no, Richard, not you again,' she says, though she is smiling.

'Actually,' his voice is low, conspiratorial, 'it's my friend. With an altogether different, er, dilemma.'

There's an hour's wait for the results, and rather than going back to college, Rick and I sit in the pub with a half of beer that I cannot force down.

'I'm pregnant,' I tell him. 'I know I am.'

There's the new curve to my stomach, the heavier, fuller breasts, which are painful at times, the complete absence of a period, which should have been signal enough. If I hadn't been so absorbed in my work, I might have noticed.

'Not such a big deal these days,' Rick says.

I see him gazing at me intently, trying to read my reaction, trying not to say the wrong thing. Neither of us says the word *abortion*; that's for the clinic nurse to mention when she confirms my pregnancy, Rick sitting beside me like an anxious husband.

'Nine weeks, I'd say, maybe ten. Does that make sense?'

'None of it makes sense. I'm on the pill.'

We've had this conversation already, the nurse and I, the fact that the pill is only ninety-nine per cent effective and it's always recommended to use condoms as well, but no one ever does. I think, but do not say, that neither have I been as diligent about taking my daily pill as I might. I'm a fool. I have no one to blame but myself.

'There's still time for an abortion,' the nurse says. 'But we need to get you booked in. Come back tomorrow if that's what you decide and we can sort out the paperwork.'

Rick shepherds me out of Marie Stopes, arm around my waist.

'Want me to come back to the flat with you?'

'No. You've been amazing. I need to tell Jake on my own.'

'He loves you, Al. It'll be fine whatever you decide.'

The new Disciples album is finally finished, and to celebrate Jake is roasting a chicken and has a bottle of cava chilling in a makeshift ice bucket, bucket being the operative word, though he has filled it to the brim with water and ice.

He unwraps the foil hood and slides the cork from the bottle with a triumphant pop, and I watch as the wine fizzes right over the top of both our glasses. Jake raises his to mine and we clink.

'To us. To *Apparition*. To your debut show.'

He is feverishly happy today, almost too much. There is a craziness to him as he talks and talks and paces around our tiny flat. And while I listen, I am thinking: how am I ever going to tell him?

According to his label, Island Records, Brian Eno has transformed what was already a great record into a 'smash'.

'They think it's going to be huge,' Jake says. 'They actually said that and normally they don't forecast. So Island are pushing for an earlier release. They want to get "Cassiopeia" on the Radio 1 playlist at the beginning of February. We might need to do the launch sooner if you can manage it.'

I follow him out into the kitchen, leaning up against the counter, watching as he takes the chicken from the oven and bastes it, my head full of the things I cannot say.

'You're quiet,' he says, sliding the bird back into the oven, and I tell him, 'Just tired,' though the words scream through my brain. Pregnant. Abortion. Abortion. Baby.

I watch Jake flipping through his box of records, as he does every night, sitting back on his heels, pulling one out, considering, replacing. It is part of our daily routine, this; it can take him five minutes or more to make his choice. In Italy, Tom and Eddie christened him 'the vibes master', but sometimes he took so long to choose, all three of us would shout at him, 'Just play something!' For Jake, though, it always has to be exactly right. So when he selects Leonard Cohen, *Songs from a Room*, opening track 'Bird on the Wire', an anthem of freedom we both love, without warning I find myself crying. So much of our time together has been about freedom and liberation, about finding ourselves and proving ourselves, and now there is a tiny fragment of human that could change everything for us. And in some crazed way, I want it to.

Jake catches me brushing the tears from my cheeks and is across the room in moments, kneeling before me. He takes my hand.

'Is it the pressure of the show? If it's too much, we can delay the launch, I'm sure. I forget how young you are sometimes, Alice. I'm sorry.'

'It's not that. I'm excited about the show.'

'Then what, tell me.'

'It's hard.'

'Alice, whatever it is, you need to tell me.'

Give it to him straight, just like they did at the clinic.

'OK. I'm pregnant. Ten weeks pregnant. Almost three months.'

Shell-shock words.

'Pregnant?'

'Yes.'

'But how?'

'I don't know. Sometimes I forget to take the pill. It's my fault, I'm sorry.'

'You're sorry?'

I'm in shock, I'm confused, I cannot comprehend the expression of utter joy that transforms his face.

'Why on earth would you be sorry?'

He's grinning wildly and holding my hands, now kissing them, and I'm smiling too; in fact, all of a sudden I'm laughing.

'You think it's a good thing?'

'Not good, no. Fantastic. Incredible. Amazing. You're having a baby. *We're* having a baby. Alice Garland, this is the best news I've ever had in my life.'

Now

Luke

The separated adoptee and birth parent are, by definition, strangers to one another. How can you understand who someone is and what they might be capable of when you have missed all the nuances, behavioural complexities and fundamental background that has formed their persona?

Who Am I? The Adoptee's Hidden Trauma by Joel Harris

On Saturdays, Hannah gives me a lie-in. Sundays are her turn, though she rarely takes it.

'I can't bear to miss out on any time with Samuel,' she will say, appearing downstairs in the kitchen while the two of us eat our unvarying breakfast: milk and baby porridge for him, toast and Marmite for me.

I sleep late on this particular Saturday, exhausted perhaps by the combined stress of my job – will they, won't they close down my record label? – and my ongoing disillusionment with Alice.

I find my girlfriend and son sitting together in our small paved garden, Samuel leaning against Hannah's stomach, cradled between her thighs.

He laughs in recognition as soon as he sees me, and Hannah

says, 'Yes, he's pretty funny, your daddy, isn't he? Do you realise you've slept for almost twelve hours? You must have been shattered.'

She stands up, passing the baby to me.

'I was going to make bacon sandwiches, and then we can go to the park.'

'Sounds good. I'm starving.'

It's only once she's gone that I take in the retractable washing line, hung with a neat row of sleepsuits, all white, the colour Hannah likes Samuel in best. Eight babygros stretched out by pegs, drying in the midday sunshine, and at the end of them a teddy bear. There is a threatening tightness in my chest as I walk towards the line and unclip the bear, a sodden toy that now smells not of Alice's perfume and old times but of Persil.

I walk into the kitchen where Hannah is frying bacon, Samuel under one arm, the wet bear in the other.

'You washed the bear.'

She turns around from the cooker, smiling.

'Yes, and I cut off its eyes. They're lethal, those glass ones. I'm going to embroider some black ones on instead.'

'You cut off its eyes?'

I put Samuel down on his sheepskin rug as carefully as I can. And then I stand in the middle of the room, damp bear clutched to my chest, while the years drop away. This bear was mine. This ruined, disfigured bear belonged to me back in the days when I belonged to Alice. The days when Alice cared about me the way she now cares about Samuel.

I am struggling to breathe and there's a pain in my chest, sharp and insistent. I collapse onto my knees, arms wrapped around myself.

'Luke?' Hannah says, but she sounds distant, as if I'm underwater.

Her voice becomes shrill, frightened.

'What's happening? What's going on?'

The pressure in my chest is so strong I feel as if my lungs might explode. A panic attack. I've had them before, but not for years. Not since Hannah.

Breathe in, hold and count to four, breathe out. One two three four. I know the routine.

'I think this bear was mine,' I say, kneeling up as soon as I can, surprised by the wetness on my cheeks. I hadn't realised I was crying.

Hannah takes the bear from me and strokes its wet, matted fur, a gesture of unbearable tenderness.

'This is about Alice, isn't it?'

'I'm not coping with it, H. I feel like I've barely got to know her in all this time. You seem to get on better with her than I do.'

'That's only because we're women, we bond in the way that women do. And we've got the art thing, that's all.'

'No, it's more than that. There is a disconnect between me and Alice, I'm sure of it. I feel like all she cares about is Samuel and maybe you, a little bit.'

'Oh babe.' Hannah squeezes my hand so hard it's almost painful. 'This is so tough on you, isn't it? But Samuel is a baby who needs looking after. And Alice is wonderful with him, but it doesn't mean she cares about him more than you.'

'You're right,' I say, thinking: you're always right. Thinking: why can't things ever be as straightforward for me?

'What just happened? Was that a panic attack?'

'I think so. I used to have them when I first started my job. Stress basically.'

'Is this about Spirit? And Reborn?'

'It's partly the whole Alice thing. But also there's so much pressure at work. I'm worried Michael is going to take Spirit away from me.'

'In my bones I know that's not going to happen,' Hannah says. 'And I'm not going to let you ruin your weekend stressing about it. Come on, can't we enjoy being together, just the three of us?'

'Welcome to Nappy Valley,' the estate agent said when we signed the contract, which made me want to rip up the paperwork then and there. But he had a point. We merge into the background wallpaper, my micro family and I, as we reach the new souped-up playground on the common, hailed by shrieks of joy.

Here on a Saturday afternoon, the weekend dads are out in force, the loud, look-at-me ones in their off-duty shirts. Something in the City probably and unable to blend, weaned on a diet of competition and self-belief, they talk as if to instruct the entire playground.

'Well done, Pandora, see if you can get to the next bar. I know you can.'

Five-year-old Pandora is being forced across the monkey bars, failure not an option. She'll rise to the top, wrenched all the way, unless she's like me, the definitive square peg, a wimp at the monkey bars and all that followed.

But we have a campaign of our own this afternoon. Samuel has just started sitting up and Hannah wants to try him out in the baby swings. All four swings are taken, a trio of babies and one oversized three-year-old whom I resist the urge to eyeball. *Get out of the swing, kid.*

While we wait, we watch, still new enough to the whole scene to be fascinated by playground dynamics. One mother counts to ten each time she pushes her baby in the swing – one, two, three, four – and moments later the mother next to her starts counting too, vacuumed into the land of tiger parents without even realising it.

A swing becomes vacant and we lower Samuel into it, fixing both tiny hands onto the bar in front. His face creases with confusion. What? Why? And when we give him a gentle push, oh so small, momentum too minuscule for the naked eye, he continues to stare at us with a furious hauteur, as if the whole thing is beneath him. But then Hannah pushes the swing a little harder – 'See, it's meant to be fun,' she says – and I wonder if soon he, like me, will believe everything that comes out of this woman's lovely mouth. If she says it's fun then it must be. There's a widening of those dark brown eyes on the upward swing, an anxious brow on the return journey, this the roller-coaster ride of a six-month-old. Then suddenly he gets it and he's doing his belly laugh. And the woman next to us, the unwitting tiger mother, starts laughing too.

'Isn't it amazing when they start to laugh?' she says.

She's blonde and pretty, wearing a floaty white top, jeans and New Balance trainers, a classic Clapham mum, a few years older than us probably. She and Hannah start talking and it turns out that our babies are just a few months apart and Sarah lives on the next-door street. I feel Hannah's radar zipping up. Since returning to work, she worries she's missing out. On her days off, she'll wheel Samuel up to Starbucks and sit there with her solitary latte next to a gathering of intimate, laughing stay-at-home mums, wishing she could join them. But theirs is a different world, with their day-in, day-out meets at the library and the park and the music class. The doors are closed, Hannah an outsider looking in.

'Trouble is, you can't have it both ways,' Christina said when

Hannah mentioned she hadn't become friends with any local mothers. And I remember thinking: but why not?

While Hannah and Sarah talk, I take over the swing-pushing, rewarded each time by Samuel's laughter. I push him higher, nothing controversial, but this boy is a daredevil, and the harder I push, the harder he laughs.

'He's a thrill-seeker,' I say, returning to the conversation, and Hannah says, 'Well, just look at the parents.'

Sarah says, 'I've seen your baby before in the library. Only he was with an older woman. I noticed her first, she's tall and glamorous, impossible to miss. Is that your nanny? I remember thinking how fantastic she was with the baby – actually, I thought he was hers and she was one of those older mums you see around.'

'That's Alice,' I say with the complicated blend of emotions that always accompanies this statement.

'Well, you're very lucky. She had him on her lap and she was opening and shutting books and he was roaring with laughter. It was mesmerising. It's his laugh just now that reminded me. She seems great, where did you find her?'

The seconds before I speak feel paralysing, but Sarah doesn't seem to notice.

'She's a friend,' I say, and Hannah jumps in with, 'Do you fancy meeting for a coffee on one of my days off?'

'I'd love to,' Sarah says, fishing her mobile out of her bag to exchange numbers.

As soon as they've made a plan to meet, Hannah scoops Samuel out of the swing and we say goodbye.

'See you next week.'

'Bye, Hannah. Bye, Luke. Bye, CHAR-LIE.' Sarah laughs, pleased with herself. 'I remembered his name without you telling me.'

'Oh, actually, he's Samuel,' Hannah says, voice casual, as though this small slip-up means nothing, as though it isn't the first solid evidence of what I have suspected all along.

Then

Alice

Pregnancy is a time of intense romance for Jake and me. My second trimester, when I feel extraordinarily well, coincides with a period of successive power cuts, and we live by candlelight. Jake always has thirty or forty candles burning in the sitting room, stuffed into wine bottles with wicker casings or the battered candelabras he collects from Golborne Road. Now we bathe by candlelight too if there is enough hot water, and if there isn't, we go to bed early and he reads to me, book in one hand, candle in the other, held close to his face like a Dickensian protagonist.

Sometimes he reads poetry – not Blake or Keats or Coleridge, but the lyrics of Bob Dylan, Joni Mitchell, James Taylor, James Brown. There is one song in particular that he reads more than any other on these nights, Dylan's 'The Man in Me'. When you hear Dylan singing this song, it is elevated to something heart-rending and insightful, the story of a woman who comprehends all the things her lover tries to hide; flat on the page the words look surprisingly schmaltzy, but its message is not lost on me.

Night after night we stay in together, working or lying on the sofa listening to records. And I get used to it, this intense domesticity, a new grown-up-ness to our lives. Arriving home from college to the scent of something Jake is cooking for our supper: a Bolognese he has simmered for hours, lasagne to rival the one we loved in Siena, the fish stew, which means a trip to Billingsgate. He keeps a bowl filled with apples and oranges and encourages me to eat as many pieces of fruit as I can. He buys a baby book that details every stage of the first year of your child's life, and while I have an extended bath, refilling it for as long as our hot water lasts, he will read out sections from it.

'He'll be laughing by the time he's twelve weeks old.' Or, 'When he's seven months he'll be crawling and trying to pull himself up on the furniture.'

There is no question in Jake's mind that we're having a boy. I hope he won't be disappointed if it turns out to be a girl.

As Christmas approaches I feel hurt that my mother still hasn't tried to get in touch. My parents don't know I am pregnant and I cannot face telling them, I can imagine my father's rage and I won't sully our happiness with it. Instead I send them a card I've made myself, a schmaltzy, hand-painted winter scene, the kind of thing they like. Inside I write the most innocuous message I can manage.

Dear Mum and Dad, hope you have a good Christmas. Love from Alice.

But nothing comes back. They know my address; I had to give it to them so my post could be diverted here. It would have been easy for my mother to send a card in return. But she is in thrall to her husband's diktat just as she always was and always will be. And my father never goes back on his word. He made me choose – Jake rather than them – and mostly I am glad that he did.

Naturally, Jake goes into overdrive with his Christmas preparations. We buy a tree and he lugs it home single-handedly, its tip trailing along the pavement. He won't allow me to carry anything 'because of the baby', even though we've both read the books and have learned that essentially I am meant to carry on exactly as before. In Berwick Street market we find coloured lights and baubles and tinsel and we pile them on the tree so that hardly a single strand of spruce can be seen.

'It's a disco tree,' Jake says when we turn the lights on for the first time and discover they flash on and off. 'Very now. Very seventies.'

I've taken so much trouble over his presents for this, our first Christmas together. In the Record and Tape Exchange I find a Jimi Hendrix single, an original pressing of 'The Wind Cries Mary' from 1967, with 'Highway Chile' on the other side. It was expensive, which I'd expected; after Jimi's death, his records quadrupled in price overnight. But worth it just to see Jake's face when he opens it.

One lunchtime I take Rick to Liberty with me, an old-fashioned Christmas paradise with beautifully decorated trees on every level, themed in silver and white, the opposite of our cut-price disco extravaganza.

'So what's it going to be? Jewellery? Scarf? Shirt? Watch?' Rick asks.

'He has all of that. I'd like to give him something he can wear every day that reminds him of me. For when he's away on tour.'

'Why don't you get him some aftershave?'

The lady at the fragrance counter is dismissive at first. Rick and I are dressed in our paint-spattered art-student clothes – lemon-yellow dungarees for him, a loose white top and flares for me – and she clearly thinks we have no money. But I have been saving my student grant with exactly this intention, to splash out on something perfect for my lover.

When I reach for a bottle of Eau Sauvage – price £7 – the

woman seems more interested. Rick dabs it on his wrist and holds it out for me to smell.

'Bloody gorgeous, isn't it? I wish someone would give it to me. Maybe you could drop a hint to Tom.'

'It's not Jake, though. It's too … I don't know, suit and tie.'

The shop assistant laughs.

'So what's he like, your boyfriend?'

I get a little lost in my description.

'Well, he's tall and thin, with long dark hair and a romantic kind of face, angelic, a bit like a Botticelli painting.'

Rick is tittering, though the woman manages to keep a straight face.

'He's a musician, a singer and songwriter. He's artistic. He wears shirts with bell sleeves and velvet suits and lots of scarves and jewellery.'

'He might like a unisex fragrance?'

'Nothing too feminine,' I say.

'But frankly nothing too masculine either,' adds Rick, and this time the woman joins in with our laughter.

'How about something Italian?' she asks, and Rick and I, in unison, cry, 'Perfect!'

'He's obsessed with Italy. We both are. We spent the summer outside Florence.'

She produces a beautiful turquoise bottle with a cobalt-blue lid.

'This is Acqua di Parma, a cologne. Very fashionable in Italy and worn by women just as much as men.'

Rick and I inhale deeply.

'Wonderful, smells like ferns,' Rick says, 'and lemons and cedar trees.'

'It's exactly right for him,' I say, opening my purse to find the right amount of cash.

*

We wake up late on Christmas morning (no church, another luxury) and Jake insists on bringing me breakfast in bed: cappuccinos in polystyrene cups and fat slices of panettone from Bar Italia, which stays open every day of the year.

'On the house with Luigi's love,' he says, getting in beside me.

He lifts the blankets and inches down to kiss my stomach.

'Happy Christmas to you, baby,' he says.

He counts up the months on his fingers.

'Next Christmas you'll be six months old. Imagine that. I wonder if we'll still be here in this flat.'

'We'll never leave Soho, surely?'

'Never. I can promise you that. Unless we move to Italy.'

It is a perfect day, just the two of us. While a chicken is roasting, we listen to classical music, Brahms first, his violin concerto, and then Vivaldi's *Gloria*. It reminds me of my father for a moment – anything choral and churchy always does – but I push away the image of my parents sitting down to a turkey alone. My father hogging an expensive bottle of wine, my mother cowering as he pours his third, fourth, fifth glass and the spectre of incandescence rears its head.

'What were your Christmases like as a kid?' I ask, without thinking, and beside me Jake goes still.

'Well, that depends on where I was. Sometimes it was just me and my mum on our own and that was fine. But usually we were at my grandparents' farm and quite often my mum left me there alone. She liked to get the sun at Christmas if she could afford it; she went to Spain, Morocco, the Canary Islands.'

I can sense the change in his breathing, and my own heart begins to pulse in return. I reach for his hand.

'I'm never going to ask you to talk about things you don't want to talk about.'

'I know that.'

'But sometimes I think it might help you to exorcise the past. And I would listen. I love you. And I want to help.'

'All right,' he says, and he gets up and walks over to our tree with its twinkling, flashing lights and its baubles the colours of Quality Street. He picks out a package, flat, square and wrapped in shiny red paper.

I read the tag: *For you, Alice, with all my love.*

Inside there's a framed photograph, an instant bullet to the heart. It is a school portrait of Jake aged nine or ten, a beautiful boy with short hair and solemn eyes. He is wearing a grey V-necked jumper, a white shirt and red and grey striped tie, and the thing that strikes me most about this picture, this textbook, cheesy school picture, is his refusal to smile.

'I found this photo and thought you might like it. I know you're curious about when I was a kid.' He leans forward to kiss my face.

'I love it. You're so beautiful,' I say, looking at the photo. 'But you don't look very happy.'

'Well I wasn't.'

He gets up from the sofa and starts pacing around our tiny sitting room. I can hear the breaths he is taking, deep and longer than usual. My heart clenches in empathetic distress.

'My grandfather was into punishment. I think we can safely say he was a sadist. There were the regular beatings – he broke my ribs several times – and there was the locking me out of the house in the middle of winter. I slept – or rather didn't sleep – in the car. But the thing that made me miserable was the way he talked about me, as if I was disgusting, the lowest form of species, corrupt, sinful, all of that. When I was young, it was difficult not to believe him. Sometimes it still is. Sometimes his is the only voice I can hear.'

I am crying as I stand up and walk over to him.

'Is that why you …?' I leave the rest unsaid.

'Yes. He made me feel worthless. That life wasn't worth living. And it's hard to shake that feeling sometimes.'

'Oh Jake, I can't bear it for you.'

My arms are wrapped around him, my face pressed against his chest. I hate the factualness of his voice. When he states these feelings, it's as if he believes they are true. For the past year I've longed to understand his demons; I've thought, naïvely, that I could help him overcome them. Now I am beginning to understand how deep-rooted his self-loathing is; I'm not sure the baby and I will be enough to fix it.

'Please don't cry. I hate you being upset. Can we talk about something else now?'

'Why didn't your mother help?'

'I suppose she was a bit frightened of my grandfather; she must have known how violent he could be. But I think she was so committed to her quest for freedom, she didn't care about anything else. And then she met someone and she wanted to start over. And that meant leaving me behind. I just wish she'd had me adopted. I used to dream about it sometimes, this wonderful older couple turning up to take me away. I'd imagine their house, an old ramshackle farmhouse with a huge garden and lots of animals, ponies and dogs and cats.'

'You honestly think it would have been better to be adopted?'

'Of course it would. It was just me on my own dealing with my grandfather's rages, and this went on for years, all the way through my childhood. But you know what that's like. An only child, with no other siblings to take the edge off.'

'Sometimes I think I hate my mother more than my father, for not standing up to him. Never trying to protect me.'

'We are exactly the same, you and I. And it's the thing that brought us together.'

When Jake goes out to baste the chicken and check on his roast potatoes, I sit back down on the sofa, the framed photograph balanced on my knees. It gives me a feeling of vertigo, this picture, not just the past, his past, the past that up until now he has kept hidden, hermetically sealed inside him. I also feel, as I stare and stare at ten-year-old Jake, that I am looking into the future and in some bizarre sense I am time-travelling forward to meet our unborn child.

Now

Luke

As expected, Alice has a mini nervous breakdown when she sees the bear. I'm standing at the sitting-room window, Samuel in my arms, waiting for her to arrive. Samuel is holding the bear, face outwards, with ugly new eyes on show – Hannah did her best, but essentially it's cut-price plastic surgery. A bear with caring black and amber eyes made of glass now has the flat, cold glare of cross-stitch.

As soon as I hear Alice's knock, I bring Samuel to the door with me, our daily ritual. She makes her funny face, he laughs and reaches out for her, and then I'm off in a swirl of anxiety about the day ahead. This time, though, she spots the bear immediately and cries out.

'What did you do?'

Samuel is rolling his R's like a gift, but Alice ignores him.

'This, you mean?' I point at the bear, acting casual, ignoring the dramatic plunge of my heart. 'Hannah has a thing about glass eyes. She's thinks they're a choking hazard.'

But the words come out like sawdust. Dry to me and to her. I understand the cruelty of the crime.

'The bear was yours, Luke. It means a lot to me. Perhaps it was wrong of me to give it to … Samuel.'

Her hesitation is enough.

'Alice, let's have a coffee. I feel like we should talk.'

In the kitchen, I set Samuel down on the floor and he begins his exhausting new semi-crawl: face-plant, press-up, chest forwards, face-plant. Alice spreads the blue rug out across the floor and relocates Samuel to its soft woollen stripes.

'The floor is too slippy, little bird,' she says.

The kettle is reaching boiling point, thunderously loud it seems to me as I strain to catch the tone of her voice. How quickly the bear has become symbolic of the wrong we cannot right. Alice giving me away, me being taken from Alice, is a pie chart without an intersection, two spheres that cannot be blended, just like the worlds we inhabited. Separated, that's the word they should use for adoptees. A separated child. A separated mother.

I bring a cafetière of coffee and two mugs to the table, milk from the fridge. My hands are shaking. I abhor confrontation of any kind. I'm an adoptee, by nurture a people-pleaser.

We sit down opposite each other and it's an effort for me to look up into Alice's face. But when I do, I find that, as usual, she is calmer than me, assuming her role of adult.

I watch her bring her mug to her mouth, setting it down without taking a sip. Perhaps it's too hot. Perhaps she's just thinking.

'You loved that bear,' she says, and each word lands on me like ointment. 'Rick gave it to you, and from about two weeks old you used to sleep with a fist curled around an arm or a leg. You were too young for me to worry about glass eyes, or perhaps I was too young to understand about them. After you'd gone, I kept the bear with me. For years I slept with him on my pillow, and then I relegated him to a shelf, a reminder but nothing more. I told myself that was progress.'

It's the most she has ever said to me about the past.

Samuel is making small moans that will soon evolve into full-blown tears, a little 'he-he' noise that is hard to ignore. Alice gets up from the table and stoops down to collect him.

'Come on up, my friend,' she says, and she settles him on her lap, finds him the salt and pepper pots to play with, kisses the side of his face.

'What was I like?'

She looks at me, surprised.

'You were just like him. Happy. Always smiling. And laughing.'

Happy. Always smiling. I think of the way Christina often describes my first weeks – 'you cried and cried, you wouldn't stop' – and it cracks my heart a little bit more.

'Alice?'

Her face, lovely as ever, is impassive.

'You call Samuel Charlie sometimes. Did you know?'

'Oh, that. Yes, I can't help it. He's so similar to you at that age, I get confused.'

I'm nodding my head, too many times, trying to find the right words.

'I'm beginning to feel as if we've got this the wrong way around. You looking after Samuel instead of getting to know me. It was our fault for suggesting it in the first place, but I really think it's churning us up. Well, me anyway. I'm not sure it's very healthy.'

'It's about as healthy as you can get. We're family. Isn't that better than farming out your child to someone you don't know?'

I nod again, unconvinced. Suddenly, for the first time, I am really quite concerned by the depth of her love for my child. And the thing is, I don't know Alice. Not really.

'You don't want me to stop looking after him?'

There's anxiety in her face now. Burning eyes. I can't look at them for long.

'I know I don't talk to you enough about those weeks when we were together. I know you mind. Sometimes I try to talk about it, but there's just this great big block, memories I still can't cope with all this time later.'

'You can't imagine how much I want to hear about it. The circumstances of my birth seem so mysterious.'

'I remember you being born as if it was yesterday. It was very quick for a first baby, just a few hours.'

'What did we do together? I know it's about sleeping and eating in the first weeks, but is there anything you can remember apart from that?'

Alice smiles. 'Actually, you loved swimming. Well, not swimming exactly, but lying on a little blow-up boat. You liked the sensation of floating, I think, and the sound of the waves.'

'Waves? Surely we weren't in the sea?'

There's something here, a slight nervousness that I pick up on but cannot understand.

'I meant the sound of lapping water. Sometime I'd like to take Samuel swimming. I think he would love it.'

Alice is smiling now. When the light comes into her face, when you see those straight white teeth and the indentations around her eyes, she looks extraordinary. Heart-stopping. Head-turning.

'I feel embarrassed to say this, but sometimes I'm jealous of Samuel. Because he gets to spend time with you and I don't.'

'Oh Luke.' She reaches out and squeezes my hand, just for a second. 'How could you be jealous of this little thing? But I do understand. The whole situation is a little strange, isn't it?'

Samuel starts trilling like a bird and we both laugh; it lightens the atmosphere.

'Yes, you are very clever,' Alice says.

When the phone rings, I leave the answering machine to pick up, not for one second expecting my other mother to call.

'Hello, darling. I called your office and they said you weren't in. Just ringing to make sure you're not ill. Kiss that beautiful boy for me and say hello to Alice.'

We regard each other, Alice and I, when the machine clicks off, me wretched at the duplicity.

'It's a bit like having an affair,' I say, 'only much, much worse.'

Alice smiles.

'Maybe you should tell her?'

'Not sure I can. The lie just gets bigger the longer it goes on.'

I look at the kitchen clock; it's 10.30.

'I should get going, I'm already late. I hope it was OK having this talk?'

'More than OK. We needed it. Luke?'

Alice's eyes are her strongest feature. A deep black-brown, framed with thick, long lashes, cartoonish eyes.

'I am churned up. Same as you. But this helps.' She drops a kiss onto Samuel's head. 'Being with him helps. Thank you for inviting me into your family. It was very generous of you.'

I'm trying to process this as I walk to the Tube station, trying to understand why these final words of hers slither in the base of my stomach with the dull ache of unease.

It was very generous of you.

Then

Alice

It is a cold night in late January when the phone call comes in. Jake and I are midway through a black and white thriller on BBC2 called *The Deadly Affair*.

'Leave it,' Jake says when I start to get up from the sofa. 'They can call back.'

The phone rings on and on. It stops, then starts again ten seconds later.

'Oh for God's sake,' Jake says, crossing the room and snatching up the phone.

As soon as he realises who the caller is, Jake turns his back on me. He is silent, listening to the voice on the other end of phone.

'I see,' he says.

He talks only occasionally and I sit on the sofa, ignoring the television, trying to make sense of this one-sided conversation.

'No, I can't do that.'

'Why don't you go if you care so much?'

'I don't owe her anything.'

'All right, I'll think about it. But, believe me, I'm not going to change my mind.'

His voice crescendos on this last line, he slams the phone down and throws himself out of the room without another word.

In the kitchen I find Jake pouring whisky into a wine glass, he fills it to the brim. I see how his hands shake as he puts the glass to his lips and swallows down an inch or two of liquid.

He puts the glass down on the table; he still hasn't looked at me.

'What's happened?'

'My grandmother died yesterday. My mum wants me to go to the funeral.'

'Isn't she going?'

He shakes his head, meets my eye for the first time.

'She's not coming back from Canada. The flights home are too expensive.'

'I'd go with you if you wanted.'

'I am not going anywhere near that bloody hellhole. Why should I?'

Standing a few feet apart, divided by our little Formica table, I can see that his whole body is shaking, with anger or fear.

I think of his confessions at Christmas, the childhood beatings, being locked out of the house on a freezing winter's night a bit like this one. I walk around the table and wrap my arms around his waist. He allows me to hold him for a few seconds before he wrenches away and I watch him pacing around the kitchen in tiny restricted circles. He picks up his glass and downs the whisky in three or four gulps.

'Talk to me, Jake.'

He sits down at the table, body curved away from me, face in hands, a cliché of despair.

'There's nothing to say,' he says and he fills up his glass again, though he lets it rest untouched on the table. 'Nothing.'

Thoughts and ideas run through my brain but I'm scared to mention them. I am thinking, doesn't this mean it's over? Both grandparents dead, Jake freed from his childhood. What if he went back to that house as an adult with his lover, with his child soon to be born, and faced the ancient horrors that still haunt his dreams, those quiet unguarded moments of sorrow?

'Let's watch the rest of the film.'

He picks up his glass and holds out a hand to me and we return to the sofa, but it isn't the same. Jake might be watching the screen but I know he sees nothing but his past.

Grimness settles upon Jake like a cloud of dust. He is silent, preoccupied, haunted. The morning after the phone call, he says not one word to me. We shower and dress in silence as if we are flatmates and not lovers and I see that the effort of acknowledging me is more than he can manage.

We leave the flat together and when I walk towards Bar Italia, he says: 'I'm not going to bother with coffee today. You go.'

He reaches into his pocket and hands me a pound note for my breakfast, but I shake my head.

'I won't bother either.'

'I'll see you later,' he says. Then, 'Sorry.'

I stand in the street watching him walk away, examining the stoop of his shoulders, his laboured gait. I don't know what to do.

At college, I try talking to Rick about it.

'He seems so down. One phone call and he's like a different person. I can't get any sense out of him.'

'Maybe it's brought everything back. He probably just needs space, Al.'

At lunchtime, I go shopping for our supper. Jake always cooks, but I think that tonight I will surprise him. I will make my mother's chicken, mushroom and courgette casserole, the one fail-safe dish she taught me.

Jake isn't in the flat when I arrive back in the late afternoon and I miss walking in to the strumming of his guitar or the blast of The Rolling Stones or Fleetwood Mac from the record player. But I'm contented enough as I begin to prepare the casserole, rolling chicken thighs and drumsticks into a plate of seasoned flour. Frying mushrooms, onions and courgettes into a soft, sticky mush, then browning the chicken pieces.

By eight the casserole is ready and Jake still hasn't come home. I turn the oven down to its lowest setting and then I pace around the sitting room, too stressed to listen to music or read or draw or do anything except stare out at the street below, my whole being waiting for the sound of his key in the door.

In desperation I ring Rick and catch him on his way out to meet Tom at The Coach and Horses.

'Thank God,' I say. 'If Jake's there ask him to ring me. I am going out of my mind. Tell him I've cooked.'

'Alice, my love,' the unexpressed laughter in Rick's voice soothes me. 'Do you think you might be overreacting just a teensy bit? You are nineteen not forty. So what if Jake wants to go out and get smashed?'

'You're right,' I say. 'I know you're right. But Rick—'

I catch him just before he hangs up.

'Phone me if he's not in the pub. Please?'

At a quarter to nine I turn the oven off and take out the casserole. I have no appetite for this greasy pale-grey sludge which used to be my favourite thing to eat not so long ago. I return to the sitting room and resume my wait, an unopened book on the sofa beside me, the television on with the sound turned low.

Rick calls at ten. He's been at The Coach and Horses and now he's in the French House and there is no sign of Jake.

'He was here with Eddie earlier, they've probably gone on somewhere else. Maybe they went to get some food.'

'Why hasn't he called me?'

We are interrupted by the beeps as Rick's money runs out.

I sit in darkness for a while, the street lamps below throwing occasional stripes of light across the brown carpet. Jake is out getting drunk with his oldest friend, the one person who knows the truth about his childhood. There is no reason for me to worry.

Why then as I lie in bed is my chest so tight it's hard to breathe, my mind a blizzard of fear and anxiety I have no wish to examine? Beneath the romance and the passion and the euphoria of our love, there has always been this stubborn, inextinguishable truth. The man I love is unstable. He once tried to take his own life. I live in dread of that ever happening again.

Now

Luke

Michael is in the States this week and there's a holiday atmosphere at work. At lunchtime, we all disperse in different directions, some to the pub, some up to Wandsworth for an hour of retail therapy and me to Soho for a liquid lunch with Ben.

First to Liberty. It's Hannah's birthday in a couple of weeks and I'm doing a recce of ground-floor accessories: scarves, necklaces, bracelets, hats. She has unchanging but definite taste, which makes her easy to buy for; if it's crafted and hand-made she is certain to love it. Almost immediately I find the perfect thing – a black beaded necklace with hand-painted wooden discs, slightly gothic, shades of Madonna in her eighties incarnation. Hannah will love it.

Without quite knowing why, I find myself taking the escalator up to the fragrance department on the first floor. The necklace was steep (£130) and Hannah would be cross if I bought her anything else. Why then am I uncapping bottles and spraying my wrists, quick sniff, decisive shake of the head, no that's not it, nope, nor is that, on and on until I've tried around twenty fragrances.

'Can I help?'

The woman behind the counter looks kind; I think that's the

deciding factor. The truth blurts out before I've had time to recognise it.

'I'm trying to find this scent I keep smelling. It's driving me mad. But it's none of these ...'

I wave my hand at the ranks of Chanel, Guerlain, Dior.

'Can you describe the smell? Who is wearing it?'

'It's nothing like these perfumes; they are all too sweet, too heavy. It's light, lemony, spicy and smoky. Hard to describe. And it's a woman I know who wears it.'

I hate the smile she gives me; I feel ashamed. She thinks I'm trying to buy the perfume of someone I've fallen in love with; perhaps she pictures me dousing myself in it each day like some kind of weirdo. One step away from wearing women's pants to work.

'Could it be cologne? Or aftershave?'

I nod, glad that someone is taking me seriously at last.

'I think it could. But I don't wear aftershave, so it's nothing I recognise.'

She picks up a sheet of cardboard and begins spraying its corners – Dior Homme, Eau Sauvage, Gucci, Prada. It's none of these.

'Sharper,' I say. 'Fresher.'

She points to a bottle. 'Long shot,' she says, 'but this is Acqua di Parma, an Italian cologne that's been around for decades. A lot of women wear it.'

She uncaps the bottle and holds it out for me to sniff. And there it is, the scent of woodlands and lavender and cedar and lime; it is all of these things, but, critically, it is also the smell of my past.

'That's it!'

I'm not sure which of us is the more jubilant.

'I'll take it,' I say, and while she wraps the bottle, I pick up the tester and dab it on my neck, my throat, my cheeks.

Of course, when I get to The Coach and Horses and find Ben at the bar, he steps back from me in surprise.

'What the fuck? You're wearing perfume.'

He looks so shocked, I can't help laughing.

'I've been buying presents for Hannah in Liberty.'

He hands me a pint.

'Drink up. And man up while you're at it.'

Oh it's good to be here in the company of my oldest friend, the two of us quietly celebrating. Him the fact that he has just finished a couple of commissions – 'Jude Law's kids. Bit too pastel and cherubic for my liking, but it paid well.' Me because Michael is away and I can take a longer lunch than usual. I've been working flat out these past weeks, desperate to clinch the deal with Reborn and keep Spirit safe. At night I dream about it; I dream of Michael appearing in my office, twisted and vindictive as he fires me. 'You're utterly hopeless,' he tells me, 'a complete waste of space.' This happens night after night after night. Yet when I wake, I understand that the dreams are not about work, not really; on a deep level they connect to my concerns and fears about Alice.

Two pints turns to three in less than an hour. Lunch is two bags of cheese and onion crisps and a shared packet of KP nuts.

'I've missed this,' I say, raising my pint. 'We never get a chance to go to the pub any more.'

Ben is silent, sipping his ale, watching. I don't need to tell him I'm close to the edge; he's been right here on the brink with me many times. At school, he was the only one I ever cried in front of when my acute homesickness cut deep. We were eight, if that sounds lame, incarcerated for weeks at a time. I've come to understand, as an adult with my own child, that boarding school is little more than abandonment on repeat.

'It's Alice, isn't it?' he says eventually. 'Ever since she came into your life you've seemed … messed up.'

'Hold it there,' I say. 'We need something stronger for this conversation.'

I return to the table with doubles of Jameson's and more beer.

'I don't think Alice is in the slightest bit interested in me,' I say. 'All she really cares about is Samuel. Hannah can't see it – or won't see it; she needs it to work with Alice so she can carry on with her job. The one thing we know is that we are leaving Samuel in good hands each day.'

'But what is it you want from her? She can't be your mother again, not after twenty-seven years apart.'

'It's more that there's no connection between us. None whatsoever, and that seems strange to me. She never talks about the weeks when we were together. Why not? It's the one thing we have in common.'

'What about Rick?'

'What about him? We've had a couple of lunches. He's great, but I haven't got to know him. He doesn't feel in the least bit like my real father.'

I see Ben's hesitation. I know him well enough to understand that he is weighing up whether he should tell me something.

'What?' I say, impatient.

'Elizabeth doesn't think Rick *is* your father. You know what she's like, she never minces her words. For a start, you look nothing like each other. Rick has blonde hair and blue eyes. Also he's gay. Go figure.'

'I'm dark, like Alice. Why would Rick say he was my father if he wasn't? Why would he be on my birth certificate?'

'Just a hunch Elizabeth had. Probably nothing.'

'Answer me this. Am I just being jealous and needy and insecure? Or do I have a point?'

Ben stands up.

'More whisky needed, I think. And yes. You have a point.'

It's almost six when our session breaks up; I remember nothing of the ride home, London blurring past. All I can think about, all I can feel, is a sort of disaffected rage, a venomous self-pity for my confused identity, my lone wolf-ness. Probably not the right state of mind in which to meet my birth mother, and it doesn't help that I can't get my key in the door. After a few minutes of scraping and scratching and rattling, the door opens and I lurch through it, almost toppling into Alice and my small son.

Oops.

'Goodness,' Alice says. 'Are you OK?'

'S'fine,' I slur. 'Sorr'm late.'

I reach out to take Samuel, and Alice actually backs away from me. What I see is the way she curves her arms protectively around him as if he is her child, not mine.

'Why don't you have a lie-down,' she says. 'I'll wait here until Hannah gets back.'

'Gimme m'son,' I say, or at least I try to. I'm blind drunk, I realise now, without the fallback of Ben, who was so pissed himself we could communicate perfectly, a contrapuntal wave of sound unintelligible to all but us.

Alice shakes her head. 'It's not safe. You might drop him. I'm not judging you, don't think that, just trying to make sure Samuel's OK. Hannah will be home soon.'

And now I am inflamed with rage, hurt, disappointment, self-loathing, of course, and it makes me vicious.

'Is my child, not yours. You gave yours away, remember?'

I am crying as I haul myself up the stairs, clinging to the banister, step by step, until I reach the bedroom and throw myself on the bed, and mercifully my world soon turns black. But in the countdown to unconsciousness, in those final seconds, I am sure I see Alice's face at the door. My mother standing there, my child in her arms, silently watching.

Then

Alice

It seems unfathomable to me now, four days into Jake's drinking binge, that there could have been a time when I didn't know him this way. We are living separate lives. In the mornings he is too deeply asleep to hear me leave for college, and I go straight to the Slade, forgoing my morning cappuccino, for I cannot bear to be in Bar Italia without him. In the evenings he is never at home and I have learned to go to bed, forcing myself into sleep if I can, waiting for the slide and scrape as he attempts to fit his key in the lock if I can't.

He is lost to me, but I understand he is drowning in torment. I know this from the notes I come home to, the desperate scrawls in a page ripped from his notebook.

Alice. Forgive me. I'm so sorry. I hate myself. This will stop, I promise.

But it doesn't stop. Four days turns into five. I ring Eddie and he suggests meeting for lunch. We go to a caff near college and he orders a full English: undercooked bacon, pallid sausages, beans, fried egg, tinned tomatoes and a rack of white toast. It makes me nauseous to look at it. I drink a cup of tea and try to eat my hot buttered toast, but I can't manage more than a couple of bites.

'You must be going out of your mind,' Eddie says.

'Pretty much.'

'He does this sometimes, Alice, when it all gets on top of him.'

'I don't understand why it has to carry on. He made the decision not to go the funeral, why isn't that the end of it?'

'It's not about the funeral any more. This is Jake's depression. It's a self-hate thing. A self-perpetuating thing. You might not understand this, but Jake is punishing himself.'

'But why?'

'Goes back to his grandparents. Jake still hears the things they said to him as a child. He still believes them.'

'It's like he's avoiding me.'

'He is avoiding you. He's ashamed. He doesn't want you to see him like this.'

'When will it end?'

Eddie shrugs. 'He'll burn himself out sooner or later.'

'Shouldn't he see his doctor?'

'He should but he won't. What will happen now is that he'll come to his senses and he'll quit drinking. And for a while everything will be fine.'

I wake in the middle of the night and sense Jake's presence even before I see him sitting with his back against the bedroom door as if he has simply slid down it, his knees pressed high against his chest.

'Jake?' I whisper and he says, 'Hey.'

I can tell from this one word that he is sober. His face, lit up by the moon, seems so beautiful to me and I am overwhelmed with longing for him.

'I miss you.'

I cannot stop myself from crying.

'Will you come to bed?'

He shakes his head.

'You want to know about that time when I was sixteen?' he says and his voice is so sombre I feel afraid.

'Yes. If you want to tell me.'

He takes so long to begin that I am drifting towards sleep when his voice cuts into the darkness.

'My grandmother knew about the beatings. And she blamed me for them. She used to say, "Your grandfather is a good man but you push him to the limit." She resented me living with them and she told me that most days. She'd say: "Even your own mother doesn't want you. Don't you think you ought to try and be more lovable?"

'I tried to change, but whatever I did it wasn't enough. And whenever my grandfather beat me up, she would tell me: "Look what you've made him do now." So I grew up thinking I was flawed. But I had an escape route and that's what kept me going.

'When I turned sixteen, I was going to live with my mum in London. "Just wait till you've left school," my mum would tell me, "you and I will have so much fun." I was going to get a job and earn enough money to buy myself a decent guitar. And then I could join a band.'

I know that I mustn't talk or touch Jake or do anything to stop his story. But I move noiselessly from the bed and I sit on the floor, just a few feet away, in a pool of moonlight.

'My mum came to stay on my sixteenth birthday, she gave me a Van Morrison record and my grandmother made a cake. And in the morning my mum said she had some news. She told me she was moving to Canada with her new boyfriend and I could join her in a year or so if I wanted. She'd bought her plane ticket and was leaving in a month. She had known for weeks but she didn't want to spoil my birthday ...'

He stops speaking for a moment and this heartless betrayal, a decade old now, lingers in the air.

'I didn't mean to kill myself. It was an impulse thing. I saw the kitchen knife and I was drawn to it. But the doctors thought I was suicidal. Next thing I knew I was in a secure psychiatric unit in Epsom. I was locked up there for nine months.'

'Jake.'

I inch towards him, needing to be closer.

But he says: 'I'm going to finish, Alice.'

His voice is determined, almost chilling, and so I stay where I am, just out of reach.

'My mum came to see me a few times before she left for Canada, but she never stayed long. She was too scared.'

'What was it like?'

'Do you really want to know?'

I nod my head, unable to speak.

'It was like hell, or worse maybe. I was so out of it to begin with, I lost my grip on who I was, I just existed in this crazy place where people banged on the walls and shouted and wept and moaned all day long. There was one young guy and he used to talk to the wall, a proper conversation with pauses, like he was addressing an invisible alien or something. There was a woman in the room next door to me who used to howl every night, these long, awful cries of anguish. The Screamer they called her. So much anger, everyone fighting and shouting and arguing, the patients, the staff. And sadness. It was like bathing in it all the time. These people had nothing and no one cared about them. And suddenly I was one of them.'

'Did you need to be there?'

'Not for nine months. I was depressed not dangerous. But the doctors didn't care. They kept me pumped so full of drugs I just lay around in a ball of apathy. Those pills stopped me from feeling, from living. All I did was exist.'

He pauses.

'Eddie saved me. He visited me every week. And he kept telling me "you don't need to be in here." He was only sixteen himself, but if he was scared he never showed it.'

'Why didn't you tell me this? Why didn't Eddie?'

'Because mostly I can pretend it didn't happen. But then my grandmother died and it came rushing back, and the feelings I had, the memories, were too much...'

At last he stands up and holds out a hand and pulls me to my feet. And I am in his arms, my face buried against his neck, my tears wetting his skin.

'Promise me you'll never let me go back to a place like that.'

I understand so much about Jake on the strength of this one conversation. I know now why being with him has always felt so potent. He inhabits every moment of his day, from the morning cappuccino to the songs he listens to and the food he cooks at night. Jake's terror, I realise, is blankness.

'I lost you,' I say when I am able to speak. 'You left me.'

'I'm sorry.'

His mouth against my hair, his arms holding my waist. We'll go to bed and we'll make love until the light begins to press against the windows and we will fall asleep, wrapped up so tightly that our faces touch and our breath becomes one.

'Don't ever leave me again,' I say.

'I won't,' Jake says. 'I promise I won't.'

And I believe him. Because I must.

Now

Luke

Self-sabotage or acts of destruction are a common response in adoptees. They will put themselves in a situation and push and push until the thing they fear most happens. We call it self-fulfilling prophecy.

Who Am I? The Adoptee's Hidden Trauma by Joel Harris

On the outside it must look as if my life has never been better. Reborn have rejected Universal's offer and their manager, Steve Harris, has told me Spirit is back in the race. I should be ecstatic with relief and excitement at the prospect of potentially working with one of the hottest unsigned bands in Britain.

And yet I am clenched with a feeling of doom from the moment I wake.

Ever since I came home drunk, Alice has barely spoken a word to me. I'm convinced I have offended her, but I can't remember anything about that night other than me storming off to bed when she wouldn't let me hold the baby. Even Hannah, my glass-half-full, twenty-four-seven optimist, thinks she is being distant.

'Is everything OK, Alice?' she asked one evening while Alice was packing up her things to leave.

'Yes, of course. Why wouldn't it be?'

'You've seemed a bit quiet the last few days.'

'Oh no, you're imagining it.'

What I noticed was the way Alice managed to avoid eye contact with both Hannah and me; I saw how she rushed from the room the moment her bag was packed.

But as soon as she had gone, Hannah said, 'There you are. Nothing to worry about.'

I keep up my lunch-hour surveillance, sandwiches on park benches, a little light shopping on the high street. Sometimes I see Alice and Samuel, sometimes I don't. Even on the days when she doesn't appear, there's a tantalising cloud of Acqua di Parma in the air around me; I hear snatches of a lullaby she often sings to Samuel with her sweet, clear voice.

> Moonlight so sweet and pale from heaven falling,
> Wavelets that murmur low to us are calling.

I've heard it so often that the words and melody have saturated my brain. I fall asleep hearing it, I wake up anticipating it. Once, worryingly, I walked downstairs one morning and heard Alice singing in the kitchen. Of course, by the time I got there, the singing had stopped, which raises the obvious question: *Dude, are you imagining things?*

I haven't told Hannah about this. But my silence is driving a wedge between us. More and more, I catch her watching me with that little stripe of anxiety between her eyebrows. Not long ago, I used to crave her concern; now I want to avoid it. I won't let anything come between me and my lunch-hour sleuthing, my daily fix of Alice and Samuel, this flatline into my past.

*

I arrive home at six o'clock to find Hannah and Alice sitting at the kitchen table.

'Tea?' Hannah asks, gesturing at the pot.

'Beer,' I say, heading for the fridge.

Alice says, 'Right, I must be off. I'm already late.'

I say, popping open my can, 'Where do you go, Alice, when you rush off like this? Is there someone you have to visit?'

I'm not even sure where I'm heading with this, but since Ben raised the suspicion that Rick might not actually be my father, I'm wondering if someone else is going to come out of the woodwork. At this point nothing would surprise me.

I look into her eyes as I speak, just to see what's there. Her face is expressionless, as always, but I detect a wariness.

'I rush off to my studio, Luke. I have work to catch up on.'

'Please stay for a few minutes. I feel like I never see you.'

'Sure,' Alice says, but there's no warmth to her voice, none at all.

I join them at the kitchen table, where Samuel is in Hannah's arms, having his bedtime bottle of milk, eyes darting from left to right like he's reading a hymn sheet. And the instinct to self-sabotage rises within me, serpent-like, impossible to ignore.

'What did you and Samuel get up to today, Alice?'

'Oh, the usual. We went to the library this morning. He's obsessed with books; I think you've got the makings of a real bookworm.'

'Did you go to the park? Did you feed the ducks?'

'Yes, how did you know?'

'You sing to Samuel, don't you, Alice?'

'Sometimes. But—'

'There's a song you sing. "Santa Lucia", it's called. I looked it up. Did you sing it to me when I was a baby? It's just, when I heard you singing it, I felt something. Perhaps it was recall, a memory. Do you think that's possible? Do you think I might remember?'

I'm asking too many questions. I've stood up now and am pacing. Unable to stop.

Alice says, voice calm, 'But when can you have heard me sing it?'

'Today in the park.'

'You were there today? And you saw us? Why didn't you come and say hello?'

Hannah is staring at me, aghast, no other word for it, and Alice looks a little horrified herself. But the strange thing is, I just don't care. I am unravelling rapidly, and I no longer mind – me, the anxious people-pleaser – who gets to see it.

'I was in a rush.'

Alice stands up from the table, squeezes my shoulder perfunctorily and says, 'Well, another time please join us. We'd be so thrilled to see you.'

We.

Alice and Samuel. Alice and Charlie. The mother with the interchangeable baby.

The moment the front door has closed behind Alice, Hannah says, 'What the fuck is going on?'

I sit slumped over my beer, head in hands.

'Why do I think you're following Alice in your lunch hour?'

'Because that's what I am doing.'

'Why? For God's sake, Luke.'

'I don't know. Something about her is making me uneasy. Don't you feel it? Can't you tell how obsessed she is with Samuel?'

'And that's why you're stalking her around the park? Your mother and your son. Can you hear how that sounds?'

I sit scrunched up, arms wrapped around myself, a primal curl.

She reaches across the table for my hand.

'Babe,' she says, 'this whole Alice thing has really taken a toll on you, hasn't it? I wish we'd never asked her to look after Samuel in the first place, but he adores her. And we feel safe with her looking after him. That counts for everything, doesn't it?'

'Does it?'

'I think we need to find someone for you to talk to. I think this situation has triggered some kind of ...' she breaks off to choose her words, 'psychological collapse.'

'You're not listening to me, H. Alice is taking our baby away and you can't even see it.'

Then

Alice

I have learned so much about Jake in these weeks and I understand how to look after him. I am watchful, like Eddie, but I never mention his depression or the shadow of his childhood. There's a new comprehension between us, that's all. I encourage him to avoid alcohol and to take up exercise and he obliges, most days he runs in Hyde Park. When he is quiet, when a look of sorrow falls upon his face, I am quiet too. Silent but present, that's my intention. I can soften his solitude, I can show him that he never needs to feel alone. And we are happy again, the blip of his five-day drinking binge, almost, but not quite, forgotten.

I am six months pregnant by the time of my show and the dress I choose to wear at the opening, a long, silky thing in vivid poppy red, clings to my swelling stomach. I stand in front of the bathroom mirror admiring my profile while Jacob blind-shaves in the bath.

'Definitely pregnant now,' I say, and he laughs.

'Why, were you thinking you might not be?'

'I like that it shows. I like people knowing.'

'Me too,' he says. 'But there will be press tonight and that means photos ...'

He trails off; no need to say the rest. For I still haven't told my parents that I, an unmarried girl of nineteen, am expecting a baby in May. This shouldn't matter in 1973, but to my father it will be the worst of crimes. I am jolted back to one of his more cringeworthy lectures, post-church, mid-wine, during a lunch to which I had foolishly invited a school friend. The wine, as always, was just for him, the morality sermon custom-designed for the two teenage girls at his table. The most odious part, I recall, was his slurred, clichéd repetition of an old biblical verse: 'Who can find a virtuous woman? For her price is far above rubies', or words to that effect. The friend, Matilda, dropped me soon after that and I never invited anyone home again.

Even so, I feel a little melancholy getting ready for the biggest moment of my life knowing the woman who gave birth to me, who brought me up to the best of her beleaguered ability, will not be there to share it. And Jake, as always, knows what is in my head.

'Soon we'll have our own family,' he says as we set off for Robin's gallery, 'and that's what matters.'

In both of us, a deep desire to give this unborn baby of ours everything we didn't have ourselves. Beyond words, beyond bone; he will be confident, loved, listened to, encouraged, allowed to veer from any path. Choice, freedom, unequivocal support, oh we can get really quite evangelical on the subject of what makes for a perfect childhood. The opposite of ours is the shortcut.

How to describe the feeling of walking into a gallery where my painting of Jake and Eddie hangs in the window, where my name is spelled out against the white walls in huge capital letters: ALICE GARLAND. As instructed, we are half an hour early, yet there are already several people walking around, glass in hand, observing the art. It makes my stomach swoop just to see them.

'I'm not sure I can do this,' I say low-voiced to Jake.

'You've already done it,' he says, with a brief kiss to my cheek.

He throws his arms open to take in the gallery, its walls covered in my art.

'Your time has come,' he says. 'And you, Alice Garland, are one hundred per cent ready for it.'

Rick is already here, drinking champagne and chatting to Robin's guests. Unlike me he is entirely at ease amidst a room full of art lovers, thrilled to be introduced over and over again as Robin's 'latest discovery'. If he carries on with his avant-garde portraiture, Robin has intimated that the next show will be his.

'Your paintings look so beautiful,' he says, hugging Jake and I in turn. 'I actually wept when I saw them. See that guy?'

He points out a collector he recognises.

'The one in the red corduroy jacket and black polo neck? Robin told me he dropped eight thousand pounds in this gallery last year.'

Corduroy Jacket seems fixated by the pietà, titled *Apparition*, me seated with Jake asleep in my lap. I like the way his dark hair flops over my left hip, his hand curled between my thighs, his face, eyes closed, so beautiful in repose.

Robin comes over carrying two glasses of orange juice (Jake has avoided alcohol for three months now and is in better shape than ever).

'I invited Jasper to come before everyone else,' he says, nodding at the man. 'Early reports are favourable. He'll buy a few tonight, I think, but that's the one he likes best.'

With his established artists, Robin takes a sixty per cent cut of the sales. As a lowly second-year art student, I was awarded a generous advance, but all the takings go to the gallery.

'If we sell the lot, there'll be a big bonus for you,' he said at the time, 'and dinner at San Lorenzo either way.'

'I don't want to sell that one.' The words are out before I can stop them. Both Robin and Jake look at me, confused.

'But, Alice, my dear,' Robin speaks slowly, as if to a child, 'all the work has been priced up. I bought it from you with the advance, I thought you understood that.'

It's a moment before I can speak, irritated to find I'm fighting back tears.

'It's so personal. Me and Jake. I don't think I want it hanging on someone else's wall. Can't we put a red sticker on it?'

'It's the best painting in the show. With the highest price tag.' Robin's voice is neutral, patient; he wants to be kind.

'You can do another one,' Jake says, a whispered aside.

I shake my head and have to wait before I'm able to speak. Even so, my voice cracks a little.

'You can't just knock out copies. It doesn't work like that. The reason I love that painting is because it holds all my feelings about you. Why would I want someone else to have it?'

Jake says, 'Robin? Could we keep it? Alice will give you back some of the advance. How about that?'

'The whole thing,' I say, 'if you like. I haven't spent any of it. I just want to keep that painting. It's too personal to sell.'

I wonder if my pregnancy hormones are getting the better of me, but I don't think so. I need to protect Jake's vulnerability; this painting leaves us too exposed. My love for him, my desire to keep him safe from the darkness he tries so hard to hide. The self-loathing I now understand. It's all there in this picture.

At exactly this moment, Jasper turns around and catches sight of the three of us talking, Jake with his arm wrapped around me.

'Ah,' he says, 'the artistes.' He pronounces it with an exaggerated accent. 'Congratulations. Your work is wonderful.'

We shake hands, and although I avoid Robin's eyes, I can

feel his fierce scrutiny. I know what he is thinking: *please don't mess this up*. He may be at the top of the food chain, but he still has bills to pay; he can't allow an overemotional girl to get in the way of his business sense.

'I'm particularly interested in *Apparition*,' Jasper says. 'The style is reminiscent of classical religious art. Is that what you intended? You spent the summer in Florence, I believe?'

And so I tell him about my visits to the Accademia, my obsession with the work of Stefano Pieri and in particular his pietà.

'There was something so sad in that picture, sad but not in the slightest bit sentimental, almost as if it had been caught off camera. That's what I wanted to capture with this show.'

'And why the title, *Apparition*?'

'I suggested that,' Robin says. 'I'm not sure exactly why. I just got this peculiar sense of déjà vu when I first saw the painting.'

'It's a very private piece,' I say, and Jake squeezes my hand.

'Exactly,' says Jasper. 'That's what I like about it. It's full of emotion and love and pathos. I've made up my mind. I'm going to buy it. And a couple of the others too.'

'Wonderful news.' Robin has a firm smile for me as the two of them walk away to secure the deal.

Jake says, 'Please don't let it ruin your night. We can do as many pietàs as you want. I am your forever life model.'

The gallery is filling up now with the young and beautiful, Robin's hand-picked crowd of artists, musicians, actors and models, art buyers and journalists, photographers with cameras slung around their necks. Jake is more used to this, and when a photographer from the *Daily Express* approaches us as we stand beside the pietà with its little red sticker, he puts his hand around my waist.

'Could you just turn towards Jacob a little, Alice?' the photographer asks, framing the shot.

Instinctively, I rest one hand on my stomach, emphasising the pregnancy in that unconscious way of new mothers.

'A little closer together, please.'

Other photographers have begun to gather around now, and they join in, calling out requests.

It's easiest for me to look at Jake instead of the photographers, and so I stare up at him and he drops a kiss on my forehead, both arms curved around me, and this is the shot that will make most of the papers tomorrow, the one my parents will see.

Now

Luke

The childhood of an adoptee is characterised by its secrets. Rarely, for example, is the true genetic identity of the child revealed. A successful reunion between adopted child and natural parent relies upon stark honesty between both parties.

Who Am I? The Adoptee's Hidden Trauma by Joel Harris

Rick has a studio in Clerkenwell, a few blocks down from his apartment. I know exactly where to find him. I'm intrigued to see this place and a little bit excited to catch him unawares, but I hadn't counted on having to deal with his abrasive assistant first. Of course Richard Fields has an assistant. Doesn't Damien Hirst have about fifty of them? I should have expected this.

The studio, actually the ground floor of a former factory, has an intercom beside its locked double doors, announcing several companies and the intentionally misleading 'Fields'.

I press the buzzer and a male voice, not Rick's, floats towards me.

'Hello? Can I help?'

'Yes, I'm here to see Rick.'

See my cunning employment of the abbreviation by which he is known to his friends.

'Do you have an appointment?' The man seems unimpressed.

'No, but if you tell him Luke is here, that will be enough.'

'Look, Luke, I'm sorry, but Richard cannot be disturbed when he is working. And if you were someone who knew him well, then I wouldn't need to tell you that.'

'Perhaps you should tell him his son is here to see him. That might help change his mind.'

Electrifying silence between us, then the buzzer goes and I push open the front door. Behind another closed door I hear male voices, Rick's slightly raised and his assistant's more of a murmur. They come out together, Rick frowning, the assistant, a tall man around my own age, with undisguised curiosity on his handsome, model-like face. He's wearing a white T-shirt that reads *Love is the Drug*, with paint-spattered Evisu jeans, the iconic 'E' visible on both arse cheeks when he turns around.

'Luke, this is a surprise. Just to say, I hate, loathe, detest being dropped in on, and if it wasn't for your shock declaration about our relationship, you'd never have got past my assistant. This is Henry, by the way. But now that my concentration has been well and truly wrecked, what can I do for you?'

I struggle, momentarily, for words. Why am I here disrupting this intensely famous artist, who looks fucked off to say the least? But then I remember. Actually it's *me* who is fucked off.

'Shall I say in front of Henry?'

My voice is as hostile as I feel. Rick considers me in silence. He looks at the watch on his wrist, an elegant thing I've noticed before, silver with a navy-blue face.

'Is this your lunch hour? Shall we grab a coffee? I won't be long,' he says to Henry, who is watching this interplay virtually open-mouthed.

I follow Rick out of the building and along the street and neither of us says a word until we reach a café with bleached wood floors, white walls and two hostile-looking baristas standing behind a counter.

'Best cup of coffee in London,' Rick says. 'There's a roastery out the back.'

He orders two espressos without consulting me about my choice and we carry them through to a little courtyard at the back. Rick, who has always been warm, welcoming, *fun*, is none of these things. It's unnerving, this cool and silent scrutiny; he's not going to make it easy for me.

'I suppose I should tell you why I'm here,' I say, and Rick just nods and takes a small sip of his espresso.

It's hard to begin with, to enunciate the interior chaos, the slow and steady collapsing of my world, but once I've started, I find I cannot stop.

'Things aren't going well with Alice.'

'Tell me about it,' Rick says, voice heavy with sarcasm.

'We grow more distant from each other every day. I don't even feel like she's an au pair any more; she's become a complete stranger. And it hurts me that she cares so much more about Samuel than about me. I don't seem to interest her at all.'

'I'll stop you there, shall I? Can you actually remember what you said to her the day you came back pissed and tried to have a fight over Samuel?'

A small nugget of unease that has been lodged in my gut ever since that day flares up. I'm dizzy with dread.

'No? Well, you reminded her that she had no claim on your child since she'd given her own away.'

'Fuck.'

I don't bother to hide the fact that I'm crying, tears that tip down my cheeks, and I couldn't care less.

'She didn't give you away. She gave you up. With good reason. Can you really not tell the difference?'

'You're angry with me.'

Rick shakes his head.

'More worried than angry. Why do I feel like this whole thing is about to blow up in our faces?'

'I didn't mean to hurt Alice. I lashed out because she's hurting me with her indifference. Isn't it obvious?'

'I warned you about this. But you rushed in, you and Hannah, like a couple of bulls in a china shop. No thought for what might happen if it didn't work out. You're bloody idiots, the pair of you.'

'I'm not sure how to patch things up with her.'

'You could try saying sorry. That usually works.'

'I'm not sorry. I'm angry.'

'With us for giving you up?'

Rick's voice has softened, his eyes too. There's the gleam of tears, a crack in his voice.

'For that, yes, and for the fact that neither of you will ever tell me about the weeks when we were together. Where did we live? What did we do? Where are the photos from that time? You're my father, for God's sake. Why won't you tell me these things?'

I glance up and catch a look of shame or guilt or fear on Rick's face, I'm not sure which. And suddenly I know, with absolute certainty, that Elizabeth is right.

'You're not my father. Are you?'

'I'm on your birth certificate, aren't I?'

'That's not what I asked. You've been lying to me all along. Why would you do that?'

The rage is back. I slam my hand down on the table and my little espresso cup rattles in its saucer.

'Do you think we're trying to deceive you? Or protect you?'

'I need to know the truth. I need to know who I am. Is that so hard to understand? Are you my father? It's a simple answer, Rick. Yes? Or no?'

We are staring at each other while our coffees cool on the table between us. Rick's face is kinder now; he attempts a smile. In the seconds while he chooses his words, I feel the rhythmic beating of my heart: tell me, don't tell me, tell me, don't tell me. I watch his mouth and his eyes, searching for clues. I'm not even sure what I'm hoping for. Do I want Richard Fields to be my biological father or not? The hesitation, the seconds of waiting, are too intense for either of us to breathe or take our eyes away from each other's faces.

'The answer is no. No, I am not your father. And yes, we lied to you. Your father, Luke, is ... someone else.'

Then

Alice

Disciples are playing a showcase gig at the St Moritz on Wardour Street. Twenty music journalists plus Robin's elite guest list of beautiful people, guaranteed to make me, at seven months pregnant, feel fat and insecure. Rick is my plus-one, resplendent in mulberry velvet loons and a patchwork jacket of emerald green and gold; it's a reality check for us both that in an hour's time our lovers will be appearing on stage.

This is the first show Disciples have played in a while, and it sold out instantly. They have been rehearsing the new songs for weeks, and even though the first single went straight into the Top 10, I know Jake is anxious. He is preoccupied almost all of the time. We'll spend a whole night together and he might only speak a few words to me. I'll be glad when the gig is over, except that then I am counting down the days until the band's three-week European tour.

At the St Moritz, Rick and I are checked off the guest list and allowed backstage to the dressing room, a tiny, smoke-filled pit, ashtrays brimming with butts, an unhoovered carpet and nowhere to sit. They are all smoking, and passing a bottle of Jack Daniel's from one to the other, and I watch, alarmed, as Jake takes a sip.

'You're drinking,' I say in as measured a tone as I can manage through the panic that throbs in my veins.

'Just a little bit. I always drink before a show. I can't do it completely sober. I'm nervous. What if the new songs bomb?'

'You'll be brilliant,' I say, wrapping my arms around him, but only briefly. I can tell he needs the freedom to pace.

'See you on the other side,' he says, and I hear the instruction to leave.

'He's drinking,' I say to Rick the moment we're outside the door.

'Jake is in a good place now, you don't need to worry. Like he said, it's just a bit of Dutch courage.'

The St Moritz is a dark, subterranean, cellar-like space, so thick with smoke my eyes sting. We find Robin at the bar ordering wine, looking at the bottle in distaste when it arrives.

'Utter plonk. I'll have to hold my nose to force it down. Want some?'

The three of us push our way through the tightly packed crowd until we're almost in front of the stage, bodies pressing in all around us. I feel a little panicky here, that sense of not being able to fight my way out.

'I'm a bit claustrophobic,' I whisper to Rick, and he takes my hand and says, 'Only for half an hour. I'll look after you.'

Robin points out the editor of *NME*, a reporter from *Sounds* magazine, the music critic from the *Evening Standard*, someone else from *Time Out*.

'Jake's nervous,' I tell him. 'I've never seen him like that before. He's always so confident about his music.'

'There's a lot of pressure from the record company. They need album two to go well. But don't worry. They were brilliant in rehearsal.'

A surreal, out-of-body experience, seeing my lover walk onto the stage, standing just metres away from us. He is a beautiful man; I know this, of course, but seeing him raised up on stage like this emphasises it even more. It takes me back to that first gig at the Marquee, to the feeling of being vacuumed towards him. He raises one hand in salute and the audience cheers its welcome.

'Tonight we're playing the new songs from our album *Apparition* for the first time. We hope you like them.'

And with that, they're straight into 'Sinister', the rockiest number on the record. Jake is instantly at ease as he powers through the lyrics, mouth just centimetres away from the mic, his voice that addictive (for me, anyway) combination of purity and rawness.

I should know by now how assured he becomes on stage, no hint of self-consciousness as he struts from one side to the other and dances with his head thrown back, oblivious to everything except the music.

The audience is loving it, as far as I can tell. I'm scanning the faces of the journalists and I can see they are engrossed, eyes trained on the stage, no one talking.

We are four songs in, just two more to go, and the mood shifts as the opening chords of 'Cassiopeia' strike up. I'm looking at Rick when Jake begins singing, his rant against homophobia concealed as an ambiguous love song. I wonder what Rick is thinking as he listens to the story of our night in Southwold. I turn back to look at Jake, who is now sitting on the edge of the stage with his guitar, just as he did the first time we saw him.

When he sings the first chorus – 'They built each other up but you tore them back down' – Rick takes hold of my hand and squeezes it.

The fight comes out of nowhere. We are shoved from behind, Robin, Rick and me, as the crowd presses in against us, no space to fall. I find myself down on my knees, being hauled up by Rick, who is screaming, 'Pregnant woman here! You're going to crush her.'

But it's almost impossible to stay upright as the shoving and pushing continues. I feel the sharp thrust of an elbow in my stomach; my feet are trod on, painfully, again and again.

'Rick, help me!' I cry as I fall once more to my knees, a blur of bodies around me, and he hoists me up again.

'Stop shoving!' he is shouting. 'For Christ's sake, she's going to get trampled.'

The music stops, there's the hiss of static, and then Jake's voice through the microphone.

'Chill out everyone. This is a peaceful show. Please can you all just calm down.'

And then his voice explodes.

'My girlfriend is down there. She's pregnant. Chill the fuck out.'

I'm in blackness now, head down in a mass of bodies, partially held up by Rick, who is soothing me as you might a child.

'It's all right, I've got you. I won't let anyone hurt you. We'll keep the baby safe.'

The evening collapses. Security men, four or five of them, a cliché of bulk, push through the crowd, yelling, 'Everyone out. Show's over. Everyone leave now.'

Rick and I stand in the middle of the room, wrapped up together, while the storm dissipates. It is only now that I notice my breathing, ragged and uneven as if in the aftermath of tears. Rick says, 'Oh Alice,' and I rest my face against his chest.

'I thought I was going to lose the baby.'

'Me too. But you're all right.'

'There was a fight at the back, apparently, and everyone started stampeding away from it. Could have been really nasty,'

Robin says, coming to find us minutes later. 'Alice, my dear, are you all right? Let me get you some water.'

When I've drunk my glass of water and my breathing has returned to normal, the three of us go backstage.

'Well, that was a disaster,' Eddie says, tipping his head back and pouring a stream of whisky into his mouth.

I watch in horror as Jake snatches the bottle from him and does the same.

'Jake? Don't drink any more.'

'Those fuckers,' he says. 'They could have hurt you, Alice. And the baby.'

'Well they didn't,' Robin says. 'Let's be thankful for that.'

'Robin's right,' Tom says. 'No one got hurt. We should try and forget about it.'

'How about we go somewhere we can get a decent drink? I'll take you to the Chelsea Arts Club,' Robin says.

'Jake? Can you and I go home? Please?'

He sighs.

'I need to be on my own for a bit. Sorry. I can't shake this off as quickly as you all seem to be able to. You could have been badly hurt.'

But I won't let him go down, I won't allow it.

'Jake?'

I wait until he looks at me.

'That was pretty scary. I really need you right now. Please can we just go home?'

I watch as the clarity comes back into his eyes; I feel as if I am dragging him back from the pull of darkness.

'Of course we can,' he says. 'It was just so hard, knowing you were in that crowd, not being able to help you.'

He passes the bottle to Rick.

'You're right,' he says. 'I don't need to be drinking this.'

233

When I glance over at Eddie, I see that he is watching me. He dips his head in an almost imperceptible nod, and I understand. Eddie and I are in this together, we always will be. Crisis averted, he seems to be saying. For now.

Now

Luke

I take a taxi from Clerkenwell to Clapham, too wretched and confused to face the Tube or the office or anything apart from the confrontation that must come next. My head is filled with Rick's words – 'I'm not your father'– and then his refusal to tell me anything else.

'Do you think she kept his identity from you for no reason?'

His frustration had returned, this man whom I've admired so much, first as art-loving bystander and then with what I believed was some biological claim upon him.

'Well, if you won't tell me, Alice will have to,' I said, all bravado, though I don't feel like that now.

It's around 2.30, several hours before I am due home from work, and as I put the key into our front door, I wonder momentarily what I will find on the other side. I hear singing from the kitchen – oh God, that bloody song again, an anthem that penetrates right through to my core.

Alice has a lovely voice, and she sounds happy as she sings, happy and absorbed. When I enter the kitchen, for a moment she doesn't see me. She's sitting at the kitchen table with her sketchpad, Samuel in front of her in his bouncy chair. She has her head to one side, examining him, a small smile on her face. I feel as if I could watch them for hours, but perhaps I am signalling something through the airwaves, for she glances up and gives a shriek of surprise.

'Luke! Don't creep up on me like that. You gave me such a shock.'

There's something in her face here, something I can't identify: guilt perhaps? As if I've caught her at something.

'Why aren't you at work? Are you ill?'

You could say that. Ill in the head, sick in the heart.

'Why did you lie to me about who my father is?' Less of a question, more of a rant. 'Why would you do that?'

And here's the thing: her face collapses instantly. She puts her hand across her mouth and stares down at the table, and I see the telltale tremor of her shoulders.

'You asked me if I was ill just now and I'm beginning to think I might be. Hannah thinks I'm having a breakdown.'

'She said that?'

'In so many words. She thinks this reunion of ours has pushed me over the edge.'

'Same here,' Alice says with a small smile.

And something about that smile, her casualness, snaps the final string. My rage is volcanic, bigger than me, bigger than everything. I can do nothing but submit to it, shouting like a tormented child.

'Who is my father? Tell me! TELL ME.'

Alice shrinks away from me; I see it, yet I cannot stop. I feel ... violent. I slam my hand down on the table so hard it hurts.

'Tell me who my father is. You have to.'

I'm wailing, I'm demonic, and Alice has her hands against her face.

'All right!' She's shouting too. 'Sit down, Luke. And, for God's sake, please calm down. Think of Samuel, if not me.'

Through all this yelling, the baby has remained asleep. And

the sight of him – I can just see the top of his head peeking out above his chair – soothes me. I sit down opposite Alice. I breathe in slowly and let the air out in a long rush.

'Christ. Sorry. I lost control.'

'You don't need to apologise. I understand how hard this is on you. But I haven't been able to talk about your real father for a long time. Twenty-seven years, in fact. Your lifetime. I haven't said his name out loud in all that time. I'm not even sure that I can.'

'Then write it down. Write me a letter. Just tell me the truth. Please, finally, can I know the truth?'

'A letter is a good idea. There's so much to explain.'

'Are you my mother, Alice? Or is that a lie too?'

'Of course I am!'

'I don't understand why you would lie to me about Rick.'

'Because your real father had gone by the time you were born and Rick stepped in and cared for you and loved you as if you were his. He was like your father.'

'So he left you? My dad? Your lover?'

'He did. And I never got over it.'

'Who was he, Alice?'

'I'll write you a letter, Luke. I'll tell you everything, I promise. I'll do it tonight.'

'Thank you. I'm sorry for shouting. I only want ...' I hesitate, unsure of how to continue.

Alice says, 'Go on.'

'I want things between us to improve.'

She nods, but I see that again she is on the edge of tears.

'I hope that your knowing the truth is the right thing, then.'

'Let's start again. Can we do that?'

I remember now I've said it where this phrase comes from:

my other mother, Christina, the words she always used when we'd had a fight: 'Shall we start again?'

And perhaps Alice recognises its childish connotations too, for she laughs and holds out her hand for me to shake.

'I'm on for that,' she says.

We smile at each other, and there's a glimmer of understanding; you might call it progress.

'I should probably get back to the office.'

And that might have been it, the most constructive, bonding talk we've had for weeks. The promise that at last I'm going to find out the truth.

I stand up and peer over the top of Samuel's bouncy chair at my sleeping son. And, in that moment, everything slides, my world pivots and this momentary warmth between us is replaced with the bone-freezing suspicion of old. For Samuel is dressed not in the Gap T-shirt and combat trousers we favour, nor even in one of his sleepsuits, but in old-fashioned orange and yellow striped dungarees that seem too small for him. Clothes that are old, dated, hand-made. Clothes that belong to another time, another era. Another baby.

'His clothes,' I say, and I find that Alice is watching me intently.

'Just for the drawing,' she says, but I know with a gut punch of instinct that this is not the truth.

She is dressing up my baby like her baby. This little chat we've just had means nothing. All she wants is for Samuel to be me, to be hers. Alice wants her baby back.

Then

Alice

Had my father been watching the flat, waiting for Jake to leave, witness to our long-drawn-out goodbye on the doorstep as he headed off for the European tour? Did he see the way he crouched down to kiss my eight-months-pregnant belly – 'Goodbye, baby, be good, don't come out before I'm back' – or our final kiss, which lasted longer than any I can ever remember?

The prospect of being apart is unbearable to both of us. Jake because he is obsessed with every aspect of this, my third trimester of pregnancy, the final countdown until our baby is born. Me because despite his efforts to hide it, I sense a creeping darkness in him, silences that last too long, a listlessness that is entirely out of character. Apart from the gig at St Moritz, he's managed to stay away from alcohol. But I can't help worrying about the damage he could do to himself without me to keep him stable.

'Don't let him drink,' I begged Eddie the last time I saw him.

Eddie just shrugged.

'I'll do my best. You know what he's like.'

When we finally part, I watch Jake walking off up Dean Street with a pit of fear in my stomach.

After he's gone, I walk around our flat picking up things that belong to him. The half-finished book by his side of the bed – *Fear and Loathing on the Campaign Trail '72*, Hunter S. Thompson's vitriolic coverage of Nixon's second win. Jake, Eddie, Tom, Rick and me – in fact everyone I know – are violently opposed to Nixon, to the continuation of the Vietnam War, its senseless wasting of life. Jake's black army boots, discarded at right angles to one another, still seem to contain his essence. I'm staring at them, wondering if I should sketch them, when the doorbell rings. It takes a moment for me to register it. Another pressing of the bell, longer, more insistent.

As I walk towards the stairs, I pick up an apple from the fruit bowl – an unusual Snow Whitish red – and take a bite of it, thinking only of Jake and how much I already miss him. I fling open the front door, and there, hovering on the doorstep, black shirt and trousers, the off-duty-vicar garb he favours, is my father. The apple falls from my hand, bounces onto the doorstep and rolls to a stop at his feet.

'Are you going to invite me in to the love nest?' His mouth twists on the words.

I am eight months pregnant, no Jake or Rick to protect me, alone with this man who has cowed and persecuted me for most of my life. I don't say no, I don't slam the door in his face and double-lock it from the inside. I stand aside and let him into the dark corridor where once upon a time Jake kissed me so passionately that my sketchbook slammed to the floor.

He follows me upstairs and into our flat, door opening into the orange, red and purple room that has become my home.

'Dear God,' he says. 'It's even worse than I thought. Like some kind of bordello, I'd imagine.'

'It's called fashion, but it probably hasn't reached Essex yet.'

'If you can't be civil, I'll just come straight out with it. Sit down, Alice.'

'I'd rather stand.'

'In your condition?' Again the twist of distaste. 'I'll cut to the chase, shall I? Your mother and I want you to have this child adopted so you can get on and finish your degree. After all, you're doing rather well, aren't you, according to the papers. There will be plenty of time for children with this *musician* of yours if that's what you want. But you must not throw your life away. We won't allow it. You're not quite twenty and you have many opportunities ahead.'

'Since when did you care about my opportunities? I thought I was a disappointment – academically and otherwise, according to you.' I am clasping my stomach as I speak, for comfort, for reassurance, but aside from that, I feel calm. For the first time in my life I'm not afraid.

My father has his leather folder with him, a zipped thing he takes wherever he goes. I watch as he unzips it and brings out some kind of document.

'Sure you won't sit down?' he says.

He is in his late forties – twenty-eight when I was born – but he looks much older. His hair has thinned since I last saw him, greased wisps combed over a naked pate, the lower half of his face dragged downwards, too much flesh around his chin.

'No thanks.'

He hands over the papers.

'Have a look through these forms. I've taken the trouble to get in touch with a very good adoption agency, one with an excellent reputation. They have a couple in mind, respectable middle-class people from Yorkshire who would be perfect. So if you and your … lover decide you want to have the baby adopted, which in my mind—'

My scream, long and shrill, surprises me as much as him.

'Get out! Get out of here.'

'For goodness' sake. Don't overreact.'

'How dare you? How fucking dare you?'

My father strikes me hard with the back of his hand, a sharp smack to my left cheek that lands just beneath my eye, the sound of flesh meeting flesh. I crumple to the floor. He hauls me up.

'Foul-mouthed little ... *whore*.'

Violent eyes too prominent for their sockets, skin an alcoholic purple. I have seen my father's rages many times, but this is the first time he has hit me. And the strength of the blow, his choice of insult, reveals the depth of his hatred.

I turn away from him, throw myself down on the sofa, face buried in the cushions. My sorrow is acute.

'Just go.'

When I force myself to look up again, he is still there, staring at me, a concentration of disgust gathered in his face.

'You will leave,' I tell him, 'or I will call the police. You are not welcome here.'

I curve my hands around my stomach. I do not think the fall will have hurt my baby, but the surge of poison, the stress and anger coursing through my blood, what of that?

My father points at the papers before he leaves.

'I'd advise you to look over these,' he says, and I hold my breath until I hear the click of the front door closing behind him.

How many hours pass? One, two? I sit motionless on the sofa, too shocked, too downcast, to think of crying. I miss Jake with a savage ache, but I won't tell him about my father's visit. I will never share the things that might push him down. I feel I can guard him when we are together, I can watch over him with vigilance and make sure he is safe. But I have no control with him away on tour. All I can do is make sure each phone call we have is a good one, and he hangs up feeling positive, calm, reassured.

'What's wrong?' Rick says when I call an hour or two later.

For a second or two I am too choked to speak.

'My father came.'

'What did the bastard say?'

Rick knows my father as a bully, not an abuser; I hadn't realised that myself until today. Not that I care, not that it matters. I'm a little flattened by it, that's all.

'Can you come over?'

'On my way.'

I haven't bothered to look in the mirror, and when I open the front door, Rick takes a step back and yelps in surprise.

'Alice! Your face!' He screeches it and then he makes a sequence of noises I've never heard him make before, a gasping, wheezing sound that turns out to be Rick crying.

We sit on the sofa with a bowl of ice and water and a flannel that Rick presses against my swollen cheek, tears running down his face until I tell him, 'This isn't really helping, you know.'

'You're right, I'm sorry. But I hate the fact that he did this when Jake was away. He'll kill your father when he finds out.'

'He won't find out. Rick, you have to promise me that. He couldn't handle it.'

'I think you underestimate him sometimes.'

'Hardly. Are you forgetting how he disappeared on a bender for almost a week? He's so fragile, I'm only starting to realise how much. I'm worried about him being away.'

'You've got to stop stressing, it can't be good for the baby.'

'I just need him home.'

'And he will be. Come on, let's forget about your father. Stop worrying about Jake. Can't we do something normal and everyday? Just you and me.'

I watch as he lights all the candles in the sitting room, the way Jake usually does, so that this orange and red space is filled with a calming night-time glow. He makes tea in the cream and gold pot I bought at Portobello Market and flips through the stack of records, selecting *The Dark Side of the Moon*, a perfect choice.

While we drink our tea, he flips through our book of baby names, reading out the most outlandish ones. Jake and I have already chosen our names: Charles for a boy, Charlotte for a girl, both shortened to Charlie. But I indulge Rick while he suggests Aristotle and Prospero, and Cassiopeia for a girl.

And soon I'm laughing, the horror of today almost forgotten as I sit drinking tea and laughing with my best friend and his pitch-perfect interpretation of 'normal'.

The last time, as it turned out, that my life would ever be normal again.

Now
Luke

It begins as a perfect Saturday. We sleep late, all three of us, or rather the late that is 8.30 and not 6 a.m., woken by Samuel, who rolls over and pokes his feet into my stomach. When I open my eyes, he is staring at me intently. I grin, a nought-to-thirty-second response when faced with this joy-giving human being, and he does his uproarious laugh, which is how Hannah wakes.

'Hello, laughing boy,' she says, kissing him.

She reaches for my hand and pulls it up to her mouth.

'It's Saturday,' she says. 'Two whole days of just being us.'

'Breakfast in bed?' I say. 'For three?'

We get the weekend papers delivered, so I carry up a tray laden with tea and toast and the Saturday *Times*, a warm bottle of milk for Samuel. I open our curtains and the early-autumn sun spears in through the window, a *Star Wars* beam of gold.

We prop him up against the pillows and he reaches out for his bottle, snatching it rudely and shoving it into his mouth, a daily gesture we still find amusing. He guzzles with that fixated gaze of his, as if we starve him and this is his first bottle of milk in days.

'Tea?' Hannah says, kneeling up in my Cult T-shirt and looking heart-achingly lovely with her flushed, healthy skin, her smile, her wild bedhead hair.

'Hannah?' I say, full of the moment, and she looks at me, still smiling.

There are so many impulsive things I might say. 'Marry me' pops into my head on a regular basis, but Hannah has her own unswerving beliefs on that score. Marriage is more likely to lead to a break-up, she says, though she has no statistics to back this up. It's just her hunch, her distrust of anything official; she, always, the Cornish hippy at heart.

I settle for 'I couldn't love you more,' and she laughs and blows me a kiss.

'Ditto, you ridiculous man. Luke?'

Her hesitation is enough; I know what she is going to say.

'Are you feeling OK?'

I shrug. 'Yes and no.'

Last night, when I recounted the shocking revelation that Rick isn't my father, Hannah burst into tears. I think she is beginning to realise that I might have been right about Alice all along, and for once she is on my side, not hers.

'But it's the weekend,' I say, accepting my mug of tea. 'Let's have a break from talking about Alice.'

We drink our tea reading Hannah's review of a new play at the Donmar Warehouse; second reading for me, twentieth for her as she checks for any last-minute subbing catastrophes, that inveterate ability to exchange lyricism for flat, joyless accuracy.

When Samuel finishes his bottle, he flings it across the bed like a despot.

'Looks like breakfast is over,' Hannah says.

We plan our day while we shower, dress and pack up the despot's essentials – more milk, a miniature pot of frozen puréed pear, the plastic set of keys he loves, his cross-eyed bear. Coffee first at the North St Deli, which has a little garden in the back, then a walk around the common, stopping off at the playground for half an hour or so on the swings. We'll buy lamb steaks from the butcher for dinner and a bottle of our favourite wine from Oddbins, and by the time we get home, Samuel will have fallen asleep and we'll allow him to snooze in the buggy while we nip upstairs for a little siesta ourselves.

The thought of this siesta, which might last an hour and a half if we're lucky, permission for the kind of slow, elongated sex of before, gives both of us a glow. I press my lips against the inside of Hannah's wrist and she exhales in that way she has, telling me everything I need to know. I like the silent, shared programming of sex; it has its own eroticism. No, we can't fall into bed whenever we want to, leaving theatres and catching cabs on nothing more than a shared glance or a whispered desire as in the old days. But we can look forward to it for several hours, allowing the moment between us to build and build.

Hand in hand we walk through our neighbourhood, where our long summer of heat has forced the trees into a premature burn of red and gold, with the occasional shock of canary yellow. When Samuel is older, he'll leap in the air to catch a falling leaf, and we'll tell him to make a wish. In Larkhall Rise, we admire, as always, the tall grandeur of the four terraced houses, each one three storeys with a generous slash of garden at the back. We notice how the last one, the shabbiest, which we had earmarked for our future, has a For Sale sign, and we forecast how there will soon be a couple of bankers in it, Farrow & Balling their front door, and putting out planters with miniatures trees like a couple of full stops.

By the time we reach the deli it's almost eleven o'clock and my head is beginning to ache a little without its early-morning injection of coffee.

We never come to the North St Deli, although our friends rave about it. Hannah is a sucker for the vintage china, loose-leaf tea and chocolate eclairs of the French Café on the high street. So it's a surprise when the owner rushes forwards to greet us.

'*Ciao*,' he says. 'You've brought my favourite baby. I don't normally see him at the weekend.'

We're both smiling, ready to explain, when the man crouches down to Samuel's level.

'*Ciao*, Charlie, where's your beautiful mamma today?'

The moment stills, the air freezes; there are whole seconds before either of us reacts.

'Did you call him Charlie?' Hannah says, and her voice is harsh and un-Hannah-ish.

'Yes, it's Charlie, I know him very well.'

The man stands up and holds out a hand for us to shake.

'I'm Stefano,' he says. 'His mamma Alice is a friend of mine; she comes here every day.'

What to do with this information? My beautiful trusting girl: I see first shock, then horror flashing into her eyes as she registers the full repercussions of this.

I say, 'Alice is his au pair. I'm not sure why she's allowed you to think she's his mother.' My voice doesn't sound much like me either, gruff, macho, unfriendly. In any other circumstances I'd be ashamed of our rudeness.

'There is some mistake?' says Stefano, confused but wary. 'Would you like some coffee? Some cake? We have a lovely little garden in the back.'

'Yes,' Hannah says, 'we know about the garden, thank you. And I'm sorry, but I'm finding this information a little hard to get my head round. So just to be clear, Alice, your friend, our au pair, comes in here with our son, Samuel, but she says he is hers? She pretends, in fact, to be his mother?'

Stefano looks crestfallen and trapped in the face of Hannah's cold interrogation.

'I'm sorry.' He shrugs. 'I don't know what else to say.'

Hannah shakes her head; she seems to have run out of words. She bends down to the buggy, where Samuel is sitting wide-eyed and oblivious. She puts her hand against his cheek, just for a second, a heartbreaking gesture that says just the one word: mine. Then she stalks out of the café.

A few doors down, beside the entrance to the new gym we both belong to and never attend, she slows to a stop, hands to her face, curved over the pushchair, weeping. Guilt, shame, sadness, fear; the whirlpool is full as I put my arms around her, wondering, dreading, which bit of this terrifying new development she hates the most. It's a good minute before she can speak, and when she does, she says not the thing I'm expecting – 'How dare she? How. Bloody. Dare. She?' – but something else.

'Samuel thinks Alice is his mum.'

I'm so surprised, I almost laugh. Samuel is eight months old. His thoughts are centred on food and sleep; he doesn't yet have the cognitive power to assess who is and who isn't his actual mother. Does he?

But Hannah's outburst is far from over.

'I should never have gone back to work, it was so selfish of me. I love him more than anything and yet I've allowed a complete stranger to look after him day after day just so I could carry on with my stupid fucking career. When your mother, your actual mother, the woman who brought you up for the first eighteen years of your life, was generous enough to offer us financial support if I stayed at home to look after him like any normal, caring woman would, given the choice. And I've wanted to, oh you don't know how much I've wanted to be with him, but I put my job first. And now this has happened and it's all my fault.'

'How could it possibly be your fault? Samuel is too young

to understand about things like that. He loves you. He knows you're his mum.'

I'm trying to hold on to her, but she shoves me away.

'You don't get it, do you? You don't understand what this is about.'

'Yes I do. You're worried that Samuel loves Alice more than you. And I'm telling you that's crazy. Babies don't have thoughts at this stage in their lives. They don't remember one day to the next.'

'How can you say that when you're so *fucked up* about the first months of your life?'

I step backwards, a physical defence; the wash of shock makes me cold and alert. I can hardly look at her, this woman I love.

Hannah starts crying again.

'I'm sorry, I didn't mean that.'

Samuel, marooned and motionless in his pram, begins to wail, and Hannah wiggles the handle, distractedly, demonically.

'We used to be so happy,' she says.

'We still are, aren't we?' Please say yes. I cannot stand any threat to my existence, surely she knows that. I'm an adoptee, I'm addicted to the status quo.

I watch as she bends down to take Samuel out of the pram, unclipping his straps, kissing his face. The minute he's propped against her, he stops crying. Isn't that proof enough?

'See? See how he loves you? Shall we walk up to the common? We can talk as we go.'

Hannah looks at me now, her focus absolute.

'I really hope you fully comprehend what just happened,' she says, and there is a coldness to her voice I don't like. 'Alice needs to go. Alice needs to be sacked or whatever it is you do when it turns out that your *birth mother*' – nasty, hostile emphasis of the words – 'has been stealing your son.'

'Hardly stealing, H. But she's definitely weird around him. I tried to tell you.'

'Why didn't I listen to you? Why didn't I see it? What kind of woman pretends another woman's child is her baby?'

'And dressing him up in my old clothes. The whole thing is strange. She seems to have zero interest in me, her actual son; her entire focus is on him.'

'Do you think she's dangerous?'

'Christ, I hope not.'

I'm relieved Hannah has finally come around to my way of thinking, but she's making leaps here that are bordering on the extreme.

'Come on, it's not like she's a psychopath,' I say, expecting her to laugh, but she doesn't.

'I really hope you're getting the magnitude of this. Should I spell it out for you? I want that woman out of my life.'

Then

Alice

Jake's deterioration is easily measured through his phone calls: the ones he makes, then the ones he doesn't. I can always pick out the alcohol in his voice, even if I don't hear it at first. At the start of the tour he seems mildly drunk, high after his shows and a late dinner with the band. But within a week the drinking has accelerated into something else. Night after night, his voice is so slurred and indistinct it's hard to understand at times. He tells me he loves me, that he misses me, that it's so hard being away. I lie awake long into the night after these calls, while our baby wriggles and shifts inside me, heels and elbows erupting alien-like from my stretched stomach, and I worry. Is this it, the start of his decline? Is he going to become ill again? I am counting down the day until the tour finishes.

When Jake calls, I often ask him to put Eddie on the line, but he never does.

'You're not looking after yourself,' I say one night when I've woken up at three to take the call. 'You're drinking too much. You need a break. Remember how depressed it made you last time? You have to stop.'

But Jake rarely listens on these phone calls.

'Love you,' he says, his voice thick with booze. 'No need to worry 'bout me.'

He hangs up without saying goodbye, too drunk, it seems, to remember he's in the middle of a phone call. My demons are at their peak in the middle of the night, my brain a cinematic projection of all the things that might go wrong. Jake staggering into the middle of the road, where he is mowed down by a truck. Jake overdosing on sleeping pills like Jimi Hendrix. Jake choking on his own vomit while he sleeps.

Eddie sounds the alarm just a few days before the band are due back.

'Alice, it's Eddie.'

My heart freezes over.

'Oh God, please tell me he's OK.'

'He's a mess. We've had to cancel tonight's show. He's been off his face for the past two weeks. We've been telling him to cut it out, but he won't listen. He's ruining the tour. But it's his mental health I'm worried about. He's a bloody fool.'

'Come back, Eddie. Cut the rest of the shows. Please. Do it for me. Do it for the baby. We need to get him home.' I realise I am crying, but it's painless, unconnected, just a wetting of my cheeks.

'I think you're probably right. I'll talk to Tom.'

Jake's call comes in much later the same night. It's three in the morning, but that doesn't matter, I'm instantly awake on the second ring, waddling into the sitting room and snatching up the phone by the fourth.

'Hey.'

How can one short syllable contain such profundity? I know from this greeting just how far Jake has fallen.

'I've been so worried about you.'

'Alice …' He breaks off; is he crying?

'Jake? Are you there?'

Nothing.

'Please talk to me. I've missed you so much.'

There's a gasp, that's all, and then his voice, so weak and stilted I find I am crying myself.

'I'm fucked, I think. So scared. Scared of everything.'

'What things? Try to tell me.'

'The trip home. Talking. Thinking. Going to sleep. Waking up. Having a shower. None of it seems ... possible.'

'Are you on your own? Where are the others?' My voice sounds frantic even though I'm trying to stay calm.

'In the hotel.'

'Jake, go to bed. Please promise me you'll do that. Everything will seem better when you wake up. And as soon as you get home, I'll look after you. You're going to be OK.'

'Am I?' he says, his last words before the line goes dead.

Sleep is an impossibility; instead, I lie on the sofa waiting for the pitch black of 3.30 in the morning to move towards dawn's pale-grey sludge. The rattle of taxis, I long to hear that. Stallholders shouting out to one another a couple of streets away. The Bar Italia opening up for morning custom. In Soho's silence I hear nothing but gloom.

A telegram arrives at nine in the morning and I'm almost too frightened to open it. I sit on the sofa, Jake's sofa, our sofa, a sofa with so many memories, holding the envelope between hands that shake.

We've cut the tour. Arriving home tonight. Eddie.

Half an hour later, telegram still clutched in my hand, I realise with an energy my heavily pregnant self has almost forgotten that I need to get the flat ready for him. Oh, the relief of having a purpose, as I haul my bulk from one room to the next, changing sheets, cleaning the bath, plumping cushions, replacing candles. In the afternoon, I walk to the Iranian shop on Beak Street and buy tins of soup, bread and two bottles of Lucozade, invalid food. I think of my mother, briefly, as I unload the Heinz tomato soup into the cupboard, sliced Mother's Pride into the bread bin. As a child, with recurring tonsillitis, all I ever wanted was tomato soup. I remember how my mother sat by my bed, right through the night when the pain was at its worst, and I wonder how we have got to here.

The doorbell rings at six o'clock and I find both Jake and Eddie on the doorstep. Jake looks like a ghost, that's the first thing. His skin is blue-white and his eyes slither from side to side, unfocused.

'Jake!' I say, reaching out to embrace him, but he takes a step back.

Eddie, I realise now, has been supporting him with one arm around his back, and he says, 'Let's get him to bed. Then we'll talk.'

How I have longed to see this man, this thin, gaunt ghost, and now, as he and Eddie climb the stairs ahead of me, one step at a time, I do not know how to feel. They stagger past the sparkling sitting room with its brand-new orange candles just waiting for a match, past the record player with *The Dark Side of the Moon* ready on the turntable. At the bedroom door, Eddie says, 'Best to stay there, Alice, while I settle him. I'll only be a minute.'

How can this be happening? How can he have fallen so far in less than twenty-four hours? He sounded desperate last night on the phone, but today he is catatonic.

'Heavy dose of Valium,' Eddie says, sitting down next to me and taking my hand. 'They had to sedate him to get him on the bus. He's a fucking mess, the worst I've ever seen him. Did you know he'd stopped taking his medication?'

There is no tone of accusation in his voice, but that's what I hear, and I plant my face into my palms. All I can see is Jake popping out his sachet of pills into the lavatory.

'Yes, I knew. He hates it so much. I should have made him take it. I didn't understand.'

'Alice?' Eddie's voice is sharp; he has picked up my remorse. 'This is no one's fault except Jake's, and not even his. He's a manic depressive and he has to keep taking his medication to avoid extreme episodes, or whatever this is. The doctor in Paris called it psychosis.'

'What's going to happen?'

Eddie sighs. He keeps hold of my hand.

'When's the baby due?' he says.

'Ten days.'

'His timing's really off, isn't it?'

'I don't care. I'm just glad he's home.'

Eddie nods, several times. I can tell he's trying to choose his words.

'Alice,' he begins, and then he stops himself.

'What is it?'

'You do understand what this means, don't you?'

'He's depressed. He needs medication. He needs peace and quiet. Of course I understand.'

It seems to me that the look on Eddie's face is one of un-utterable sadness, and this time he takes both of my hands between his.

'He won't be allowed to stay here.'

'But why not? I love him. I'm going to look after him. We'll be fine.'

Eddie shakes his head. 'They'll make him go to hospital. And he won't want to go. You know as well as I do how he feels about hospital.'

'Then he won't have to go. Why are you looking at me like that? I don't know what you're saying.'

'I think you do. Tomorrow they'll probably section him. You have to be prepared for that. Tomorrow they will take him away.'

Now

Luke

The adult adoptee longs to experience the absolute love a mother has for her child at birth. But this is never going to happen. You cannot overcome the layers of defence that build up over twenty or thirty years. You cannot replicate the newborn experience.

Who Am I? The Adoptee's Hidden Trauma by Joel Harris

By the time I arrive at Alice's studio (I haven't called because she never answers her phone on a Saturday but works without fail in her studio), I am in a frenzy to get the deal done. I intend to burst in, surprising her at work, delivering my missive as I walk through the door, short, sharp, brutal, a rebuttal to match my own.

Leaving the taxi, I stand for a moment outside the red-brick ground-floor flat. The studio is an open-plan space, I'd imagine, four rooms knocked into one, although this is conjecture, because last time I was here she wouldn't allow me through the door. I hover. I ponder. My hand reaches up to press the bell and pauses just a centimetre or two away, frozen with indecision. My heart rate, now that I'm attuned to it, has definitely speeded up. I feel breathless with anger but also fear at the confrontation that comes next. The man who has carved a career out of maintaining the equilibrium, about to implode it with a few hostile words: 'Alice, we don't want you to look after Samuel any more.'

I try the door handle, for it is easier this way. Just walk in, I tell myself, and say what you need to say. The door opens easily, which is a surprise. Nothing could have prepared me for what I find inside.

How can I describe to you these first seconds of shock as I take in the images of Samuel on every inch of wall space, every surface, a vast half-finished canvas in the middle of the room. Like a hall of mirrors, or a nightmare, my boy laughing, sleeping, crying, one whole wall dedicated to Polaroid snaps with their eerie, ghostly light.

My eyes swivel from one canvas to the next, so many, such likeness, such accuracy; the skill and depth of artistry is astonishing. Here is Samuel propped up against a tower of cushions on an unfamiliar blue and white blanket, his bear beside him with eyes of glass. Now he wears a top of mustard yellow and brown stripes, a pair of orange shorts. In another he sleeps in his bouncy chair, dressed in the tiny dungarees of before. To me he seems a little sheepish in his seventies garb, as if he understands the equation, the alchemy that takes place here in Alice's studio, the transformation of Samuel into me.

'Luke!'

Alice enters the room with a small, half-pleased cry of surprise. But then I turn around and she sees my face.

'I can explain,' she says, but she has no words, no defence.

I am having the strangest experience, out of body almost; I look at Alice and feel all connection to her dissolving away. In front of my eyes she becomes the thing that deep down she has always been: a stranger. Who was I trying to kid in this wretched attempt to turn her into my mother? I have a mother, one I've treated pretty badly of late.

'What the hell, Alice? This place is a shrine. It's weird, devotional shit. Like, I don't know ...' I wave my arms around, 'kind of psycho stuff.'

Our worst fears are realised is what I'm thinking, but as always, Alice's face remains impassive, her voice quiet.

'Can you really stand there and say that to me?'

'As a matter of fact, I can. Shall I tell you what happened today?' My voice is bitter, cruel, loathsome. 'Hannah and I went to the North St Deli for a coffee. Ring any bells?'

I watch the shame flooding into her face; I'm glad of it.

'I see that it does. So what happens when Hannah ...' my voice falters a little on her name, 'and *Samuel* – arch over-emphasis – 'and I walk into the deli is that a friend of yours, I believe he's called Stefano, rushes over to say hello to Charlie. He asks where Alice is, Charlie's mother. He says the two of you go there all the time. Can you even begin to imagine how that made Hannah feel?'

I am full of indignant rage and yet I'm crying. I feel as I speak with such contempt to my mother as though my heart is immolating. I am angry and ashamed.

Alice says, 'I'm sorry.'

'Sorry? For stealing our son and pretending he's yours? Sorry for wanting him to be me?'

'Look, I can see how upset you are and I can explain.'

'Explain what?' I gesture to the studio with its wall-to-wall Samuel. 'The evidence is all here. You want Samuel to be me. You want my baby to replace the one who was taken away from you.'

'No, Luke, it's not like that, I promise you.'

But I don't want to listen to her. I know she is not to be trusted.

'You can't look after him any more, that's what I came to say. This whole thing has been such a big mistake.'

Alice gasps. 'You don't mean that. Who else will look after him? You know how Samuel adores me.'

'We'll work it out. My mother will help us to begin with.'

This incendiary word, *mother*. One I have stumbled on so many times. But not now. The difference between Christina and Alice has become starkly clear. One the woman who has looked after me my whole life, the other a virtual stranger. A dangerous one, it seems to me now.

Alice begins to cry, both hands concealing her eyes, but I see how her shoulders tremble. I wish I could step towards her and put an arm around her and make things right between us. But here in this bizarre setting, with my tiny son looking down at me from every wall, I know things have already gone too far.

'I'm sorry, Alice. But Hannah is completely freaked out. She doesn't want you around Samuel any more. *I* don't want you around Samuel any more.'

Such hostile words, but I can find no other way to say them. There is a fury in me and it's not all to do with this blatant idolatry of my small son. For Alice has done nothing but lie to me all along.

'This isn't just about Samuel, it's about the way you've treated me. Can you imagine what it feels like finding out who my father is after twenty-seven years of not knowing, only to discover that actually it's not Rick, it's someone else entirely and you won't even tell me his name?'

'You're right,' Alice says, not looking at me, her gaze directed somewhere near the floor. 'I've made some bad mistakes. But I'm trying to fix them. I don't expect you to understand, but I've spent my whole life running away from it. It's so ... incredibly painful for me to face it.'

'Oh Alice,' I say, and I think that in this moment perhaps there will be a way back for us. But then she blows it, utterly, with her next line.

'Please don't take him away from me. I won't be able to bear it. When can I see him again?'

Not 'you' but 'him'. Not me but Samuel.

'Goodbye, Alice,' I say with a cruelty I don't recognise in myself.

Then

Alice

Jake is asleep, curled on his side, facing the window. He has a hole in one of his socks and the three middle toes have broken free. Something about those toes, that sock, breaks my heart. I sit down on the bed more heavily than I intended. I roll my bulk towards him, my arms wrapped right around his waist, our unborn child filling the gap between us, and this is how he wakes.

He turns to face me; instantly he's crying, tears that will not stop.

'Oh Jake,' I say, crying too, 'I love you so much. I wish I could help.'

He doesn't speak, not for a long time; the sadness in him is just too big. By the time the doctor arrives mid-morning, he has said only one word to me – *sorry* – and I saw the effort it cost him to speak. So much pain and sorrow and he has no way of expressing it. He is caged within his body, his mind in torment.

The doctor is with him for almost an hour, and I spend the time pacing back and forwards from the kitchen to the sitting room, making a cup of tea that turns cold as I stare out of the window.

'Shall we sit down?' the doctor says, finally coming into the sitting room and gesturing at our brown sofa. 'I'm sure you must be very anxious with your baby almost due, and so I'm sorry for what I have to tell you. Jacob is very severely depressed. The important thing is that we've caught it. We need to get him into hospital right away and on to medication. I'll be able to organise a bed for him within a couple of hours, probably at the Maudsley.'

'Not the hospital. Please, Jake hates hospitals.'

'I'm afraid so. And as a matter of urgency. You do understand, I hope, the severity of this depression?'

'Will I be able to visit him?'

'Of course. Perhaps not a good idea for the first few days, until we can stabilise him.'

'What if he doesn't want to go? Have you talked to Jake about this?'

'He knows he needs to go into the hospital for a while. He's fairly resistant to it. But, Alice, it's the only way. If he refuses to come voluntarily, then we would have to section him to keep him safe.'

He pats my arm before he leaves.

'Once the medication starts to take effect, you'll see a huge change, believe me.'

Jake is staring up at the ceiling when I return to the bedroom, but even from the doorway I can see the constant slide of tears running down his cheeks. He watches me come into the room, he taps the space beside him. I put out a hand behind me and lower myself in stages, a lumbering manoeuvre that would have made him laugh not long ago. He turns to face me and we lie there holding hands, not speaking. Sometimes the baby kicks or shifts position and I'll capture his hand and hold it to my belly so he can feel it too. He doesn't smile, but he leaves his hand there long after the baby has stopped moving.

The clock beside the bed is measuring out our time; three hours turns to two and then one and a half. And still we haven't had the conversation about the hospital. I don't have the strength for it.

Eventually I get off the bed and start pulling clothes out of his cupboard. Underwear, socks, T-shirts. Are these the right things? I come across his long, skinny scarf, the one emblazoned with a feather design; he was wearing it the day he came to find me at the Slade. I hold it out to him.

'Remember this? You were wearing this the day I fell in love with you.'

He nods but doesn't smile, and I put the scarf on top of the chest of drawers, knowing I'll need to look at it later.

'What are you doing?'

I hear how hard he has to dig for each word.

'They want you to go into hospital today.'

I feel treacherous saying it, this word 'hospital' which he loathes and dreads and fears.

'No.'

I return to the bed and sit on the edge. I reach out for his hand, but he shifts away from me, a sullen child.

'NO.'

'Jake. Please. You have to do what the doctor says. You're so unwell. They only want to make you better.'

'What about ...' He breaks off, the effort of speech exhausting him. 'What about our baby. Can't miss it.'

'It will probably be late. First babies often are. You'll be back by then, I know you will.'

He turns his face away from me.

'So you're on their side?'

'Of course I'm not. How can you say that? All I want is for you to get better so you can come home again.'

'What if I say no?' He speaks the words to the window. And he knows the answer just as I did.

'They are going to make you.'

We're both crying now, and I lie down beside him. This time he does let me hold his hand.

'It will be all right,' I say. 'It won't be like last time because now you've got me.'

Jake manages to nod before he turns away.

I finish packing his bag. A pair of jeans. Toothbrush and toothpaste from the bathroom, a brand-new bar of soap. I reach for his razor and snatch my hand away, thinking better of it but hating myself a little more.

It's almost 2.30 by the time I've finished. Robin and the doctor are arriving in half an hour: Robin to drive him, the doctor to enforce his admittance if required. My heart is bleak.

'I'll go with you,' I say, but Jake shakes his head.

'No. Come here.'

I lie back down next to him, and this time he wraps his arms around me just as he used to.

'I don't want you to see it. I told you what those places are like. It will frighten you.'

'I don't care.'

'But I do.'

'You'll let me visit you, though?'

He squeezes my hand. 'I'm counting on it.'

'You know how much I love you?'

'Same, same.'

'Could you eat something? There's enough time.'

He nods. 'Something small.'

'Soup?'

He smiles for the first time in twenty-four hours.

'Soup would be perfect,' he says.

*

Did anyone ever prepare a tin of soup with such care? As if I can deliver all my love and hope and reassurance into this small bowl of vivid orange, the toast crisp and hot and buttered from corner to corner. While I wait for the soup to heat, I make myself a cup of tea and remember that I haven't eaten anything since a slice of toast at eight o'clock this morning. I chide myself for not taking better care of the baby. I think that with Jake away I will go to the greengrocer and pack in all the healthy ingredients I can get my hands on, a last-minute nutrient boost for our almost-born babe.

It's a quarter to three by the time I make it back to the bedroom, enough time for him to eat the soup, which I have taken care not to over-boil. I push at the door with my foot, but it doesn't budge; there's something jamming it from the other side. I put the tray down on the floor, a difficult move at nine months pregnant.

'Jake?' I call, pushing harder at the door so that it inches forward, but there is still something pushed against it, some-thing heavy and hard to shift. Everything in my body – bones, blood, skin, heart, lungs, stomach – turns to ice. I shove against the door with my full weight, all nine and a half stone of me, and then I see on the other side of it his feet, still in the holey socks, three toes exposed, and I know, oh I know, what I am going to find. He is leaning away from the door, face tilted up grotesquely, neck looped to the doorknob by a slip knot in his cream feathered scarf.

I'm sobbing as I try to release the noose with hands that shake.

'You're alive,' I say, talking to myself, talking to him, talking to anyone who might be able to make this true.

And his skin is still warm, that's the thing, but his body

slumps forwards across my lap the minute he is released from the scarf, and his eyes are staring into nothing. I sit down on the floor, cradling him in my lap, my lover, my love, my darling.

Now
Luke

Luke,

I used to tell you stories about your father while you slept, whispering them into the darkness so your dreams would be filled with colour and light and love.

Of course you couldn't understand, but I wanted to somehow pass on to you the strength and passion of this most amazing human being as if by osmosis.

I loved him, and not just because I'd fallen in love with him so passionately and intensely as a girl of nineteen. My first love. My only love.

He was the person who inspired me and understood me, my mentor and my saviour.

You look just like him. So much so that when I first saw you in that restaurant, it was like him being brought back to life. It still is sometimes. The re-emergence of you, such a happy event, one I have longed for, has also brought me to the brink of despair. I'm not always sure I'll be able to bear it, this constant reminder of what I lost.

And so I must tell you the truth about your father, write the words that I can never speak. The horrible, ugly truth and my part in it. I will spare nothing.

Your father was Jacob Earl, the lead singer of a rock band

269

called Disciples, set for great things. Their second album had just come out and after he died it went to number one in the charts.

Jake had severe depression, which stemmed from a troubled childhood and pursued him as a young adult. He had good patches when he was happy and creative, and it was during one of those times that we met. He really believed he'd kicked the depression once and for all and so he threw away the medication that was meant to keep him stable, and I allowed him to do it. I didn't understand.

I want you to know how excited your father was about my pregnancy; an accident, it's true, but we both wanted to keep you. He said it was the best thing that had ever happened to him. And it would have been, I know that.

Jake fell into a deep depression while he was on a European tour; by the time he came back he could hardly speak. The day he was due to go into a psychiatric hospital he hanged himself from the bedroom door while I was in the kitchen.

That he died on my watch is something I shall never forgive myself for. Please just know this. He loved unborn you with all his heart. He was the best man imaginable and you are just like him.

Alice

The letter from Alice heralds my breakdown. Letter, photographs and an old newspaper cutting of the two of them at a gallery opening, caption: *Jacob Earl, singer of Disciples, and artist girlfriend Alice Garland at Robin Armstrong Gallery in Mayfair.*

In the photograph you can clearly see the swell of Alice's pregnant stomach, but the thing that derails me is the way these lovers are looking at each other, inflamed by love, at the height of their beauty, on the precipice of success, a snapshot of greatness. I hold Alice's letter in my hands and I weep for the man I never met and the life that was taken away from her, and for things I cannot name. The crying lasts all day and I can't explain it to Hannah, who fusses over me, trying to understand the mix of hopelessness and sorrow that has swept over me; how could she when I cannot comprehend it myself?

It's dark when my mother arrives, summoned by Hannah at some point during the day. She sits beside me on the bed, holding my hand between hers; she calls me 'my poor boy'. Her hands are warm, dry and cracked from gardening; she smells of lavender soap.

'Don't try to talk,' she says when I begin to apologise. 'There's plenty of time for that. And don't feel you need to explain either, because you don't. I understand.'

'Alice ...' I say, and she shushes me.

'It's all right. Hannah told me who she is, and I understand, completely, you wanting to find her. Don't feel bad about not telling me the truth; I understand that too.'

Her kindness is hard to bear, of course, and somewhere beneath the encircling madness I realise that it is guilt that pins me to the bed. Guilt about Christina, guilt about Alice. The man who hurt two mothers, that would be a better title.

Who knew that a mental breakdown would affect the body just as much as the brain? For the all-encompassing dread I feel has given me limbs made of lead, a tight, bronchial chest, palpitations, sweats, dizziness and a surfeit of panic attacks, one after the other, which convince me I am about to die.

An emergency doctor is called out and I weep for the duration of his visit while Hannah and my mother whisper to each other in low-pitched, anxious voices. I am crying for Jacob and Alice, of course, for the destruction of their dream, for the life the three of us were not allowed to have. I am crying for a man who was once so desperate he hanged himself days before his child was born. But I cannot find the words to explain any of this, and the doctor diagnoses burnout and prescribes anti-depressants and a fortnight off work.

After he's gone, Hannah lies down on the bed next to me and holds my hand while I cry.

'You'll feel better as soon as the pills start to work,' she says, and I manage to nod.

'Do you think you might sleep?' she asks, and I close my eyes, feigning tiredness, relieved when she gets up and goes downstairs.

All I want is to get back to Jacob. I cannot explain it, this bizarre communing with my dead father, but it is the only thing that matters, the only thing there is right now.

Alice sent me a photograph of Jacob in school uniform, aged around nine or ten. There is something about this picture that draws me in more than the others; I cannot stop looking at it. He is a handsome boy with his dark eyes and his sharp cheekbones and his full mouth; indisputably like me in this image. When I showed the photograph to my mother, she burst out crying, this woman I cannot once remember crying in my childhood.

'It's you,' she said, when she was able to speak. 'He is you.'

Now when I look at the photo, I absorb his solemnity, an adultness that belies his age. This boy who looks out at me knows more than he should; his life is not bikes and football and chips and chocolate. He looks at me and I look at him and in some bizarre, unexplainable way we are connected by pain; we know each other, we are each other; it is enough.

Then

Alice

He is dead. Not dead when I found him, not exactly, not clinic-
ally, not thoroughly. That happened in the ambulance minutes
later, I am told. But my mind cannot contain this information
and so instead I lie in our bed, curtains drawn against the light,
a covering of his shirts, the arms of them wrapped around me.
Rick is here with me as the hours turn into days, and he doesn't
say anything apart from my name occasionally, a whispered
Alice, because he understands there is nothing to say.

People come and go. Eddie. Tom. Robin. I talk to no one,
Rick deals with it all.

They speak of the funeral, a horrid, pulsing word, but I will
stay here in my frozen state and Rick will know, without me
telling him, that this is all I can do.

He makes me drink water and eat food, tiny doll's size
mouthfuls of bread – 'for the baby,' he says – and though the
child in my belly moves and kicks and seems ready to fight its
way out, I am no longer connected to it.

Rick says, 'Alice, are you going to stay here in this flat? Robin
will cover the rent until you know what you're doing to do,' and
I don't like this conversation because he is forcing change right
in behind my eyelids.

'Stay here,' I say, because although I am thinking of nothing,

273

nothing is my chosen state, somewhere in the hinterland of my consciousness I believe Jake is still away on tour. And I am waiting for him to come back.

Rick runs a bath for me, water just above lukewarm – 'We don't want to boil the baby,' he says, holding me steady while I step into the tub. He picks up the shampoo and massages it into my hair, and when I get out, he holds a towel for me and wraps it around me as if I'm a child. When I am dry, he passes me an old blue dressing gown of Jake's to wear, and it smells so strongly of him, the scent of cedar and ferns and lime, that I am jolted into real, painful tears, as if I am crying for the first time.

We sit together on the brown sofa, Rick's arms around me, and we cry and cry as the light changes in the window.

'What will I do?' I ask him, and he shakes his head.

'Somehow we'll get you through this. We'll take it minute by minute if we need to.'

The baby comes that night. I wake to find the sheets soaked beneath me and I hobble through to the sitting room, where Rick is asleep on the sofa.

'My waters have broken,' I say, and he is fully alert before I've finished the sentence.

Unbeknownst to me, Rick has been studying the baby books and he knows exactly what to do.

'We'll call the hospital and let them know we'll be coming in. But we don't want to go too soon or they'll just send us away again. We need to wait until your contractions are five minutes apart.'

It's almost comical sitting here with Rick, drinking tea in the middle of the night, him timing my contractions on his watch.

'That was a huge one, it lasted thirty seconds. Won't be long now.'

And though the pain is exquisite, I react not at all as each wave breaks over me. This is all I've wanted, for my body to be ripped apart by pain.

The first hurdle at the Elizabeth Garrett Anderson Hospital is that they try to send Rick away.

'Only family members or spouses,' they tell him, and when I begin to cry, he shouts, 'But I'm the baby's father, for God's sake. Doesn't that count for anything?' and I don't know if they believe him or if they are just trying to put a stop to my unending tears, but he is allowed to stay.

The midwives think I am odd, strange, disturbed. The pain crescendos as my cervix dilates and my womb contracts and the muscles around my belly turn into a coating of iron. And I am addicted to it.

'No!' I shout through another contraction, waving away the gas and air, the offers of other medication: pethidine, an epidural. But otherwise I am entirely silent – 'stoical', the midwives tell Rick – just the slide of a solitary tear when I think how Jake will never see this baby.

The final moments of delivery, the overbearing desire to push – not that I want to, just that I have to – and Rick crying out, 'Here's the head. Oh my love, the baby is coming.'

The baby is out, the cord is cut, there is a newborn cry, tiny, tinny, a kitten's mewl.

'It's a boy, Alice,' Rick says, and I don't need to look because I always knew that.

He's first to hold the baby, wrapped up like a package in a perforated white blanket, just a flash of deep pink skin to behold. He walks around the small, hot room gazing down at the bundle nestled in his arms.

'You look like Joseph in the school nativity,' I say, and he laughs, his loud, shouty laugh.

'Here you are.' He places my son on my chest. 'Your turn.'

He unwinds the blanket from the baby's face and we look at him properly for the first time. And right at this moment he opens his eyes and then there is no mistaking him, and I bite my lip, but the tears won't stop coming, and Rick is crying too.

The midwife is back with a clipboard.

'Mother's name Alice Garland, father's name Richard Fields, time of birth six seventeen. Just checking all the details before we send this off.'

I see Rick look at me and I give a tiny, sharp nod.

'Yeah,' he says. 'That's right.'

'And do we have a name for baby yet?'

'Charles Jacob Garland,' I say after a moment's pause, and my voice comes out strong and steady even though I've spoken his name out loud for the first time since he died.

When the midwife has gone, Rick leans over the bed, over the baby, and puts his mouth against my ear.

'Alice Garland, you are a survivor,' he says.

And the thing is, Jake said the exact same words to me once before.

And if he said it, if he believed it, then, I tell myself, it must be true.

Now

Luke

It is not unusual for an adoptee to wait until the wheels have fallen off and the car has crashed catastrophically before he seeks help. This is because an adopted child grows up masking or burying their true feelings; in effect, they lock them up in a safe and throw away the key.

Who Am I? The Adoptee's Hidden Trauma by Joel Harris

There are whole days when I cannot get out of bed. The tasks of showering and brushing my teeth and getting dressed overwhelm me. Sometimes I am paralytically sad, grieving with ceaseless tears that drop down my face for a man I never met. Other times I am subsumed by panic. Not the short, sharp attacks I am used to, two or three minutes of raggedy old-man breathing before the anxiety begins to subside. This is different, a pervasive terror that can last hours at a time. I cannot voice it because mostly I am unable to speak; words have become meaningless and impossible, a language unknown. I feel as if I am slowly losing my hearing, my vision and my mind. If only I could speak, I might break the penetrating quiet that surrounds, engulfs and suffocates. Instead I wait in desperation for Hannah to come and see me, thinking she will understand.

But when she does come, I turn my head away and look at the wall, and after a while she kisses me and goes back downstairs to my mother. I am drowning in ignominy.

The doctor comes back again and this time he prescribes Xanax to be taken regularly throughout the day. These small blue pills bring the first moments of relief, knocking me into a thick, exhausting sleep. I sleep through the day and night, waking for water and sips of soup before plunging back into chemical darkness.

On his third visit, the doctor tries to find out more about my genetical history. My mother is present, which is just as well, for I am unable to speak about Jacob's depression without crying, unable to speak full stop.

'We only have the patchiest details from Alice – Luke's birth mother – about what happened,' Christina says. 'We know that he was a depressive and was prescribed medication, which he stopped taking. It was during an episode that he killed himself.'

'It sounds like he was bipolar – a manic depressive as it was known back then. This kind of depression is often determined by genetics. You say Luke's breakdown has been triggered by finding out about his natural father, but it's also likely that it has been coming for years. Has he had depressive episodes in the past?'

My mother turns to me with so much compassion in her face I have to look away.

'He's very sensitive,' she says. 'He always has been. He takes things to heart, if that's what you mean.'

'The real danger with manic depression is that it can tip over into a state where someone is so full of negative feeling they present a threat to themselves. I think Luke is ill enough to warrant inpatient care. I'd like to organise a place at the Priory Hospital in Roehampton.'

'No, no, no. That is *not* going to happen.' My mother jumps up from her chair, her face lined with anger. 'I am here by his side and I do not intend to leave until he is fully recovered. Luke is not suicidal. He is depressed, and with good reason. There's a difference.'

The doctor nods. 'I thought it wise to point out the risks. Let's keep a close eye on his medication and find him an outpatient appointment as soon as possible.'

Once the doctor has left, my mother returns to her bed-watching post. I'd like to thank her for this outburst of loyalty, I'd like to apologise for not realising how much she loved me. But words are as unstructured as cotton wool and I say nothing.

Next door, Samuel begins to wake up, and my mother smiles at his midday coos, the clucking and trilling that signals not just his alertness but also his sunny, optimistic mood. The baby who loves to laugh.

'Shall I bring him in?' she asks, and I nod.

I'd speak if I could, and I do try moving my tongue around my mouth, but it's as if I have forgotten this most fundamental of skills. She stops at the door and turns around to look at me.

'This is a blip,' she says. 'Brought on by traumatic circumstances. But you are strong and you will get through it.'

'How do you know?' My voice when it comes is thick and rasping, an old man's voice.

There is no doubting the tears in my mother's eyes.

'I know because you are *my* son,' heartbreaking emphasis of the pronoun, 'and you have always got through everything.'

Then

Alice

I suppose my parents would always have found out. They could have rung all the hospitals on a daily basis. Or perhaps the hospital rang them, informing the parents of this young, un-married, seemingly deranged mother, who cries so hard when she feeds her baby, his small, soft head is soaked in tears.

They arrive on the third day of my hospital stay, Charlie asleep in his tiny cot on wheels. I love it when they bring him in from the neonatal unit, wheeling him through for his four-hourly feed.

'Your parents are here at last, lovey,' says Penny, my favour-ite nurse, with her soft Scottish accent and her bleached Norwegian-blonde hair.

My father is wearing a suit and tie, which seems oddly formal for a hospital visit, and my mother too is dressed in a matching skirt and blouse, her rarely worn pearls a note of discordance, a hint of something I cannot comprehend. She is carrying a cellophane-wrapped bunch of carnations – did I never tell her how much I hate those flowers? – and I wave it away.

'On the table, thanks,' I say.

My mother tries to take my hand, but I snatch it away.

'I'm so very sorry,' she says.

'Look at the baby,' I say, gesturing to Charlie in his

see-through cot, asleep with one small fist resting beneath his cheek, lips curved in a rosebud pout.

'Lovely,' says my mother, looking.

'Now, Alice,' says my father, sitting down next to the bed, not looking.

I stare at my beautiful sleeping boy, Jake's boy, and I try to blank out the noise of my father talking.

'We're here to help you. And we forgive you, absolutely. Let's start with a clean slate for all of us. I'm sure you want this baby—'

'Not this baby, *my* baby.'

'Your, er, child, to have the best chance. And so we've asked Mrs Taylor Murphy from the adoption agency to meet us here. Just for a chat, a preliminary chat, you understand, so that you have options.'

'Fuck off. I'm not giving my baby up.'

This time he ignores the swearing (I never used to swear, it's been a surprise for us both), though I see the purple flooding his face, the violence in his gaze.

'But have you thought about how you'll manage without your … er … boyfriend to support you? And as your mother said, we're very sorry about all that. Alice, you'll have nowhere to live and no money. Please be sensible. Don't throw your life away. You could have a summer at home with us to recover and then go back to college in the autumn, and it will be as if none of this ever happened.'

'Get. Him. Out.'

No one reacts. My father sits in his chair, regarding me with his high colour and his popping-out eyes; my mother gazes out of the window with her practised mask of a face. Her life like one long uninterrupted meditation.

Into this scene of joy trips Mrs Taylor Murphy, dressed as if for a garden party, with a voice to match.

'Alice, my dear, what you have been through. I do hope you don't mind me popping in?'

She exclaims at the vision that is my sleeping child – 'Isn't he a beauty?' – and asks my parents if she can have some time alone with me.

'Is that all right with you, Alice?'

'It would be better if they didn't come back at all.'

Despite the floral dress, the perfume – too strong, too sweet now that she is standing next to me – the dark red lips and the patent heels, I like the woman instantly.

The moment my parents have left the ward, she pulls the curtain around my bed.

'Let's have us a bit of privacy,' she says.

She sits in the chair just vacated by my father and observes me with her head tilted fractionally to the side.

'How on earth are you coping? Motherhood and grief all rolled into one, you poor darling.'

I allow her to take my hand while I sob, and she tells me, 'Let it all out now, that's the only way. You'll feel better if you have a good cry.'

She doesn't speak but continues to hold my hand, and I like her for that. What is there to say? What words of comfort can she possibly offer?

After a while, I begin to tell her things.

'He was so excited about the baby,' I say, while Mrs Taylor Murphy nods and listens. 'We used to sit up in bed every night choosing names – Charlie was the one we both liked, for a girl or a boy. We would chat about our future, how we'd manage with my art and his music. How I'd finish my degree. How I'd cope when he was away on tour. We had it all worked out.'

'I'm sure you did.'

'He didn't mean to kill himself. I know he didn't. He just didn't want to go to the hospital. It was an impulse thing. What he wanted was to be there for me and the baby, it was one of the last things he said to me.'

'It's such a tragedy. I cannot imagine what you must be going through.'

'I don't want to give Charlie up. He's all I have left.'

'I can understand you feeling like that. I know I would feel exactly the same. I will tell you something though about babies, Alice. They soak up their environment like a sponge and this acute grief you're experiencing, it's going to affect him. I wonder if you can step outside of your own situation for a moment and imagine these two choices that Charlie has and see which one you think is better. He could grow up with you, his natural mother, who would love him with all her heart and who would struggle and fight, I'm sure, to provide him with a good life. But it would be hard, for you and for him. Hard to find enough work to support yourself. Hard to get back to your career as an artist. Hard to find anywhere decent to live. I think I'm right in saying your parents don't support your choice to keep the baby?'

'My parents are shits.'

'And then,' Mrs Taylor Murphy carries on regardless, 'Charlie could grow up with two parents who are desperate for a child, particularly a little boy, and have plenty of money to give him the best possible education, and a beautiful house in Yorkshire with acres of land and a swimming pool and a tennis court.'

'I don't care about money. It's my child's life we're talking about.'

'Exactly. You do see, Alice, don't you, how different those lives would be for Charlie?'

And the thing is, I do. Her words, her pitch, her bid for my boy: just this, it makes so much sense. I'm not sure I will manage to bring him up on my own. Where would I live? How would I finish my degree? How would I ever support us? I might be able to draw a single-parent allowance, but would it be enough to cover rent, food, clothing, heating, all those things I've never had to think about? I am twenty years old and I don't know where to start.

Penny comes in now and wheels Charlie away for his bath.

'Cup of tea for you, my darling? And one for your visitor?'

And perhaps it is simply because my son is out of sight that when Mrs Taylor Murphy brings out the 'preliminary' adoption papers for me to look at – so much emphasis on that word today – I say, 'Just tell me where I have to sign.'

I don't see my parents again, although I am sure Mrs Taylor Murphy will have imparted the good news, the impending handing-over of my son.

Just before she leaves, she asks why I put Rick's name down on the hospital certificate instead of Jacob's.

'The nurses only allowed him to stay with me because he said he was the father.'

'You know what, Alice? Maybe it's a good thing. Maybe in the future, when your child wants to contact you, he'll find two parents ready to meet him instead of one.'

And she gives me that little fantasy to hold onto, the prospect of meeting my child again once he's an adult.

In our last days together, the nurses, aware that I'm having Charlie adopted, ration the time I spend with him.

'Don't let her get too attached,' I hear one of them telling Penny, who smuggles him in outside of feeding time. 'It will only make it harder when she has to say goodbye.'

Goodbye. How is that even possible? I have an acute pain

in my heart, physical, like the gouging of a javelin, every time I contemplate it. During the night-time feed, three o'clock on the dot, I am left alone with him in the darkness. And I whisper my secrets to him, filling his tiny ears with hopes and dreams as the stars stud the sky outside our hospital window.

'You'll be like your father. You'll be tall and handsome and funny and brave. You'll be musical. Artistic. I will love you all the way through your childhood. And when you're eighteen, we will find each other again.'

On our last day – Mrs Taylor Murphy is due to arrive at ten the next morning, to take Charlie off to his foster parents – Rick comes to visit.

'Tea and biscuits, Richard?' asks Penny, who loves Rick and always gives him extra custard creams.

'You're a wonder woman,' Rick says. 'And do you think we could have a few minutes undisturbed? Just want to make sure Alice is all right about tomorrow.'

'Leave it to me,' says Penny, pulling the curtains around the bed.

For a moment we just look at each other, no need for words.

'Don't bully me, Rick.'

'He looks like Jake even now at a few days old. Imagine how much he will look like him when he's older: twelve, eighteen, twenty. And you won't be there to see that happen. How can you bear it?'

'I don't have a choice. Not if I want what is best for him. And I do want that, more than you could ever imagine. Where would I live? In your squat?'

Rick shakes his head. He grins, then grabs hold of my hand and kisses it.

'The thing is,' he says, 'I've just had the most genius idea.'

Now

Luke

Adoption is one of the last great taboos. No one talks about the fact that the adopted child might carry their relinquishment wound into adult life. It's like a conspiracy, everyone contriving to present a united view. Adoption is a good thing, a fantastic thing. How could you possibly think anything else?

Who Am I? The Adoptee's Hidden Trauma by Joel Harris

If you're going to go nuts, you may as well do it in the company of Kate Moss and Robbie Williams. I'm to be treated as an outpatient at the Priory, infamous rehabilitation centre to burnt-out celebrities but also home to some of the best psychotherapists in town.

I am in my mother's car, with all its checkpoints of familiarity: the flower dangling from the mirror, once a tasteful air freshener now a defunct piece of cardboard; the folded rug on the back seat; the tin of sweets on the shelf beneath the glove compartment. Samuel is in the back, asleep in his car seat, one fist closed around his squinting old bear, a needle of pain each time I see it.

A moment of misgiving when my mother drops me off in

front of this palatial white building (turrets, arches and Doric columns for the celebrity breakdown). She offered to come in with me, but that meant bringing Samuel too, and somehow I couldn't bear the thought of it.

'Good luck, darling,' she calls as I get out of the car, as if I'm going for a job interview or about to sit my physics GCSE.

The first thing I notice as I am taken on a tour of the facilities – ping-pong tables and instant coffee, just like a sixth-form common room – is the friendliness of all the other patients. On every turn there's another unasked-for greeting, 'Hi there,' a smiling face, an infrared beam of reassurance, the unified, silent message: 'Come let us help you over the start line.' It's a bit like joining the Moonies, I'd imagine.

My first session of the day is group therapy, the terminology alone enough to trigger queasiness in days gone by. But I am too tired, too forlorn, to bother with cynicism.

Our group of eight, seated in a semicircle of comfortable chairs, is led by Marion, who introduces me – 'Everyone, this is Luke' – to resounding support. It is too much to respond; their kindness, their congeniality, coupled with the reality of my being here, brings me to tears. I nod my greeting instead and they seem to understand.

'Before we get started,' Marion says, 'I thought it might be useful to tell Luke what we gain from these group sessions. How helpful the act of talking can be.'

A dark-haired girl around my own age says, 'The brilliant thing about group therapy is that you bring your fears and anxieties into the open and you find out that other people feel exactly the same way. And that makes them less frightening. It makes you feel less alone.'

The session gets under way and I tune in and out while those around me speak of mortification and self-sabotage with the same insouciance I once reserved for planning our Sainsbury's shop. There's a tea break halfway through and I am besieged with new friends. Don't get me wrong, I appreciate their efforts to make me feel at home, but it makes me want to cry. Everyone is so goddamn tactful. No one asks me why I'm here; they know through experience how to steer a safe conversation. Dark-haired girl tells me she has the same pair of Reebok trainers as mine at home, only hers are the grey version. A woman called Kate jokes that the instant coffee is a brilliant way to break a Starbucks habit: 'We'll save ourselves a fortune when we get out of here.'

After the break, Marion asks me if I feel ready to share a detail about myself with the group.

'Don't feel you need to tell us why you're here just yet. We would love to learn even one thing about you.'

'I don't much like being looked at,' I say, scorching in the intensified heat of eight pairs of eyes.

'Very few people do,' says Marion. 'But in these sessions the first rule is to assume support. When we look at you, we're supporting you.'

The dark-haired girl, whose name I discover is Lisa, says, 'My first day I started with a list of things I liked. I could only find one and it was dark chocolate.'

'Music,' I say. 'My job is in music. I listen to it all day. Sometimes I think I can only express my feelings through other people's music. Like I can only connect to emotions other people have had first.'

'That's interesting,' Marion says. 'What kind of music do you like?'

'David Bowie. The Rolling Stones. The Doors. The seventies is my era, I don't know why. Bob Dylan. Led Zeppelin. The Who.'

Pink Floyd are my undoing. I remember Alice telling me how she'd been to see them on their *Dark Side of the Moon* tour. I realise that Jacob must have been with her, and I am flattened by a vision of the two of them in their cheesecloth and flares, high on beer and marijuana and the saturation of new love.

Here's a thing I didn't know about group work. If you wobble, no one jumps up to comfort you, no one says a thing. They want you to have your moment, and how quickly we have come to mine.

'My father was a musician.' I gasp it out. 'My real father. He killed himself a few days before I was born.'

Crying without consolation, a new experience for me. The rest of the group observe me quietly, without interruption; even Marion takes her time to speak.

'You must wish you'd known him.'

'I wish that more than anything. I have this sense he was like me and he would have understood me. Because I'm adopted and I feel ...'

A pause while I struggle to say the words that make sense of my entire life.

'I feel that I've never fitted in anywhere.'

Then

Alice

I am always left alone during the 3 a.m. feed. This is Charlie's hungriest time; he'll suckle for forty-five minutes, first one breast, then the other. The nurses tried him on a bottle the moment I'd signed the adoption papers, despite my protests, but he wouldn't take it.

'Here's your crosspatch,' says the night nurse, lowering a screaming Charlie into my arms. 'I'll leave you two in peace.'

I detect the pity in her voice. Everyone knows that later on this morning is our big goodbye.

The moment she has gone, I manoeuvre myself out of the bed, one arm held beneath Charlie as he continues to feed. The slightest disturbance and he'll yell out his fury and wake the whole ward. I'm barefoot, according to the plan, and dressed only in a nightdress, but I do swaddle him in the green cashmere shawl Rick brought for me.

In the darkness, at first glance, the baby is obscured. I'm just a girl finding her way to the bathroom in the middle of the night. I stand behind the curtain for a moment, gathering my strength, while my heart slams against my ribs and Charlie continues to suck in his emerald cocoon.

There are five other beds in this ward, all with their curtains drawn around them, and I force myself to walk slowly in what

I hope is a soothing, rocking motion for the baby. Through the swing doors, pause, allow myself to experience the nauseating surge of pure fear. To my left, just metres away, is the reception desk, where two nurses are talking. They are facing the opposite direction, but just a 180-degree swivel of one of their heads and I would be spotted. To my right, a corridor with wards on either side, and at the far end a door that leads to the staircase where Rick is waiting. I continue with my stealth-like walking, the mild squeak of flesh on linoleum, the baby sucking, my breast slowly emptying.

I am almost there, the door in sight, when a nurse comes out of the last ward, wheeling a cot in front of her.

'Where are you going?'

'To the bathroom, bad stomach.'

There is, mercifully, a bathroom a few feet away, and I slam open the door with my free hand. Inside, leaning back against the door, panting with fear, I somehow manage to dislodge the baby, and he yells out in protest. Forcing my nipple back into his mouth, stifling him mid-yell, praying that he will latch on straight away. The desperate thud of my heart. Did the nurse hear his cry? I am too frightened to open the door to find out. I wait, trying to steady myself with long, deep breaths, and each second that passes is interminable. There is so little time; I have to get this right. I count to ten and force myself to ease the door open, inch by inch, each squeak like a gunshot. No one there. Across the corridor, running now, heart squeezing painfully, through the door to Rick waiting on the other side, his frozen, fearful face a match for mine.

He wipes his forehead to mime relief and takes my free arm to help me down the staircase, one step at a time. We mustn't rush, we cannot risk jolting the baby again. Three flights of stairs, our progress painfully slow. And at the bottom, more terror as we open the door to the ground floor with no idea of what or who we will find. But at 3.30 in the morning the hospital is dead, and no one sees us escape through a back door into the night air. We are unchallenged, Rick wandering around a hospital where he has no right to be, me an undischarged patient, and the tiny package in my arms a baby with a new adoptive mother to meet tomorrow.

Charlie has fallen off my breast now, but he seems quite content as I hoist him up over my shoulder, rubbing his back in soothing circles the way Penny taught me on the first day. I hear his sweet little belch against my ear – such a small, small thing, but it makes me cry, tears that drip down my face. To think I might have missed this.

'Almost there, my love,' Rick says, pulling a key from his jeans pocket as we approach the car park. 'Check out our wheels, if you please.'

A dove-grey Morris Minor with red leather seats and chrome wing mirrors that beam out in the darkness.

'It's perfect. Where did you get it from?'

'Robin gave me the cash. I bought it this afternoon.'

'Robin knows?'

'Only that we're leaving, not where we're going. No one knows that.'

'Not even Tom?'

He grimaces. 'Definitely not Tom. We are no more. We both lost heart after … after what happened. And don't look at me like that. Tom is the least of our problems.'

Charlie and I get into the back seat, and the moment the car pulls away he falls asleep. I press my lips against his head, inhaling his smell, just the lightest touch so as not to wake him.

'I didn't know you could drive,' I say.

'Of course I can. Just haven't got around to taking my test yet.'

We lock eyes in the rear-view mirror, allowing our smiles to grow.

'Richard Fields, I love you,' I say, and he blows me a kiss.

'Same here, Alice Garland.'

We arrive at the beach at sunrise, as if we'd timed it so that our new beginning would be filled with pink and orange and stripes of gold. Charlie wakes the moment the car stops, but instead of wailing for food, he gazes up at me with Jacob's eyes.

'Let's sit on the beach for a while,' Rick says, and he takes Charlie from me, still wrapped in his green blanket, and passes me his jacket to wear over my nightgown. We arrived at this beach as the sun rose once before, Jake, me, Rick and Tom. The sorrow is acute as we walk down to the water's edge, the crunch of sand beneath my feet, the salty air whipping my face, and I understand that it always will be. But I also know we'll be all right. One day. Some day.

I reach for Rick's hand and we stand together, the three of us, with the heat of the new sun on our faces.

Now

Luke

> The real architect of the brain is experience. And if you are abandoned by your mother at birth, your first experience is a sense of danger. Fear of the unknown can become truly terrifying to the adult adoptee.
>
> *Who Am I? The Adoptee's Hidden Trauma* by Joel Harris

Joel Harris has become something of an expert on adoptee trauma; he has even written a report on it. An addiction counsellor for almost thirty years, he explains he gradually became aware that adoptees were overrepresented in his clinics.

In the following decades of research, both practical and theoretical, he realised that the trauma of adoption – or 'the relinquishment wound', as he calls it – is stored within the body. Adoptees, he says, are born with a trauma personality.

'It's quite common for an adoptee to have a fear of abandonment – for obvious reasons – but coupled with the contradictory hunger to attach. And that abandonment feels life-threatening – is there any bigger trauma than being separated from your mother, the one person you needed at the beginning of your life? I don't think so.'

I cry openly through these one-to-one sessions, partly with

sorrow but also relief. For the first time in my life, my fucked-up-ness is beginning to make sense.

Joel explains about the trio of grief that marked my beginning. Mine at being separated from Alice, Alice's at losing her child and Christina's at her failure to have a baby of her own.

'You begin life,' Joel tells me, 'with an impossible job description. From the word go you have to be a son to parents you don't fit with genetically and you are there to fix an enormous grief in them at not being able to have children. As an only child, the onus is entirely on you to make things better.'

'My mother admitted yesterday that she's never really got over losing her baby,' I say. 'He was stillborn in her final month of pregnancy and I now think she was battling depression right through my childhood. And that made me feel guilty. I knew, without her telling me, that she was mourning her dead baby. But to me it felt like I was a constant disappointment because I wasn't him.'

'Do you think you would have felt different if you'd grown up with Alice? And Jacob?'

Jacob, this man I never knew; just the mention of his name triggers instant painful tears.

'I don't even know why I'm crying. Jacob died before I was born.'

'Is it possible to feel grief for someone you have never known? Absolutely. You are grieving for a man you believe would have made a perfect father and a woman who wanted very much to be your mother.'

'I'm poleaxed by sadness, but I didn't even know of Alice's existence until a few months ago.'

'That's part of it. Adoption is based on secrets and silence and nobody talks about how they're feeling. How ridiculous is it that you spend your entire childhood without knowing who your real parents are and not feeling that you can ever ask? And without having the facts, you start to believe you must be flawed, because why else would someone have given you away? Sound familiar?'

'As if you're looking inside my head.'

Joel laughs. 'You'd be surprised how many people say that to me. The problem is that everyone from the adoptive parents to the birth parents to the social workers bands together to protect the myth that it's a great thing. "You were so lucky to be adopted," how many times were you told that? I bet your parents said they "chose" you, didn't they?'

'My mother told me she'd gone to a hospital ward full of babies and picked me out because of my spiky black hair and my dark eyes.'

'But you know that couldn't possibly be true, don't you? There's no ward full of babies ready for adoption, like a supermarket pick 'n' mix. It's not a litter of puppies we're talking about.'

'And anyway, Alice managed to keep me for the first few weeks of my life.'

'Did she tell you what you were like?'

'Happy, always smiling. I never cried, apparently.'

'And when you arrived in your new home, what were you like then?'

'I cried day and night for the first three weeks. My mother thought it was colic.'

'I listen to a story like yours every week and it amazes me that this great conspiracy still exists. Why don't people understand the trauma of relinquishment? That pain you felt as a baby is still there, Luke. It's locked away inside you.'

I've been crying almost without noticing for the last ten minutes. Now I press a tissue against my face, holding it there with the palms of my hands. Inside me there is a shaft of such intense sadness my heart is actually hurting.

Our time is probably up, but Joel lets the silence run on; he waits until I take the tissue away from my face. We gaze at each other while I try to find the right words.

'Will I ever feel better?'

'I think so. You're already beginning to understand the reasons why you feel the way you do. That helps, doesn't it? With therapy you can learn to manage the trauma so you spot it the moment it walks through the door rather than waiting for it to knock you down.'

Most days my mother picks me up from the Priory, waiting in the car park in her navy-blue Golf, with my small son and his ragged bear strapped into the back. Samuel always smiles as soon as he sees me. He has mastered his version of a wave, one hand flung out in recognition, accompanied by a whoop of delight.

Sometimes I get into the back beside him. I kiss his face, his tight, smooth cheeks, his unfeasibly long eyelashes. My mother likes to brush his hair into a 1950s sweep-over. Hannah jokes that he looks like Laurel from Laurel and Hardy.

'Hello, Laurel,' I whisper as Christina starts the car and pulls away.

And Samuel laughs and claps his hands, his latest trick, waiting for me to do the same.

Then

Alice

The hundred pounds I earned for designing the Disciples album cover, the advance from my show at Robin's gallery, means that Rick and I can survive the first few months of parenting.

Stick it in the bank or something, you might need it someday. How long ago was it that Jake spoke those words, as if he had seen the future, could picture me alone?

For the moment, a few months at least, there is a kind of freedom in this tiny seaside cottage of ours. The place belongs to Rick's elderly great-aunt, who has been on the brink of death many times but is proving, at eighty-nine, to be a survivor. We're glad of this, of course, but the situation sheds uncertainty over our future. The minute she dies, the house will be sold, its profits split between her nephews and nieces.

Now, though, Rick and I have it to ourselves, a pale-blue two-up, two-down in which to learn the roles of mother and father. Every day Rick surprises me with his aptitude for fathering, although why wouldn't he make a good parent, with his unfaltering good humour and his huge, all-encompassing heart? It is because of Rick, I am sure, that Charlie begins to smile at a few weeks old. How could he fail to mirror back that daily injection of warmth?

Without saying anything, Rick also gives me the space to

grieve, acres of it when I need it, constant companionship when I don't. From the moment we arrived here in Southwold, I made a decision to hide my pain, to let it out only in private, at night when the rest of the world was asleep, or on my solitary walks along the beach. It was partly Mrs Taylor Murphy's words about babies soaking up their environment 'like a sponge' and my determination that my son would not have his beginning marked by sadness, but also my need to find some light for myself. Just glimmers of it, just sometimes.

Midnight is my crying hour, and I look forward to the relief of being able to let out my grief and rage and guilt. I'll hold Jake's shirt to my face and inhale the scent of him, getting fainter each day, and I'll whisper into the blackness, 'I'm sorry, I'm so sorry,' until I eventually become so exhausted I know I can fall asleep.

One night as I'm crouched weeping in the corner of the bedroom, the door opens and the room floods with light from the corridor.

'Alice.' Rick kneels beside me, taking hold of both my hands. 'Why didn't you wake me?'

And I tell him the thought that always comes at this hour.

'It was my fault.'

'I wondered when we'd come to that.'

'Don't bother telling me it's not. I was there, I could have stopped it. I should have stayed with him.'

'Suicide is never anyone else's fault. How can it be? You might have prevented it. This time. But in the lifetime of someone with manic depression who had already tried to kill himself once? I'm not so sure.'

'We'd have had more time. He would have met Charlie.'

'And he would have been the most brilliant father. It's so unfair.'

'How can I carry on, Rick?'

'You just have to, my love. Because you've got Charlie. And Charlie will always be a part of Jake. Do you know what I was really worried about? When you were having him adopted, I thought you'd have nothing to live for.'

That night Rick sleeps in the double bed with me, the baby sandwiched between us, holding my hand across his tiny back until I fall asleep.

And in the morning, when I wake to strong sunshine arcing in through the fine linen, the smell of coffee being brewed downstairs, the prospect of another day spent with my child, there is a kind of peace.

After a couple of weeks, I write a letter to my parents and Mrs Taylor Murphy, which Rick posts to Robin in London to avoid our secret location being exposed. I tell them I'm sorry, that I couldn't separate from my son in the end. Babies are happiest with their natural parents, I say.

And it does seem to be true. Charlie has the sunniest of natures. Fed on demand instead of the cruelty of the regimented four-hour wait – how I hated hearing him cry just along the corridor; I could always pick him out from the other babies – he is content to lie in my arms gazing up at me for most of the day.

Rick gives him his first toy, an old-fashioned bear with eyes of amber glass, and he curls his tiny fist around its leg, holding fast. The bear goes everywhere with us: to the beach; to the cannons, where we picnic most days; on our daily pilgrimage to the shops in the high street.

I learn how to make clothes, sewing them by hand, first for Charlie and then for myself. I buy fabric from the brightly coloured bolts in the haberdashery shop on the high street and fashion dungarees and shorts and tops of orange, red and yellow.

Sunshine colours for my boy. I make purple bell-bottoms for myself with flower badges stitched all the way along the outside seam, and when he sees them, Rick says, 'You know, I think you could sell these.'

We begin thinking of ways to make money. We drive to an art shop in Norwich and buy an easel, oil paints, sketchpads and canvases for Rick. He's trying his hand at seascapes to sell to the local galleries, and being Rick, they are wonderful. But I can tell his heart is not in it. I try not to think about what he has given up for me and Charlie, his place at the Slade, his career at the Robin Armstrong Gallery. But it's there all the time, a pulsing, low-level guilt.

In high summer, Southwold is transformed with crowds of holidaymakers, the beach segmented by windbreaks, a huge, colourful British mess, particularly when viewed from the pier, where Charlie and I love to go. There is a hall of mirrors right in the middle, and it is here that I first hear Charlie laugh. Every day I take him out of his pram and hold him up in front of each mirror in turn so that our bodies transmute: wide and short, tall and thin with elongated legs, or tiny as Lilliputians. I smile at him in each mirror and he always smiles back, ready to embrace the joke, and then, at eleven weeks, he laughs. Can I have heard properly? I make crazy faces at him in the mirror and he laughs again, louder this time, half gurgle, half belly laugh, a pure, sweet sound. Oh my beautiful boy. In this moment I am utterly happy.

I buy a tiny blow-up boat with a perfect baby-sized space in its centre. The first time I take Charlie swimming, he lies back and stares up at a sequence of flitting, Raphael-shaped clouds. He smiles, absorbed in his sky-gazing, and I tell him, 'You are your father's son.' I look up too, memorising the exact colours, and I think that soon I will be ready to paint again, and when

I am, I will make huge sky pictures, in remembrance of my lost love.

In the evenings, Rick cooks supper for us. He has perfected the spaghetti vongole I craved from Florence, buying clams straight off the boats in the harbour and cooking the pasta to al dente perfection. Sometimes we share a bottle of wine, but most often we sit in front of the second-hand black and white television set we bought, laughing at the simple humour of *Dad's Army*, *Are you Being Served?* and *Man About the House*. We sit on the sofa holding hands while our baby sleeps in his carrycot, and we joke that we are man and wife, just without the sex.

'We'll always have each other,' Rick tells me when Charlie and I go up to bed. He says it every day, almost every hour, my dear, darling friend, as if by repeating it often enough he can simply erase my grief.

Now

Luke

My mother and I are in the kitchen preparing supper when Hannah walks in and delivers her bombshell.

'I resigned from my job today.'

'Oh Hannah, are you sure that's what you want?' asks my mother with surprising tact (she is learning; we all are).

'I've never been surer of anything. This whole situation with Alice has made me realise how I feel deep down about leaving Samuel each day. And, actually, I hate it. I feel sick with guilt and ashamed that I've been putting myself and my career first. And missing out on the chance to be with my son.'

'But you're doing so well,' I say. 'And you love your job.'

'It's not for ever. Just till Samuel goes to school. And the paper is being fantastic. Mark has promised me a freelance piece every week. I'm still keeping my job title. I'll make all my phone calls when Samuel is asleep and write in the evenings.'

'Well, if you're sure, then I'm very glad,' my mother says. 'I hope you'll let me supplement your income. And any time you need babysitting, you just have to ask. Samuel and I are used to each other now.'

We have come so far in two weeks, my mother, Hannah and I. Christina has helped me through this terrifying breakdown pretty much single-handedly, sitting by my side during the worst days and driving me to my appointments at the Priory. I feel closer to her now than at any time in my childhood. I am proud of the way she cares for Samuel, ashamed that I once considered her old-fashioned and out of touch.

Hannah walks up to her and puts her arms around her, unthinkable not so long ago.

'Christina, you have been a lifesaver,' she says. 'And we are so lucky to have you.'

Two things of note happen in my first week back at work.

On day one, Michael sends me the usual terse summons: 'Can you pop in for a minute?' and, as always, I arrive in his glass-walled office pumped with dread and expectation.

'Sit down, Luke.' He gestures to a chair. 'Tell me how you are. What's been going on?'

'Everything just got on top of me, I guess. It's hard to explain. Things at home, things at work. The doctor said I was emotionally exhausted, and that's how it feels.'

'I can understand that. I've sometimes struggled with the pressure myself. I'm no stranger to the therapist's chair.'

He laughs at my shocked expression.

'Yep, even a tough old bastard like me. Well, you'll be glad to hear I've had excellent feedback from Reborn. They are this close ...' he pinches his thumb and forefinger into a minute gap, 'to signing to us. I've promised them you will put together an A&R pitch to seal the deal. Spend this week getting your ideas sorted and we'll present it to them next week.'

Tuesday, Wednesday and Thursday pass in an enjoyable haze of research. I'm listening to seventies Bowie, Chic and James Brown, trying to unpick the production, listening for sounds that will work in a revitalised noughties interpretation. *The Dark Side of the Moon* (with an accompanying jab of regret) lives on the turntable, Bob Dylan and The Rolling Stones too. This is the part of my job I love the most.

On Friday, just as the rest of the office is decamping to the pub for the weekly piss-up, a courier arrives with a square cardboard package for me. Nothing unusual in that; we're a record company, we get sent vinyl every day of the week. There's something about the writing on the front, though, that makes me look at the envelope for a long time. It's familiar, I know that, and my heart is aching even before I've opened it up to pull out a card and an old album from the seventies. The album is called *Apparition*; it went to number one in the charts when my father died. I've done my research, I know the facts.

Nothing could have prepared me for the picture of my two young, beautiful parents on the cover of this album. An oil painting shows a teenage Alice cradling the head of her lover in her lap. He's asleep, or at least faking it, eyes closed, lips slightly parted, his long dark hair flopping over the side of her knees. She is leaning against a terracotta wall and wearing a forest-green dress with thin straps, one falling from her shoulder. Bold, jump-out colours, it's a stunning sleeve. But it's Alice I can't take my eyes off. She's not smiling in this portrait; instead she looks out in utter contentment, her smooth, almost babyish face lit up by an internal joy.

I open Rick's card with hands that shake.

I am so very sorry at the way things have played out between you and Alice. And I hope with all my heart that you'll be able to fix it. In the meantime, this album belongs to you.

I extract the album carefully from its cover. I walk over to the record player and place it on the turntable with the exactitude, the reverence, of a high priest.

I sit, leaning against the office wall, with the album cover face up in my lap. I force myself to look at those lovers and to listen to Jacob's voice, my father's voice, and I tell myself as my heart breaks all over again that this is what I owe them at the very least.

Then
Alice

Jacob's birthday at the tail end of August is my hardest challenge yet. I'm determined not to cry in front of Rick or Charlie, and I've kept quiet about the date even though I've thought of nothing else for the past week.

This time last year we were in Italy. I got up early and walked into Fiesole to buy croissants and cappuccinos from our favourite café and brought them back home. I undressed again in the darkness, the room still blacked out by its heavy velvet drapes, and got back into bed and covered Jake's naked body with my own. I lay exactly on top of him, groin to groin, shifting from side to side, my breasts pressed against his chest, my mouth brushing his chin, his cheeks, his closed eyes. By the time he was fully awake he was inside me, exactly as I'd planned. He opened his eyes and said, 'Christ, you're amazing,' and the memory of this lovemaking fills me with a grief so raw and insistent I cry out.

When I go downstairs to make breakfast for Charlie, Rick is already up, a pot of coffee on the stove.

'Good morning, my love,' he says, and I can tell instantly from the way he says it that he knows.

And then I do start crying, even though I have tried so hard not to, and Rick comes over and puts his arms around me.

'Oh Alice,' he says. 'I cannot bear it for you.'

'I just want today to be over.'

'It's still a special day. We'll find a way to mark it.'

It's beautifully warm, this August day, and we take a picnic to the beach and sit beneath the sun with all the other summer tourists. Families with foil wrappers full of sandwiches, packets of crisps and flasks of squash. Beside us a little girl is solemnly eating a Jaffa Cake while her father rubs suncream into her shoulders. A few feet in front, a man is building a sand car for his toddler; an empty Ski yoghurt pot marks the steering wheel. Jake loved Ski yoghurt; he could eat two or three pots at a time, and I turn away, scorched.

Charlie dozes in the shade of the buggy while Rick and I eat our sandwiches, and after lunch, Rick begins sketching, zoning in on a couple sitting close to the water's edge. I watch over his shoulder as he exaggerates the woman's roundness, her husband's angularity, all elbows and shoulder blades cuddling his mountain of flesh.

'You're mean,' I say, and he laughs.

'This is for me, not them. Why don't you go for a swim while the baby's asleep?'

I miss my chance, sitting beside Rick, watching him finish his sketch. Charlie opens his eyes at the exact moment I'm looking at him. Instantly he's smiling. There you are, his smile says.

'Come on, then,' I say, picking him up. 'Let's take your little boat out.'

The water, the warmest it has been all summer, soothes me. I wade out to my waist, pushing Charlie in front of me, and he gazes up at the cloudless sky and I try to think that somehow, somewhere his father can see him. For me, the sea is magical; the water soaks up my pain, and soon I am swimming, kicking my legs behind me, arms outstretched as if I am holding a float.

When I look back, Rick is just a tiny dot on a blue and white blanket. I could do this forever, the physicality so absorbing that for a while I am able to think of nothing; it's just me and my child and the motion of my legs through the water.

It's only when Charlie begins to wail that I realise how far I've travelled. I turn the boat around and swim back to shore, kicking as hard as I can, but each cry of Charlie's cuts through me.

Rick is waiting for us at the edge of the water, squinting through the sun.

'For God's sake, Alice. You were ages. How can you be so selfish? You shouldn't take him out there for so long.'

It is the first time he has ever shouted at me, and my anger fires in response.

'He's my baby, not yours,' I say, hurting him in the only way I know how. 'And he's fine. Here, you take him.'

I storm up the beach, intoxicated by rage, by anger. I walk all the way up to the cannons, where we have picnicked with Charlie so many times, and pace around them in tight circles, sobbing, sobbing. I want to hurt someone; maybe just myself. I feel like smashing my fist into the black iron barrels until my knuckles splinter and my flesh rips.

'I can't do this any more,' I scream to the ancient guns.

I don't notice a woman sitting on a bench close by until she calls out to me, 'What's wrong, my dear?'

'My boyfriend is dead,' I tell her. 'He died. He's dead. And I need him. I need him so badly.'

And I cry and cry and this old lady, whose name I will never know, tells me to sit with her on the bench, and she holds my hand and says over and over again, 'You poor thing. You poor little thing.' She tells me to keep on crying; she says, 'Tears help,' and perhaps she is right, because when I finally stop,

I feel exhausted but the pain is almost gone, it's muted and distant, and I know I can last for one more day.

Back in the cottage, Rick says, 'Alice, I am so sorry,' as soon as I walk through the door.

'No, *I'm* sorry. I didn't mean it.'

'There's tea in the pot,' he says, pointing at the table, and neither of us mentions my swollen eyes.

After supper, Rick takes a bottle of wine from the fridge. Vivid green glass, extended swanlike neck. He flashes the label at me.

'Muscadet,' I say, though what I really mean is: how could you? How could you remind me of that perfect weekend, you, me, Jake and Tom eating mussels and playing cards and drinking this wine as if our lives would continue to infinity?

'Sometimes we need to remember,' he says.

We wrap Charlie up in a sweater and coat and hat and take the wine down to the beach. It's dark now, and we sit beneath the charcoal sky watching the stars come out, checking off our favourite constellations one by one. We don't mention Cassiopeia, but he sees it and I see it and I think that he was right to make me come here, drinking the same wine and watching the same stars of a year ago, linked together in the universe at least.

After a while, he says, 'Do you know why some stars are brighter than others?'

And I shake my head, although I do know, because Jake told me.

'It's because they're burning up hydrogen at a much faster rate. They last half as long as all the other stars. Live fast, die young. To be fair, we're talking millions of years rather than billions.'

'Nice try. But it doesn't help.'

'I think it does. You lived so intensely, you two. You experienced more love and passion than most of us find in a lifetime.'

I don't say anything, because I can't, but I do hold Rick's hand, I do drop a kiss on my sleeping baby's head.

'I can't bring him back for you, Alice. I wish more than anything that I could. But you will always have me.'

Now

Luke

In my experience, adoptee and birth parent reunions go wrong more often than they go right. Sometimes catastrophically.

Who Am I? The Adoptee's Hidden Trauma by Joel Harris

My mother is installed for her fourth and final week of childcare, and I have to admit she's pretty good at it. She has somehow managed to get Samuel sleeping in his cot at night, and here's the thing – both Hannah and I love it.

'The freedom,' she'll say, unbuttoning her pyjama top while I watch from the bed.

'Exactly,' I'll agree as she leaps on top of me, covering my naked body with her own.

My mother has also got Samuel to wake later each morning – seven instead of six – by bolstering his diet (how many mashed bananas can one boy eat?) and by putting him to bed an hour later each night, which means we have more time with him. We will miss her when she goes.

On Friday, once the paper has been put to bed, there's a leaving party for Hannah at Le Pont de la Tour. Champagne and lobster for the whole of the Culture team, subs included. She'll come back slightly pissed and tearful and I intend to wait up for her, to soothe away any regrets about leaving. With Reborn poised to sign to us – a big meeting this morning should clinch it – I'm glad it's her giving up work rather than me, but I do feel guilty about it. I offered to cut back on my days, but Hannah refused, as I knew she would. She understands how vital work is for my self-esteem. Music defines me, it gives me my identity, and without it I'd be lost.

'Good luck,' she says, kissing me goodbye at the door. 'I know you'll nail it.'

She looks irresistible in her black Joseph trouser suit and boots, her curly hair tamed temporarily, an unaccustomed stripe of lipstick on her lovely mouth.

'Hannah?' I say, and she turns around, door half open, light from the street pouring in.

'You're amazing,' I say, and she laughs.

'You're a sentimental fool, and that's what I like about you.'

I dress carefully for the meeting with Reborn in my dark-grey Kenzo suit with a white T-shirt and my Reeboks. I know Michael will be in a suit instead of his jeans, a ploy he uses both to impress and to disarm; I'll do the same. My mother is in the kitchen with Samuel, preparing our supper while he sits beside her on the floor banging a saucepan with a wooden spoon. It's been nice seeing the calm, unhurried way in which she parents a small child, so I can imagine myself at the same age. Always there's the piercing that is Alice, the painful recall of her brilliance with our boy, but I tell myself it was complicated. It's not over, just on ice, a fraught mother–son relationship that can be rebuilt at any time. And this is how I sleep at night.

The band arrive early, and they've dressed up for the occasion too, the boys in shirts, the girls in dresses. Steven Harris – thank you, God, spirit being or whoever you are – is away on business in LA. There are handshakes all round, no kisses or hugs, which underlines the sombreness of this meeting. But Michael is not the CEO of the biggest independent in the music business for nothing.

'Great to have you here,' he says, a small Mafioso figure in his black suit and shirt. 'There's breakfast in the meeting room; let's get straight to it, shall we? And Janice?' he adds to the receptionist as we pass. 'Categorically no interruptions for the next two hours. Just take messages for us, please.'

The table is crammed with plates of croissants, pains au chocolat and Danish pastries. There's a platter of beautifully chopped fruit: pineapples, peaches, a volcano of berries in its centre. None of this will be touched. Instead I pour everyone a coffee from the cafetière – pleased that my hands do not shake – and we begin.

I've been in this situation with Michael several times and I know that he doesn't do small talk. He has zero tolerance for conversations about anything other than music.

'I can't tell you how glad we are that you are seriously considering signing to Spirit,' he says. 'You'll know, of course, how passionate Luke is about your music, but the whole company, from distribution to the art department, is excited about your record. I know the decision will come down to money in the end and I wanted to assure you that we can come up with a significant deal.'

'If I can jump straight in,' Daniel says, 'we've come to a decision.'

This is unexpected. My physiological response – heart banging, blood rushing – almost deafens me. I am straining to hear.

'We're going to sign to Spirit. We're flattered by the interest from other labels, but you're the best fit for us. We have a few conditions, though, and I'd like to set those out.'

My pulse is heart-attack fast as I listen to the band's require-ments – all of them reasonable – but I don't really get beyond the first one.

'We'd like Luke to A&R the record exclusively. We really feel he connects with what we're doing in a way no one else has; in fact that's the whole reason we want to sign to you.'

I catch Michael's eye and he smiles at me, minimally; he always was the master of understatement. But I can't help myself. I jump up from the table and start hugging the band, one by one.

'This is incredible news,' I say. 'There is literally nothing I would like more than to get involved with the next record. I've got so many ideas.'

Over the next couple of hours, we brainstorm the new album – hands down my favourite part of this job – and I have a suggestion for them. There's a record player in the meeting room and I tell them I have something to play them. I feel a confusing mix of emotion taking *Apparition* out of my bag, knowing none of them will ever have heard it before. Proud, yes, but also wretched, sorrowful.

'This band had short-lived success in the seventies,' I say, flashing the album at them.

Bex says, 'Oh my God, I love the cover. Is that an oil painting? Weird. I feel like I've seen that guy before; he looks familiar.'

'Disciples were a rock band, but they sang ballads too, and the songwriting is sublime. There's a track called "Cassiopeia" and you can hear the influences of the time; it sounds very seventies. But there's also something about the song that stops you dead. And I've been trying to unpick what that is. Have a listen.'

I glance at their faces and I see that they are rapt, entranced, just as I was the first time I heard it. But mostly I'm communing with my dead father; I'm telling him, Jacob, I think we've got this. You and me together. Father and son.

'Well done,' Michael says, when we've seen the band off the premises a couple of hours later 'This is totally down to you and your musical integrity. One of the reasons you're so good at your job is because you understand about songwriting and you can talk to musicians about it. You'd be surprised how few A&R men actually can.'

I am sunning myself in this unfamiliar praise, deeply attuned to each word he speaks, trying to remember it exactly to tell Hannah later, when Janice calls out to me from reception.

'Hey, Luke, you need to call home right away. Your mum rang a few times and also Hannah. They need to get hold of you.'

And right there my world fragments into a thousand tiny pieces.

I take my phone out of my pocket and see I have eleven missed calls, six from my mother, five from my girlfriend.

Hannah picks up on the first ring, which is in itself enough to terrify. Why isn't she at work?

'For God's sake,' she says, but she is crying too hard to finish the rest of the sentence.

'Christ, what's happened? Is Samuel hurt? Hannah?'

'He's … gone.'

The sound that Hannah is making is horrible; not crying, more of a demented wail, the howl of a mother whose child has died.

'Gone? What does that mean? Who has gone? Samuel?'

My mother comes on the phone, also crying, and this, more than anything else, acts as a trigger warning. My mother is not a woman who cries.

316

'Someone has taken Samuel from his cot. It happened when I was in the garden. I didn't have the walkie-talkie thing, but the back door was open and I always hear him.'

'Alice.'

'It must be. She still had keys, didn't she? No one else could have got in. And also he would have recognised her, so it wouldn't have been a shock. I'm so sorry. Luke? Are you there?'

Am I? Not really. I am bent double, arms round my ribcage, searching, searching for my breath.

Alice has stolen my baby. And somehow, somewhere down deep inside me, I always knew this was going to happen.

Then

Alice

In September, the tourists leave and we have this sedate seaside town back to ourselves. The weather is beautifully warm and we spend most days at the beach, Rick painting, with his easel set up on the sand, Charlie and I playing with shells and pebbles and dipping our feet into the sea.

He laughs at the cold water, never cries. Not when a seagull flies almost into his face as he dozes on the rug. Not when a fat elderly Labrador comes over to investigate and lands a long rivulet of drool on his face.

He is such a genial baby that we often take him out in the evening, wrapped up in a little woollen coat I knitted for him in rainbow stripes. Sometimes we walk up to the pier, stopping for fish and chips at our favourite stall, then spending the coins we save all week in the slot machines. Charlie's favourite is the moving shelf of pennies; he watches transfixed, waiting for the coins to clatter onto the shelf below, surprising people with his wild, uproarious giggle when they do.

The nights are beginning to darken, but there's still enough light for our favourite walk to Walberswick, across the marshes and past the water tower, Southwold's famous beacon of ugliness. We'll always stop for a half of cider at the Anchor and share something to eat if we're feeling rich enough.

We never talk about Jake, because I can't. As the weeks pass, it has become impossible for me to even say his name out loud, and Rick doesn't mention him either. It's as if there is a block in my throat; I can carry on, just, so long as I never speak of him. Say his name, Jake, or the fateful words *he died*, and I will fall apart.

Alone in the blackness of night is when I think of him. I remember our most passionate moments: the first time we said we loved each other here in Southwold, that beautiful lunch in Italy when he asked me to marry him. The day he turned up at the Slade out of the blue asking to see a student named Alice. But most of all I love to recall those daily insignificances: the cappuccinos, the pizzas at Kettner's, the ritualistic lighting of candles. I think of us buying groceries in the shop across the road, or choosing our Christmas tree, or sketching and songwriting in silent companionship. That's where I go in my head at night, back to the days when taxis rattled beneath the sitting-room window, and the air was scented with chicken and patchouli, and Jake was still alive.

It is mid-October when a quiet comes over Rick, indistinct perhaps to anyone but me. But I know him and I can tell he is worried.

'Something's up,' I say one night at the Anchor as we wait for our shared chicken chasseur to arrive.

'What do you mean?'

'Something's wrong. Come on, we tell each other everything.'

'We've only got a hundred pounds left. What will we do when it runs out?'

'You'll sell some paintings, won't you? I'll start making clothes.'

Our pipe dreams of the summer seem just that, fantasies we spun beneath the hot August sun.

'I spoke to Robin a couple of days ago. I asked him if he'd buy some of my seascapes. He was … pretty harsh. He's a businessman and sometimes we forget that. He said, "You know that pedestrian shit doesn't interest me. And it doesn't interest you either. Are you really going to wreck your career for a child that isn't yours and a woman you don't love." But …' He holds out a hand to stop me from speaking. 'He is mine, isn't he? In a way. And I do love you, Alice. In fact I've been thinking, why don't we—'

I know what's coming before he says it, and I reach out and put my palm across his mouth.

'Don't say it, you beautiful man. You don't need to. Everything you're doing right now is enough.'

I take his hand and kiss it, and he smiles.

'All right,' he says. 'But you're allowed to change your mind. The offer stands.'

If Rick and I were to marry, it would go some way to healing the rift with my parents, and also his, who still aren't speaking to him after he confessed to his love affair with Tom. I'm still old-fashioned enough to think it would be a good thing for Charlie to have two married parents. But how could I marry anyone who wasn't Jake? And how could I allow Rick to give up the chance of finding happiness with someone else? It's a sacrifice I could never let him make.

The next day he takes three of his seascapes to a local gallery in town and they offer to buy two of them on the spot for five pounds each. They take fifty per cent as commission, and he comes home and throws a five-pound note onto the kitchen table.

He's laughing as he says, 'That's what they think I'm worth round here,' but I cannot bear it for him: Rick, the star of the Slade, whose self-portrait hangs in San Lorenzo, who had a career lined up at Robin Armstrong if only he'd finished his degree and stuck with his edgy, instantly recognisable portraiture.

But we carry on, Rick, Charlie and I, as October turns into November, bringing with it a new chill and the prospect of a cold winter in our tiny damp cottage. I'm worrying too when we are down to our final fifty pounds, when the gallery says it has enough seascapes and perhaps Rick could try somewhere else. When Charlie gets his first cold, a nose that permanently runs, a cough that seems to get worse, not better. He doesn't cry but nor does he laugh; he lies in my lap, listless and miserable.

The impromptu fish and chips, the suppers in the pub, are forgotten now as we ration ourselves to a weekly budget of ten pounds and eat baked potatoes and baked beans on rotation. At night I hold on to Charlie in the darkness, his tiny fist in mine, wrapping myself around him for warmth. I talk to Jacob, tearless now, asking him, 'What shall we do? What shall we do?'

And then one morning just before the end of November, the answer comes.

Now

Luke

Hysterical, frenzied, ferocious: I cannot find the right word for my passive, peace-loving girlfriend, destroyed, utterly, by the taking of her small son. When I walk into the kitchen, she screams at me, 'Where the fuck have you been?' and collapses, sobbing, into my mother's arms.

'The police have just left,' Christina says, looking at me over Hannah's head. 'And Rick is on his way; he's going to Alice's house and studio first.'

'The police? Already? Christ. What did they say?'

'They're taking it seriously, thank God. Classifying it as an abduction even though she's a member of the family. Biologically, anyway.'

'Are we sure it's Alice?'

Hannah lifts her head to scream, 'Of course it's Alice. Who else had keys? Who else would do something like this? You said it yourself, she's completely obsessed with Samuel. I just hope ...'

She breaks off, weeping, and I put my arms around her.

'Hannah?'

She looks up, face streaked with mascara tears.

'This is the worst thing that could ever have happened, but we need to stay strong for Samuel. We need to think clearly

322

so we can find him. And we need to keep reminding ourselves how much Alice loves him. That's a good thing, right?'

Samuel is everywhere in this room – the clean bottles on the draining board, the bouncy blue chair he is now too big for, the hand-painted fruit bowl, irregularly stamped with his tiny newborn feet. We laughed so much that day, dipping his naked feet into pots of paint, the look of haughty disgust that spread across his face when flesh met gloopy cold.

'When did you notice he'd gone missing?'

My mother puts her hand to her forehead as if checking for fever.

'I always put him down for his morning nap at ten thirty, and I wake him at around eleven fifteen. I never let him sleep more than forty-five minutes. But it was such a beautiful day, I thought I'd get on with some gardening. And when I went to get him up …' her voice catches, 'he was gone. I tried to ring you, but the receptionist wouldn't interrupt your meeting. So then I rang Hannah and the police.'

I look at my watch; it's already 1.30. He could have been missing for almost three hours.

Hannah cries, 'Luke, they could be anywhere by now. On a plane, boat, train. How will we ever find him? What are we going to do?'

'I will find him,' I say. 'Trust me, Hannah. We need to be out looking for them. Did you try the café, the playground?'

'I rang Stefano at the deli, but he hasn't seen Alice for weeks. Sarah and all her mum friends are searching the park and the library and the high street. But it's pointless, they won't be anywhere obvious.'

'We have to think why Alice would have done this. Is it vengeance? To give us a fright? Or is she actually thinking she can steal him?'

'Do you think she's capable of that?' my mother asks. 'She seemed a very reasonable sort of person to me.'

'Dressing our baby up in weird clothes so he looked like Luke? Hardly reasonable.'

'But not dangerous,' my mother says. 'That's what we need to hang on to.'

There's a knock at the door, short and aggressive. All three of us jump.

'Police,' my mother says.

'I'll go.'

I need to grasp back some control from this horrifying situation, and I throw open the door expecting two policemen, but instead I find Rick, still in his painting clothes, smears of colour on his cheeks, his hands, his hair.

'Christ, Luke, I'm sorry.'

He opens his arms and we embrace, and now, for the first time, I am able to cry, unexpected tears that run down my face. I am unselfconscious here in the arms of a man I briefly thought was my father, a man who still holds all the clues.

When we part, he says, 'I've checked Alice's flat and studio and, of course, I've rung her mobile countless times. I also did a whistle-stop tour of all the places that mattered to her. Soho basically. Bar Italia. Kettner's. The French House. No one has seen her.'

We go through to the kitchen, where Rick apologises to my mother and hugs Hannah, who, like me, finds herself weeping in his arms.

'It's definitely Alice, isn't it?' she asks, and he nods.

'I'm sure it is. She's been increasingly unwell these last months, and since you guys fell out, she's sort of lost it a bit. All she could talk about was Samuel and how she wanted to say goodbye to him properly. The thing is, in some strange way, I think she's reliving what happened with you all those years ago. She has tipped over into fantasy.'

'But where would she go? Do you have any idea?'

'I think I do. It's a gamble and I could be wrong ...'

He hesitates for a second or two, and Hannah cries, 'Tell us, Rick. Please.'

'I think she's gone to Southwold.'

'Southwold!' Hannah and I speak at the same time.

'That's miles away. Why on earth would she go there?'

And it's the strangest thing, because Rick is looking at my mother and not us, and she is staring back at him with an expression I cannot read. As if they know something that we don't.

'Cards on the table time, I think, don't you, Christina?' Rick says, and my mother nods. 'You see, Alice did this once before. Only that time the baby she stole was you.'

Then

Alice

We do all the things we normally do, Charlie and I. We walk down to the pier, stopping off at the hall of mirrors for our daily cheap laughs, extreme thinness, fatness, shortness our shared, fail-safe joke. I take some scraps of bread to feed the seagulls, a new fetish; the birds swoop down right next to the pushchair and Charlie whoops and catcalls his excitement.

On the way home, we stop off at the phone box on the high street and I park the pram outside it. I call Directory Enquiries and scribble down the number they give me and dial again before I can change my mind. When I give my name, it's obvious that the girl on the other end of the line knows exactly who I am. She sounds intrigued, excited; she begs me to wait while she fetches Mrs Taylor Murphy.

'Alice, hello.'

There's a pause now where I am unable to speak, and after a while she fills the gap.

'You've been so brave,' she says. 'To try and manage by yourself. You must love your baby very much.'

The deal is struck. Tomorrow at eleven o'clock. No one else. No parents, just her and Charlie and me.

'We'll meet on the beach,' I tell her, because we have been at our happiest there, me, Charlie, Jake.

When we get back to the cottage, Rick is finishing a sketch of Charlie, asleep in his cot with one fist curled beneath his cheek.

'What do you think?' he asks. 'I'm thinking love-struck new parents with dosh to spare. Reckon I could get some commissions?'

He sees my face.

'What? Alice?'

My voice is wooden as I reveal the facts. I can tell it no other way.

'The woman from the adoption agency is coming to collect Charlie tomorrow. Eleven o'clock.'

'No!'

He hurls himself from his chair to the ground, face down on the carpet in a fit of melodrama. It's real, though; his pain is exactly the same as my pain.

'He's mine too, you always say so.'

'You gave me these months with him, Rick, and I'll always have that. One day he will come and find us. And when he does, he'll belong to you just as much as me.'

Rick sits back on his knees but doesn't look at me.

'Are you sure?'

'I'm sure. You need to go back to the Slade and have the career you were meant to have. And Charlie needs stability, security, the things we can't give him. This house could be sold at any minute, and then where would we live? Your squat? I don't want that life for him.'

'How will we bear it?'

'We'll take it minute by minute, as we have done all along.'

I don't sleep much, curled around my baby for the last time, whispering to him in the darkness.

'You will have a big garden to play in and a pony to ride and a brand-new bicycle. You will be loved and happy. And I will wait for you.'

In the morning I feel strangely calm, waking to the sound of the gulls outside our window. While Charlie sleeps on – he has turned into the world's best sleeper – I pack up his clothes and nappies and bottles, keeping back a few of my favourite things. The little orange shorts, a yellow and brown striped top, his dungarees.

When it's time to go, I hand him to Rick and tell him I'll be waiting for him outside the cottage. I'm not going to stand around and witness his private farewell. I've already said mine throughout most of the night, holding Charlie's tiny fist in my hand. Goodbye, my love. Goodbye.

Walking down to the beach, baby in one arm, plastic carrier full of clothes in the other, I think I will make a funny face so that Charlie laughs one more time, but it's too difficult, my facial muscles will not obey. And perhaps it's true what Mrs Taylor Murphy said, because this contented, happy child of mine is solemn and unsmiling, as if my sorrow has somehow transferred itself to him.

She is there waiting for us, wearing a flowered dress with flat shoes – I did wonder about those heels on the beach – and she waves, though she seems rather sombre too.

I hand over the plastic bag of clothes. 'These are his things.'

And then I remember. His bear is still sitting on the kitchen table.

'I've forgotten his bear. He can't be without it.' My voice is frantic, my eyes have blurred over with tears.

Mrs Taylor Murphy puts her hand on my shoulder.

'I promise I'll buy him one exactly the same. I think you're going to need it more than him.' She looks at me. 'You'll want some time to say goodbye,' she says, and I shake my head because I can't speak, I can't see, and if we delay by even one second, I won't be able to do it.

I pass Charlie over and he tries to cling to me, grabbing at a strand of my hair.

'I know you'll see him again, Alice,' Mrs Taylor Murphy says as Charlie starts to cry. She places a hand over her heart. 'I can feel it.'

I watch them walking away, the flowered dress getting smaller and smaller, the plastic bag just a white dot in her hands. And above the shriek of gulls I listen to my baby, programmed so acutely to hear him as he cries all the way along the beach.

Now

Luke

The guilt at giving up a child is ravaging and inescapable and a birth mother will normally react in one of two ways. She will become deadened inside, closing off her grief in order to carry on. Or she will become utterly tormented by it.

Who Am I? The Adoptee's Hidden Trauma by Joel Harris

The drive to Southwold takes less than three hours, powered by Rick's silver Alfa Romeo and maniacal driving.

He tells me about his and Alice's flight from the hospital, in an old Morris Minor with red leather seats.

'You and Alice slept in the back seat the whole way, and you woke up just as we arrived at the beach for sunrise. In spite of all the heartbreak, it felt like a new beginning. Like we'd been given a second chance.'

I learn on this journey how Rick was, to all intents, my father for a short while; Rick, Alice and me, a team of three.

'You and I spent a lot of time together in the first few weeks. I wanted Alice to have the space to grieve and so I'd take you out wrapped up in a shawl and tied to my chest. We'd walk for hours along the beach and over the marshes, and when we got back, Alice's face would be red from crying, but she always made a point of smiling for you. She never cried in front of you; she said she wanted you to only know love and happiness. I'm not sure how she managed it.'

'Poor Alice.'

'She never got over it. A love like theirs is a rare thing. They weren't just lovers, they were connected on a much deeper level. For one thing they'd both survived abusive childhoods and they held each other up. Together they were strong, but without Jake, Alice couldn't function. I asked her to marry me once; I thought it was the solution after he died. But she wouldn't have it. She's never loved anyone except Jake. I don't think she ever will.'

'Did you have to give me up?'

I see the way Rick tightens his grip on the steering wheel. I understand that the question hurts him in the same way it hurts me.

'Perhaps not. Perhaps we could have found a way through. It was a decision that wrecked her life. Even more than losing Jake, I think. She closed off, lost her character, became someone else. I kept thinking she'd recover, but she never did.'

We are silent for a long time after this.

Hannah and my mother are at home waiting for the police, all of us clinging to Rick's conviction that there is only one place Alice would go. I didn't want to leave Hannah, but nor could I sit around waiting. It is a relief to be in this car, driving at ferocious speed, believing, or at least trying to, that every mile covered brings me closer to my son.

It's Rick who speaks first.

'You look just like Jake, same voice, mannerisms, everything. It's almost unbearable at times, even for me.'

'You think I remind Alice of him?'

'I know you do. She told me she cried herself to sleep the day you first met. So happy to find you, so devastated all over again that she'd lost him.'

'Why did she get so obsessed with Samuel?'

'Because he's exactly like you. It was hard for me too, seeing Samuel the first time, don't you remember? It was like we'd got our baby back. Alice hasn't been very well these past years – that's obvious, isn't it? And I think she used to disappear into a fantasy world when she was looking after Samuel. In her mind, she allowed Samuel to become you, the baby she'd lost. She didn't mean any harm. It was the escape of a rather sad and heartbroken woman. But she went rapidly downhill when you stopped her seeing him. She was talking about Southwold all the time, the months we had there, the things we used to do, and I just wish I'd realised where it was all heading. She was fixated on saying goodbye to the baby.'

'And did she call him Samuel?'

Rick turns his head to look at me for a second.

'Nope.'

'I could see it happening, but no one believed me. I started following Alice around the park most days, and I know how that sounds. But I knew something was wrong, something I couldn't put my finger on.'

'Her mental health has been fragile for a long time. The reunion with you, something she'd longed for, tipped her over the edge. It was as if Jake was back in her life again and she's missed him so much. Only, of course, he wasn't. Obsessing over Samuel was easier than dealing with all that pain again.'

'I wish we'd had this conversation before it was too late.'

'It isn't too late. We're having it now.'

'You don't think …' I break off. Fear has vacuumed up the words that cannot be spoken. But Rick needs no explanation.

'She loves him. She wouldn't hurt a hair on his head.'

We have arrived in Southwold now, in good time; there's still plenty of daylight left, there's still heat in the sun. I've never been here before, don't know what to expect, am slightly amazed by the chichi-ness of it, although I don't know why. Architecture in colour-coordinated pastels with Farrow & Balled doors. Delicatessens and second-hand bookshops and hip-looking cafés that probably specialise in chai and almond-milk lattes.

'Notting Hill on Sea,' I say.

'Not in our day. Back then it was deeply unfashionable and all the better for it. Fish and chips on the pier, candy floss, an arcade with slot machines. There was one machine you loved; it used to have a moving shelf of pennies – you know the kind? – and when the pennies tipped over the edge, you laughed your head off.' There's a wistfulness in his voice, and it makes me sad to think of Rick and Alice, those two young art students with their baby.

'Rick?'

He turns around from the steering wheel, tears in his eyes as I expected.

'Maybe everything can be all right between us.'

'It can, Luke. I know it can.'

He is turning down a side street, and now the sea is ahead of us, a silver skin dissected by a cloudless sky. We pull into a little car park in the showstopper car, the beach in front of it lined with a row of candy-coloured huts: pink, yellow, blue and green. My heart is surging with hope and fear.

'This is our beach. The first time we came here, Alice and Jake and Tom and me, we drove through the night and arrived at sunrise. We made that same trip the night we ran away with you. This beach means so much to her; it's the last place she was with you before she gave you away.'

A thought strikes me.

'Can I go alone?'

Rick looks at me. 'Are you sure?'

'Yes, I think it's important. Just me and him and her. I want to get it right.'

He nods. 'Understood. I'll wait here.'

I get out of the car and walk towards the beach, past a family making their way back to a bright-orange camper van with faded gingham curtains in its windows. The kind of van, I'd like to think, that Alice and Jake might have had back in the day. A mother, a father and two small girls, wet hair plastered to their heads, bodies shrouded in towelling robes. One of the girls is carrying a shabby-looking panda, and it's like an electric shock to the heart. I need to find Samuel; I need to find him right now.

There's a sloping cement path down to the beach, and I find myself running down it, scanning the space between the breakers: late-afternoon picnickers, dog-walkers and a young couple hand in hand, but no woman and child, not that I can see. My despair is instant, fierce, vengeful. Bloody Rick for leading me on this wild goose chase, I think as I scan the beach again, more slowly this time. He seemed so sure they would be here. And I believed him.

A red flag is flying down by the shoreline, and two policemen stand close to it, looking out to sea. I know what they are waiting to tell me. No Alice, no Samuel.

There is a fizzing in my veins, a tightening, a blurriness that warns me to stop and take my time. Breathing in the smell of salt and seaweed, familiar and intoxicating, but not today; hold, count, exhale all the way out. I repeat this several times until my vision sharpens and my heart begins to slow.

I won't cry, I tell myself, gripping my hands together in a

tight clasp, trying to stay strong. They could be on the pier; in the arcade, playing with one of the penny machines that used to make me laugh. In a moment I'll go back to the car and get Rick and he'll know where to look. We'll exhaust every nook and cranny in this postcard-pretty town.

I take out my phone and read a text from Hannah.

No news here. Call me as soon as you get to Southwold.

I consider phoning just to hear her voice, but I want to extend her hope for as long as possible, and for the same reason I stand still, allowing myself whole minutes of procrastination before I approach the policemen.

'Excuse me?'

The pair turn to look at me in surprise.

'I'm Luke. The father of the missing boy.'

'A missing child?'

They look at each other. The taller one, prematurely balding but around my age, shrugs.

'We haven't been told anything about that.'

'Are you sure? He disappeared in London a few hours ago, but we think he might be here in Southwold. The police are involved.'

The bald one shakes his head. 'There's been an accident on the beach this afternoon, that's why we're here. See the red flag?'

He nods at the shoreline, and for the first time I take in the violent foaming waves.

'A drowning. Happened about an hour ago. A woman and her baby got caught in a rip tide and carried out to sea. Absolutely tragic. Sir? Are you all right? Sir?'

When the world ends, as you know it, you will find that all the clichés are true. Your head will swim, words that are un-containable darting before your eyes like little black dots. Your knees will buckle, you will collapse onto the sand clutching your heart, while above your head seagulls wheel and screech their sombre song.

Epilogue

The pilgrimage to Southwold at the end of August marks also the end of the school holidays. We don't observe the actual day but the closest Saturday, and we always stay the night at the Swan Hotel, which the children adore. We book the family room, year on year, and the staff know why we come.

Rick comes too, driving down in his pillar-box-red Ferrari, bought, we suspect, for the sole reason that our son was in love with it.

We mark Alice's drowning not with sorrow, not any more, but with flowers and music and a picnic, even when it rains like today. We sit on a rug, holding umbrellas over our egg sandwiches and toasting the children's grandparents with Coca-Cola and champagne.

We douse ourselves in cologne – Acqua di Parma in its bottle of vivid blue – and Rick tells us that smell is the sense most closely connected to memory. We all inhale, and this particular fragrance is delicious and achingly familiar to me now: lemons and cedar and woodland. The scent of Alice and Jake.

Rick cues up *Apparition* on his iPod with his fancy new Bluetooth speakers, and when 'Cassiopeia' comes on, he tells us about a night of stargazing on this same beach long ago.

'Alice and Jake were so happy that night. It was the first

time she had told Jake she loved him. And we lay on our backs looking at the sky while Jake pointed out all the different stars. Did you know that Cassiopeia was a queen who thought she was the most beautiful woman in the world?'

Rick talks about Jake, everything he can remember, he brings out new details each time like a gift. Sometimes it's the food Jake cooked, spaghetti vongole, which he pronounces with a wildly exaggerated accent to make the children laugh. Or it might be about the songs he wrote. But mostly he tells the love story of Jake and Alice.

'They made each other strong,' he says, 'the way the best couples do.'

Sometimes I wonder what it's like for our children growing up with these fictional characters whom Rick puppets to life each August. But then it's the same for me. For I didn't know Jacob or even Alice, not really. And to ponder too much on the Alice I could have known, the Alice I misunderstood, feared and lost, is to ache with regret.

Samuel has a story of his own, one he loves to embellish.

'Alice had taken me to the beach for the day,' Samuel says and we smile now and allow him this twisting of the truth. 'And there was a family with a little sea float a bit like the one Alice used to take Dad in when he was a baby. So she borrowed it.'

'She went paddling, didn't she?' asks his sister Iris, always keen to have some involvement in this tale, however small.

Samuel gives a solemn nod.

'But it was windy and the float got caught in a current. And we were blown out to sea. Alice tried to swim back, but she wasn't strong enough.

'The man on the beach ran into the sea to help us, even though his wife was screaming at him to stay. And when he reached us, Alice begged him to save me.'

The man – Thomas, he's called – bears a lifelong scar about that desperate split-second choice: save the woman or save the child. There was no choice at all.

'I thought I could go back for her,' he told me afterwards at the hospital, and his face as he said this was broken, Alice's last moments an ineradicable image scratched onto his eyes. I didn't tell him what I thought, deep down: Alice didn't want to be rescued.

Sometimes Rick cries, sometimes I do, but as the years pass and the children grow and our strange family with its surfeit of grandparents – some dead, some alive – continues to flourish, we think, we hope, that Jacob and Alice got the ending they would have wanted.

Acknowledgements

First of all a huge debt of thanks to Frances Ronaldson for being so understanding about this book and allowing me to subvert her joyful reunion with John for my own dark fictional purposes. The real life story has been the happiest event. Enormous thanks to my amazing agent Felicity Blunt. I count myself so lucky to have you on my side. Thanks also to Lucy Morris, an absolute rock of strength through the rollercoaster of publication.

Francesca Pathak, my editor at Orion, thank you again for your absolute connection with this story and for helping me to make it immeasurably better.

You make the editing process such a pleasure.

Thanks to the whole team at Orion and special thanks to Leanne Oliver and Amy Davies for all your hard work on both *Him* and *Mine*. Thank you Lucy Frederick for working so hard on this manuscript.

And to Jane Selby for doing such a fantastic and sensitive job with the copyedit. Emily Burns my thanks for your dedication and professionalism and for being the loveliest person to work with.

Kishan Rajani thank you for coming up with another spectacular cover!

I have had so much help with the researching of *Mine*. First and foremost I must thank the psychotherapist and addiction counsellor Paul Sunderland of Outcome Consulting Ltd for his insightful wisdom into the hidden trauma of adoptees and for generously sharing his knowledge with me. Joel Harris is a fictional character largely inspired by my conversations with Paul and his groundbreaking research into this area.

Thank you to the adult adoptees for allowing me to join your equine therapy workshop and for sharing those most poignant and memorable days.

Claudia Navaneti for your insights into adoptee psychology and Dr James Stallard for fielding endless psychiatric questions.

Professor Andrew Stahl, my thanks for your memories of the Slade in the early 1970s, I loved hearing them. Thanks also to Jo Volley for the same.

The artists Brian Rice and Jacy Wall thank you for talking to me about life and art in the 1970s I so enjoyed the day we spent together.

Portrait painter Saied Dai, thank you for allowing me to join your life class and for your invaluable insights into painting and drawing, I could have listened to you talking all day.

Dave Meneer, my most wonderful friend, for your exacting and elephantine memory of student life in the early 70s. Who else would know the price of a pint of bitter in the Coach in 1972? (10p).

To Caroline Boucher for perfectly rock and roll recollections of the 70s but also for your generous and continuous support.

Anna and Pete Banks, I began Mine in your beautiful house in Southwold. Thank you for lending it to me, for introducing me to this incredible town and most of all to Anna for a lifelong friendship which means everything.

My thanks to Billy Jones for providing me with a writing sanctuary when I needed it most alongside unwavering friendship. Victoria Upson, the loyalest and funniest person I know, for showing me what true friendship is.

Thanks to Susy Pelly and Chloe Fox, my writing sisters in Smug HQ, for sharing the joy and angst daily. Harriet Edwards and Lucinda Horton for your humour, brilliance and always making everything better. Hattie Slim, my secret weapon, I'm so glad I found you.

Thank you to the readers, bloggers and authors who enjoyed *Him* and told me so, I am so grateful for your support.

To Jane and Anna, for always standing beside me. I'm so glad I have you in my corner. Jake, Maya and Felix. Thank you for putting up with your distracted mother and for being the kind, funny, quirky and wonderfully individualistic people you are. I will always be more proud of you than anything else. And to the inspirational Diana Empson who is greatly missed.

Finally but most importantly Lucinda Martin and John Empson, this is not your story but it is your book. It comes to you with love.

Credits

Clare Empson and Orion Fiction would like to thank everyone at Orion who worked on the publication of *Mine* in the UK.

Editorial
Francesca Pathak
Lucy Frederick

Copy Editor
Jane Selley

Proof Reader
Jade Craddock

Audio
Paul Stark
Amber Bates

Design
Debbie Holmes
Joanna Ridley
Nick May

Editorial Management
Charlie Panayiotou
Jane Hughes
Alice Davis

Production
Hannah Cox

Marketing
Amy Davies

Publicity
Leanne Oliver

Finance
Jasdip Nandra
Afeera Ahmed
Elizabeth Beaumont
Sue Baker

Rights
Susan Howe
Krystyna Kujawinska
Jessica Purdue
Richard King
Louise Henderson

Contracts
Anne Goddard
Paul Bulos
Jake Alderson

Sales
Jen Wilson
Esther Waters
Victoria Laws
Rachael Hum
Ellie Kyrke-Smith
Frances Doyle
Georgina Cutler

Operations
Jo Jacobs
Sharon Willis
Lisa Pryde
Lucy Brem